RHYMER: HOODE

BAEN BOOKS by GREGORY FROST

Rhymer Trilogy
Rhymer
Rhymer: Hoode

To purchase this title in e-book form, please go to
www.baen.com.

RHYMER: HOODE

GREGORY FROST

A Baen Books Original

Baen Publishing Enterprises
P.O. Box 1403
Riverdale, NY 10471
www.baen.com

ISBN: 978-1-9821-9349-2

Cover art by Eric Williams

First printing, July 2024

Distributed by Simon & Schuster
1230 Avenue of the Americas
New York, NY 10020

Library of Congress Cataloging-in-Publication Data

Names: Frost, Gregory, author.
Title: Rhymer. Hoode / Gregory Frost.
Other titles: Hoode
Description: Riverdale, NY : Baen Publishing Enterprises, 2024. | Series: Rhymer trilogy ; 2
Identifiers: LCCN 2024005452 (print) | LCCN 2024005453 (ebook) | ISBN 9781982193492 (hardcover) | ISBN 9781625799685 (e-book)
Subjects: LCSH: Thomas, the Rhymer, 1220?-1297?—Fiction. | LCGFT: Fantasy
  fiction. | Novels.
Classification: LCC PS3556.R59815 R594 2024 (print) | LCC PS3556.R59815
  (ebook) | DDC 813/.54—dc23/eng/20240209
LC record available at https://lccn.loc.gov/2024005452
LC ebook record available at https://lccn.loc.gov/2024005453

Printed in the United States of America

10 9 8 7 6 5 4 3 2 1

DEDICATION

To the Philadelphia Liars Club past and present.
So many dangerous minds, so little time...

ACKNOWLEDGMENTS

A number of people contributed to the final version of *Hoode*. First and foremost is fellow writer and friend Oz Drummond, who followed the progress of the draft over many months and then set aside her own novel-in-progress for several weeks to work with me during revisions as beta reader and continuity editor, chapter by chapter, via text, email, and even Zooms. Thank you more than I can say for helping locate the true path for Thomas once again. This book would not exist without you.

Next, my thanks to author Rick Wilber who, during an early online conversation about the book, said, "You're including the caves of Nottingham, right?," which in turn led me to *Sandstone Caves of Nottingham* by Tony Waltham, an invaluable resource for anyone wanting to write about medieval Nottingham (or learn about the oldest pub in England). Similarly, *A Palace for Our Kings* by James Wright (Nottinghamshire Local History Association) proved to be a critical study and depiction of the King's Houses (now generally known as King John's Palace).

And finally, as always, to my ever-tenacious agent, Marie Lamba, and to my editors on this volume, Toni Weisskopf and David Butler, for fine-tuning Thomas throughout.

PART ONE:
THE WOODWOSE

I. Thieves

There was something off about the prelate. Even Little John sensed it. Clothed in simple sackcloth, the bishop waddled south along the King's Great Way through Sherwood, the only obvious item of value being the ivory-topped crozier he handled like a walking stick as he approached the huge split-oak tree behind which John and his companions hid. Yet, if he was just a journeying palmer, why was he accompanied by two knights dressed as if fresh from a crusade in red-cross-adorned surcoats? Knights Templar? What *did* he have worth stealing? Robert Hodde had to be wondering the same thing.

In front of John, lean and scruffy Hodde leaned on his quarterstaff. John and, behind him, the third member of their little band, the rabbity-faced Much the miller's boy, watched the trio approach over his shoulder; in the depths of the woods, their clothes of green with red trim rendered them nearly invisible.

The knights wore quilted gambesons beneath deep brown brigandines, presumably plated, although at this distance it was hard to tell—they might just be thick leather. Either way, the two layers would probably stop an arrow, certainly at the distance Hodde's team preferred to work. That meant close fighting if the prelate chose to be feisty, and only Hodde had brought his quarterstaff. John and Much only had their bows. At least the knights didn't sport fauchards or crossbows, just flat-topped steel-pot helms with gold crosspiece decorations on the front protecting their heads, and arming swords at their hips.

"What you think, John?" Hodde muttered. "Something in that satchel?"

The prelate carried a small satchel on a baldric slung over one shoulder. It might have contained his more elaborate dalmatic or folded cape, but not much more than one of those—still hardly cause for the presence of the knights.

Granted there were other outlaws lurking in the High Forest between the River Aire and Nottingham. Hodde's band knew them all; John and he only forayed into Sherwood for quick robberies, after which they headed right back to Barnsdale Wood, where the sheriff or the King's men were less likely to pursue much less find them. Even the occasional deer they slew they carried off to Barnsdale, leaving no trace that they'd trespassed in the King's preserve. Life was safer that way.

The prelate drew nearer. Little John read Hodde's profile—he was chewing on the tip of his brown beard. John knew he was reconsidering. Robbing a priest, even an unaccompanied one, could bring all kinds of trouble. The Church simply had no sense of humor. And this was . . . peculiar.

Then the prelate's sackcloth shawl flapped open and Little John saw two flashes of color beneath it. He remarked, "'E's got 'im a king's ransom on that cincture 'round 'is middle. *Look* at them sparklers, Robbie." He pointed. The sackcloth obligingly flopped open with his next step, and a dangling section of knotted silk cincture swung into view. It flickered red and green where the sunlight caught it. Small jewels in settings had been worked into the wide rope. Hodde had to appreciate that for all of his pretense of poverty, the prelate had not been able to deny himself one tiny act of vanity. Or maybe it was the only cincture he owned. Of some value, certainly, but it did not explain the need for the company of two knights.

The prelate and his guards were drawing even with the split oak. John said, "Well?" He looked to Robert Hodde for a sign.

Hodde turned his head and started to speak. But he'd barely breathed, "We should—" before naive Much, as he had done successfully a dozen times before, strode swiftly out from behind the tree. Hodde hissed his name and tried to reach around Little John to grab him, but it was too late. Much scrambled right up into the road ahead of the travelers, his bow nocked and, though pointed at no one, an obvious threat.

John muttered, "Come on, Robbie, put down yer staff an' grab yer bow."

Much called, "Good sirs," as he blocked the prelate's way. "Forgive me, but I am obliged to ask for some charity from the clergy for my friends and me." He gave a slight nod, and the knights as one turned to behold Robert Hodde and Little John step out from behind the broad tree and circle onto the road behind them, bows likewise nocked though not aimed at anyone in particular yet. Hodde was cursing under his breath that this was a terrible idea.

"Merciful God!" exclaimed the prelate. "How dare you threaten to rob a poor man of the Church such as myself, sirrah."

"Not so poor as to waddle alone from Wentbridge, secure in the knowing that you carry nothing of interest to the likes of us," Much replied.

Hodde gave his head a small shake at that. Even Little John recognized that the lad's phrasing hardly passed muster. Hodde took a step forward to wrest control of this situation. "A quick look in the satchel is all we need," he called, "and then ye can continue on tha way."

The prelate turned about. "Show you that, I will not, Robbehode," he replied. He beamed triumphantly. "Oh, I know your name, cutpurse. It is not a name to be proud of."

"It is also in fact not my name, good metropolitan, so you may use it as ye like." He held the bow to the side, one finger hooked over the arrow, and extended the other arm as if in friendly gesture. Worry poured off him like heat. "Surely, a mere neb inside cannot harm."

The knights said nothing, but one of them and the prelate turned to face Much, while the other continued to stare at Little John and Hodde without moving. A dull ache vibrated in John's head, and he saw Hodde wince as if the same pain plagued him.

The facing knight drew his arming sword. The blade flashed with sunlight in rainbow colors like that of no steel John had ever beheld.

Hodde withdrew his friendly gesture, and gripped his bow again. Little John was certain now that they should have let this group pass by. The knights were sinister in some way he could not pinpoint. The one facing Much had drawn his blade, too. It glinted with its similar sheen. If he hadn't been fixated upon it, he wouldn't have seen what happened next, though it was as if he didn't see it at all, but only its effect. The length of the blade seemed to strike like a snake, plunging straight through Much. The lad went up on his tiptoes, his mouth opened in a gasp, while the sword was merely an arming sword again, held at the knight's side although now coated with blood that looked to be . . . vanishing, as if into the blade.

Hodde called out Much's name, but Much did not seem to hear, instead stumbling forward and back, eyes pleading helplessly with him and John. Then he collapsed.

In that instant Little John reached over, grabbed Hodde by the quiver strap, and yanked him aside just as the second knight's blade sprang the distance. He wasn't quite quick enough. The impossible blade slashed straight through Hodde's side instead of his middle, gone again so fast it all seemed an illusion; the blade extended from the knight's hand like a normal sword, and now it, too, was soaking up the blood that stained it. Hodde's blood.

Little John let go of him, aimed and shot the prelate in the back. The jolt flung the miter from the priest's head, and he staggered in a circle, clutching at the arrow driven through him. Both knights turned to him.

The prelate wheezed, raised an arm as if about to bless or curse Hodde. Then a weird mist of red blood burst through his sackcloth cloak, and his face seemed to ooze from his head. John took this in as he charged the nearest knight before the fellow could direct his magical blade again. He hammered a fist against the crusader's pot helm hard as he could, and an unusual thing happened: Instead of falling off, the helmet retreated into the brigandine like a snail drawing into its shell, as if it was a soft gardcorps and not solid at all. It revealed a long, spiky, and coarse gray face surrounded by silvery hair. The knight stumbled and went down on one knee. John stepped past him and grabbed the strap of the satchel from the melting, collapsing corpse of the prelate, as the second knight turned from Much's body, sword arm extended. That was when Hodde's arrow pierced the knight's wrist, and the magical sword fell out of his grasp. Otherwise, John would have been skewered.

The spiky-faced knight started to rise, and John clubbed him down again, a blow that should have shattered his neck. Behind him, Hodde cried, "Take it! Run, John!"

Little John needed no further urging. He hurled himself into the woods, through the trees on a path they all knew to use. But when he looked back, Hodde wasn't behind him. Two other figures were—if they were the knights, they'd transformed into white-haired, greenish-gray faced demons, sheathed now in strange black armor that gleamed like steel but hugged them like full-body hauberks. The one in front carried one of the weirdly gleaming swords; the one in back clutched its wrist. Their running was jerky, as if they'd never done it before.

Dodging ahead, he dared another glance just as the flashing blade shot forward. He leapt, almost kicking his heels together, and the blade stabbed into the ground beside him, then as quickly snapped back.

John picked up his speed and raced away through the forest, into a landscape he knew from a lifetime of thieving and outwitting pursuit.

What were these creatures? Devils they must be, guarding a prelate who'd ... who'd *melted*—had he actually witnessed that? He could only hope that Robert Hodde had fled in the other direction and made good his escape, because whatever was in this old satchel he'd snatched, the knights had both come after it. A king's ransom at the very least, he imagined. It had cost poor Much his life.

What had they all blundered into?

II. Fontevraud, 1185

Janet was dying. The tall and imposing Abbess Gilles told Thomas herself, but he knew already, just as he knew there was nothing he could do this time to cure her. Something had been in her lungs for months, and it was getting worse.

She was seventy-three now, a remarkable age. He could still see in her thinner face the woman he remembered. Janet's skin was like moist parchment pulled over her bones, her lips prone to cracks, and her hair gone completely white. Her skinny wrists and arms made him think of birds. But Janet's reaching the end of her life was natural. What was unnatural was his own failure to do the same.

Even Morven, their daughter, was older in appearance now than he. Morven resembled Janet as she appeared after his return from Ailfion: the same slope to her nose, the same wide jaw. He'd taken care not to unglamour in her presence. He'd been careful with that right from the first.

Two decades earlier when he'd brought his sister, Innes, back to Ercildoun from Cluny, he had looked the part of her younger brother naturally. However, because he was going to have to masquerade as their nonexistent relative, Ainsley Rimor of Alwich, for a short time, he'd had to reveal to her how because of the elves he could change his appearance. Poor Innes had already long been the victim of elven magic, labeled a madwoman and shut away with the truly mad, initially by the Yvag that had inhabited their father. Damaged by their cruelty she might be, but mad she was not, despite that they'd stolen

her baby and told her it was dead. How she withstood that loss, he did not know, but she accepted Thomas's power to transform as if it were the most normal thing in the world. She grasped immediately how he must pretend to have aged in order to match his Janet. He had believed the discrepancy was due to the way time ran here versus in Ailfion: Janet had waited twenty years for his return while for him their separation had lasted a handful of months. So he aged himself to match his beloved, to let her forget.

Innes took charge of the family estates. He remained nearby at Cardden's keep with Janet only long enough to determine that the Yvag had gotten his message never to return to Old Melrose: For months none came through the invisible gate there. No fiery green ring appeared near the ruins, and no grotesque gray sleepers lay among the tombs of St. Mary's Abbey. No doubt Yvags were emerging through a gate *somewhere* to collect their *teinds*, but they weren't invading *his* territory or harming those who mattered to him any longer. His private war with Nicnevin was done.

Innes continued to oversee the Rimor and MacGillean lands while Janet and he divided Cardden's holdings including the keep between the two Lusk brothers in return for a promise of semiannual proceeds from the profits. Finally, he bid Innes farewell; they gathered up their belongings, including Janet's loom, his bows and stonecutter's tools, and headed off for the Abbey of Our Lady of Fontevraud where their daughter lived.

Morven had long since accepted that no one was coming for her, and had taken her vows. She was married to the Lord, devoted to the abbey, and in particular to the current abbess, Audeburge de Hautes-Bruyères, who'd been in charge now for fifteen years, more than half of Morven's life. For the abbess, and for Sister Marguerite—which was what Morven answered to now—Thomas's elves were plainly demons, and he and Janet had been right to rescue their daughter from such influences. Witchcraft and malevolent spirits were everywhere these days. And hadn't God's knights fought two crusades to conquer such dark forces?

Knowing next to nothing of any crusades, Thomas could only acquiesce in the abbess's opinion. Morven had never seen an Yvag. Her only memory of a near encounter was of a voice outside their door the night that Janet had whisked her from their home. While

she wanted to believe her parents, her reliance now fell upon the Order of Fontevraud. These strangers might be her parents, but what did that word even mean? The busy abbess assigned Sister Marguerite to take Janet and Thomas on a tour of the abbey.

Fontevraud was a double monastery, Sister Marguerite explained to them, with monks living on the grounds in the Priory of St. Jean de l'Habit and working in support of the nuns, as unusual as that sounded. They all labored side by side while living separately. Altogether, the community numbered close to three thousand, with far more nuns than monks. She showed them the gardens of healing herbs, of vegetables and fruit trees, the smokehouse, the leper house of St. Lazar, and the abbey itself with its bone-white sculpted capitals. "Near one hundred of them," said Morven. Thomas replied reflexively, "One hundred two," then apologized for a facility he couldn't control.

They wandered the grounds, past a well, and a sepulchral chapel being erected, where nuns were to be interred. He couldn't help being suspicious at the sound of that, wary of anyplace where it seemed the dead lay sleeping. Crypts could never be trusted.

The abbey was built on a slope, and part of the lower wall surrounding it had collapsed after the spring rains. Thomas noted that as they strolled past.

When Morven returned them to Abbess Audeburge, he offered to rebuild the wall where it had fallen in. He and Janet, he explained, had moved into a small house in Chinon nearby, so that they could be close to their daughter. He would apply to join whoever was constructing the chapel building as well. The abbess asked if he wasn't past his prime with regards to working in stone. He looked, after all, like an old man of fifty years or more, matching Janet's appearance. It was Janet who spoke up then, to say that her husband knew more about the working of stone than anyone she had ever met and that the abbess would not regret taking him on. "You'll be working with monks," the abbess said. He replied that he had worked with them before, at the abbazia di Santa Maria di Lucedio in Italia. The abbess knew of that Cistercian abbey. If anything its mention suggested he was even older than she'd thought. Nevertheless, she agreed to take him on.

❈ ❈ ❈

By the time Innes died, Abbess Audeburge had also passed on and been replaced by the Abbess Gilles. Because of his masonry skills, Abbess Audeburge had referred Thomas to the seneschal of the Château of Chinon, and he had gone to work there for King Henry. Portions of the château remained unfinished, and it was often unoccupied in that time, but the work was suspended on numerous occasions while Henry battled his own sons and his queen.

Thomas watched the staff and advisors for any hint of Yvag habitation, but circumspectly, so as not to reveal his own identity. To the household of King Henry he was simply Tàm the Old Mason, whose wife wove lovely shawls and small tapestries, and who had a daughter in the abbey nearby.

That he could do the work of a much younger man was remarked upon, however, and so he started to do less. Routinely, he feigned exhaustion, a perfect excuse to spend even more time in the company of his wife. She had grown more frail.

Janet's hair by now was all white. At her loom, she did not pass the shuttle with anything like the agility of old. Her fingers were long, thin, and knobby, and often seemed to pain her. She and he lived well enough, with money coming from Filib Lusk twice a year to bolster what Thomas earned with his mallets, chisels, and trowels, and she with her loom.

Kester Lusk had died and his son had taken over his role as a tenant-in-chief, but Thomas didn't learn his name until word of Innes's death reached him, and he felt he must go home and settle things. He knew Janet would not come with him. Before he'd even asked, she told him, "These old knees of mine will never make the journey. You needs must go on your own, Tàm."

He didn't like being away from her. Too much of his life had been spent away already. But Innes was gone and the estate must be settled. In her last letter to him, she had stated that she'd put it about that a cousin of hers was expected, one Thomas Learmonth, thus covering his identity locally. Through her the unseen Learmonth had already purchased a small cottage in Ercildoun, so no one would be surprised by his arrival. Briefly, he considered cutting open a portal, using the ördstone of Alpin Waldroup he'd found long ago on the path through Þagalwood, and simply stepping from Chinon to Ercildoun, but worried that such an act would send ripples, alerting the Yvags to his whereabouts. They might follow him back home or, worse, arrive here while he was gone. He made sure that Janet was looked after in his absence. Abbess Gilles and Morven would ensure that.

So by horseback and by ship he returned to Ercildoun, which he'd never intended to see again.

There, for the first time in years, he went about without any glamour. After all, he was neither Thomas Rimor nor Tàmhas Lynn anymore. Now he was this new Thomas of his sister's creation. Stopping to give his horse a drink, he studied himself where the water was still: a young man with a short beard and thick dark hair, muscular and handsome. He disbelieved his own eyes. Surely this was more a memory of who he'd once been than a reflection of who he was. *This* was the Tàm of Janet's dreams. And anyway, it was impossible, wasn't it? At twenty years Janet's junior now, he was nearly fifty. Perhaps so long under glamour had a lingering effect, or maybe he hadn't fully thrown it off yet. Perhaps over the next few days he would advance to his proper age.

The town of Ercildoun had doubled in size, in part due to land Innes had gifted it. Their castle had become a manor, surrounded by nineteen workers' houses, a small church, fields of barley and oats, and even a small mill of their own operating on the Leader River. Innes had already been buried. She had left him instructions for the parceling and distribution of the land, lots large and small, naming to whom each should be distributed, and who would handle all of this for her. She had used her influence in order to have the property deemed adjudged a *fee simple absolute*. As such, it was hers to do with, and now his.

But Janet was ill, and so he remained only long enough to see a stone erected at Innes's grave and to visit Filib Lusk, now residing in Cardden's keep, to make one more request of him, that he follow up on Innes's instructions. Filib, near an ancient sixty, looked worn down, his hair thin, his teeth nearly gone. There had been no further business with the elves. So far as he could say, they'd stayed away. But, oh, how effectively Thomas was glamouring himself to appear young in his role of Learmonth. Thomas said nothing, but upon his return trip to Ercildoun, he paused at the pool on the Teviot where he'd once watched Janet swim, to look again at his impossible reflection. Who was this staring up at him? Not someone who had known more years of life than old Filib—Filib, whom he should have resembled by now.

He all but fled the pool.

In the morning, he would depart for Tynemouth but thought to pay a final visit to The Gorse and Hare, which was still a going concern in the same location where he and Alpin Waldroup had once spent the night. He hadn't heard the voice of that ghost in so long that he could no longer remember it accurately. When he'd sailed across the Channel with Janet, the spirit of Waldroup had remained behind.

In the tavern he confessed to being Innes's cousin, and was asked in turn if he intended to stay on at the manor. He started to explain that, no, he was entrusting a local party to execute her will, when his eyelids fluttered and the world seemed to tilt on its side. His head turned ice cold and lightning flashed through it, rattling his skull. The fit was so unexpected he couldn't fight it.

As if down a deep well, his own voice echoed to him.

"The eldritch gone for now return one day for all.

When the Thorn Tree of Ercildoun on the Common here doth fall."

He came to himself on the floor. A crowd of people encircled him and more were arriving. In the few minutes he'd lain unconscious, word had gone out that Thomas the Rhymer himself was back among them, here in the tavern.

He sat up and they pressed back, as if fearful he might use some mystical force against them, or cast a spell, or otherwise curse them for sussing his identity. He pulled himself up against the nearest table, then gripped onto it to stabilize himself while the world tossed off tiny sparks and tilted itself upright again.

Then the taverner stepped forward, put one hand upon his shoulder, and said, "Oh, sir, give us another—tell us our fortunes. When will that tree fall? Who are the eldritch?"

"I don't know." He shook his head, confused already as to what it was he'd said. "I don't know any of it."

He backed away. The crowd parted for him, and he turned and fled out the door, ran down the High Street to where his small cottage stood. They called to him all the while to come back and tell them more.

He knew what would happen next. Without him there, conflicting recitations would fill The Gorse and Hare—not just of this riddle but of many others, most of them things he'd never said. The two simple lines he'd spoken would mutate, until people were fighting over what they'd heard. The Thorn Tree was known to them all, but even he didn't know what the eldritch were.

What had he, Thomas Learmonth, meant? What was the secret of his riddle?

He had only minutes before the arguing factions banded together and marched off down the High Street in pursuit of their new True Thomas. He needed to be gone. His satchel was packed, his horse ready.

Now he heard the crowd approaching down the lane; as he'd imagined, they were arguing over what the *eldritch* could be: "Witches!" "Queer forces!" "No, creatures never made by God!" And someone drunkenly rejoined, "How can there be creatures never made by God?"

Quickly, Thomas cut a portal straight from Ercildoun back to Fontevraud. In his terror he had no trouble concentrating on his destination, turning, and sealing it up again. And if by some chance it alerted the elven now, so what?

Janet was dying. . . .

III. Hodde

Janet was dying and he'd known it instinctively. He could hear the rattling of her breath from across the channel.

He sliced open the night and stepped through. In the narrow gate, the imagined slavering Yvag warriors failed to materialize; the elven weren't expecting him, did not so much as notice him any longer. Of course they didn't. Probably they thought him dead, long dead; it had been forever since he'd handed Ainsley Rimor of Alwich over to the Lusks and brought back Innes. After that, Thomas Lindsay Rimor de Ercildoun vanished, rightly and truly dead, a living corpse of no concern to anyone, neither elven nor human, because no one alive other than Filib Lusk remembered him (and Filib was long dead now, too); they remembered only Thomas of the ballads, recalled only whimsical sayings that he'd never uttered, while they smeared and coated him with the daub and mortar of "True Thomas," obscuring the *true* Thomas, the Tàm of Janet's devotion, the father of Morven—identities long-buried and him nothing but a fading ghost of them, safe from prying elven eyes so long as he lurked in the shadows of this hut, so deep in the forest of Barnsdale that hardly five people knew of him, almost never encountered him. Those five surely counted him mad, which was such an easy disguise, for he *was* mad, wasn't he, living forever in the past where he crossed from Ercildoun to Fontevraud in two terrified strides, and his Janet hovered between life and death, her brown eyes full of love but mostly pain.

He'd had to let her go, couldn't find a way to rescue her another time. She'd whispered to him that she would meet him in Heaven. But he knew now that he would never reach there. Heaven was as far from him today as it had been as he watched the light go out of her eyes. He used to see her eyes so clearly. Now they were just shiny spots in the darkness; he was remembering the memory of them, and soon all of her would be gone.

He rolled into a ball on the sack of leaves that was his bed, gnawed on his beard, and ducked his head to hide from his own memories—except, someone was pushing at his door. Had the Yvag found him finally? Did it matter anymore if they did? Who was left to protect?

Outside the door, a voice groaned like some awful ghost and then called softly, "Woodwose? *Woodwose.* Tell me you're about." He squatted there in the dirt and stared as if the words were in some other language than his own. Memories fluttered around the periphery of his awareness. Then came a sigh and, "Please! Oh, dear Christ, I haven't much time."

The desperation of it banished the last of the past world where his wife lived on, his daughter, too—where he dwelled.

He uncurled, lay flat. He was in the hut he'd built, a monk's beehive hut that led most who encountered him to assume he himself must be an ancient monk; his mattress was a wool bag stuffed with leaves; he remembered filling it. He glanced around. There wasn't much to see.

Most of his belongings lay in a single chest that had once held Janet's weavings, themselves eaten by moths and so no different than his tattered recollections.

"Please," came the appeal once more from outside the door.

Why hadn't whoever it was already opened the door? Ah, but he'd thrown the wooden bolt, locking the physical world out. He couldn't recall doing it but knew he did it quite often. Besides, there was no one else, not even the ghost of Waldroup, who had never yet returned to tease or torment him. Someone was leaning against his door and soughing. Finally, he returned fully to the here-and-now.

To become again the nameless Woodwose, mad denizen of the forest, he had only to grizzle his long black hair and beard, both grown out so long that he seemed made of hair, and thin his body, making it seem ancient and decrepit. His clothing was hardly more than half-rotted linen braies, but needed no glamouring for a mad hermit. He stood up, spent another moment gathering his wits, then pushed open the creaking door.

Into his arms fell Robert Hodde.

Thomas gently lay the body down on the woolen bedding, ignoring the bow that clattered down as Hodde's fingers released it. Hodde's hands were covered with blood, and clutching at something balled up and pressed against him, itself drenched and dark.

"What's happened to you?" asked Thomas. His voice grated and creaked like the rusty iron hinges of his door. When was the last time he'd spoken a word to anyone? He sounded like—like when Nicnevin had robbed him of speech for weeks or months at a time. But Hodde was answering and he was missing it all. A prelate—Hodde's little trio had been engaged in a robbery. Then he was telling of a sword that could leap through the air. It was what had done for him, he said—the dance of that sword blade right through his side. Thomas carefully unlaced his short green cotehardie to see the wound. Indeed it was long, thin, and terrible, the gift from a sword blade thrusted straight through him. The magic sword seemed to be real.

Robbery gone awry was always the likely outcome for an outlaw such as Hodde, though all of his band pretended otherwise. And as outlaws went, Hodde had always showed some small kindness to Thomas, as if understanding instinctively the depth of his loss, the core of his madness, though Thomas had never told him of Janet and Morven.

Hodde hardly seemed to notice the investigation into his wound. "Little John saved me, Woodwose. Pulled ... pulled me aside."

Thomas chewed some more on his beard. What sort of sword could fly across distance?

Hodde looked at nothing as he babbled out his story. "'Twas John saw through the prelate's disguise."

"His disguise?"

"Aye, in pauper's sackcloth, like some ... penitent. But underneath, oh, jewels." His eyes shone excitedly, remembering. "An' spun gold thread. Here. See?" He pushed the blood-drenched bundle at Thomas, then lay his head back and rested.

Unfolded, the wadded material proved to be a long maniple covered in a motif of gold crosses; crushed up inside that was a rope cincture decorated with set stones, jewels. It had been white before Hodde's blood soaked it. At first glance the quality of the polished gems looked impressive. Certainly it hadn't belonged to any poor wandering mendicant, of that Hodde was right.

He set down the cincture and examined the maniple more closely. There was something hard in the middle of it. He ran his fingers and thumbs along it until he'd defined the hard round spot. Straightened and turned it over.

On the backside of the maniple, which indeed looked like spun gold, there was a hidden pocket with a small slit at the top. Thomas pushed up with his thumbs, forcing the object toward the opening. Whatever he expected—a larger jewel, a papal seal of some sort—it wasn't the large ördstone that popped out, and for one instant he didn't comprehend what he'd found. The tiny blue gems flickered at him. Whispers of machine intelligence tickled his brain.

He flung it across the hut. It struck the wall and bounced on the packed dirt of the floor.

No, no, no, no, not Yvags here. For the love of God, hadn't he left them far enough behind, left his war with them behind in order to live, to have a life with Janet and Morven?

Hodde had raised his head at the noise but sank back.

But he'd *had* that life, hadn't he, the years he was still clinging to. Janet was . . .

No, that life was over. Janet was dust, Morven, too, and him the mad monk of the woods north of the Shirewood because he had kept himself from returning to Ercildoun and all the confrontations he would certainly have had with them.

He glared at the black twinkling stone. He wanted to smash it, but also remembered the power that could unleash.

The unattuned hum of the thing still echoed faintly in his head, like a hornet trapped under a cup. Was it calling out to his own sleeping ördstone where it lay wrapped up and hidden in the chest in the corner? Over time this awful thing was sure to burrow into his mind the way Waldroup's collection of such stones had once invaded him. He must be rid of it. Even now it might somehow be seeking its owner, nearby Yvags. They wouldn't hear it . . . unless they'd followed Hodde. And what would he do if they had?

With effort Thomas swept away the clouds of the past. The

flickering stone couldn't be destroyed, and if it had signaled others, he must be ready.

An old tunic and shirt lay draped across the wooden chest of his meager belongings. He leaned over and grabbed the striped linen tunic, balled that up and pressed it to Hodde's wound. "Push with this," he said. "To stop the bleeding." He had to guide Hodde's hands around it.

What should he do? Who else was coming?

Gently, he asked, "Hodde, where is the prelate now?"

Robert Hodde opened one sunken eye and grinned again, showing that he still had most of his teeth. "You're not half so mad as tha let on, are ye, Woodwose?" Then he said, "Oak tree, split trunk, King's Way." He reached up and grabbed Thomas's arm. "Killed him, us, and like candle he just melted." He let go, dropped his arm.

A skinwalker. In possession of this stone . . . What else could he be? Fear leaked into his stratagem. "He melted."

"Doubt me?"

"How can I doubt a man who walked across the Shirewood all the way here? Why did you do that? Why come here?"

He spoke now without opening his eyes. "Much is dead, Little John run off for 'is life. Anybody else'd strip me naked, steal everything ah 'ave."

"No, we'll get you . . . a poultice, something."

"Yer daft. You go now—Great Limewood a Barnsdale. Tha remember Great Limewood. I showed it tha. 'Ole in it as big as th'ead, at second split. All mah treasure. I've family in Nottingham. Tanners all. You carry mah takings. Find Little John if them knights haven't killed him—"

He sucked in his breath. "Knights? You mentioned no knights."

"'Twas them two as wielded swords. Dressed for a crusade. I know it's mad."

Not mad. Yvag knights, of course. No crossbows now—new weapons to brandish. "You rest here and push on that." The wadded tunic was already saturated, and Hodde's color deathly gray. "No one will find you. I need to go have myself a gander at this prelate."

Hodde opened his eyes. "Nah," he insisted. "Great Linden—I mean, limewood. Swear."

"Yes, I'll see to it, I promise."

"Good man," he murmured.

Thomas found his shoes tossed beside the wood chest. He couldn't remember the last time he'd worn hose and shoes. Years it must be. No surprise then how stiff the leather was. He grabbed the linen shirt.

He picked up Hodde's bow now and studied it: well-crafted, but smaller than a warbow. He laid it down next to the outlaw. "In case you need it," he whispered. Hodde gave no indication he heard.

Outside the door, he paused to put on the shirt. It was ragged but hung over his braies at least. Hodde might have led the knights right to his door, but there was no one visible in the woods, no black-armored creatures approaching.

He'd resided here for decades, long enough that he'd likely encountered most every outlaw who made these forests their home, and probably half of whom had been captured and hanged by shire reeves or the Keepers of Sherwood Forest in the time he'd lived here. They all knew him for the reclusive mad monk, just a part of the woods, and left him alone. He wasn't on the King's preserve and posed no threat. They might also have thought him supernatural, given that he sometimes made his hut disappear altogether, throwing off the appearance of a thick cluster of vines. Most of the outlaws avoided him. But not Hodde.

Now, however, he was venturing out into their world, where he might not so easily explain himself—certainly the mad old Woodwose didn't belong out here. In that moment he exhaled, releasing the glamour. His long hair and beard turned dark again, and beneath the loose shirt his body remolded, lean and hard. He would look perhaps like another down-on-his luck outlaw. At least, unarmed, he could not easily be accused of poaching nor of slaying a prelate. And that was another good reason for leaving the bow behind.

He gave the nearby abbey a wide berth, unable now to recall its name. There must be a good half dozen abbeys and priories scattered through what he thought of as "the Shirewood"—what Hodde called Sherwood. Abbeys and priories were places he'd avoided in particular upon arriving—every abbey was Fontevraud, every priory Wariville. He was quit of such places forever; all they represented to him was loss, death, anguish.

He tracked through the wetlands along the River Poulter, heading toward a vast expanse of birch and oak. By now he would be well inside that wood.

Three roe deer paused in their foraging to watch him, then bounded away into the deeper shadows. He watched them vanish before he walked on.

He found the great split oak beside the King's Great Way, and if there'd been any doubt, Hodde's quarterstaff was leaned against it. He took the staff and walked out onto the wide pathway beyond it. Just as Hodde had described, two bodies lay there. The nearest was that of Much, the poor son of a miller and as harmless an outlaw as he could imagine, which this encounter with true evil certainly proved. That ushered him to the other body, though "body" was hardly the word for it. A dressed skeleton lying in a pool of stinking stew. With the staff he nudged it over. He knew what this meant. It brought up from the darkness of his past the death of Baldie, drowned and then inhabited, only to liquefy upon his second demise . . . the first time Thomas had encountered what the Yvags called a *conveyance*.

From the evidence of the miter and crozier lying near, this one had been a bishop—a skinwalker bishop in the company of two Yvag knights. Not so ancient a habitation as to rot and crumble away; he'd only been occupied for a few years, then.

Careful to avoid the "soup," Thomas squatted and tugged at the sackcloth robe, which rolled the body halfway over. There about its neck hung a gold cross. Hodde in his panic or haste had missed this. Thomas took it now, then stood away and breathed the clear air.

No sign of Little John or any knights, although it was easy enough to discern where they had run. In pursuit of him the Yvags had abandoned their bishop. Had that been in haste or had his usefulness ended the moment he was struck down? It seemed that what he carried was of more importance to them. Yet, if it was so important, why carry it through the forest when they simply could have opened two gates and jumped from point to point?

He wondered then: Was it possible that inhabited skinwalkers couldn't pass through their green-fire gates that way? Certainly, they stood on hand for the collection of *teinds,* but did any of them actually pass through the portals themselves? Then he remembered

Alderman Stroud stepping through the ring at Old Melrose after Thomas's brother, Onchu, had been walked through it. Hadn't Stroud sealed himself up on the far side of the ring, or had that been an illusion? Thomas had run into it at full tilt and been blasted through time. His memory was jumbled. What if Stroud had not actually left, had simply stepped behind the fire? The other times he'd observed them the knights and the Queen of Ailfion had returned through the portal, but the skinwalkers all went back to their assumed lives. What if Stroud had stepped through simply to draw him out?

He set the matter aside—something for another time. Right now, before the knights returned, he must be gone. It would be injudicious to be found anywhere near here. They would kill him whether armed or not, not even aware of who he was.

Of that he had no doubt whatsoever.

IV. Into the Woods

Hodde lay dead.

It came as no surprise. That wound likely had bisected his liver and skewered a kidney for good measure. The leaf-stuffed wool beneath him was soaked through with blood, and from his pallor Thomas guessed it was the last he'd had in him. Covering the distance to the hut had cost him dear. He'd never have reached Pontefract.

Thomas sat down beside the corpse. Hodde had treated him with common courtesy, more than could be said of many outlaws. Whatever else, he'd shown the "mad monk" some kindness—had even left him food on occasion.

Thomas needed to get far away from here—first to the Great Limewood and then, presumably, to Nottingham. He would have to do something with the chest of his possessions. It contained the few things he had left of Janet's. Leaving that chest for the Yvags to find was out of the question, but he couldn't very well haul it about with him.

He opened it, lifted up the small, moth-eaten tapestry that covered the rest; beneath it lay the black Yvag armor he'd kept all this time and which showed no deterioration from the last time he'd worn it, a lifetime ago. He quickly shoved the armor aside.

Where it had been lay his own ördstone, the one he'd recovered in þagalwood. He picked it up. The row of blue gems pulsed as if the stone were saying hello, communicating in some fashion though he hadn't beheld it in more than thirty years. He felt as he always had, that it was somehow attuned to him. Despite that he'd been transformed, he never understood what it was imparting. He sensed only pressure, a feeling of it moving about inside his thoughts.

He took out the two Yvag daggers he'd acquired over time, then gathered the very few things he would need. Hodde had conveniently presented him with a useful bow and a full quiver of arrows. His own and Waldroup's, which he'd kept, were likely too old and brittle to be of much use. Everything else must vanish for now, especially the bishop's ördstone, which went into the chest and under the black armor in place of his own. It flickered almost angrily, and its pressure pushed at his temples. He was sure that, if he slept in its presence, it would invade his dreams the way Waldroup's collective of such stones had done to him long ago.

He took his pointed stone hammer and mortar hoe blade (the handle had long since been lost), and went around the back of the hut, behind a large birch tree. There he knelt and chopped up the earth with the pointed end of the hammer, then dug out a long trench with the hoe blade, making one end wider and much deeper. Returning to the hut, he brought out the chest, and his mason's tools in the old, patched bag where he'd always kept them. He put the tools in the chest, too, and laid the off-the-shoulder bag aside. As he had no idea the size or nature of Hodde's "treasure," it would be wise to have something in which to carry it. Finally he placed his and Waldroup's bows, wrapped in cloth, in the hole. By hand then he pulled the dirt back over the trench, stood and tramped it all down, and kicked leaves and debris over it until he was satisfied that it was undetectable.

Hodde's body was another matter. The knights would undoubtedly track him here eventually. For one thing, Hodde had spilled too much blood along the way, but burying him in the woods was problematic. If he gave them any cause to look for the body, they might find everything else he'd just hidden from them. And a buried body meant someone cared enough to cover it up, which would send them looking for the true occupant of the hut. Better to let them have their body but not their answers.

Also, he had no desire to go about perpetually glamoured but half-naked in a linen shirt so old it would tear apart if anyone looked at it wrong. He needed clothes. Hodde no longer did, and while he'd proclaimed that Thomas was the only one who wouldn't strip him naked, under the circumstances it was exactly what he needed to do. After all, he was carrying out his outlaw friend's last request.

So he stripped the body, discovering as he did that clothing had changed somewhat since he'd last been aware of fashion. For one thing, Hodde's olive-colored leggings extended much farther up his legs than any hose Thomas had ever worn. And the braies tucked into the tops of them, which allowed them to be attached to the braies' girdle rather than being held up by bands (in his experience those almost never worked for long before the wool was piled around his ankles).

He bundled the clothing up and carried it to the nearby stream, where he knelt and washed it against the rocks. Blood snaked away on the water from the tear in the cotehardie. Most of it came out, and the red trim on the green wool more or less disguised the rest. The prelate's cincture and maniple were another matter. The white cloth remained pink with blood. Thomas studied the jewels more closely—mostly cabochons, they would fetch a pretty penny. Hodde's family would be well set up for a time.

He laid the clothing out in a patch of sunlight, then took an Yvag dagger and began sawing off his hermit hair and beard in repeated passes until both were as short as he wanted to go. The face that looked up at him then was a stranger, someone he hadn't seen since he'd last visited Ercildoun. *Janet was dying.* He banished that memory, and the echoes of people calling for The Rhymer, pleading for more of his fits, his nonsense verses. He'd only been plagued by fits a few times since settling in here.

He shook his head, glad he had not gone back there. Here the fits when they came were simply something he weathered. Most occurred when he was alone, although they seemed to be tied to anxious moments—especially to the intrusion of others. Far fewer of them plagued "the Woodwose." The worst was probably the one that had overwhelmed him in the company of Hodde's band, but it had also revealed Robert Hodde himself to be a trustworthy confidant.

He traded another look with the black-haired face in the water, leaned close to see the blue eyes, the pale scar on the right side of his head. Who was that? Surely not him. He was ancient, as old as Taliesin.

He finally plunged into the cold water, destroying the reflection. Then he bathed, and soaked his head to rid himself of loose bits of hair, held himself under long enough to drown all fleas and lice. When he crawled out on the bank again, he felt renewed. His lean torso ached from disuse. He'd lost muscle mass, although not as much as he would have expected.

Hodde's clothes did not fit him well. Hodde was skinnier than he was even now. The woven shirt stuck to him. The cotehardie was looser; the armpits had been left open for movement and flexibility that an archer would need. Even so, it was tight on Thomas, and he left it loosely laced over the shirt. He was sure he would split the shoulder seams of the shirt the first time he drew his bow. In Nottingham, perhaps he would engage the services of a seamstress.

Fortunately, Hodde's feet were about his size and the leather shoes fit well enough, better than his own.

The wet wool leggings were certain to itch, but at least this new method of attaching them to the braies' girdle was more comfortable. He tied the long belt around the cote, then tugged down on the fabric to hide the rent in it. Had anyone laid eyes on him then, they would have thought him one of Robert Hodde's merry band of cutpurses, or maybe the ghost of Hodde himself.

Returning to his hut, he attached his quiver to the left side of the belt, strung the two Yvag daggers in their sheaths to the right, then slid Hodde's bracer onto his left forearm.

Grabbing the quarterstaff to lean on, Thomas left his hut, circling into the trees away from where he was headed before doubling back, deeper into Barnsdale Wood. If the Yvags came this far and tried to track him, he would make sure they knew no joy at all.

Hodde's Great Limewood figured prominently in Thomas's brief history with the outlaw.

Hodde and his band—it was seven men at the time—had come upon Thomas's hut one chilly afternoon. They had been tracking an enormous buck and it had conveniently bounded off the King's preserve, meaning that they could legitimately kill it without running afoul of Isabella Birkin, chief Keeper of Sherwood Forest, and her forces. It was the deer that led them to the old stone hut and the "man of the woods" who dwelled within. They felled the buck within a few yards of the beehive hut. The commotion drew the recluse out. He saw what had happened and, without thinking, insisted he be given a portion of the quarry. All of them laughed at him, but Hodde immediately agreed—provided the Woodwose (as he called him) would accompany them back to their Barnsdale camp.

Thomas had reluctantly agreed, but had not been in their company five minutes when his head became cold as ice and jagged light flashed behind his eyes, mushrooming darkness in front. He fell to the forest floor.

When he came to, Robert Hodde was the only person with him and he was back inside his hut. "Sent others on wi' that buck so they'd no' see what I'm lookin' at."

Thomas looked at his hands. His glamour, of course, had deserted him.

"Nah then, what are tha?" There was awe but no fear in his voice. "This be fairy glamour?"

Thomas nodded. It was close enough to the mark.

"What did riddle mean?"

"I spoke?"

"Oh, aye. An' riddle to be sure 'twas." Hodde scratched his chin as he recalled it. "'A parting of ways, the band dissolves. Before is met a new friend, the survivor t' the Great Limewood will be summat.'"

Thomas nodded, listening to the riddle's retreating echo. "Summoned," he said. "Not summat. 'The great limewood,' what's that?"

"Our camp. Where we're goin'. Come on." Hodde reached down to him, drew him to his feet. "Well, put yer glamour back on first. T'others are nah ta know."

Then Hodde led the old Woodwose through the woods, across a broad heath, and then back into more trees. Soon they walked beneath a canopy of oaks, birch and ash, with a fairly clear forest floor. Thomas wondered who the "new friend" could be.

Even if their camp hadn't encircled it, the Great Limewood tree was unmistakable. Its massive trunk divided into five boles, easily climbable. Two displayed what he thought of as squirrel holes—from fist- to head-sized, enough of them that he could easily have mounted the lower half of the trunk until he was up among the foliage.

They had drunk ale, eaten charred venison and field fare, and probed him with questions: how long had he lived in Barnsdale Wood, had he had run-ins with the so-called foresters (who did not consider themselves outlaws, but representatives of the King's preserve, but mostly culled herds that "needed the trimming"). They'd returned him to his hut at evening's end with a cooked rump of venison, unharmed, and addled with drink for the first time in decades. Within months Isabella Birkin's Keepers had driven the band elsewhere, and probably arrested a few in the bargain. But not, it seemed, Hodde himself.

Now Thomas considered the riddle anew. Robert Hodde had hidden what treasure he had in one of the hollows in that limewood tree.

"The survivor to the Great Limewood will be summoned." The opaque riddle from years gone by was finally coming true: He was the survivor and Hodde himself had done the summoning.

V. The Bridge
Over the Maun

The limewood tree was massive and ancient. Even after many seasons, Thomas recognized it. There were mostly oak here. Limewood abounded elsewhere, south in particular, in Lyndhurst Wood. He could recall Much, who must have been twelve or thirteen at the time, climbing up into it quick as a squirrel, disappearing in among the leaves where he "magically" found a ram's horn that he blew into, sounding a thin trumpet blast that sent birds leaping from branches all around them.

"Care tha t'go up?" Hodde had invited him. "All manner of surprises in old trees." He'd declined. Much, clinging casually to a branch, grinned down at him.

Now, standing before the limewood tree once more, he wondered if Hodde had meant to tease him with his treasure way back then.

All signs of that camp were gone now; the forest had reclaimed them. The area around the tree was grassless and flat, not even a hint of a cooking fire. All the same, this was the tree Hodde had meant and no mistaking it.

He scanned the woods once more. Then, satisfied that it lay empty of spies, he leaned his staff and bow against the tree, put down his bag, and started climbing. The diverging boles made it easy to reach the higher branches off the main trunk within the canopy. Like Much that day long past, he disappeared within the leaves, the colors of his cotehardie and leggings blending into them. He reached a point where the bole split into two, which fit with Hodde's description. Now he was looking for a larger hole—one "as big as his head," but looking straight up, he didn't see it. There was a fist-sized knotty hole in front of him. He grabbed onto it and swung himself around the main trunk. There, on the backside of the tree bole, was a hole the size of a hornet's nest. Gingerly, he reached into it. You never knew what might have taken up residence in such a tree.

His fingers brushed against soft leather. He patted the shape, trying to judge its size. Then he closed his fist around the tied-off neck of the large pouch. It jingled when he lifted it. He swung back against the trunk of the tree, and the heavy pouch chinked against his thigh. He climbed back down, then knelt and untied the thong that secured the neck of the pouch. Inside were all manner of coins, mostly short-cross silver pennies. He quickly tied the neck again and clambered up the tree a second time.

He swung around the trunk once more and reached into the hole. The first thing he touched was the ram's horn. He drew it out. He was tempted to blow into it as Much had, but overcame the urge to draw that much attention to himself. He set it aside, reached in again. Sure enough, he found a second pouch. He lifted it out, then patted around in the hole. There was nothing else in it. He put the ram's horn back.

The second pouch proved to be much smaller, a belt pouch with a thick drawstring. Inside it were more coins, a few of gold.

Thomas returned to the larger pouch. He stuffed the maniple, cincture, and gold cross in with the cache of coins, then laced it closed again. He placed it into his empty mason's bag. The smaller pouch he tied onto his belt ahead of the two Yvag daggers. The prelate's possessions and the large bag of coins and jewels would provide for Hodde's family. The small pouch would do for him in Nottingham—a delivery fee. He picked up his bow, thanked the tree for its bounty, and set off on his way.

He must stick to less traveled routes and keep off the King's Way near where he'd found the bishop's bones. He'd no desire to meet those two knights. By now, he suspected, they would have slain Little John and be looking instead for Robert Hodde and the ördstone he had inadvertently snatched. They would not be easily satisfied.

Keeping to less-traveled routes meant also that he did not cross the River Maun at the village of Mansfield. Another bridge lay near the so-called King's Palace, a Romanesque complex in the king's deer park at Clipstone that he'd heard of but never seen. Thomas feared both of them would be too visible and too busy. If other skinwalkers or glamoured knights were about, they might be watching such crossings—especially for someone dressed like him. He circumvented the deer park, or at least what he remembered of its boundaries from decades ago, and followed the course of the river from there. The first crossing he came upon was a much more restrictive rope bridge. It hung from stakes driven in at each end and had planks tied in place every few feet above the fast-flowing water.

Wearing his bow across his back, he carefully worked his way from one plank to the next. He reached the middle of the bridge when a knight appeared on the far bank.

Thomas stopped. If this was one of the two knights who had attacked Hodde, a strange sword was about to be drawn. But the knight did not draw a sword. Like Thomas he held a quarterstaff.

On a closer look he appeared shabby. His surcoat, blue displaying a white cross, was filthy, as were his hose. His shirt of mail bore signs of rust; in places rings had separated altogether. He wore no helm, and his graying brown hair was long and matted, his short dark beard peppered with white. This was no Yvag. This was someone living in the forest. Not one of the elven then, though possibly a threat all the same.

The knight called out, "There is a fee to cross this bridge."

Thomas replied, "How so? The bridge at Mansfield requires no fee."

"Yet, you choose not to cross there." The knight pointed with the staff. "What is in thy sack?"

Thomas glanced at it as if only just discovering its presence. "Well," he remarked, "whatever it is, at day's end *you* won't possess it." As he spoke he let his foot find the previous plank, then took a step back.

"Surely one such as yourself knows the price of travel." The knight stepped onto the bridge, and took a second step. He wore no sword at all that Thomas could see. No weapon but the staff. That suggested he was persuasive with the staff.

Stepping back off the bridge, Thomas said, "I believe I'll seek passage elsewhere."

"Ah, but already you walked onto the bridge. Your fee cannot be waived."

He nodded, knowing it would go this way. He would not turn and run although he could certainly outrun a man in mail. He shrugged off the shoulder bag. "You really ought to post a sign, you know."

"Oh, but then nobody would *ever* cross."

"I do not see them lining up as it is." He pulled the bowstring over his head and set the bow down, the arrows from his quiver beside it.

"Well, there's some truth in that. You could just pay me." He was in the middle of the bridge now.

"I couldn't." He stepped back onto the bridge, then took one, two planks and suddenly jumped to the next; at the same time he swung his staff past his right ankle and straight up hard, but the knight blocked the strike at his genitals, turned the staff aside, continued the movement in an arc, and struck Thomas in the shoulder. He lurched off-balance, turning as he stumbled, his back to the knight, a seemingly helpless target. Guided by instinct then he thrust the staff straight back. The knight had taken the bait and lunged forward, and the staff drove into his belly, doubling him over. One foot slipped between planks, and he desperately grabbed a rope to yank himself upright.

Thomas swept the staff around his own legs as if describing a skirt. The tip caught on one of the ropes or he would have knocked the knight's feet out from under him and finished it. As it was the staff only nicked one ankle while the knight danced aside and thrust at Thomas, who batted the strike away.

"You've had practice," wheezed the knight. He swung at Thomas's knee.

"Not for a"—he parried the strike, directing the other's staff to slide harmlessly along his—"very long time." Quickly, he flicked his staff up into the knight's chin. Even as it struck home, the knight's staff rebounded off the plank beside him and caught Thomas's knee as he stepped forward. He missed his footing and fell, against and over the ropes. He glimpsed the knight tipped backward, feet off the boards, as he toppled into the river.

The current grabbed hold of Thomas. He stabbed his staff hard into the riverbed and let it drag him around it, out of the main current, then swam for a large boulder. Slowly, he hauled himself over it and to the riverbank, where he crawled out, spitting and coughing. He lay there a moment to gather his breath. "Four seasons full, I did not bathe," he muttered, and, using the staff for leverage, pulled himself into a seated position. "And now twice in one day."

With a groan, he climbed to his feet.

"I think I do not need another." Unsteadily he squelched back to his things. Of the knight he saw no sign. The weight of that mail hauberk had probably dragged the fellow to his death in the Maun.

Thomas gathered up his bag, his bow and arrows. He wiped water off his face. He turned to step onto the bridge . . . and there stood the knight on the far side, soaking wet and holding his chin carefully as if ensuring that his jaw still worked. One of his leggings was around his ankle.

Thomas shook his head. "Another round? Or do you waive your fee for the outlaw who bested you?"

"Bested me? You're soaked to the bone."

"And you're much cleaner than when I first set eyes on you, sir knight."

The knight considered himself. "Very well. A draw, then," he proposed.

Thomas stepped out onto a plank. The knight didn't move.

He continued across the bridge and as he neared the opposite side said, "Let us agree to no more man-to-Maun challenges today."

Laughing, the knight agreed and offered a hand to Thomas, who accepted. The knight pulled him the final step. "Free passage."

Thomas glanced back. "Do you do much business on this little bridge?"

"None at all, I'm afraid," replied the knight. "Everyone else has run away at the sight of me."

To which Thomas laughed. "Two outlaws, then."

"Well met." They strode off together. The knight introduced himself as "Sir Richard atte Lee. By preference I'm not an outlaw, you understand, purely by circumstance. I am, ah . . . out of favor, you could say. You fight well with a staff. Who trained you?"

"A man named Alpin Waldroup. He was a mercenary archer."

"So, dead, I take your meaning. I do not know his name. Was he a Crusader?"

"No. This was . . . some time ago."

"Not that long surely. You are, what, thirty years of age?"

He made a smile. "A little older."

"And your name?"

Thomas, out of practice, had no false name at the ready. Besides, by now, he thought, nobody would know his name any longer. "Thomas . . . Thomas Rimor," he said.

Sir Richard raised an eyebrow. "As in the ballads?" He half sang:

"'True Thomas the Rhymer did on Huntley Bank sit,
Plucking the strings of his lute, hey ho.
Met he there the Queen of Fair Elfland,
She seeking a worthy tithe to recruit . . .'"

"Ah." So, the songs lived on. "The names are similar, yes."

Sir Richard seemed to accept this. "Well, then, Thomas Rimor," he said, "come to my camp and let us break bread and crack cups of ale. It's too late in the day to wander deeper into these woods no matter where you're bound."

"And my sack?"

"Upon my word, I won't touch it."

Thomas walked along awhile before replying, "Some bread would be very nice."

VI. The Knight

The encampment seemed to be for more men, with a semicircle of five lean-tos around a central fire. The only thing missing were walls and a roof. The bread, Sir Richard atte Lee explained, one of those absent men had bought that very morning in Mansfield.

"Not stolen?"

"Where possible we don't steal from those we know. Certainly not from those on whom we depend. Bread and ale sustain us." He patted two casks placed side by side against the nearest tree.

"And the occasional King's deer?"

Lee opened his hands. "Well..." he said, and laughed. He collected two glazed cups from among the leafy forest floor. "Who can say how many inhabit the deer park?"

"Isabella Birkin, I imagine." Thomas watched to see what reaction mention of her brought.

Lee continued filling the earthenware cups, then plugged the first keg again. He handed Thomas a cup of ale, turned to the second cask, slipped a finger into a knothole in its lid, and pulled the lid off. He reached down inside it and came up with a half-eaten boule of bread, which he offered to Thomas, at the same time saying, "So, you know Isabella, then."

Thomas shook his head. "Only her name. We've not met."

"And dressed in the colors of Robert Hodde, you'd best not."

He glanced down at himself. "Then you knew Hodde."

Sir Richard leaned back his head. "You say 'knew'?"

"Yes, he's dead this very day."

"The foresters or the Norman reeve?"

37

"Neither. He was slain on the King's Way by two knights dressed, according to him, as for a crusade."

For a moment Lee pondered, finally giving his head a shake. "The King's Way tends to invite robbery. But crusading knights, I know of none in these woods save for me." He plucked at his tunic. "Crusaders' ghosts more like."

Thomas gestured at the tunic. "What crusade was that?" he asked. "They seem to have lasted forever."

"'Twas more than one, or perhaps less. What they call now the Children's Crusade when I was but fourteen. And from there a late plunge into the Albigensian Crusade, which was truly no crusade at all from my perspective."

"I know little of either."

Lee gulped his ale. "Nicholas of Cologne and another, a French boy named Stephen, brought together twenty thousand of us, children and adults, with the intention of retaking Jerusalem, something the papal-backed Crusaders had been trying to do for years. There had been four, you know, by then. The first two were fairly successful in reaching Jerusalem. The third, led by King Richard, reached but did not take the city. The fourth was an utter fiasco. The knights went off and sacked Constantinople instead. Christians murdering Christians.

"Stephen and Nicholas meant well, but they understood nothing of the real world, where their ideals meant less than nothing. We lost hundreds in the Alps on our way to Genoa. Many simply vanished without a trace. There came a point, I confess, where I thought something was stalking us to get its hands on the littlest ones. In that rarefied air of the mountains, you see things, imagine things. Shadow figures and green fire."

"Green fire?"

"I know, ridiculous."

"No," replied Thomas, "not at all." He imagined the Yvags overjoyed at the opportunity to steal children without the need to leave changeling creatures behind, though he had to admit he knew nothing of how they selected their *teinds*. Would they have insinuated themselves among the Crusaders in order to choose their prey? Glamoured or skinwalkers? He wondered, as he often had over the years in Barnsdale, how far from a sleeping Yvagvoja the occupied victim could travel before the connection was severed, and whether this king's forest was far enough away from Melrose. Then again, why assume Melrose to be the only portal?

"We were penniless by the time we arrived in Genoa. The Pope made it clear that he considered us misguided. He told us all to go home. Papal money had funded all the others and was even then funding the Albigensian Crusade; but for the zealous children following Nicholas and Stephen there was to be nothing. Many of them ended up kidnapped by slave traders, I fear. Genoa was not a friendly city for abandoned children. Nicholas was a naive and trusting fool."

How convenient a group of exhausted, destitute children would have been for the Yvags. Would one of Sir Richard's company have been a glamoured knight? Thomas asked, "What happened to this Nicholas?"

"I've no idea. I left. Joined up with a force on its way to the south of France to fight against the Cathars for Pope Honorius. I boarded a ship and never saw them again."

Thomas reflected upon all those soldiers he'd fought alongside with Waldroup, many of whom had come to be more than mere acquaintances. They would all be dead now, like everyone else he'd known.

Lee continued. "I escaped from one false crusade by myself attaching to another. We were being lied to. We were supposed to be fighting for God against a heretical sect that rejected Christ and believed in both an evil God and a spiritual God who did not concern Himself with the matters of the world. Already more than four hundred Cathars had been burned as heretics. That was how the crusade had begun, but by the time I joined, it had all become an excuse to steal land, often from people who'd nothing to do with the Cathars. We sacked Avignon, attacked Toulouse, killed more people, and in the end we proved nothing and advanced no cause for God. De Montfort, our leader, was obliterated by a catapult missile that landed on him, crushed him right in front of me. God did nothing to protect him. All of that carnage so that some houses, some property could change hands. There was I, a knight who'd enlisted to fight in the Holy Land for Christ, God, and the Holy Spirit. For all my efforts I'd not found an army engaged to do that anywhere."

Thomas took the information in. "You remind me of that man who taught me the quarterstaff and the bow." He was thinking, too, that Sir Richard must be the "new friend" of the riddle he'd babbled at Robert Hodde many years ago: He'd assumed it referred to Hodde's band being dissolved, but considering the men Sir Richard counted absent from his camp, perhaps not. The riddle had definitely pinpointed Hodde's treasure in the limewood tree, though.

"Was he a disappointed knight, your mercenary friend Waldroup?" asked Sir Richard.

"In some ways, very much so."

"And did he also return home to find the land which should have been his had been mortgaged to the abbot of St. Mary's to pay off debts his family had incurred?"

"Is that what happened?"

Sir Richard atte Lee nodded. "The abbot is also a former knight. When I attempted to assert my birthright, he had me dragged out, beaten, and left in the woods. Such a man of God that he is one of the largest landowners from York to Doncaster and called by some 'Red Roger.' It takes little imagination to see why. Nothing and no one stands in his way."

There was the same old pattern again: influence, power, holdings, property. Ercildoun revisited. He said, "Your abbot sounds as if he might be associated with the killers of Robert Hodde. Or with the prelate Hodde dispensed with at the very least. He was journeying from the north."

Sir Richard unbunged the keg and poured more ale for them both. Then he sat down beside Thomas, and seemed to dismiss his own travails. "Now you know enough about me. Tell me of yourself, Sir Thomas."

"I? There's so little."

"Oh, I think you lie. You are fashioned of stories. That much even I can see." He drank some ale.

Fashioned of stories he might be, but there were none he could describe. How was he to compress or make sense of his life? What could he tell about Janet? Or Morven? The true portrayal would be disbelieved by anyone, this disillusioned knight included. To tell the truth was to proclaim "I've lived more than a century and hardly aged a day"—a conclusion he'd almost managed to hide even from himself.

In the end he chose to say simply, "I had a wife and a daughter once, but no more."

"Ah, forgive me. I did not mean to make you relive such loss."

He shook his head. "No, nothing to apologize for. It is past."

"As much as anything ever is."

Thomas drank more of his ale. "True," he agreed. "We carry it with us into the present." He drank again, then asked, "And might I ask, what year exactly is this?"

Sir Richard guffawed. "Been in the woods awhile, Sir Thomas?"

"Aye."

"Well, it is the year of our Lord 1252."

All Thomas could think to say was, "Oh."

VII. Little John's Night

With night coming on, Little John returned to the split oak tree. He'd led the two knights a chase all the way to Bilhaugh Wood, evidently losing them there. The only bodies on the road belonged to the foolish Much and to the prelate, who had indeed melted. The evidence lay there for anyone to see. Magic was afoot. The less John knew about it, the better.

Apparently, Robert had escaped. Little John identified the place where he'd fallen; and blood on the ground and crushed ferns indicated that he'd made it back to the oak and retrieved his staff before continuing on—in any case, the staff was gone. Little John followed.

He anticipated at every turn in the path that he was going to come upon Hodde's body. The sky grew ever darker, the telltale spatterings of blood becoming harder to see, but by now he had an idea of where his friend was headed—to The Saylis, where he might hide out and be looked after. But Pontefract was an absurdly long walk for someone with so awful a wound as had been inflicted upon Robbie.

Instead, the trail into Barnsdale ended at the hut of the Woodwose. That queer old man couldn't possibly help, could he? But maybe Robert had reached the end of his tether here.

The door to the hut hung open. The interior was dark as a cave. Little John grabbed some dry grass and sticks, then ducked into the hut. Inside, he sparked a flint until he'd lit a small fire.

The corpse of Robert Hodde lay pale in death on a blood-drenched wool-covered bed tick, stripped of his clothing. The terrible wound in his side was a jagged blackness. He'd simply bled out. Yet, someone had taken his clothes, his staff, and his bow. Maybe the knights had come, and they'd captured the crazy Woodwose as well. They weren't human. More like demons who'd snatched their victim and Robert's soul back to hell. Terrible to contemplate. Robert and Much dead because the lad had been too impetuous. He should have listened to Robert and let the prelate and his men pass. Even that bishop he'd killed had been something unnatural.

John sat with the body awhile; at first he contemplated staying with it, but feared the killers would come back. They would kill him, too, despite that he had no idea what he'd stolen. The prelate's satchel contained three squat pyramids of four sides each, reminding him of the bodkin heads of certain crossbow arrows. Unreadable markings covered them—nothing to tell him what they were, what they did, why they were important. But the knights had come after him, abandoning the body of the bishop, so whatever the things were, they mattered to the fiends, and he had no idea what to do with them.

The longer he sat beside his dwindling fire, the more uncomfortable he became remaining there. He should head for Nottingham, put as much distance as possible between himself and those demons. If they could change shape once, they could easily do so again. Best also to travel in the night. He knew Sherwood better than almost anyone, well enough to navigate it in darkness. Doubtful the knights could match him.

For a minute, he stood and said his farewells to the spirit of Robert Hodde. Then he kicked ashes and dirt over the small fire and walked out. Taking a moment to orient himself, he identified a small path to the south, and set out.

Little John had barely walked half a mile back into Sherwood when the darkness lit up in the distance, a weird unsteady glow. He changed his course to creep up on the fire, thinking it must be someone's encampment, but the light vanished before he could reach the source. A will-o'-the-wisp, had it been? Those usually bloomed over a marsh, and there was wet marshland past the trees here. He glanced up at the moon. Bats flitted about, tiny forms crisscrossing the bright white disc. Seeing them made him uneasy. The Devil was about. Everybody knew that bats carried messages between witches and the Devil. Even as he thought this, another spark ignited, this time out of the trees and among the heather-clad heath, and he raced to see it before it vanished again, only to dive to safety in the heather.

The light came from a spitting green ring that hovered in the air. Two mounted knights sitting jet-black steeds flanked it. They might be the same two who had chased him—he could not see if they carried those swords—except their surcoats were different, presenting alternating red and black panels. Underneath those, however, their armor was black like the armor of the two who'd given chase that morning. The presence of these two suggested there could be even more of them about.

The light from the flickering ring played upon their shiny black helms. The fire made them look green and dazzling. However, they and their horses remained as still as statues while tiny things pouring from the hole flitted about them. He thought the flying objects were more bats—evidence of the Devil's work—but these darted and wheeled about, not at all the way bats flew. More like a small murmuration of starlings above and around the opening. Something else then, but he couldn't say just what.

The center of the ring seemed to be empty, like a well that had been tipped on its side, when suddenly a new figure emerged out of it. This was a woman, golden-eyed and flame-haired. She wore a deep green sideless surcoat and a tall, filigreed gold crown. Her features were unnaturally extended. It was as if someone had stretched her virescent face, tilting and enlarging her eyes in the bargain. Her hands, resting upon the shining silver bridle, appeared to have extra joints. He could not say why, but everything about her exuded a threat. Could the Devil be a woman?

The tiny imps flocked about her. *Queen of the Faeries*, he thought.

Two more figures followed her—more mounted knights, these without surcoats at all over their black armor. Their jaws, visible beneath the helmets, were long like hers, but sharp-chinned and spiky. And their fire-eyed mounts were no horses at all. Demons, he was certain. This was what they looked like, wasn't it? A convocation of demons.

Then the one he thought of as the Queen spoke to the demons—at least he assumed she was speaking. The sound of their conversation reached him as a strange chirring, as if they had filled their mouths with beetles. The Queen gestured about herself, pointing to various directions. When she pointed at Little John, he ducked even lower, startled and ready to flee. But, no, the Queen was turning about and riding back into the circle. Some of the flying imps dove in after her, but others continued to flit about.

One of the mounted soldiers then swung down, and faced the hole, knelt and slashed one hand from the ground up. The hoop of fire collapsed and disappeared. It was all magic. How it worked, John did not know, but he'd no desire to investigate it further, else they capture him and drag him to hell.

Before the knight had regained his mount, Little John was away, on a path too small for a horse. He knew all such paths and that no one would come riding after him. Soon he branched off, and then did so again, to make sure that no one could follow as he headed for Nottingham.

VIII. Fontevraud, 1207

The ale from Sir Richard must have been very strong, and they consumed a goodly amount of it. Thomas remembered only crawling beneath a lean-to in order to pass out. By then the conversation with the knight had stirred up his memories of Janet again in ways he did not want, but not wanting to think of these things meant only that he could not *keep* from thinking about them. He drifted, perhaps into slumber, but soon enough into the depths of memory....

Abbess Gilles found Thomas's swift return from Ercildoun quite amazing. He should have been weeks longer. That said, he was right to have come back so soon, because his wife was losing ground rapidly and nothing to be done about it.

Morven and the abbess had moved Janet to the abbey's infirmary. The nuns grew poppies in the garden, an extract of which allowed Janet to sleep comfortably, hopefully to regain her strength. But each time she woke from these long induced naps it seemed as if she had lost a little more energy, not gained. Upon waking to discover Thomas at her side, however, she rallied. Her brown eyes shone with joy, and for a few days she was up and about, denying that anything terrible plagued her, although her skin remained clammy to the touch and her brow feverish. She wished to return home. She remained so insistent that the abbess advised Thomas to take her to Chinon. "She will not last a week regardless of where she is situated. Better with you, her good husband, than in our infirmary surrounded by ailing lepers." She added, "I'm sending Sister

Marguerite with you. Ministering to the sick is one of her duties." At least this meant the three of them would be together, however long she endured.

Death was in the air, it seemed. News had arrived at Chinon that King Henry's son, Geoffrey, had been trampled by a horse in Paris. He would normally have been interred at Fontevraud, but his father was quite content to have his most adversarial son buried at Notre Dame cathedral instead.

After two days, Janet's newfound energy failed her. She was at her loom. She abruptly became confused as to where to pass the shuttle. She met his gaze with alarm, then simply fell forward. He was there to catch her. He lifted her up and carried her to bed. Janet weighed hardly more than a sparrow.

Father and daughter maintained a vigil from then on, one of them always awake with her. Mostly they just watched her sleep and listened to the crackle of her breathing. She didn't need the poppy tincture now to sleep. At one point, he stood in the shadows and beheld Morven in a pool of candlelight at her mother's side, and it was for a moment like seeing Janet twice.

When the change came, it was slight, a shift in the rhythm of her breath. Both of them knelt beside her, speaking to her as she slept. Her breaths became softer and softer until, finally, they ceased.

He clutched Morven to him as he wept. She received him stiffly and shed no tears.

Morven left to inform her abbess. Gilles suggested they bury Janet in one of the cemeteries near the Chapterhouse, beside but distinct from the cemetery of nuns. She could be placed there, where others of the small town surrounding the abbey had also been laid to rest.

Thomas was bathing Janet's body when his daughter quietly returned. More than a few minutes passed before he realized she was there; when he did notice her, the combined look of confusion and shock on her face stopped him. He set the sponge down in the bowl of water and drew a sheet to cover Janet. He'd been so intent upon cleansing Janet's body that he had neglected to glamour himself into Tàm the Old Mason, Tàm her father, Tàm who wasn't yet thirty.

Head bowed, he said nothing, and waited for her to speak.

"What are you?" she asked.

"Your father," he replied. "Altered by my time with the—"

"Demons."

"Worse than any demons, Morven. Calculating and sly, murderous things."

"Did Mother—"

"She knew, yes. But I kept it hidden mostly, from her, from everyone. Not because it's something evil. I did not want to remind her of what had happened, how we'd been separated for near twenty years—her years—but only a handful of months for me before I managed to escape. Time in Ailfion, it doesn't run the same as here."

"Ailfion?"

"It has many names." He rattled off the ones Alderman Stroud had given it: Elfhaven. Álfheim. Ildathach. Then he added, "One of the elves suggested its true name was Yvagddu."

She stared at him as if she'd just discovered he was mad. "Elves. You escaped from *elves*?"

"Yes, from elves." He glanced down at Janet. "I didn't mean to keep it from you. I was keeping so much from her so that we could go on being together. Otherwise, my appearance would have been a constant reminder of my difference, the distance dividing us. That would have been too cruel. And people would have noticed, wondered, whispered." He shuffled where he stood, and in an instant he was his old self with gray hair and hollowed cheeks. "I'm sorry I forgot."

Morven asked him to remove the glamour again.

Reluctantly, he did so, head bowed.

She came closer. He watched her without turning his head. "But you are younger than *I* am," she said. "Twenty years younger at least."

"I . . ." He considered what to tell her, how to tell her. "The Yvag— that's what the elves call themselves—they have a pond, the changeling pool, where they immerse human babies stolen from our world, like my sister's child. Changelings. Its waters turn those babes elven."

"What has that to do with this?"

"In my escape I hid from them in that pool. I knew not its magical properties, nor had any idea that the waters were changing me, too. I returned home believing our differences—your mother's and mine—were all down to the inequities of time here and in their world. As your mother aged, I began to see it was more than that. She grew older while I . . . "

"You were hiding this from yourself, not from my mother."

Her accusation stung. "You're right, of course. I didn't want to face what happened to me, what I've become."

"And what is that, Father?" She seemed impatient with him.

"Forever a new cousin, forever an arriving stranger." He stared into her eyes. "What they took from me was time itself. Very soon now everybody I've ever loved will be gone from this world. I lost you, Morven, years ago. You and she were stolen from me. It was how it had to be if you were to go on living. The elves would have murdered you both. And now I can't have you back, I can only hold onto you going forward for however long that lasts."

"You're right, Father. You lost me so long ago, your reasons no longer matter. You made the choice. I was left behind. No one reclaimed me from the Church. Now all we have is the time ahead. There is no time before."

After a minute, he cleared his throat. "I would remain here with you, if you'll let me stay."

She nodded and stated very matter-of-factly, "Abbess Gilles wanted me to assure you that you can be buried beside Mother."

A smile quivered on his lips. "Your abbess will likely be disappointed."

Thomas remained at Chinon for eight more years, an old man attended to occasionally by Sister Marguerite. King Henry was dead and entombed at Fontevraud; Queen Eleanor was in residence at the chateau. Tàm the Mason was too old to work; he lived reclusively in his cottage. The money from the Lusks ceased arriving, which he suspected meant that Filib had finally succumbed to old age. But Thomas had saved enough of it that he could still pay for the few things he needed to live. Morven was now supervised by a new abbess, Mathilde of Flanders. Caring for elders in the villages of Fontevraud and Chinon allowed Morven to visit him. She brought him vegetables and herbs from the abbey gardens, but never stayed long.

Abbess Mathilde died in her turn and was succeeded by a further Abbess Mathilde, this one from Bohemia. Almost immediately upon arrival, she selected a group of nuns to populate the Priory of Wariville, a part of the Order of Fontevraud north of Paris. Because of her work on behalf of the needy all the way to Chinon, Abbess Mathilde named Sister Marguerite to be prioress.

Morven broke the news to her father. "At least you can shed your glamour awhile," she said. "No one in Wariville will know you."

By then he had gone about so long looking ancient, gray-haired, and gray-bearded that he could hardly recall what he looked like otherwise. Morven, at fifty-one, was also gray-haired, like her mother.

He had to sell his cottage, the last place that anchored him to Janet's memory or anything on Earth. Could he do this and begin again? He wasn't sure. There seemed no point to it all. He wasn't fighting the elven, though he knew they wouldn't have given up taking innocent souls as sacrifices; he wasn't at his wife's side—in fact in his isolation he felt that she was already blurring, fading like a ghost in sunlight. He thought he heard her voice in Morven but could no longer be sure. Janet had been the one who spoke French well. He still stumbled through it, as he stumbled through reading and writing. She had taught him a great deal. He'd relied on her for so much.

It was difficult interacting with people now. He was unused to it. He doubted he would ever get used to it again. Nevertheless, in short order he sold the cottage and purchased a cart, loading what little he would take. That included Janet's loom, from which hung the half-finished tapestry she had been working on when she died. Morven had, once or twice, offered to finish it, for the pattern was clear, but he didn't want it finished, as though if he left it like that, Janet might somehow return, drawn perhaps to its incompleteness. The loom was the largest thing he owned. He left behind most of the furniture, save for one trestle table and a stool, a chest with his winter cloak and boots in it along with Janet's few possessions, her shawls and hangings, and of course his and Waldroup's bows.

He headed north ahead of the Fontevraud nuns. He hoped the town of Wariville or one of the lords of Clermont would be able to offer him some employment.

He was fortunate that Count Raoul of Clermont, prior to departing upon a crusade alongside Phillipe Auguste, had made arrangements to see that the priory was supplied with wood for their fires. Thomas kept silent rather than ask about the crusade, lest they think him an idiot. The count's foresters were shy a man, and the young, muscular Tallis Maçon was exactly what they were looking for. Many of the men were housed together on the count's estate. Thomas, when asked about himself, told the others he had lived many years in Chinon near the Abbey of Our Lady of Fontevraud. It was all that he knew of France any longer, and he dared not invent some other story, certain that one of the other men would be able to see through any fabrication. Yes, he told them, he knew the priory for whom they were cutting the wood was of the Order of Fontevraud, and nearly added that his daughter was to be the new prioress before he stopped himself, realizing how absurd his claim would seem. Instead, he rattled on nervously at length about working for King Henry on his chateau. One of the men asked how old he was. Fortunately, the others then waxed on about what life as a king must be, and he clamped down on his desire to blend in. No one could know his stories. There was no one who could ever know the truth of him, and none who would have believed.

When Morven and the other nuns arrived in October, he was delivering cut wood for their fires and hearths. She saw him, but said nothing. Her duties as prioress kept her busy, responsibilities further limiting her freedom to visit him. The count never returned. Word of his death arrived borne by Gerard de Saint-Pierre, a baron who had accompanied him. The man stood before them all and announced the death of their count during the siege of Acre, proclaiming it the death of a noble man blessed by God. It had been a long time since Thomas had heard such speeches, most of them on battlefields in the aftermath of some engagement or other where lords or knights, never infantry or bowmen, had fallen. This proved no different.

It was as he watched the baron afterward that he began to suspect something was not quite right about him. In particular, it was the way the man leered after Count Raoul's widow and daughter—a look with which Thomas had become too familiar. His own father had worn it, and the one who played at being his cousin from Alwich. It was the look of an Yvag steeped in lust within the human shell they inhabited.

"Of him be wary," he warned Morven. "Your flock, too, else he's likely to cull a *teind* from the priory, but not until he's used her as he likes."

The baron married the widow, and Thomas found himself released from the count's service. He moved his belongings to an abandoned hovel nearer the priory and glamoured himself once more into an elderly man, albeit one who was still sturdy enough to handle himself. Tallis Maçon was gone, never to be seen again.

Morven was over sixty herself now, and arthritic. He would see her shuffling through her journey from priory to ville to minister to the sick and needy, but did not intrude upon her solitude.

Then one morning in May of the year 1207, she did not appear at all. He stood in the doorway for a time, watching. None of the other sisters were about that morning, either.

Finally, he walked to the high-walled priory himself. It was immediately clear that something had occurred. The sisters were all gathered in the yard. One of them began to wail. Thomas became afraid to move.

A nun came rushing up to shoo him away. He asked what had happened. "Oh, so awful. The abbess of Fontevraud has died—"

"Oh, I see." Morven had probably been called home—

"No, indeed you do not," said the nun. "We brought this terrible news to Sister Marguerite before matins only to find that she had died in her sleep this very night as well." Another nun cried out in anguish behind her. Thomas stumbled back against the stone wall. His chest felt as if it was splitting down the middle. Not Morven, not her, too. Had there been signs? Of course there must, there had. Her body had been giving out for such a long time. He'd watched, unable to do anything else. She didn't want his help, didn't want *him*. And now he couldn't even ask to see her, could he? Would these sisters allow him in?

"Impossible," the sister answered his request.

"But she was my . . . my child."

The nun looked at him in some mistrust, and quietly suggested he go home. When he tried to protest, she said, "Sister Marguerite, I'll have you know . . . Oh, my dear God preserve us!" She clutched the cross at her breast. "Devil!"

It took him a moment to understand that in his grief, he'd shed his glamour right in front of the nun.

He backed away, out of the open gate. Turned and fled, his head down, tears streaming from his eyes. He could not bid his daughter farewell, could not kneel and pray beside her body. Could not remain here any longer. Morven, the last attachment he had to anyone or any place, was gone. All of them gone and him a stranger in everybody else's world. He would never be buried beside Janet.

Thomas acquired a horse to pull his cart, drove it to Boulogne in Flanders, and there bought passage across the channel to Sussex. In his anguish, his madness, he intended to go home, to be Thomas Lindsay Rimor again. But the nearer he got, the more oppressive became his terror at arriving where no one would know him or acknowledge him as anything other than Thomas Learmonth, Thomas the Rhymer, the True Thomas of make-believe.

He was dead thrice over at least and cursed to remain on Earth until God took him.

Near Doncaster, he abruptly turned away from his journey northward and headed across Sherwood Forest and into the depths of Barnsdale Wood, where he intended to lose himself completely and forever. "Forever" had lasted forty-five years.

IX. The Waits

At dawn Sir Richard and Thomas arose in Lee's camp, both groaning over the bruises they had sustained in their river contest. The knight leaned on his staff as he hobbled about. Neither man commented upon the injuries, as if such discomfort was merely part of their daily tasks.

"What now for you?" asked Thomas. "More guardianship of your bridge?" He tore a hunk off the remaining bread, winced, and chewed it.

Sir Richard made to smile but immediately winced as if the act was painful. "No," he answered. "I have five men to hunt up who should have by last night arrived here. Something has forestalled them."

"I would offer to help you look, as a courtesy to my generous host, but I've given my word to a dead man that his family shall receive his proceeds."

"And that's something you must honor. If I'd understood that yesterday, I would not hurt so much this morning."

"You gave as good as you got," Thomas assured him.

Sir Richard filled the two cups with ale, handing one to Thomas. "To equality," he said. Thomas laughed and drank it down.

"So, tell me, good Sir Richard," he asked, "which path takes me to the King's Way?"

The knight pointed to the southeast. "That one, follow it between the birches. It will lead you across open grassland, and into the oaks again before Clipstone. You might even catch sight of the King's Houses along the way."

Thomas picked up his mason's bag, pulled the strap over his shoulder. "I'll be off, then. May we meet again where I can return your hospitality."

"Good hunting, Sir Thomas," said Sir Richard and they parted ways.

As promised, the path led Thomas to the King's Way, well south of Robert Hodde's split oak tree, even though he eventually lost his way and somehow missed both the place called Clipstone and the royal hunting estate.

As he arrived on the broader road, he found that he was not alone, and paused at the edge behind a tree.

A wagon was rolling along from the north. Poles projected up from its four corners, with colorful pennants at the top of each, and large dyed sheets of linen canvas hung between them. Six men walked alongside and behind the wagon, dressed in patchwork kirtles, smocks, and one in a long red robe. One of them at the back whistled a tune briefly, then repeated it. The man in front of him put words to it, singing, "Oh, my dear Catherine, she must be..." The younger man in front of *him* finished it: "... the ugliest witch in the north country." Objections followed along with laughter. "Oh, now you're stealing lyrics, Warin! At least invent your own, you thief."

"But it *rhymes*," insisted Warin, and the others piled on with their opinions in a blustering but friendly way. It was into this raucous debate that Thomas inserted himself by stepping out onto the road.

Horse and wagon drew up. "Thief, thief, armed to the teeth," recited the heavyset driver. The six on foot left off arguing to look him over.

"Are there more of him, Benedict?"

"Out, outlaws!" called the red-robed man, who towered over the rest. He turned to them. "That would make a good title for a little play, no?"

"So 'e's alone, then. I must say, very brazen."

"Brazen?"

"To pull a robbery by himself."

The man nearest him, balding and gray-bearded, placed a firm hand upon his shoulder. "Thy bow and thy staff, they comfort thee?"

"In Latin, for God's sake, Elias!" cried the tall one. "Do you want to get us hanged before we've even rehearsed?"

"How so, Geoffrey? He's neither bishop nor cardinal, but bedecked in Lincoln green."

"I repeat, *thief.*"

"Shush, Benedict. For all you know he's in excellent standing in the Pipe rolls. Good sir," said Elias, "are you a traveler?"

"Ask him does 'e 'ave any musical talents?"

"What? Why, Osbert?"

"We might be able to rid ourselves of Warin."

"Oh, an' thankee, ya lout," Warin answered, others laughing.

The one called Elias asked Thomas, "Where are ye bound, stranger?"

"Nottingham."

"Oh, ho," crowed Osbert. "Then ye must enlist in our company."

"Or accompany our list." Geoffrey leaned to one side.

Someone at the back blew a raspberry at that.

"But . . . forgive me," said Thomas, "who are you all?"

Replied Osbert, "Why, sir, we are the Waits of Nottingham." They all bowed theatrically.

"You've heard of us, naturally," said the tall Geoffrey. He made a great show of bowing.

"I am sorry to say I have not."

"You see?" whined Warin. "We are less and less relevant with each passing year."

"Well, *you* are," called one at the back.

"What are the Waits?"

"Ha' ye been living in the woods or someplace on the moon?"

"Hush up, Osbert. After all, if he hasn't visited the town yet, he's likely no experience of us," Elias said. He seemed to be the leader of the troupe. "The Waits," he explained to Thomas, "are the watchmen of Nottingham. For example, we blow horns—"

Geoffrey had reached into the wagon, drawn out a long straight brass horn. He blew it so loudly that Elias jumped and Osbert glared.

Elias cleared his throat. "And we bang drums and generally sound the alarm if the town is besieged."

Thomas asked, "Is that effective when you do it from here?"

"Oh—"

"He has a point."

"Ahem!" Elias cleared his throat with extra vigor. The others fell silent. "Four of us are on watch in Nottingham at all times. Which determines who makes up the company, for we're also in great demand as traveling players these days."

Geoffrey chimed in, "We have just completed three days in York and another in Warsop. I'm surprised you ain't encountered us somewhere."

"I've been living in the woods."

"Ah, heh-heh, I apologize for that remark," Osbert replied.

"Why?" asked Thomas. "It's true. I have been."

"What? Really. Well, for how long?"

"On that I'm a bit vague. Long enough that I seem to have missed four crusades."

They silently exchanged confounded glances. Then Osbert began to laugh and the others joined in. Geoffrey insisted, "We must steal that. 'I stayed out so long I missed the *Crusades*!'" He howled with glee.

As the laughter died down, Thomas said, "So you bang drums and play horns in other towns and villages, too? Do they not have a watch of their own?"

"You're a true marvel, sir, don't mind me saying."

Warin said, "We perform music, plays, stories. Yes, we do *Robyn and Gameleyn*, about three boys with deadly archer's skills. Everyone dies in the end—it's very satisfying."

"And there's *Thomas of Erceldoune's Prophecy*," added Elias. "That's ever the crowd-pleaser, because of course we simply make up new items to fit where we are. But you trade on a name such as that and everybody believes."

Thomas had to work not to react.

"And of course the tale of *The Monk and the Devil*. You *must* know that one."

"Sorry. I don't."

"Really? What has happened to education? Well, it's about a monk who wants to be a great healer and so he bargains with the Devil for knowledge of the curative powers of every plant. He becomes the great healer, warding off many plagues and terrible illnesses—until the Devil inevitably comes to collect his soul, and the monk, opening his final bottle of wine, hands the Devil a potion to drink because he has fashioned an elixir that keeps the Devil away, a bottle prepared years ago in anticipation of this very day. So he drives off the fiend and goes on healing the sick."

"Speaking of which," said Benedict with some urgency, "we need to go on, too."

"Oh, apologies. I've held you up."

"He held us up. Told you 'e was an outlaw!" cried Benedict to the amusement of almost no one.

"Yes, you did," Elias replied heavily. "Please walk along with us if you like, sir. Those of us who are *not* Benedict, including young Calum way at the back, would enjoy your company." The wagon lurched forward and they all continued down the King's Way.

Warin said, "Perhaps, too, we can convince you to join the Waits. If you're staying in Nottingham, of course."

Osbert strode forward. "Are you by chance at all good with disguise?" He drew a hand across his face and where it passed his features seemed to transform. "Like that?"

Thomas studied the ground. "Not really, no," he lied.

"Oh," Osbert replied. "Well, we could teach you."

"Let the man be," said Elias. "Forgive us, but the forest is queer today, and has unnerved us all a bit."

Geoffrey said, "Tell him of the body." To Thomas he added, "'Twas the most unnatural of spectacles."

"I was..."Elias paused, making an effort to keep control of his temper.

Osbert interjected. "About five mile back, we come across a body in the road."

Thomas tried to look surprised. He was, after a fashion—surprised the Yvags had left it there. Did that mean they were still in pursuit of Little John and whatever he'd stolen? He hoped so.

"A skeleton, it were," said Osbert.

"But dressed up in bishop's robes and miter. With an ivory crozier to hand," Warin added. "That we, ah, brought with us. Wonderful prop it'll make."

Benedict said, "I'm still thinkin' it's some outlaw's prank."

"Sure and if 'is name's Till Eulenspiegel."

"'Tweren't owls nah mirrors a part of it."

"What if 'e were the bishop of Skillington, then?"

A collective of groans followed that. Geoffrey blew another blast on the horn.

"But e'en before that," called one of those in back, "were a very strange night in the high forest."

"What was so strange?" Thomas asked.

"Lights. Odd fires. Odious small flying creatures that harried travelers, pulling at their hair and biting them."

"And the ghosts o' knights on black steeds wi' hot coals for eyes, straight from hell."

"You saw these?"

"Well, *we* didn't," admitted Geoffrey. "Maybe one weird fire off in the distance, and Warin swears one of them flying *fae* bit him while he sat on watch. Show him the marks, Warin." While Warin pulled up his sleeve, Geoffrey went on. "Nah, others we passed this morning told us they had been assaulted by them ghosts."

"Ransacked their belongings, ne'er said a word."

"Couldn't just be more outlaws, could it?" he asked.

"That is precisely what I said," Elias replied, obviously happy to share an opinion at last.

"Don't forget how the little flying beasties went tearing open sacks of grain."

"More like elves or fairies, *I* think," argued Benedict.

"Or mice," suggested Thomas, though he knew exactly what flying beasties these must be.

Geoffrey lurched in closer to the conversation. "I wager e'en now we are under observation."

"But you always think that," countered Osbert.

"In Sherwood, aye, I do," Geoffrey agreed. "The size of our company is the only reason we're not robbed coming and going. Too many of us. Plus, we have weaponry." He reached into the wagon and drew out an arming sword that might have been a prop. He slashed with it as he continued walking. The others, as if wary of him armed, immediately allowed him more room.

In that moment, blond Warin ran up and showed Thomas where he'd been bitten on the forearm by something with tiny needlelike teeth, a perfect oval. "You see? I didn't imagine it, an' that's no bat nor bird."

Thomas had to agree. Even as he nodded, for a moment he felt a dull pressure in his head. He braced himself, expecting a fit to drop him in his tracks and a new riddle to come spewing forth, but the sensation dwindled as they walked along, and he wondered if Geoffrey wasn't perhaps right and they had just passed hidden Yvag knights or even a cluster of those hideous little hobs in the woods.

"In that case," he said, "I'm doubly glad to be in your company."

Elias's response was to ask, "And what do we call you, sir?"

Unprepared as he was, he knew he couldn't be Sir Richard nor himself now, and if they performed some sort of *Thomas of Erceldoune* play, they might even know both of Learmonth and his Tàm Lynn guise. In desperation, he reached for a name the Waits had themselves thrown out only minutes earlier. "Robyn," he said. "The same as in your play."

"Of course." Elias smiled in a way that suggested he knew it for a lie but would let the name pass.

Thomas saw the look but was far too focused on what they'd told him about the weird night. The flying homunculi and the described knights were all too familiar, and he found himself wondering again what Little John could have stolen that had brought those eldritch creatures openly into Sherwood Forest.

X. Sir Richard's Mistake

Sir Richard atte Lee removed his armor before he headed north in search of his comrades. In cotehardie and hose he could move much faster. He brought his sword along and his staff, but not the items that announced his relationship to the crusades. After all, the costume had failed to strike any fear into his most recent opponent.

His band ought to have crossed the River Maun in returning, but none of the five had. One or two delayed he could perhaps understand, but all five gone missing—that was too peculiar.

There were plenty of places they might have camped, places that he and others used, for instance the so-called bramble fort, a naturally cultivated barrier that had warded off many unswerving pursuers who didn't know that the entrance was tiny and could only be used by someone crawling on their belly.

There were sinkholes and crevices of various depths hidden in the veins of surface rock amongst the heath of Sherwood, too. All the outlaws knew the same hideouts, the same hollow trees, the same meeting spots.

He was approaching Edwinstowe when he came upon the first body floating facedown in the water among the reeds. Hugo Eylmer was one of his band. Turned over, Hugo's eyes were open but seeing nothing, his final expression that of pain or fear, somewhat relaxed in death. Yet nowhere was there a mark upon him, no obvious wound. More likely he'd been drowned, held under, which suggested more than one man had been involved.

Sir Richard hauled the body out of the water, seeing then that more reeds had been smashed ahead. Not far away, he found Hugo's brother, also seemingly drowned in the shallows of the wetland.

The third, Fuckebegger, had at least made it to the nearest trees. He had a terrible wound right through the center of him. A sword thrust. It had to have been made by someone strong. Or else Fuckebegger had been unable to move.

A thorough search of the area turned up their camp, well-secluded though apparently not secluded enough. It had been ransacked, the lean-tos smashed, satchels and sacks torn apart, one small ale keg splintered, and every bow and every arrow broken. So Hugo and the others had been on their way back from the manor of Leeds with ale, with supplies, when these brigands had struck. Three good men of the woods had been surprised. He shook his head in dismay.

Thomas, the Lincoln-green outlaw, had said that knights—crusaders, in fact—had killed Hodde with a sword thrust. Had the same knights caught up with his men? But why? It made no sense. Were they after every outlaw in the forest or his men specifically? He felt as if someone from Avignon, or even Carcassonne, was hunting him. But that was absurd. He'd made no such enemies in battle and those battles were long over.

The latest Crusade, led by Louis IX, was ongoing, but what would such knights as the king's be doing this far from Damietta? More like thugs in the employ of the abbot of St. Mary's. After all, his true enemies were here.

Still puzzling it all out, Sir Richard walked out of the camp and straight into a trap. He was suddenly beset by a horde of tiny flying monstrosities—green and goggle-eyed, shrieking and snarling, baring their teeth. He turned in a circle, sword drawn, but the little things flitted and whirled around him, making him turn and turn as he tried to ward them off. He stumbled through the underbrush, his only thought to get away from the creatures.

And suddenly, they withdrew, leaving him standing alone among knights.

It was the stillness of the knights that struck him as odd: The several of them on horseback and their mounts did not so much as twitch. They stood like carvings of men and horses. Then others on foot, wielding spears, strode forward to close the circle around him. The little screeching things hovered overhead.

The knights all seemed to be of one army, but whose? Their surcoats displayed four panels, two of black and two of red, with no heraldic markings, dark gambesons beneath, and all wearing distinctive flat-topped heumes, so nearly identical in their total silence as to be unsettling.

Finally one of the mounted ones came to life, swung down and approached him, explaining, "We want the return of the precious gifts promised the abbot of Leicester." The knight stopped then and waited.

"Forgive me," Richard replied. "I know nothing of what you speak."

The knight's head tilted. "Yet, you are acquainted with the three men whose camp you just departed."

"Why, no," he quickly lied. "I chanced upon three bodies, which suggested there might be more, a larger party."

"You have never heard of Hugo Eylmer, then?"

"I—um, no, I don't know the name."

"So, what is *your* name then, mortal?"

Mortal? What answer could he give to that question? He looked from the speaker to the other faceless knights. These were the killers of Robert Hodde. They knew Hugo's name, and Sir Richard knew that Hugo, given the chance, would have fobbed them off with some made-up name of his own devising. Which meant that it hadn't worked. These dark knights likely knew or sought his name, and if he gave it, he would join the other three in death. The only alternative he could think of was that of the young man he'd only just met, who he knew for certain was no longtime denizen of Sherwood Forest. It was a name out of ballads and poems and plays, but what harm could it do? If they knew it, he would laugh along with them just as he had with Thomas. How absurd!

"I'm, ah, Thomas Rimor."

He was ready for the laughter to follow, but there came none. The knight stepped closer, eyes narrowed. "What did you say?"

This was the wrong reaction; all he could do now was repeat the name, invest it with the knowledge of its absurdity and with a touch of pride that it was his. He tried for that balance.

With both hands, the knight pushed at the helmet.

Sir Richard expected it to fall off, but instead it collapsed,

becoming black and fluid. It slid back into the neck of the black
gambeson the knight wore, revealing a fall of silvery white hair and
a face that wasn't entirely human. Its color was gray-green; the cheeks
were full, the jaw long and sharp. The knight drew closer until he
could clearly see the large eyes—as golden as two coins but with rings
of black around the centers instead of pupils. And while nothing of
the costume suggested one sex or another, there was something
about the face that seemed to him vaguely female.

"My goodness, Thomas Rimor, after so many years. You have
grown considerably taller since the Royal Hunt." The lips parted,
flashing a smile of sharp fang-like teeth. "My name," the knight said,
"is Zhanedd. The difference, *nuncle*, is that I haven't borrowed mine."

"Royal hunt?" Richard asked. He knew even as the question
emerged that it was the wrong thing to say. But what was the right
thing?

Zhanedd drew off a glove, revealing a hand with long tapering
fingers that came almost to points, held it up in front of him and
curled the fingers slowly. In some way the gesture caught hold of Sir
Richard's will and pulled at it. The hoarse voice rang in his head.
"Listen to me. Sleep now. Sleep."

Sir Richard's eyes fluttered. He resisted, or thought he did.

The hand drew back, fingertips together, and then it struck like a
snake. A sting in his throat. He experienced then a slow sensation of
falling back and back and never touching the ground. *This is death*,
he thought, and then thought no more.

PART TWO:
NOTTINGHAM

XI. Into Nottingham

✠

The Waits ushered Thomas into Nottingham by the Mansfield Road, which led into the market square. Well before they reached it, they passed various sandstone caves carved out of the heights and slopes surrounding the town. Some had wooden façades built onto the fronts but, according to various members of the Waits, these were lately added. The caves were much older. Some reached deep into the stone. Some, they told him, even had stairs extending up or down into the rock—some to well rooms; others, within the promontory on which Nottingham Castle stood, snaked up to the very top.

The castle was impossible to miss. It was more complex than any motte and bailey construction he'd seen before: There were three baileys at various heights, and at least two identifiable keeps as if two ruling families lived side by side there overlooking the River Leen, though both would be occupied by the more powerful and prominent Normans. Beneath the arrangement of walls and keeps, various odd caves pockmarked the escarpment itself. It looked like a giant dovecote. Elias pointed. "Sheriff's dungeons there, too."

The look of it reminded Thomas of something Nicnevin had told him once—how she had released a group of humans after showing them the sacrifice well she called Hel, and how "the fools named a goddess after it and insisted various caverns in your world led directly into her." He marveled that no one thought these caves led to some supernatural realm. Maybe because the people here had carved them all out. Then again, maybe there were some folk who did think it.

"Tell 'im about the wall," said Benedict.

"Soon enough," Elias said, which proved to be only a few minutes. Down the center of the market square ran a stone wall, approximately chest high, and with openings here and there—nine in all, with one long stretch of uninterrupted wall to the northwest.

"This side here is the Saxon borough," explained Geoffrey, "where you're welcome on account of you're Saxon, ain't yah. The other side of the wall, the Norman French inhabit. Them as is housed near the castle. It's my opinion they came here under King Henry and stayed. They put on an animal market there with goats and chickens and hogs. We kept the grains, the barley and malt an' everything else in the market on our side." He grinned, then added with pride, "So we got the ale."

"What about that?" Thomas pointed. At the far end of the wall on this side were a pond and a contraption something like a siege engine but with a seat at one end of it, which at the moment was occupied by a sopping wet woman. Two burly men stood at the opposite side of it, having just raised her out of the pond, while a third man stood beside them.

"Oh, 'at's the ducking pond," Benedict proudly announced. "And that woman, she's done summat's put 'er in that chair. Slew her babbies, killed her husband, or maybe she's a hedge-born doxy, who knows."

Osbert leaned closer and whispered, "All that's sheriff's business, and the Norman sheriff at that. Best to let it be."

"I see," Thomas replied, less than certain.

"If it's adultery she's committed, they'll send her off soon enough after the public humiliation," said Elias. "Then again, if it's murder, this is all prolusion to hanging." He pointed. "The man in the blue tunic there, he's *our* sheriff."

The sheriff had a short black beard not unlike Thomas's, but his face in profile was thinner, angular, his brows dark. His blue tunic was decorated by a small emblem on the left chest of a rough green cross against a red field. He caught sight of the Waits and waved to them. Elias waved back.

"As I said, the Normans have their own, a taller man, and red-faced like he's furious all the time," he explained. "He operates from the castle."

"Two reeves? That must be confusing."

"They stay out of each other's way."

"Which do you serve?"

"We serve the boroughs, wherever the threat comes from."

"But—"

Elias scratched at his gray beard. "I know what you're asking. We've never yet had to choose, and please God we never have to."

Thomas accepted the answer. It was time to leave the Waits and finish his undertaking. "I thank you all for your good company on the road. Now I need to find the tannery."

"Which one?" asked Warin.

"Ah, *Hodde*, I think it was."

"What, like the outlaw?"

"Outlaw?"

"Robert Hodde," said Elias. "Scourge of Sherwood. Leaves us alone as we're too many in number to trouble."

"I ... don't believe there's a relation. He's a tanner by trade. My, ah, my uncle. I bring news for him."

"So you're his nephew, Robyn? Robyn Hodde?"

"Well, we've come to spell the last name as *Hoode*." He couldn't very well take it back now. At least varying the name might provide him some distance. With luck no one here would go asking the tanner about his nephew.

"That's perilously close, don't you think?" said Elias.

"Me, I don't know any by name," said Warin, "but the tanners are all clustered along the marsh. Walk the slope down past castle wall, then ask."

Benedict laughed at that. "Tha won't need to ask." He tapped his nose. "Just follow your nostrils."

The slope Warin sent Thomas down deposited him below the town and beside the castle rock. Along the escarpment leading to it lay more caves than he'd seen upon the Mansfield Road. The rock face itself curved away around a broad marshy plain that verged the River Leen. That cliff face had been carved into dozens and dozens of openings, a few fronted by wooden façades. Others had stone houses built right up against them, as if the houses had grown out of the scarp. He followed them, initially picking up the smell of roasting barley malt. If the hanging signboards were any indication, most of the grain roasters were placed near alehouses. A great many alehouses. As with the others he'd seen, none of the openings appeared to be natural—all were scraped out of the long, winding sandstone butte. He supposed there might be an entire network of caves within the rock, including the Norman sheriff's dungeons deep in the castle escarpment above.

He asked one of the brewers where he might find the tannery caves. The man pointed back in the direction he'd come. He turned around. Initially he was accompanied on the path by many, but the numbers dwindled as he passed by the slope he'd come down and walked around the far side of the castle rock, and not long after that his eyes began to water. The air emerging from the openings ahead stung his eyes. Inhaling it made him feel he was scouring out his lungs. The openings that lay ahead stank like caves dug straight into the devil's realm. It must be an entire *row* of tanners.

Rather than torture himself further, he braved the nearest opening to ask which was Hodde's tannery. The woman he asked had a wet linen cloth covering the lower half of her face; above it her eyes were red and irritated, as was the skin of her hands and wrists. But she stepped out and pointed to a specific cave. Naturally, it stood at the far end of tannery row, as he was coming to think of this horrid stretch of caverns.

The outermost chamber of the Hodde tannery was uninhabited. A great leather cloak hung drying against a wall there. The air within was like the condensation from the piss of a hundred goats.

Thomas cupped one hand over his nose and mouth. He wished he had a piece of linen such as the woman had worn.

He entered the interior cave. The floor of it had been carved into a series of recesses—vats of various sizes dug for the processing of skins. A group of figures, most wearing aprons, knelt between the vats, some with large wood rods that they used to stir the contents. At his arrival, they looked up, all as red-eyed as any demons, and at that point he could stand it no more and ducked back out and onto the path outside, where he stood with hands on his thighs while he sucked in the comparatively tolerable air. He wiped at his eyes.

A moment later the aproned man who'd been kneeling over the nearest vat emerged after him. "How might I help thee, stranger?"

the man asked. He was inspecting Thomas's clothes. He reached over and touched the loose sleeve of the green cotehardie with a kind of wary familiarity. Thomas glanced up. There was a certain family resemblance.

Thomas asked, "You've a brother who dwells in Sherwood?"

"That I do, aye," said the man. His slightly defiant tone expressed anticipation of the nature of the news.

"He's slain, I have to tell you. His last request of me was that I deliver his takings to his family in Nottingham." He drew the large pouch of coins and jewels from his shoulder bag.

"Outlaw ways finally caught up wi'im. Well, I'll go ta Lenton Priory, give some'a this coin ta Prior Bluett that they remember his soul." Hodde took the pouch, nodded at Thomas's clothes. "An' you one a his, best take care hereabout. Sheriffs, especially Passelewe..." He seemed to debate whether to say more, then instead asked, "How fared Little John?"

He shook his head. "I've yet to locate him."

"Hmm. 'E comes 'ere, look for him in Pilgrim." At Thomas's confused expression, he pointed. "Back t'other way, way you come, far side'a malt kilns."

Thomas thanked him. "Tell me, how do you stand the reek?"

Hodde grinned with brownish teeth. "Don't notice it hardly anymore. But it keeps rats away. No plague in tanner's house."

They parted company. As fast as he could escape the mephitic air, Thomas headed back around the castle promontory.

XII. The Pilgrim

The alehouse The Pilgrim—"established 1132" according to the painted signboard above the entrance—was a cavern. A second, larger noticeboard leaned in the entryway. Thomas caught the word "prize" on one of the parchments. Two windows, carved out of the front wall, contained stained glass panels that spilled light into the main room. He couldn't help but wonder if the panels had been stolen out of some abbey or cathedral. Thomas ducked his head and stepped over the threshold.

The alehouse was doing decent business—in fact, Geoffrey and Osbert from the Waits were perched on stools around one of the pillars, and raised tankards to him as he came in. "Found your tanners then, Robyn?" Osbert asked.

"I did, thank you. Where are the others of your company?"

"Gone tae work, or else gone home."

Geoffrey grinned. "But traveling makes the two of us thirsty, as does performing." He stood and proclaimed: "Morality plays and theater, sleight of hand and all manner of rude gestures! The Waits shall perform again!"

Across the room, someone yelled, "Oh, piss off!"

Thomas took in the space around him. It was in essence one large, long room. It had been dug out around six supporting pillars, each of them broadening near the base to a wider circular shelf or table, like a horizontal skirt around which customers could stand, or sit on one-legged stools, and rest their wooden tankards. Near the back of the cave stood a winch frame over a square hole in the floor. Kegs from a cellar below were hoisted up as needed: a cave beneath a cave. Off the back end of the room were entrances to still more caves. And across the room, on the far side of the serving shelf, one familiar bearlike drinker was sleeping, balanced despite being unconscious on a one-legged stool, arms outstretched across the table as if holding it down. A cluster of four tankards stood beside his head. His costume was of a green identical to Thomas's. To Robert Hodde's. Almost certainly the burly, heavy-bearded face must belong to Little John.

He turned back to the two members of the Waits. "I see someone I believe I know," he said. "Excuse me, good yeomen. I shall buy you drinks anon for your many kindnesses, but first I must pay a debt." He made a brief bow, then headed to the shelf where the tankards were being filled. He drew the pouch from his belt and immediately sensed its lightness. He held it up higher. Some of the stitching in one corner of it had come apart—probably a result of his dunking in the water by Sir Richard. Most of the contents were gone. He had three gold coins left, likely because they were slightly larger than the silver pennies had been.

Frustrated, he bought two tankards of ale, shoved the change of silver pennies back into the pouch, and stuffed it down into his quiver where he wouldn't lose all the coins if they fell out. He carried the ale to the table where Little John sprawled and set it down, noting as he flipped another one-legged stool upright that, pressed between his knees and the base of the massive sandstone pillar, John had a worn leather satchel. Thomas laid his staff and bow across the table before leaning in the direction of his acquaintance.

"Little John," he whispered, and shook him gently by the shoulder.

John sat up all at once. Bleary-eyed, at first he didn't seem to know where he was, and said, "'Ey up," as he might have greeted anyone. Then he focused upon Thomas's cotehardie. He leapt back off the stool, which fell over as he stood. "Ghost!" he cried.

The alehouse went quiet. Across the room, Geoffrey and Osbert stared his way.

Smiling broadly as he glanced around, Thomas replied, "No ghost, Little John. Here, I've brought you another ale."

But John was having none of it. He looked Thomas up and down, then pointed at the tear in the material. "You stole his *clothes*."

"Yes, well, he came to *my* hut to die. What was I to do?"

Little John pondered that, then examined Thomas more closely. "*You* are Woodwose? I don' believe it. Why, you're no more'n thirty year, an' cut yer 'air."

"I dressed the part—poured ashes over my head, in my beard." He'd had little truck with John and the rest of Hodde's ever-changing band, mostly just with Hodde himself.

John shook his head. "You playin' old man—Robbie said Woodwose'd been there forever."

"All right, I'm his nephew. Here, drink your ale." He pushed the tankard in front of the outlaw.

John laughed. "Ah, tha had me goin' there, thinkin' yer nah human."

Thomas glanced around. Everyone in the alehouse had stopped paying attention. Quietly, he said, "I was there when he reached the hut. Hodde told me of the prelate and Much. I went and saw for myself. How did you elude those knights?"

Little John took a pull on his ale. Then he picked up his overturned stool and perched upon it again, stuffed the satchel between his knees. "I know them woods better'an deer do. Even so, those two stayed with me halfway to moonrise. Ran 'em into Bilhaugh Wood to shake them so's I could find Robbie, an' did that. In your hut like you say. Hid through night then, and later I come upon e'en more a their kind, *and* their queen."

A chill clenched his back. "You saw Nicnevin?" He wanted to urge John to show him exactly where she'd come through, although he knew she wouldn't be there now nor would have left a sign of her intrusion.

Little John asked, "That her name? Not Mabily?" The look of suspicion came over him again. "How's it you know that? Or any of it?"

Thomas contemplated the numerous ways he could explain, but all of them required him to relive all that the elven had done to him, the cruelties inflicted, the deaths he held them accountable for. Finally, he just replied, "I've tracked them, a long time. They attacked my family. My brother, I . . ." He shook his head that he didn't wish to continue. After a moment, he said, "The Yvags can look just like knights."

"*Yvags.* Demons have a name, then."

"They do."

"Well, stirred up all Sherwood now, they have. Tales flying all around taverns and inns about witchcraft in the wood, demons on road, e'en more'n I seen. Some this day are dead, I hear, from meeting them."

"Including Hodde."

He looked glum. "Poor Much were first. Stupid boy, showing off for Robbie, who neh wanted him ta step out."

"I'm sorry he died, too, but I still don't understand why. What did you three steal from that bishop?"

The outlaw slammed down his tankard and grabbed the satchel. "You tell me, 'cause I can't e'en explain 'em." He shook the contents out onto the sandstone table: three palm-sized iridescent pyramids covered in some sort of alien script.

In a panic, Thomas grabbed them up and dropped them into the empty tankards.

"How did you—"

"What the bishop were carryin', what them knights want back from me, an' what I wish I'd never clapped eyes on." He reached out and grabbed Thomas by the wrist in a grip of iron. "But you *know*, don't you, Woodwose?"

Their gazes met. John didn't believe for a moment that he was nephew to the old man of the woods. "I know," he admitted. "The Yvags use them to hollow someone out. I've . . . seen it once."

"What ya mean, 'hollow'?"

He gestured at the cavern around them. "Like these Nottingham caves. The Yvags scoop you out so they can live inside you. The way they did with your late bishop."

Little John shook his head that he didn't understand.

"He'd been dead a long time before you shot him. He was a *lich*, and a knight very like the two that chased you inhabited him, rode him."

"One a those knights . . . ?"

"No, another, somewhere else. A different knight. Hidden. Asleep. Pretending to be the bishop."

"But why?"

"To control fortunes—in this case of the church—money, property, laws, kingdoms. *Always kingdoms*," he said. That came from one of the few rhymes that he'd spouted in the house in Chinon. Janet had written it down somewhere.

Never kings, but always kingdoms.
Never thrones but always ears.
Crucial words, spoke in whispers,
from our hands put power in theirs.

As his rhymes went, its meaning was crystal clear.

John scratched at his beard a moment. "Bishoprics?" he offered.

"Oh, yes. These"—he pointed to the three tankards—"make that all possible. Right now you have kept them from taking over three people of power and influence. They had plans to do so if they had these, and your bishop was delivering them somewhere. Maybe here in Nottingham." He thought about what Little John had said about witchcraft, and glanced around. Skinwalkers only inhabited people of influence, but glamoured Yvags could be almost anywhere. "They *are* demons, and if Nicnevin's about, they want these very badly. Which means, they won't stop coming after you."

"Well, then, let's just smash the damned things."

"You don't want to do that, assuming you could. You smash these together, likely there'd be no Nottingham left—everything from the castle to the River Leen would be leveled, smoke and sand."

Little John gaped at him, continuing to stare as he picked up the tankard Thomas had bought him and drank the rest of his ale before setting it down. He belched appreciatively. "All right, you know so much of it. What do we do, then?" he asked.

"We flee."

"Listen, Robbie had a hoard of coins, all set aside. We could take it—"

"To his brother. I already gave it." John glowered at him. "It's what he asked of me before he died. Why I'm here in Nottingham."

Little John was crestfallen. "You make a terrible outlaw, Woodwose. You should'a kept it—I mean, were *already* stolen. I spent my last coin on ale. Thought maybe a buyer I'd find for these things but ne'er got that far. I'm skint."

"I'm not far behind you."

"Then what do we do? I think we don't another night dare stay in Sherwood."

The knights would be coming, glamoured and watchful. By now they'd be in Doncaster, Worksop, maybe Mansfield; eventually they must arrive if they weren't here already. He looked around suspiciously while wondering about Sir Richard and the rest of the outlaws in the king's forest. "We should drop those damned things in the sea where no one can have them." For all he knew, the Yvags might already have acquired more. The weird pyramids remained beyond his ken. How difficult was it to create a thing that sucked out the soul? Difficult enough if Nicnevin was opening gates across Sherwood to hunt for them.

Thomas saw that the two Waits had gotten up to leave but then stopped in the entryway to stare at the noticeboard. He might not be able to trust many people in Nottingham, but counted the group of players among them. At the very least they might know where he and John could hide for a night or two.

"Come on," he said to Little John. The two of them headed for the exit.

As they neared, Osbert was saying to Geoffrey, "We should ha stayed away another week, old friend."

"This is all about Benedict," Geoffrey said. "You and I are expected another duty to perform."

"What duty is that?" asked Thomas as he approached.

"See for yourself." Geoffrey thrust a hand at the large parchment nailed up on a tall slab of wood leaning against the stone wall.

This contained the word *PRIZE* Thomas had glimpsed on the way in. The sheriffs of Nottingham were heralding that on the morrow in the market square there would be a fair for both Norman and Saxon boroughs that included two contests of martial skill: One would feature the bow. The other would be the quarterstaff. The sheriffs were offering a prize of 240 gold pennies to be divided between the two winners (unless, unlikely as it was, one person should triumph at both). Thomas read it out. Little John chortled. "I ought to enter that. I'm clever wi' staff." He shook his own quarterstaff as if to prove it.

"We'll mark you down on the list. The two of us," said Osbert gloomily, "are doomed to officiating the rolls."

Thomas asked, "So then how is this about Benedict?"

"'E were champion with the quarterstaff last year. And year before."

"Did you enter this last year?" Thomas asked Little John.

"Me? I weren't e'en hereabouts. Never have entered no contest."

"Well, you're entering this one."

Geoffrey sized him up. "He might actually compete with our Benedict. What's your name, then?"

Little John tilted his head, locked eyes with Thomas. "Greenleaf," he said. "Reynold Greenleaf."

"I feel I've met you somewhere. That possible? Have you trod the boards?"

"Trod what? Nah, lots a men built like me. Like yer Benedict."

Geoffrey nodded.

Thomas asked him, "Tell me, cousin, where might be a good place to spend a night in Nottingham?"

"You're just leaving it," Geoffrey replied. "The Pilgrim's an inn'a sorts as well as alehouse. More carved-out rooms beyond." He pursed his lips. "But how is it you aren't staying with your uncle?"

Thomas smiled broadly. "Like Benedict warned me." He held his nose. "A stink to make you blind." They all laughed.

"Well, you *could* take us up on our offer," Osbert interjected. "Join the Waits an' sleep below castle wi' the Normans. Or at Chandler's Lane gaol, where we're going now."

"Be first to sign up for contest in morning," Geoffrey prompted.

"Of course, as new men, you'd be this night on watch."

"Which is what?"

"Ah, ye walk the market square, and down here," said Osbert. "Broad marsh across the London road tae Sneinton hermitage, then across tae Lenton Priory an' back again."

Added Geoffrey, "Keep watch for anything coming over Trent River Bridge." The two traded an arch look. "'Course, until Goose Fair season, nothing ever does." Then they laughed at whatever private joke this contained.

Thomas cast his eye upon Little John as he replied, "I believe you've talked me into it." At least he knew the Waits weren't glamoured Yvag and might even stand their ground, and that was one less worry, one less threat to watch. "How about you, friend Reynold? Keeps us out of the woods tonight."

Little John nodded. "Then I'm for it."

"Oh, I do hope not," said a happily well-oiled Geoffrey. "Soldiers, to the gaol, then!" he cried, and led the way as if leading a charge, Osbert laughing after him.

XIII. On Watch

His torch held high and spitting in the light rainfall, Thomas stared at the rings of the target cinched against a wall of roped-together straw before him, and for a minute or two he was a boy again, apprenticed to Alpin Waldroup, firing his first arrows in the direction of a lumpy, makeshift target. He had missed far more often than he'd planted an arrow anywhere near the thing. Waldroup warned him that he would spend his first weeks chasing down errant shots and increasingly frustrated by his inability to hit what was right in front of him. It proved to be an all-too-accurate prediction. If he hadn't been apprenticed (both as a stonemason and as an archer), he surely would have given up.

Now here he was, about to enter a contest using someone else's bow, when he had hardly fired an arrow in years.

He turned and counted off the steps across the hay-strewn square to the shooter's line: by his reckoning, one hundred fifty feet. From here the light of the torch barely suggested the location of the targets, two of them side by side. A significant though not impossible distance, he supposed.

He set down his torch, held his bow out, and drew the bowstring. It felt . . . unnatural. He'd have liked to sink a dozen arrows in the rings right then, but knew better than to damage the targets the night before the event. Besides, his were hunting arrows. Tomorrow, target arrows would be provided to the shooters, everyone's the same. Even now up under the castle the Norman sheriff had possession of them.

He plucked the cord a second time, sensing the stretch in his back and shoulder, his elbow sliding back. Then he relaxed, flexed the bow, putting one foot inside near the tip, and unlooped the bowstring. With a quick swoop he reclaimed the torch. It hissed like an angry cat. He stared down the line at the targets again.

Barring his earliest training with Alpin, had he ever taken aim at anything the way a target shooter would—calm, standing still, taking all the time he needed to prepare, aim, concentrate? Other than those first days with his mentor, he couldn't recall arrows loosed except in the heat of some sort of battle, on the run. Even against that Yvag fiend, Adalbrandr, at close quarters in Forbes's mill, there was no time to think, merely to act. Yet, tomorrow he must do exactly that—stand still and shoot—and with a bow he'd never yet used, however well-crafted it might be. Suddenly, entering the contest seemed like a very foolish idea. He and Little John should have been running for their lives right now instead.

He crossed the square and went through one of the openings in the dividing wall to join Little John at the ducking pond. The armature for punishment had been rolled aside and the narrow arch of a bridge had been assembled across the pond. The contest of quarterstaves would be decided on that bridge, and John, his own torch held high, was testing it.

Thomas watched as he performed something like a dance upon the bridge, forward and back, a turn to one side and then the other. He stumbled but caught himself as the rain spattered down, misshaping his flame-lit reflection in the cold pond below.

"Better you than me up there," Thomas told him. "I've already been half drowned this week, and I suspect by a man you could best one-handed." He wondered if Sir Richard had found his men and if they would be participating in tomorrow's contests. Those purses would surely tempt almost anyone, even the most desperate of outlaws.

"This Benedict," called John, "what's 'e like?"

"Like a bear you wouldn't want to bait. He was sitting when I saw him, though, so I can't tell you much more."

Little John came clomping down off the bridge. "'Tis a tight walk, and for any sidestepping not much room. More like you'd plunge straight off than find balance long enough ta strike. Pond's so small, you're more like to land in muck than water." For all the complaint in his description, he seemed pleased. "How'd you make out with target range?"

He shook his head. "I worry that I can't even remember how to find the distance."

Coming over, John clapped him on the shoulder. "You'll find it," he said. "Let's our watch finish, London road to Lenton Priory, agree that all's abed and then retire ourselves. I'll show you one'a the privy ways down to the Leen there." He turned and started walking.

"I thought you didn't know your way around Nottingham."

"Nah, I never said that—just that I've not entered any contest hereabout. On account of both sheriffs would be cock-a-hoop to clap me in irons first thing and hang me on the morrow. But I been here plenty enough times with Robbie when he visited his brother. I stay in Sneinton—no one there watching for me. Plenty of places to be invisible in hermitage. I'll show you."

They wandered along Chandler's Lane, passing the gaol where they had stowed their belongings, working their way to High Pavement and St. Mary's Church, at which point Thomas's torch guttered and went out.

Little John made the sign of the cross. "Ghosts in the graveyard, don't like the light, do they?" he said.

Thomas asked only, "Can we find our way with a single torch?"

"We can find it with no torches at all." He set his own torch down against a tombstone. Moonlight glowed across the layer of clouds. "Better we come with none anyway. Some'a the old fellers don't like unannounced visitors. Might run us through. We'll collect it later. What say you to that?"

"I say you're mad, but I'm at your mercy here." He placed his extinguished torch beside it. "Lead the way."

They walked on out of the town and up to the edge of another large escarpment with some small scraggly trees growing out near the edge of it. "Hermitage," said Little John. Thomas was squinting, but surefooted John led them down a narrow flight of steps cut in the sandstone. Turning at the bottom, he found himself facing still more caves, some of them halfway up the rock face he'd just descended. How the devil were those reached? They were smaller than most of the others he'd seen, but then a hermit didn't need much space. The small River Leen was at his back, as was the London road and, farther along it, the large bridge over the Trent.

"All right, John," he said. "Now I see how you've avoided the sheriffs. But how do you propose to enter the contest tomorrow if they're going to arrest you in the first place?"

Little John glanced back, giving him a pitying look. "First, I won't be found wearing *these* wet togs come the contest. We got enough coin left for a nice loose linen shirt, right? And, second, it won't be mine whose name be called. It'll be—"

"Reynold Greenleaf, yes."

"That's yer man." And he broke into a broad grin. "Come on, then, it's a long walk ta that priory. It's way t'other side of castle."

They strolled along the spit of land between scarps and slopes on their right and the River Leen on their left, and up across the London road.

Thomas had just reached the road when something came screaming out of the night sky for him. He hadn't heard such a horrible screech for a long, long time, and he responded to it on instinct. He snatched the quarterstaff out of Little John's grip and swung it hard and fast. With a wet crack, it connected with something, and a creature the size of a bat smacked into the road and skidded.

Flapping, it started to rise again. Thomas hammered it with the staff until the tip was dripping with dark, gelatinous fluid.

"Ne'er in my life heard a bat shriek like that," said John. He crouched and gingerly lifted the remains of the goggle-eyed creature by its wing. Its body was dripping, washing away in the rain, revealing a core that flexed and came apart and dissolved. "I seen these in the wood, I think, with yer queen. What are these hobs?" He glanced up at Thomas, who was wondering if by some means the hideous little thing had recognized him.

"A sign," he said sourly. He glanced up the hill toward the town. "The ones that killed Robbie have arrived."

XIV. Contests

The day broke clear to find foot and cart traffic clogging both the Mansfield and the London Roads, and all headed for the Market Square. Some were contestants for the games, but more brought things to sell such as clothing and furs, jewelry, and perfumes. There were performers of mystery plays, and jugglers and dancers and musicians to accompany, and apiarist monks selling containers of honey, while other folks brought exotic spices, and jugs of wine and mead, kegs of ale, and every manner of pies.

At one opening in the market wall, Osbert and Geoffrey sat, officiating over the combat contests, which were to begin at noon. Of course, any members of the Waits received the benefit of being entered first on the rolls: Benedict, Reynold, and Robyn, whose last name Osbert wrote as "Hoode."

"Even if it's that tanner's family you belong to, don't want 'Hodde' written down 'ere," explained Osbert. "Sheriffs will be o'erlooking the lists for outlaws, an' that name's notorious. Passelewe'd arrest you on the spot."

Little John went shopping for a shirt on the Norman side of the market. Aware that his green clothing might have labeled him an outlaw, Thomas had already upon awakening glamoured his clothing—his cotehardie now indigo with a red trim, and his leggings ochre. He could maintain that façade all week with no effort.

Ten signed up for the quarterstaves combat, and twenty-one archers. The two Waits used a blind draw to match opponents, with any odd-numbered leftover matched against whoever won the very first contest. As it was random, it was deemed fair. Benedict and Reynold would begin by fighting someone else.

Both sheriffs were on hand. Thomas had already seen the Saxon man, named Orrels, who was again dressed in his bright blue cotehardie, now paired with yellow leggings. The tall Norman sheriff proved to be both red-bearded and florid of complexion. He wore a crimson kirtle and leggings. By coincidence this made him look almost a twin to one of the competing archers, named Will Scathelock, save that the French sheriff sported a bycocket hat, also of red, and with a peregrine feather in the band while the fair-haired Scathelock had on a simple peasant's coif, the strings tied under his chin, and his tunic displayed some sort of emblem.

Knowing that the Yvags were here, Thomas kept an eye out for the two knights, though he was sure they wouldn't be disguised as crusading knights now, but as something more likely to blend in with the crowd. Of course, what did that even mean? They could have been anyone wandering through the market square, glamoured and nondescript the same as him. He knew it was a fruitless task, but it was all he had to go on. How many of their kind had stepped through in two haunted Sherwood nights and how many of those would have been directed to the harvest fair in seeking the *dights* that Little John had stolen?

Shortly before the contests were to begin, a group of four riders arrived on the market square. They were all dressed in matching surcoats of deep green with gold trim, and a circular emblem on the surcoat breast. They all wore a kind of chaperon as well, russet-colored, with a liripipe dangling over their shoulders like a braid. The emblem on their breasts was the same as that worn by the competing archer Scathelock.

Little John, in his freshly purchased white linen shirt, nudged Thomas. "That," he said, "is Isabella Birkin and her Keepers'a Sherwood."

The lead rider swung down, and Thomas realized this must be Isabella. She'd ridden her horse like any man might, made possible by her being outfitted with the same leggings as the other three. A short sword hung from her belt. Her expression was less than friendly, *fierce* he might have said. If John hadn't identified her, he would have thought he was observing a man with piercing blue eyes and a mouth set permanently in a scowl of displeasure. The belted surcoat disguised her shape, the chaperon her hair, save for a slight hint of gold around her ears.

Abruptly, Thomas realized he had met her, deep in the Barnsdale Wood, a few years before, when she and her foresters were in pursuit of Hodde, or maybe it was another outlaw—he wasn't certain of that. Her hair had been in a snood off the back of her head. She had scrutinized him, finding nothing but the mad old man of the woods he'd made of himself. The memory roared back in an instant.

He covered his surprise, saying, "She does not look friendly."

"Then you see her true, friend Robyn. An' that short blond one behind her, 'e's her son, Adam D'Everingham. Means to take her place as warden when she's done. The other's named Maurin Payne, I think."

The sourness of her expression reminded him of his own father after the Yvag had possessed him. "Would you say she's a person of power and influence?"

"She is, aye." He thought on it for a minute. "Less influence than her 'usband, though. Robert D'Everingham thinks he deserves her posting and all what comes with it."

"Does he? Deserve it?"

"Forest to him is just someplace to sport with his ladies and boys. He'd get rid'a the rest, reive the occasional deer, and pay himself well to do it."

"I see. You know a lot, John. Does Isabella know you?"

Little John replied obliquely, "I expect we'll find that out by and by."

At noon the contests began. As there were more archers, they went first, "Robyn Hoode" against a bowyer from Mansfield. He deferred to the bowyer, who, judging from his bleary gaze, had perhaps celebrated a bit too much the previous night, and whose shot struck in the third ring. Thomas, nervous as he was, had no trouble besting the shot. Even so, he aimed for the center of the target but pulled to the left, the arrow fishtailing, piercing the first ring circling the bullseye. Afterward, he floated the bow on his palm, seeking and finding the slight imbalance in it. How had he missed that before? He was rusty. Waldroup had taught him everything there was to know about the bow. He must retrieve that knowledge, and compensate.

Then came Benedict, who with his first blow knocked his opponent into the water. The crowd of onlookers cheered, Benedict being a local favorite.

And so it went. Little John won his first match, though not as handily as Benedict had. John watched Benedict's attack on his second opponent. Benedict worked a particular sidestep, a clever and quick misdirection that guided the opponent to attack where he no longer stood. By the third bout it seemed inevitable that the two of them would face off in the final round.

After the first rounds, there was open betting on both combats, with the two Waits now acting as turf accountants, taking bets—and all of it legal: The two sheriffs stood close by, neither of them objecting. Everyone had gotten a look at the competitors and now made their choices. John in his second round faced another of Isabella's foresters, who grabbed onto his staff, thinking apparently to rip it out of his grasp. Instead, when he pulled, Little John offered no resistance and simply shot forward, running the fellow right off the bridge. Cheers and boos mixed equally. Thomas observed Isabella and the Norman sheriff conferring afterward.

A blind draw had been instituted due to the odd number of entrants. This meant that one of the shooters had an extra round, an extra opponent to eliminate before the final challenge. That opponent proved to be Will Scathelock. The Keepers cheered him on against his opponent from York. Scathelock bested the man easily, once again hitting the target dead center. The ultimate contest was going to be between Thomas and Scathelock.

By now he had gotten the measure of Hodde's bow, and had hit the bull's-eye twice, but he recognized the precision of this young man. He seemed to be the darling of Birkin's Keepers. The betting was heavily weighted in his favor. If Thomas had held any extra cash, he might have bet on Scathelock himself.

Across the market, shouts and cheers erupted. Little John was facing off against Benedict. In between rounds now, Thomas strolled over to watch.

Little John climbed to the center of the bridge. In his first move, he made the same feint as Benedict's first opponent had done. When Benedict pivoted aside the same as he'd done with that man, John launched his real attack, thrusting his staff at Benedict's ankle, denying him the opportunity to balance on that leg. Benedict hopped clumsily onto the other leg, allowing Little John to draw back and aim a straight thrust to the midriff. It shoved him back, only now at an acute angle. He had to step back, but there was no longer a bridge under that foot, and the huge bearlike Benedict, staff held in both hands over his head to deliver a finishing blow, plunged straight into the pond.

A great deal of cheering but also some yelling ensued—a lot of the crowd had bet on the favorite. Osbert and Geoffrey would be paying out substantial winnings to those who'd backed "Reynold." He watched helplessly as the two sheriffs conferred while looking at John. From their demeanors, he was certain that, new shirt or no, Little John's identity had been established. But horns were sounding, the call to the archery range. He couldn't wait to see what happened.

The Norman sheriff, Passelewe, strode past him to officiate, taking his place beside Scathelock, red standing next to red. Thomas hurried to stand with them. With something like an air of indifference, the sheriff looked the two men over, then casually flipped a penny. The result: Scathelock would shoot first. The sheriff handed him his arrow.

Scathelock stepped up to the line, fitted the arrow, drew the bowstring, his form perfect; he let fly. With the precision he had exhibited all afternoon, he hit the mark, dead center. People sent up a cheer as if that were the final shot. However good a marksman the dark-blue-coated stranger might be, he could not best that and should just concede.

Scathelock must have been very pleased with himself; yet he turned and with what seemed genuine camaraderie said, "Good luck to you, good sir."

Then as Thomas accepted his arrow, he and the Norman sheriff exchanged a glance. The sheriff's eyes were cold and calculating, sizing him up in such a way that he couldn't help but wonder if the man was simply merciless or else inhuman. Uncertain, he nodded with stiff courtesy to the sheriff and ignored his unease.

The sheriff nodded back. Thomas crossed over to the line, looking out around him as he did.

The creatures were surely here somewhere, scattered through the crowd, and if he and Little John wanted to get far away, they would need these purses to buy horses and pay for passage across to France. John was likely their quarry already. But Thomas didn't know them and they knew nothing of him. They certainly didn't know he'd been an archer longer than anyone here had been alive.

He adjusted his wrist brace, nocked his arrow, and drew back the bowstring. He perceived Scathelock's bull's-eye as a feathered black dot in the center of the target now, something on which he could focus, forgetting everything else—the crowd, the sheriffs, the noise. There was him, his breathing, and the smallest of targets calling upon his skill.

He loosed the arrow. The flight couldn't have lasted more than a moment but it seemed to fly forever. His focus rode as if upon the arrow. The black dot seemed to absorb it, and abruptly grew tiny wings out either side.

No one said anything. It was as if they couldn't understand what had occurred. His arrow had been swallowed by the arrow already there. It had disappeared within it.

Then the boy on hand to retrieve arrows ran to the target; he turned, an amazed look on his face, and shouted, "He split it!"

People, including Scathelock, the sheriff, and Thomas hurried to the target. There, indeed, his arrow was lodged in the direct center of the target. It had split Scathelock's down the center and driven the front half of his arrow out the back of the target. "Well," Scathelock said, "I never."

The crowd muttered and stared at him, most of them like the boy, in wonder; a few glared. They had lost their wagers. The rest, including Scathelock, began cheering, applauding, pounding him on the back.

"*Le vainqueur!*" shouted the sheriff, a cry that echoed and was repeated around the market. The sheriff grabbed Thomas's bare wrist and thrust up his arm. In the instant they touched, Thomas could hear the insectile thrum of a dormant creature's inner voice, wherever it lay. The sheriff was a skinwalker!

The pale human eyes in that ruddy face went wide with recognition—it sensed that he could hear it. The sheriff, reconsidering him, asked, "*Ele vos a envoié?*"

Members of the crowd grabbed hold of Thomas. He peeled his arm from the sheriff's grip. "*Merci, Shérif,*" he said, and let the crowd haul him safely away, at least for the moment. *Did she send you?* From that brief connection Sheriff Passelewe believed Thomas was another Yvag, one sent by Nicnevin. How long before he reconsidered that conclusion?

Surrounded by a crowd, Thomas gave the sheriff a single brief nod as if to say "Yes, she sent me." Then he relaxed and let the crowd pull him across the plaza and toward an opening in the wall, leaving the disconcerted Norman sheriff behind.

The Yvags were here all right, and quite settled in positions of power.

XV. Arrested Development

The Malt Cross near Long Row was the platform, ten steps up to where announcements were read and where, in this instance, prize money was awarded. Climbing up, Little John cast about for Thomas, but the final competition in archery was still ongoing.

At the bottom of the steps, Benedict of the Waits stood, still dripping from his drubbing, but here to share in the celebration nevertheless. It had been a fair fight.

At the top, before the single column, stood the Saxon sheriff in his bright blue cotehardie. He smiled as though he'd personally chosen John the winner—and perhaps he had wagered on him and was truly pleased by the outcome. Little John took the purse and clambered down, still looking for and failing to see Thomas in the crowd.

He strolled over to Benedict, who, still sodden, pointed at the purse. "You're buying the ale, hey?"

"That I am." John glanced around. Even as he did, a great roar came from the far end of the wall where the targets stood. Someone had won their match; he could only hope it was Thomas. "Should we wait for him, d'ya think?"

"We might, or we could have his ale poured for him when he gets to The Pilgrim."

"Now, that's a fair idea."

They and the surrounding crowd set off. People clapped John on the back as he passed, and he smiled broadly. He was thinking he should enter more contests. The Woodwose was proving to be a valuable friend.

They passed Geoffrey and Osbert, and had just reached the pond again when, abruptly, they were surrounded by the Norman sheriff's soldiers, all wearing Passelewe's surcoat of a yellow cinquefoil on a red background. Behind him, a voice said in French, "Reynold Greenleaf, I arrest your true self, the outlaw known as Little John, accomplice of Robert Hodde, and who has this very week murdered a bishop upon the King's Great Way in Sherwood."

Some of those people nearby gasped, and the celebration of him simply melted away, the fair crowd turning before they could be identified with him. Where they fled, Isabella Birkin and her foresters remained. She said, "You *are* the one called Little John. You know I know you."

"Aye, an' that ye speak the same forward as backward. Proves nothing."

The red sheriff tore the purse from Little John's grasp. "Your winnings are forfeit." Two of the guards in mail grabbed him by the arms and a third one placed simple jointed manacles upon his wrists and locked them with a quick twist. Isabella Birkin looked on as if she wanted to strike him herself. The sheriff said, "Now, where is this partner of yours, Hodde?"

"Where you can't ne'er lay 'ands on him," he answered defiantly and was cuffed on the ear for it.

Benedict stepped in and tried to object to the rough treatment, but one of the guards jabbed a pike at him and drove him back; he thumped up against someone else, who pushed him forward. "Quiet, pig," the guard warned, "else you can share his cell." Benedict lifted a fist to slam the impertinent fellow's head but John said, "Benedict, don't." He could see that the guard was prepared to drive the pike into his friend. Geoffrey and Osbert weren't far behind, and John shook his head for them to stay back.

Benedict grabbed him by the shoulder and, leaning close, whispered, "I don't recognize these soldiers, an' we report to the castle near as often as to Chandler's Lane. Use caution."

The guards pulled Little John away, but at a nod from the sheriff, the guard leveling the pike challenged Benedict again. "It's decided, then. You come wiv us, too."

"But I'm a member of the *Waits*!"

The guard seemed to take that as provocation and slapped the side of the pike against Benedict's head even as John tried to step in and stop him. A second guard leveled his pike. Benedict was hemmed in now, caught along with him. John hoped Geoffrey and Osbert would alert Elias and the others. Maybe they could get him freed, though that woman's accusation meant "Reynold Greenleaf" wasn't going to help him here. He fell into place beside Benedict and walked forward.

On the opposite side of the dividing wall, Thomas was still being congratulated for his extraordinary shot. He asked Will Scathelock what happened next.

"Make yer way to the Malt Cross," was the reply. The blond man pointed to the stepped platform near the opposite end of the wall. "Sheriff will present yer winnings there."

"Which sheriff?" Thomas asked warily.

Scathelock laughed. "Oh, the Norman snob, Passelewe, he oversees the fair, but it's our man, Orrels, hands out the purses. I'd guess the quarterstaves purse is already awarded." He pointed past Thomas. "That's Passelewe's red-and-green cap floating along way over by the little bridge, heading for the castle. Good riddance, says I. A most unfriendly bastard." From this distance it was impossible to discern more than the hat of the Norman sheriff above the crowd, departing now that his official duties were done.

Thomas wondered aloud if Little John had won his contest. After all, he'd dunked Benedict.

"Whether or not he did, my guess is him you'll find in a tavern. 'Tis where we all go after these matches."

That sounded about right. John could certainly put away the mugs of ale.

"I thought you might have competed before," Thomas said.

"I have," replied Scathelock. "And I'm used to winning."

Orrels, the Saxon sheriff in bright blue, stood awaiting him at the top of the Malt Cross. Reluctantly, Thomas started up.

The two sheriffs had been engaged in conversation earlier; what were the chances they were both elven, both *conveyances*? Well, he would listen for an answer—not that he needed more impetus to flee.

He climbed the rest of the way up, prepared to be arrested.

The sheriff smiled as he neared. No one else stood on the

platform with him. "A fine showing," said Orrels. "I could use such marksmanship, should you ever want a job."

Thomas bowed his head. "As it happens, I joined the Waits yesterday."

"Did you?" The thin, elegant face beamed at him. "That's most excellent. I shall look forward to employing your skill, then, master Robyn."

They clasped hands and the sheriff handed him his purse while raising his other hand to the crowd, which cheered. There came no thrumming hidden voice from within the blue cotehardie, nor even the soft chirr of a glamouring Yvag. Orrels was not one of them. Quite likely he knew nothing about the true nature of his Norman counterpart, then.

At the bottom of the steps, Scathelock and some of the other bowmen remained gathered. "What do you want to do now?" Scathelock asked as Thomas stepped down.

"Should we wait for the Waits? The two of them, Geoffrey and Osbert, are around here somewhere. But perhaps their part is done?"

"It is tradition that the winner—who is now richer than all of *us*—buys the round at The Pilgrim. As men of Nottingham, they will both know that."

"Well, then, I expect we must uphold your tradition, hey-o." He could only hope that Little John was already perched on a one-legged stool and emptying a mug.

Accompanied by more cheering, the group headed off in the direction of the River Leen.

XVI. Brewing Trouble

This fair day The Pilgrim was doing brisk business, with whole families gathered at the tables carved out around the columns and enjoying an ale or two. The turnover on a fair day could be phenomenal. Thus, perhaps unsurprisingly, a number of doxies, identifiable by their striped caps, wandered among the crowd, sizing up the clientele, striking up conversations, offering company and more. They often had to shout their offers to be heard above both the many voices and the drone of a hurdy-gurdy being played by a swarthy young man beside the serving bench. The balding landlord looked on with a satisfied smile, ready to rent out a few chambers carved deeper in the rock behind the tavern. On a fair day his cut of the doxies' business supplemented quite handsomely what he made selling ale.

Thomas and his group entered, their bows unstrung, and managed to requisition a back table by bribing the current occupants with a free mug of The Pilgrim's best. Thomas and two of the others gathered at the serving bench, and he slapped down enough gold coins to cover multiple rounds. The landlord swept them out of sight with a nod of thanks.

That so many bowmen arrived together attracted attention, and it wasn't long before "Robyn Hoode," winner of the archery competition, had been identified and his name toasted repeatedly. This in turn brought the doxies circling in search of a generous vavasour or gentleman who'd wagered well. Scathelock leaned close and said, "Keep a tight grip on your purse. This lot can pluck the stitching off your braies without removing them."

Thomas replied, "Good that it's out of reach, then. I thought they dunked doxies in the pond here."

Scathelock laughed. "Never on a fair day, unless she be caught pilfering from a client."

Thomas barely heard. He was casting about and to his dismay finding no sign of Little John. He strained to hear, through the background noise and the hurdy-gurdy, the drone of at least one Yvag. And maybe he did, but it could have been the hurdy-gurdy, too. A glamoured Yvag might lurk anywhere in this bustling tavern, but for the moment he couldn't pursue it. He asked, "Is there anyone here can tell us the outcome of the quarterstaff contest?"

Scathelock asked the others who in turn asked those nearby. It was only moments before the news returned that Little John had triumphed. Even as Thomas learned this, tall Geoffrey of the Waits ducked in through the doorway and, craning his neck, spotted him and hurried over. Geoffrey knelt beside him, then described how "Reynold" and Benedict had both been arrested and John's identity as a wanted outlaw confirmed by no less a person than Isabella Birkin herself. "I came close enough to hear her ask him the whereabouts of Robert Hodde. Seems our Reynold may be someone else entirely, one of this Hodde's men. We would have objected to his arrest, but e'en I could see 'twould just get us all taken 'longside the two of them, and maybe accused of being allied with the outlaws as well. Why, such inculpation might exterminate the Waits altogether. A few of us *might* have performed deeds in the past that we, ah, regret. Osbert's gone to tell Elias." He shook his head. "I tell you, it were all queer, what with that special guard accompanying the sheriff."

"Special how?" Scathelock asked.

"For one thing, he must've hired them right under our noses. I never seen them 'afore, and us up at castle all the time."

Thomas worried for Little John. John had participated in slaying the prelate, was the only one left alive to blame. And while no one finding that body would have concluded it had even recently been alive, the Yvag sheriff, Passelewe, wouldn't care; he would be leading Little John somewhere that was sequestered, where he could be imprisoned and ensorcelled if not simply tortured to confess, not to mention give up Thomas, Robert Hodde, but most of all the bag of horrid little spinning tops. Probably in the end he would be beheaded, or snatched away to Ailfion...and all without any observers. Elias had described for Thomas the oubliettes and dungeons deep in the bowels of the enormous rock beneath the castle. It would be child's play to make a prisoner disappear there and later claim he'd been set free and sent on his way.

He also knew from experience how skinwalkers operated independently most of the time. They were often catching up on events that had transpired, on what had changed, or even what force of their kind had come through a gateway. He and Waldroup had relied on that gap in their knowledge after killing Stroud and Baldie. Might there be a way to use Passelewe's misidentification of him to get Little John out of the castle dungeons and the two of them far away from here? How long might they have? Sooner or later, Passelewe would confirm that Nicnevin had not sent him; he could close that gap just by sending one of his glamoured guards to Ailfion. Then the sheriff would come for his mason's bag and its contents. And his head.

"I have a bigger problem at the moment than identifying his new soldiers," he said. "How do I break Reynold out of that gaol?"

Geoffrey said flatly, "You don't. Even if he's innocent of the charges, you can't reach those cells except by stairwells cut right into the castle rock, going up and down. The way is guarded at both ends."

"But the Waits *know* the way."

Before Geoffrey could answer, a freckled blond doxy slid in and perched on the sandstone table between him and Scathelock, but focused her attention on Thomas. "I heard it you're the reason for this celebratin'. You got the best aim'a all these men here." As if the comment were too subtle, she added, "I like a fella can hit my target." Scathelock narrowly avoided spitting his ale.

Across the tavern, Isabella Birkin and two Keepers entered The Pilgrim. One was the one John had identified as her son. She looked as severe as before.

Watching them look over the customers, Thomas produced a gold penny and set it down beside the doxy. "By all means, buy yourself an ale on me. I would hate for you to go dry." It would afford her more than one drink, eliminating her need to come back, unless of course she meant to rob him as Will had warned. She slid it off the table and bit into it with her uneven teeth. Satisfied, she stood up and walked off. One of the other bowmen joked, "Her purse is probably bigger even 'n yours, Robyn."

Thomas was no longer listening. Birkin and her two men were threading their way straight toward him across the tavern.

She came up to Will Scathelock. "I am greatly disappointed," she said, "that my champion was bested." Then, turning to Thomas, she added, "But you seem to have found amity with your opponent." She pushed back the hood of her chaperon. Her hair was plaited tightly around her head. It looked like it might reach the floor if she unspooled it. Her previously grim expression relaxed now in a smile, and although this creased her face more, it also revealed a handsomeness her scowl and headdress had hidden. "What is your name, archer?"

He'd gotten to his feet, initially to defend against whatever challenge she meant to lay. Now he relaxed. The other two Keepers gave no hint of being prepared to attack him, either.

"I'm called Robyn, m'lady."

"Well, Robyn, you've defied all expectations in defeating our champion, Will, here. And with such an extraordinary shot. People will undoubtedly be talking about it for years to come."

He glanced at Scathelock, who was blushing. He said, "I'd no idea I was competing with a Keeper, and glad I am I didn't as it would have convinced me to stand down."

"Then we would never have known of your skill. Tell me, are you a target shooter or do you possess martial experience as well?" Her blue eyes had focused upon the scar at his temple.

"I have some slight acquaintance with battle."

"And modest. You do not brag on yourself. A crusader, perhaps?"

"In a sense, I suppose. In any case, might I buy the three of you a round? Will has emptied his mug and his thirst seems unquenchable."

"I think not but thank you for your offer. We, that is, the Keepers of the Forest, can always use someone with your skills, as Will can attest. Should you ever be looking for employment."

"I seem to be very popular with employers of late. I've only just served my first day among the Waits." He nodded to Geoffrey.

Isabella seemed amused. She hitched one leg up and sat on the projecting circular table. "Poached right under our noses," she said, mock-glaring at Geoffrey, to whom she added, "Tell Elias we have this day captured one of Hodde's men, one of the two accused of murder on the King's Way."

Geoffrey and Thomas traded a worried look, which did not go unnoticed by Isabella. "What troubles you?" she asked.

Thomas said, "Have you yourself beheld the body he's supposed to have slain?"

"I have not, what with this fair and other matters. However, I trust that Passelewe has done."

"The Waits have done." He gestured at Geoffrey as representing all of them. "It's naught but a skeleton dressed up in bishop's robes. More a corpse borrowed from a crypt than a man slain this week upon the road."

To Geoffrey she said, "What, japery? Is that so?"

He nodded vigorously.

She reassessed Thomas. He in turn listened for further hint of Yvag communication. There was none coming from her. She asked, "Why would the sheriff lie about such a thing?"

"Why, indeed? We speculated that he might have some other cause for arresting the man."

She spread her hands. "Oh, there is goodly cause to arrest the outlaw called Little John. Even should this murder prove false, I could provide you half a dozen reasons, beginning with hart, hind, and hare. The same for Hodde himself."

Perplexed, Geoffrey said, "I thought he was called Greenleaf."

Isabella shook her head. "Whatever he may *call* himself, Little John we've met before in the forests. He and Hodde and a few others. They're gifted at eluding pursuit. I daresay they know the king's forests better than we do, and we're very good. Aren't we, Adam? Maurin?"

The other two with her nodded.

"Still," said Thomas, "this crime of which he is accused is false. Perhaps staged."

"Then I'll see him in irons for his poaching, instead."

"And the Waits alongside him?"

She blinked at Thomas, confused.

"For poaching me."

Isabella allowed herself half a smile at his teasing. She stood. "Robyn. Will." Thomas stood, took her hand and politely kissed it. She met his gaze, a look of challenge, before she turned and led the two others out of The Pilgrim. He watched her leave, satisfied in his belief that, whatever else, she wasn't Yvag. Nor, from what he could sense, was her son or the other who accompanied her. He hoped he was right.

"Was it not appropriate to kiss her hand?" he asked.

"Isabella Birkin fans no flames that I know of. She's married to D'Everingham, whether he's worthy of that allegiance or not."

"I'm guessing not."

"And you would be right in every way imaginable."

Thomas appreciated how Isabella might hold to her own principles regardless of there being no reciprocity. Admirable, he supposed, if a lonely path to walk. He felt an odd affinity. Then again, perhaps it wasn't so lonely, just a way she did not share with anyone else. And why should she? Janet, too, had been private with her thoughts. He could not help but be admiring of it.

Meanwhile, the doxy returned and glided up beside Will Scathelock with two wooden mugs. She set one before him and, holding her own, balanced on a stool close against him "'Ere now, good sir, I heard how that one there moonin' after that forester cow split your perfect shot. Must be a bitter disappointment, but Molly's here ta fix it. You always got a shot with me, hey?" She smiled like a temptress as she raised her mug for him to clack his against. As he had only half drained his ale, however, Will pushed aside the mug she'd brought, and raised his own. The doxy said, "But, oh . . ."

Thomas sat back down and, finding a fresh mug in front of him, lifted it to his lips. Will was clearly engaged with the same doxy who'd accosted them before, although she seemed to have eyes for him, too, if surreptitiously, while he was feeling melancholy, dwelling on Isabella Birkin, in need of a drink.

He hardly noticed at all as the elixir in the ale slowly and inexorably wiped his mind.

XVII. In the Caves

Bits of the deeper caves flashed past him—other small chambers, some occupied by other couples. *Couples*—was he with someone? He imagined—hoped—it might be Isabella, because she sparred with him, her tongue sharp with wit, and wasn't that what appealed? It had been the same with Janet through the years . . . Should he tell her that? Probably not.

But, no, it couldn't be Isabella, because she'd left The Pilgrim. Then he'd sat down again, and . . . No idea. The figure he leaned on wore a striped cap—the same doxy? Or was she with Will and this a different one? He remembered he should guard his purse, but his arms didn't seem to work.

Whispers asked questions of him as he stumbled along. How many outlaws were in the tavern today? Was he or "the other one"— did she mean Will?—involved in the theft on the highway? Did he know someone who was? He caught mention of a bishop, of Leicester, of a Simon de Montfort, and the name D'Everingham, but the names blew away as if they'd leaked out around the questions. This was nothing like overhearing the Norman sheriff—that had been a true aberration. Thomas had been in the company of skinwalkers before without the slightest hint of connection to some sleeping Yvag. Passelewe's inner voice had been all the more startling for that, as if Thomas had interrupted a communion. As if he'd overheard God speaking and God had taken note of him because neither he nor God expected the other. His thoughts were so tangled anyway, providing no answers. Isabella had made him long for Janet, for intimacy with someone, a settled life, and this dominated his thoughts. He sensed the questioner's frustration with him, and laughed—at least in his head he laughed. He should pay attention to right now, but his thoughts slid askew.

He wasn't sure when or how he arrived in the small, very dark chamber. The world tipped and he slid into its corner.

He landed unceremoniously upon a straw-filled bed. The room was nearly circular; he wasn't alone but couldn't locate the doxy now. It was as if she'd become shadow. He should listen for Yvags, but the thought escaped him.

Fingers unlaced, undressed him. His eyes refused to focus, and anyway most of whatever was happening rushed past with a roar, so he gave in and let the current take him. At some point golden eyes that were too large and not at all human peered closely at him. He might have cried "Yvag!" but his mouth wasn't obeying him now, either.

Then began the nightmare: He'd been returned to Ailfion, where he was being ridden by Nicnevin again, that grotesque Queen of Hell. She took him; her torso shifted somewhere between human and eel while it slapped against him. Golden eyes burned lustrous in the light of candles, the rings of black pupil full wide; eager, lustful the way all Yvagvoja seemed to be once they cracked open a human body—as if they were tasting sex for the first time, unbridled and depraved. The Queen in her own body was like that, and in all the bodies she wore, bodies of those who mattered to him, who lived in his thoughts. They were stripped out and used against him. She warped and poisoned them all. As it had been with Nicnevin, beside him or above or below him in alternate moments he saw the doxy, the one who dallied with Will Scathelock, but human no more. She plucked Janet from out of him, and then Morven, to which he reacted so violently that this dissolved, transmuting into Innes, but Innes as an Yvag so that he hardly recognized her; she glared at him, lusted for him, used him the way her queen had. Finally she condensed into a distorted version of the leader of the Keepers. *Isabella Birkin?* It seemed she found that amusing. He reeled from the shifting faces pressing their lips to his, triumphantly meeting his gaze. His desire, for so long dormant, was like something that had fallen down a well long ago and been lost. But before this deformed Isabella, her shape all wrong, grotesque, he screamed, or thought he did. Nightmare blurred. It never gave him purchase before it changed again. Despite the horror of the offering, he wanted Isabella, though he hadn't until now allowed that he might feel anything for anyone ever again. Lust devoured guilt, while Scathelock's words "Isabella fans no flames" echoed through his head like a great bell tolling. *Fans no flames, fans no flames.* She was an inhuman Isabella, untouchable, yet coupling with him nevertheless, and all the while whispering her questions: *Where are the* dights? *Who has them? Where have they hidden them?* He could not answer, too full of his own rekindled desire, which must be the impossible perverting ache that an Yvagvoja felt. The questions blew past him, trailed by the same names again, *Leicester, D'Everingham, de Montfort.* He knew D'Everingham was married to Isabella Birkin, but the latter name seemed familiar, too. Who else had mentioned it before? But there was Isabella right in front of him.

Halfway between memory and dream, he watched the distorted Isabella lean close, and then it was Innes sinking her needle teeth into him until the carnal venom trickled from his wound. Why Innes again? Dead so long. How could the doxy be doing this? Capable, like the elven queen, of taking so many eager shapes?

She ran her tensile fingers over him as if she couldn't touch him enough. And though her touch pulsed with more lust, he was able to reject it as he was able to reject her questions.

Whatever she'd done to him, it masked her true nature as it hid what was happening—was she even fucking him? She plucked at his strings, distorted whatever she found, made it seem he was victim to Nicnevin again.

This time she heard the name, his acknowledgment of the damned Queen. She scrutinized him anew.

He fought to swim up out of the nightmare before he drowned in it.

Think! Not a skinwalker: She had those teeth, that venom the same as the Queen's. He tried to pull that realization into focus, but her needle-sharp teeth bit his lip and her lust surged like blood through his body again. His own blood ran down his shoulder. He hadn't dreamed the bite, but he was helpless in its thrall.

Speculations and doubts sailed on without him. No more questions from her, either. Everything funneled into sensation, down into the well again. This time they fucked and tangled and clawed for purchase. A solitary question rang in the darkness now: *"How do you know her?"*

At some point the candle must have guttered, but everything for him had gone dark already. Blind, in cold terror, he lay paralyzed, certain that when the light returned, he would be in his cell next to Taliesin, and all of this life he'd known and believed would be revealed as nothing but an insane prisoner's dream of escape, or a side effect of her venom.

The smell of her on him wrenched him awake. Not since his captivity in Ailfion had he smelled the tart sex odor of that gender of Yvag. He'd thought it belonged to Nicnevin alone.

One dim candle lit the small chamber. It stood on a shelf carved out of the opposite wall. He lay sprawled naked on a straw mattress on the floor, in deep shadow. Stripped from him, his clothes in a heap on the dark floor had transformed back into Hodde's cotehardie and leggings. How long would the glamouring have lasted? Not long, once he lost consciousness. But she hadn't noticed.

In the shadows beside him, the Yvag perched on the cheap bedding. She'd given up the façade of the blond doxy but still maintained the girl's form—a human physique but mottled gray and rough. She leaned back on her hands, one leg folded forward, her toes teasing his erection with a human foot. She still wore the striped coif. It made her look like a hooded falcon on a tree branch contemplating the field mouse she was just about to consume. Her back was to his unglamoured clothes. He tasted blood—she'd bitten his lip—glanced down to confirm the second bite in his shoulder.

She wasn't using mere glamour. This was what Nicnevin called *reshaping.* He could do it, too, though it exhausted him a thousandfold more than simple glamouring, and it could be agony to be something far from one's true self—a sheep, for instance. He remembered. For her it didn't seem any effort at all. She was comfortably halfway between human and Yvag.

"So you're a companion to outlaws, and I've got you." She pushed herself up and knelt over him on all fours. "But you thought of the Queen. I saw her clearly in your mind. When did she take you? Who *are* you?"

Her face, directly over his, was the mottled green-gray of an Yvag, with prominent cheeks, a chin elongated and thorny, and large golden eyes. Her metallic hair curtained his view. Staring up at her, he sucked in a breath, but clearly failed to express the shock he should have, the shock she was expecting. Any innocent captive would have been screaming.

When her mouth opened, the teeth were tiny and sharp. She continued to mask herself in female form, almost as if she'd taken a liking to it, the way Yvagvoja enjoyed coitus. Her face continued to remind him too much of Innes, his long-dead sister, as if having borrowed Innes from his memories, she'd decided to adopt her features. But why? Why maintain that façade out of all those she'd selected? He dismissed the likeness then, arguing that he could barely recall Innes's real face any longer. But in truth, this creature had pulled Innes and Janet into focus again. He might have thanked her for those brief glances if he didn't intend to kill her at his first opportunity.

She ducked her head and ran her tongue along his neck, repeated the questions she'd asked him before. "Where are the *dights*? And how is it you see the Queen?" The playfulness of the question did not quite hide the surging temper underneath it.

He shook his head. There was no answer he could make that wouldn't deliver his true identity. He glanced again at his clothes. She wasn't interested in them.

"When were you her *toy*?" Her fingers gripped his chin and cheeks. She was strong. She could crush his jaw. "I would know of it."

"So would I if you're offering an explanation. I'm not given to consorting with demons, succubus."

She shoved his face away. "Oh. But with whores you don't mind."

He gave a shrug. "You used sorcery. Potions rob one of any choice. I did drink a potion you intended for Will Scathelock, didn't I?" It was what Little John or one of the devout Waits might have claimed.

"They all will have their turn. So, I'm a succubus, am I? You're no more shocked at that possibility than at a dragon flying down a chimney. No, I think you are not what you seem, and I will have an answer to my questions whether you give it freely or not." She stared. He said nothing. "No? Well, we'll soon know everything about you."

She rolled away from him and stood. She held up a flexible Yvag suit of armor and stepped into it. It simply surged up her body.

Again, he knew he wasn't reacting like someone who'd never encountered the malleable armor of Yvag knights before. Whether it was the aftereffects of whatever she'd poured in the ale, or an inability after so long in isolation to feign any emotional response, the result was the same: He was convincing her of his own unnaturalness.

A moment later, she was the doxy again, clothed in a long-sleeved green kirtle. As nonchalantly as possible, he reached for his own clothes. As he picked up each item, he colored it—ochre leggings and indigo cotehardie. As she made no comment regarding them, he guessed they had been stripped from him in the dark, with such focused lust on her part that she hadn't noticed their alteration when cast aside.

His bow and belt with quiver lay against the wall. The Yvag had taken his purse of winnings. At least she hadn't dug into the quiver, where she would have found two Yvag daggers and his ördstone. She seemed dismissive of him now, certain that he posed no threat even if he knew of Nicnevin. She also seemed to be awaiting something.

As he laced the cotehardie, he learned what that was: Two of the Norman sheriff's guards arrived. The small chamber couldn't fit four without forcing Thomas to stand on the mattress. He had his bow at hand but no space to string or use it, and the soldiers had swords drawn already.

The Yvag told them, "Take him to Passelewe. Put him in a cell with the other one. I'll join you as soon as I've interrogated his allies." They closed on him. "And here, Simforax, his purse. Share it with the human guards." She tossed the winnings to the nearest one, bearded Simforax.

In that instant he sprang. He shoved her aside and grabbed the leather purse, then drove his fist straight into Simforax's face. The bearded knight fell into the second one, and Thomas heaved both of them out of his way and on top of the doxy. Behind him, she shrieked in fury.

Diving out the door, he found himself in a weaving tunnel full of carved-out doorways. Turning left, he ran down a sloping path and into a semicircular cellar cave with a knee-high thrall along the curved walls, on top of which stood barrels, a ring of them all around the room, and disappearing where the thrall curved out of sight. The bend proved to be a dead end, just more elevated barrels. He turned about, and concentrated upon glamouring himself as one of the other archers he'd competed against that day. Then he walked back out into the tunnel, where he pretended to lurch unsteadily along, back the way he'd just come.

Barely a moment later, the two sheriff's guards burst into the tunnel. The first knocked him aside; the second one, Simforax, grabbed his shoulder and spun him around, pausing to give a baleful look at this flaxen-haired and inebriated bowman, eyeing him from head to foot with clear frustration at what he saw. The angry chirring thoughts of an Yvag assailed Thomas but he kept himself closed off. The guard shoved him away and bounded ahead after his companion. If he'd any doubt that a soldier named Simforax was Yvag, that doubt vanished with the two soldiers.

Thomas quickly wove his way to the right this time, eventually turning into a corridor full of support columns, one with a cross etched in it. To the left the path sloped down; to the right carved steps led up to a closed door, and he headed for it, pushed his way through the opening, and was immediately overwhelmed by the smell of roasting barley malt in a hazy room thick with bluish smoke. Barely a foot inside, the stone gave way to tightly placed planks of a wood floor over which was strewn an ankle-deep layer of barley. Two sweating men in nothing but braies were pushing the browning barley around with besoms.

The nearest one glared at him. "'Ere, what you doin'?"

"Deepest apologies," he replied. "Wrong room." He quickly went out the door and back down the steps. Studied the other path. It led downward into what looked like a narrowing tunnel, the end of which lay right under the barley chamber he'd just exited. He could make out the red coals of a low fire going there. The two together, top and bottom, had to be a malt kiln, with grain being roasted for the ale.

Cautiously, he wandered back into the main tunnel. No point in following the guards. Let them gain as much distance as possible.

Maintaining his drunken mien, he retraced his steps past various carved-out caves including the barrel cellar, to the dim room and the Yvag doxy. He had a dagger at the ready for her.

He found the room, but the doxy was gone. He turned about. No one was following him. She could have transformed into anybody by now; he might already have passed her in the tunnels. Of course, the same was true for him. She wouldn't have known him, either.

This time he took his bow. It was time to return to the tavern. The only trouble was, the real version of his glamoured boozy illusion had been in the tavern an hour or however long ago that had been. Two of him in the same room would present a problem. He would have to change again, and soon, because she had said she would "interrogate" his allies. Did she mean everyone in the tavern? Or just Will and Geoffrey?

Nearing the tavern room then, he stepped into a shadow, where he paused, and emerged as "Robyn Hoode" in indigo and ochre once more, from then on watching for any reaction on any face and also for the two sheriff's soldiers hunting him. Those two had apparently gone, but other Yvags might yet be about. He'd heard the buzzing of their communication earlier. Who knew how many glamoured creatures might be in there? Still, no one seemed to take any notice of him.

Then suddenly he was grabbed from behind. He twisted free and turned, ready to strike, only to find himself confronting Will Scathelock and Geoffrey. Scathelock cocked an eyebrow at the barbed black dagger. "*That* looks lethal," he commented. "You seem to have sobered right up. That girl took you in the back, I thought sure she meant to rob you of your winnings. There was something in that ale, weren't there? I tried it, could tell it was off."

"You passed it to me, you know, Will."

"Er, yes, well. We didn't know where she'd taken you, so we waited for her to come back out so we could make her tell us. But she ne'er did."

Geoffrey said, "So we was waiting, you know, and these two Norman guards came pushing in, went straight past the barrel hoist and into the caves. Well, by then you'd been gone forever. We each grew the odd idea they were here for you. Silly notion, I suppose. So we stood up and went, too. Got lost. A lot of chambers in use today. Here's to fair day!" He laughed. "Good thing we were proved wrong. But the doxy prob'ly got away."

Will added, "Guards came bursting back out past us, though. Looking for *somebody*, they were." He eyed Thomas with friendly suspicion, as if still unconvinced they hadn't been hunting him.

"If they return, trust me, this time they will settle on we three. It's back to Chandler's Lane gaol for us. We need to speak with Elias and get our friends freed from the cells of Passelewe as soon as possible." He glanced around the noisy, bustling tavern again. How many Yvags did this crowd conceal? He listened but caught no hint of any communication. Nevertheless, he would get them out of there. No one else was being interrogated.

The three of them set forth.

XVIII. Of Gaols & Cells

Little John sat bent over a neck-, hand-, and leg-cuff bar that kept him from standing or even sitting upright in the small cell. The straw he sat in smelled as if twenty men had pissed in it. If they'd been trussed like him, likely they had. He'd been left hunched over, trying to work his wrists free for so long that he'd have gladly made his bed in that straw and gone to sleep if they'd just unlocked the neck cuff. Hand and leg restrictions he could live with.

Although the Norman sheriff was to all appearances human, John had his doubts. For one thing, the sheriff talked and talked about the little objects John stole—how rare they were, how important. He called them *dights*, and as soon as John heard the term he knew those little triangular pieces were what the sheriff meant. *Dights*. Somehow the word sounded like them—like dice split in half maybe. Either the sheriff was working with those demons, or he was one, maybe like that bishop on the road.

He'd expected worse torture than this hobbling, a whipping at the very least, given that the dunking pond was still covered with a small bridge. Funny how he'd gone from the champion on that bridge to the demon sheriff's captive in such short order. Hardly seemed fair. Least he could have done was let John drink a celebratory ale first.

The Norman sheriff had something else in mind.

One of the guards pulled back John's head, choking him in the neck strap, then prised open his mouth, the long fingers gripping like iron, so painful he thought they would puncture his cheeks and crush his teeth. He tried to bite them and was slapped and slapped until his head throbbed. While the bearded guard held his mouth wide, something wet and alive was all but poured in. He thought he'd swallowed a wriggling eel, sensed it sliding down his gullet.

Almost immediately it seemed that the thing reached into his brain, and the pain of that intrusion proved worse than anything he'd ever known—worse than the fire into which he'd once thrust a hand; worse than the crossbow bolt that had pierced his side; worse than the worst ague that had ever tormented his joints and sweated his body. How long it lasted, he had no idea. Hours. Days. Blinding, like a blade cutting deep into his soul, erasing even the passage of time. Voices interrogated—not him but the thing inside him. It wasn't just the demon sheriff, but someone else in his head. Was it a woman? He couldn't tell, lacking any connection to his own body. He couldn't open his eyes, couldn't look, couldn't listen to what was said.

Finally, the thing, whatever it was, seemed to let go and dissolve, with a squeal that grated through his bones.

Slowly, tremblingly, he returned to himself, now beyond exhausted. He'd fallen onto his side, neck, wrists and ankles still locked to the straight bar. This must be what it was like being on the far side of dead.

He had no idea what information he might have given up, but he suspected that he'd given up everything.

The Saxon gaol on Chandler's Lane was a rectangular building of mortar and small stones, with a projecting entryway barely a dozen yards from the Market Square. It might have been any nondescript Romanesque civic building with high arch windows, but for the door in that entryway, which was thick and studded with knob-headed bolts and hung on three huge hinge straps. A metal window in the center was barred by a grate, identical to the doors of the three cells to be found within, and providing some ominous sense that this was not so communal a structure.

The crowds had mostly dispersed in the time Thomas had spent in The Pilgrim. Hardly anyone walked along by the Market wall.

Approaching the gaol, he, Scathelock, and Geoffrey encountered Isabella Birkin and the swarthy brown-haired Keeper from The Pilgrim, Maurin Payne, coming from Halifax Lane near St. Mary's Church. Will sidled over to join his two colleagues, a move that covered how Thomas averted his eyes upon seeing her. The illusion of their coupling was all too fresh and expressed something perhaps too close to the truth of him—a truth he wasn't at all ready to acknowledge. He instinctively slowed and let the others press ahead. The cluster of five arrived at the gaol at the same time.

Geoffrey pushed open the heavy door, leading the way into the large main room, itself subdivided by six square columns. Elias had commented last night that the roof was strong enough to support a row of gallows, not yet constructed but planned.

Near the door was a stand of pole arms used by the Waits—a variety of axes and fauchards. A long trestle table occupied the middle, with stools clustered around it. The back wall contained another door like the one they'd just opened, which led to the three cells, and to pallets for use by members of the Waits. Thomas had slept on one after his rounds with Little John.

At the precise moment that they filed in, one of the Norman sheriff's guardsmen, having emerged from that door, was engaged in a heated exchange with Warin, who'd stood up from his seat at the end of the table. The Saxon sheriff, Orrels, looked on from where he still sat. His expression indicated he disliked the guardsman, or maybe just his answers to Warin.

The guard wore mail beneath the cinquefoil surcoat of Passelewe's force. His mail-framed face was wide with a powerful jaw and chin and a thick auburn mustache. He was carrying Thomas's masonry-tools bag slung over one shoulder. Seeing it, Thomas slid a hand into the quiver on his hip.

Warin was saying, "I tell ye, tha cannot remove possessions belonging to our—" He turned his head, saw who was arriving, and faced the guardsman again. "Well, here's the man himself, ye care to explain it to *him*."

Instead of explaining anything, the guard took a step back and drew his sword. It shone like a rainbow. Seeing it, recalling Hodde's description of the swords the Yvags on the road had carried, Thomas cried out, "Warin, get back from him!"

Even as he shouted the words, the guard thrust his sword arm forward and the sword stretched from its hilt, aimed right for Thomas, who flung himself to the side. The blade bit into the nearest column, then snapped back to its original size; but on the way it had passed straight through Warin. The blade withdrawn, Thomas rocked on his feet, stumbled up against a column and made to lunge at the guard, who casually batted him aside. The sheriff had tipped back his stool and tumbled away to scramble to his feet, dagger drawn.

Thomas rolled, came up running to dodge left around the scarred column. Orrels, on the right, presented the foremost threat, the obvious target, and the guard pivoted to confront him. Thomas sprang then, kicking off the column to tackle the guardsman from his blind side before he could bring that deadly sword to bear upon the sheriff. They both fell sideways. Thomas rolled away. The guard climbed to his feet, but almost immediately staggered. The sword fell from his grip. He glanced down at himself. Thomas's black barbed dagger had sliced all the way up his side from belly to armpit, through surcoat and armor. Viscous black blood flowed from the wound. The guard wheezed, sputtered, and the same black oil spilled from between lips that even then were transforming, as was everything about it, from human to Yvag. Its prominent chin grew longer, spiked, its skin a sickly green as if the creature were long dead and rotting. No mustache graced its thin lip now. The mail it wore shrank to a shiny and fibrous black with flexible joints, some of them in the wrong places as though its limbs had been broken, dislocated. Its thighs thickened and projected off its hips as a grasshopper's might. Only the torn red-and-yellow surcoat remained the same.

The Yvag bared its sharp teeth. Ringed golden eyes seethed with hatred, focusing upon Thomas. "You'll pay dearly for this," it gurgled.

"I already have," Thomas answered, "and for more to come." He watched without mercy.

Along its side, the Yvag's gills sprayed dark blood with every breath. As if only now understanding its situation, it looked suddenly terrified, gold eyes seeking some escape. "I can't die!" it insisted. Its ungoverned fear, like a scream, roared through his head. Beside him, the sheriff cringed and pressed fingertips to his temples. More fearfully still, the Yvag begged, "Don't let me *die*." But after three more exhalations it lay still.

For a moment no one moved. Then the sheriff crossed to Warin, but the kindest of the Waits had been punctured through by that wicked sword, dead when he hit the floor.

Thomas knelt beside the Yvag. First he hauled his mason's bag away from it and looked inside. Little John's three *dights* lay in the bottom. He set the bag down, grabbed and tugged at the Yvag's mail coif as he knew to do. The head covering abruptly withdrew, spilling out the strange silver-white hair of the Yvags. He reached in beneath the twisted surcoat, felt for and found the seam in the armor, then parted it enough to probe until he'd collected an ördstone from an inner pocket that he'd guessed would be there. The stone made a chittering noise audible to him. It produced a pressure in his head, one he could ignore, probably not enough that anyone else sensed it. He dropped the ördstone into his quiver, which he noted did not go unobserved by Orrels. No dagger graced this armor, but then the creature had its diabolical sword instead, a far more treacherous weapon. Thomas turned to reach for it, found a booted foot just behind him, and looked up.

Isabella had come close to see. "This is no thing of natural magic," she said, "It's a conjured demon out of hell. How can you even touch it?"

The sheriff looked queasily as if he agreed with her, although he bent down and collected the weird sword. A bemused look overcame him. "Why, this hardly weighs anything. What is it made from?" He showed it to Geoffrey and Will, but looked to Thomas for some sort of explanation.

Then, across the room the gaol door opened, and Elias entered, accompanied by Osbert and another member of the Waits whom Thomas didn't know. The moment Elias saw them all he hurried over. "What has happened here? Oh, God's love, Warin." The Waits pressed in behind him. Geoffrey pointed at the creature. "This is what we heard of on the King's Way, innit?" he said. "What people described roaming across Sherwood in the night."

Sheriff Orrels kicked at the Yvag's torso, but looked to him for some explanation. "Master Hoode?"

Thomas climbed to his feet. Passelewe's colors in that surcoat meant that Little John had given up the location of the *dights*. The Yvags would have pried open his mind and gotten everything they wanted from him. Lucky they didn't have possession of these or John would even now be lost to them, and might still be. For all Thomas knew, they'd slain him the moment he'd told them everything.

How much did he want to tell these people? How much would suffice? If they were going to take on the Norman sheriff beneath the castle, they were going to have to know more than they did right now. Not only know but believe. He supposed the "demon" on the floor was proof enough for whatever version of the facts he wished to spin for them. The world here preferred its demons, and perhaps that was the best way of explaining. It saved him trying to describe Ailfion or to express all he'd been through from the moment they took his brother Onchu. Mason, archer, mercenary, husband, hermit, all stretched over more than a century—who would understand or believe that story? Not these good people. Witchcraft and devilry versus a dependable Church sufficed for them. No doubt that accounted for why so many men of the cloth were turned. In a world of clear antipodes, simply control or replace as many of the "good" men as you can, and you're certain to win.

Orrels repeated, "Master Hoode?" inviting an answer, but still Thomas had none to offer. He refused to relive the loss of Janet and Morven again. He'd been mired in those memories for seventy years already, broken down, isolated, and benumbed. What good could come of further revisiting the time before he recognized that he no longer aged like everyone else, that he had become maybe as long-lived as the Yvags themselves? Hiding in the woods prolonged his life. Coming out into the world again risked him putting an end to an existence he'd railed against and now was not so sure of. More to the point, who in this room would believe any of his story?

At least he must reply to Orrels, whether he mentioned any of that or not. He said, "Outlaws will be the least of your worries hereafter, Sheriff."

XIX. In Ailfion

In the elven city of Ailfion, Sir Richard atte Lee sits alone in a cell. There are no bars, no locks, no doors. None is needed for there is no entrance, no exit. Just seven star-shot cells, counting his, ringing a central domed circle; all the other cells are empty.

How he has come to be here is itself something of a mystery. He recalls being led to a sort of outdoor court—and even that journey has gaps, moments or hours, even days perhaps where he can't remember just what he saw. It's as if time and distance collapsed upon him repeatedly. Brief memories of huge, strange trees, of skies full of whorls of stars, of a landscape of tall spires of glass and steel as if cathedrals have merged with blades so huge they poke at the underbelly of Heaven itself—glimpses of something vast and inhuman.

No idea how long he's been held here. Nobody has shown up to torture or interrogate or feed him. His single meal appeared out of nowhere; it wasn't there and then it was. There's no sun, no moon, no windows, no way to mark the passage of time. Inexplicably it feels as if time is hurtling past.

Then darkness descends and Sir Richard experiences the same lightheadedness as when the food appeared. Carefully, he gets up and leaves the cell, thinking that more food awaits him.

Instead, in the central circle, an astonishingly beautiful woman sits on a high-backed throne of alabaster and incarnadine. She has hair of red gold and eyes of emerald. She wears a long flowing purple robe trimmed in gold thread. Her posture, her severe expression, her aloofness bespeak her status. This is a monarch.

Beside her stands a . . . creature. He does not know what else to call it. Two guards stand behind it but he barely notices them. The creature regards him, turning its head as if to view him side on, and when it does, its misshapen skull sprouting tufts of black hair becomes almost unbearably beautiful, as if the cast of light and shadow has shifted and realigned the planes of its face. The face keeps changing thus, from demonic to angelic, as the thing studies him. Its swaying head reminds him of a cobra he once saw. It's so hypnotic that he only vaguely notices the deformed physique, uneven shoulders, and arms that end in mismatched hands—one brutishly human, the other tapered and clawed, with extra-jointed spiderlike fingers. For all its asymmetry it stands huge and powerfully built.

Finally, the Queen has one of the silent guards step between him and the creature—it's the only thing that breaks its spell over him. He looks around, blinks, comes back to himself. She speaks to him. "Thomas Rimor, is it?" The mocking voice, he realizes, is inside his head. Her lips haven't moved. But it's the identical response of the knight who called herself Zhanedd. Obviously, the name from a ballad of a man who is taken on a tour of faery is as well known to them as it is to him. He's been quite a fool.

He blushes, replies out loud: "Well, not actually."

She allows a smile. "No, of course not actually. That particular mayfly will be dead at least half a century by now."

"He lives on in ballads," he lamely protests. "Song."

"Mmm." She nods. "I regret we had a hand in that. At the time it seemed expedient to make a myth of him, that we might introduce elements as it suited us. What is a ballad after all but a story simply leaving out its motivations? It left us free to write our own. But that is of no matter to you. You are not who you claimed to be, you are one Sir Richard atte Lee, a knight who went questing as your sort do, and in the bargain lost your fortune and your future in the World-to-Be. We met you previously in the mountains of Italia, though you escaped capture then, and later again at Carcassonne. Took up with outlaws—all of them deceased now, I will tell you. Nevertheless, you still might be useful to me. Do you know who I am?"

"Qu-queen?" he stammers.

Now her smile becomes indulgence. "But of what, you're not entirely sure. Are you?"

"All I've seen . . ." he begins, pauses and begins again. "All I've seen that I can trust are these cells."

"Rejoice then that you see even this much. The last of your kind who occupied that cell conspired against us, cost us dear. Truly, I had no choice but to punish him. You know, he appeared not to mind, either, but then he was wearing out."

"What didn't he mind, Majesty?" he asks uneasily.

"His *ending*!" She comes out of her throne. "Would you like to meet him? The undigested pieces, that is. They're still visible."

Sir Richard bows and kneels. "I would not, Majesty."

"Yes, well." She resettles on her throne. "Wise you are to say so. I think we should make use of you while we have this opportunity. Don't you agree, Bragrender?"

The creature says nothing, just shifts again between beauty and horror. Sir Richard only looks at it sidelong. He hears a kind of buzzing, as if hornets have been set loose in the chamber, and in the midst of it a word, *astralis*.

Nicnevin tells him, "Bragrender is the offspring of your appropriated Thomas the Rhymer. His fabric—his *astralis*—proved sufficient to spark new life, though not, unfortunately, to shape it very satisfactorily, leaving Bragrender caught between two progenitors, two forms if you like. No one will procreate with him, either; whatever else he might be, he is as sterile as the chrysalis out of which he emerged."

"I don't understand."

"No? It's no matter. Perhaps you will surpass the Rhymer. Did you know that two of every three Yvags can alter our sex? And one of every five of those has the capacity to shift genetically to my own state, the superior stratum—the few not plagued, like Bragrender, by the sterility of our exhausted pedigree."

Sir Richard can only shake his head that the more she tells him, the less he understands.

"For you it simply means that you can potentially procreate with a minority of our kind, starting of course with those who've invested themselves in prolonged lacunae in your world. Those are our Yvagvoja. They are most favored, and deserving of reward for their sacrifice. You will be that reward for a time, serving a greater purpose while you're with us."

"Majesty?" He can barely keep up.

"Oh, you and I might suspect otherwise, but they won't. And who knows, you might impregnate one, expand the breadth of our formational pool, before I dispose of you or return you to the World-to-Be—which is to say, your world. Wouldn't that be wonderful?"

She snaps her fingers. The ceiling goes spiraling up; the three of them in the center circle rise along with it.

On the way up, she tells him, "I believe you won't be with us for very long, either way. You cannot tell us where our stolen treasure is—a situation in Sherwood Forest that must be resolved in short order. Once it is, I'm sure we'll return you. Perhaps years will have passed by then. For now..."

On the next level wait dozens of Yvags, gray-green, spiky as carved gargoyles, and looking hungry.

Sir Richard cries out, "Majesty, *please!*"

However, the Queen is distracted, contemplating Bragrender for a moment before she announces, "He's yours. But!" They stare at her, hesitant to act. Then she gives a laugh. "Oh, drain him dry as you like. It little changes how I will use him."

The elven surround him, pick him up and carry him, screaming, away.

XX. Of *Dights* & Demons

Thomas placed the three little pyramids on the table. Isabella, the Waits, and Orrels leaned in close to examine them.

"Puzzle boxes," guessed the sheriff, who then looked to him for confirmation.

He shook his head.

Orrels picked one up and turned it over and over, then held it up between thumb and forefinger to peer at it. "It has these shapes etched into every side. It's heavier than I'd expected, as if there's some hidden attachment to the floor. Even lead wouldn't weigh this much, would it?"

Thomas said, "I don't know, but I suspect you're right."

"Well, if not puzzle boxes, what are they?"

He gestured at the body. "A different demon, in league with this one, called them *dights*. All I know of them is that if you stand one on its apex and set it to spinning, it will capture the mind of the person nearest it and hollow them out such that a demon like this one can take control, occupy, *become* them."

Sheriff Orrels laughed in disbelief. He took the dight he held and tried to spin it. It fell over and rolled off the table. Thomas caught it. "You really ought not to do that."

"Why, you can't even *make* the . . . spinner spin."

"Nor would I want to," Thomas replied.

Isabella asked, "To whom has this spinner been applied? Who has fallen victim to it?" Orrels looked at her as if to say *Don't humor him.* "Well, *I* want an example," she said, then again to Thomas, "Who?"

Ele vos a envoié? echoed in his head as loudly as when he'd first heard it.

"Not this one, but another... Sheriff Orrels's Norman counterpart."

"What? Passelewe?" asks Isabella. "You can't be serious."

Thomas replies, "Who do you suppose sent this creature disguised as one of his guards to carry these off? Where do you think they were being taken?"

No one had an answer for that. Into the uncomfortable silence, Maurin said, "But we report to the man." He stared at Isabella Birkin for confirmation.

Elias added, "And we see him almost *daily*. Surely one of us would have penetrated his disguise."

Of course they didn't understand. They all thought Thomas was describing glamouring. He would need to elaborate, but then they were going to demand he explain how he knew so much, and what was he going to say: "I lived with them for twenty years though it was only a few months in Ailfion"? No, he wanted to keep everyone from asking more questions about him.

"Osbert," he said. "You and Geoffrey and the others came across a body on the King's Way through Sherwood."

"Oh, that were nothing. Somebody's joke—just a wet skellington done up in bishop's garb and covered in soup like."

He shook his head and held up the *dight*. "Whoever it was, he'd met one of these. It cored him out. He'd have gone along, looking as normal as anyone if Little John—Reynold—hadn't put an arrow through him, breaking the bond."

Orrels made a face of disbelief. "First, I don't remotely believe you. Second, if what you say is true, you've just identified your friend Greenleaf as a murderer. Not the wisest—"

"The bishop of Doncaster is gone missing."

At this pronouncement everyone turned to face Will Scathelock.

Uncomfortably, he continued, "I learned of it this morning just before the contests. Prior Walter of Felley Priory told me. Doncaster was to have stayed the night with him before the fair. He never arrived. I reported it to Isabella, but we've had no time to inquire further."

Orrels bellowed, "Well, which is it? A jape of some sort, or the bishop of Doncaster? Do I arrest your friend for murder or you for your grotesque flight of fancy? You're like one of those mad village women who swears she's flown through the skies with the pagan goddess Diana when we all know she's gone nowhere at all!" He appeared near-apoplectic.

Thomas set down the *dight*. Quietly, he said, "I told you, outlaws weren't the problem now."

The sheriff leaned on the table while he composed himself. "Is there," he asked, "not a chance you can demonstrate even one of these things at work as you describe?"

Thomas replied, "You are a danger to yourself, Sheriff. Even did I know how to start one spinning, please God and I would never want to."

"Which I take to mean that you have seen one of these put to diabolical use."

"Yes."

"Where?"

"A place far from here that was called Oakmill." He closed his eyes, knowing there was no avoiding what the sheriff would ask next.

"Who was it used on, then?"

"My wife." He raised his head and stared Orrels down. For all that he'd tried to lead the talk away from her, Janet remained inextricably bound, woven into the pattern of events forever. He could have explained that she'd escaped, but his point was better made letting them think what they liked.

The silence stretched on until suddenly Geoffrey exclaimed, "Oh, my Lord!" and pointed. They all turned to look.

The Yvag, lying in a pool of black blood, was stirring, its fingers closing and opening. And impossibly the blood seemed to be shrinking, resorbing back into the body.

"But it was *dead*!"

Scathelock took a step nearer to lean over it. "Look, even its armor is healing. How can that be?" He looked at everyone, finally at Thomas, for an answer.

Thomas turned and crossed the room as if making to leave. "Stop now!" shouted the sheriff. He drew his short sword.

Reaching the stand of pole arms by the door, Thomas grabbed hold of a Danish axe, drew and carried it back through their midst.

They all stepped aside as if fearful he might use it on them. Orrels, however, sheathed his sword. Like Will and Maurin, he peered more closely at the creature. It seemed finally that he accepted what was happening.

As he crossed the room, Thomas said, "They have remarkable healing powers, the Yvag do. So, too, their armor. It stitches itself up as if it is a living thing. If you leave this creature alone for an hour it will stand up and walk out of here to report to Passelewe. It'll be cloaked again in mail under that torn surcoat. First, though, it will kill everyone in here."

"I don't understand—you opened up its entire side," the sheriff said. "How . . . ?" He shook his head, defeated by what he beheld.

"I know. Not sure how I missed all its vitals." Then as an afterthought added: "It's not made like us."

"What is it like, then?" asked Elias.

"Like something bred with an insect, a worm, a creature out of the sea perhaps."

"But shouldn't we let it live, then?" he suggested. "I mean, in order to ask it questions. To understand. Surely, it's one of God's creatures."

Again, they had no idea what was occurring even as they looked on. This was resurrection, and they had only one model for that. "If it opens its eyes, the first thing it will do is alert Passelewe that all of you know the truth of him and that you have possession of the *dights*. If you haul it into a cell to interrogate it, you'll be overwhelmed by an urge to give it your weapons or to kill those in your company." He was recalling Old Melrose as Alderman Stroud ordered him to kill Waldroup . . . and hadn't he almost? Only a misworded command had saved them both. The Yvag knew no mercy, gave no quarter. They thought the universe belonged to them.

No more time to waste. This could all be debated after the fact. He turned back to the creature and lifted the Danish axe. Orrels raised a hand and said, "Wait," as he strode nearer.

Whether or not the sheriff's boot brushed the Yvag's arm, that arm suddenly bent in the wrong direction and its long fingers closed around his ankle with a grip so strong that Orrels cried out and dropped down on one knee. The golden eyes opened and bored into his.

With a shout, Thomas swung the axe so hard that the blade

sparked against the stone floor, and the silver-haired, green-gray head shot away toward the cell doors. Black blood sprayed the floor and ran thickly like treacle off the blade.

Isabella and Elias jumped in and dragged Orrels away. He yipped as his ankle twisted free of the creature's clutch, still inflexible in death. They set him on his stool. He was pale as parchment and sweating.

Thomas laid the axe across the table so that the blade dripped off the side of it, away from them all. He met the sheriff's pained gaze. "I'm sorry," he said. "I hope it's not broken."

Orrels pinched sweat from his eyelids. "All right," he answered, "what do we need to stop Passelewe?"

Zhanedd was confused and concerned. The human that knew Nicnevin's name had eluded both Simforax and Kunastur in the tunnels. The most likely explanation, it seemed initially, was that he had simply outrun them. Reglamoured, Zhanedd let the two of them pursue him. She had more drunken archers and outlaws in The Pilgrim to probe.

Yet, not ten minutes later the same human had emerged from the deep caves in the company of two other mortals as though there had been no pursuit, no one wanting to catch him, no one hunting him at all.

How had he rendered himself invisible to both the guards and Zhanedd? Had these other two hidden him somewhere in the caves? No one had been watching them, so that seemed most likely. She almost regretted being unprepared to stab him on his way out, but he had revealed a true memory of the Queen, and Zhanedd would know more. For instance, when had the remembered event taken place?

Of course it was well established that the Queen took the occasional human plaything. Her personal escort all knew that, when she joined those going out to secure the latest *teind*, it almost always meant that she was on the prowl for a new toy. They never lasted long. She rode them, usually to death, in the name of getting herself with child. She claimed it was to expand, even revive the line. The Yvagvoja, however (and Zhanedd knew a few), had a different opinion: They suspected Nicnevin to be overcome with the same lust they experienced when bonding with a human conveyance.

Zhanedd had now enjoyed fucking three of the humans in The Pilgrim, and had to admit it was indeed a heady mix—maybe not quite what the Yvagvoja experienced in human guise, but impossible to deny. Zhanedd wondered if, somewhere in the dim past of their so-called faery realm, the Queen had herself been Yvagvoja and had given herself completely to the pleasures of human flesh. Yvag history, with its jumps to new worlds, was so corrupt, so full of blank spaces, including a complete history of Nicnevin.

What Zhanedd knew was that one of Nicnevin's toys had resulted in Bragrender, that horror. It hardly revived their line.

The human that had contributed to the distorted half-breed must have been dead a century or more by now. So who was this other mortal who'd eluded Passelewe's two soldiers and Zhanedd, managed to disguise itself and escape? A toy of the Queen's, but not one of which Zhanedd was aware.

In The Pilgrim, the strange mortal surrounded himself with more armed humans, and they all left together. Zhanedd's curiosity got the better of her, and in a new shape, she followed them at a reasonable distance. Maybe she should have called for Passelewe's soldiers again, but this was her initiative. If it paid off, she'd no intention of sharing the glory. Nicnevin had put her in charge—at least, she thought so until being warned off by the call of another Yvag, Tozesđin, who had disguised and entered the gaol where the humans were going. Excitedly, Tozesđin announced that he now possessed all three *dights*. Zhanedd held back, waited. Being part of such a triumph was better than nothing, though it smarted to think that Nicnevin had only pretended to put Zhanedd in charge of recovering the *dights*.

And then nothing, no further communication. It seemed Tozesđin had died.

Improbable as that might be, the humans had killed one of *them*. Perhaps it was simply a "stepping through the wrong gate" scenario, and the idiot Tozesđin had been surrounded, unable to cut a way home.

When was the last time that had happened? Zhanedd could think of no such event. As for humans killing Yvag, it had been a long time since the Queen's favorite, Ađalbrandr, had been obliterated. To this day she said she regretted him. No one had dared to ask whether she meant she regretted his death or whether she regretted ever entertaining herself with the power-hungry fool. However that translated, no Yvag had perished since the death of Aðalbrandr. Until now.

The Queen had made recovery of the *dights* sound like the most noble of quests. She had picked Zhanedd for it; she said she had been watching the changelings for as long as there was memory, and Zhanedd had caught her attention. Why and how? Unknown. It made Zhanedd wonder about the identity of the humans from which she'd been taken. Despite the various gender pathways of the Yvag, Zhanedd knew instinctively she'd been a female human.

Then, as Zhanedd waited, the same group she had followed emerged from the gaol, save for the one she'd been following in the first place.

XXI. Castle Caves

Isabella Birkin and Will Scathelock followed Elias and Osbert, as representing the Waits, along the Broad Marsh to where it narrowed beneath the castle. The Norman gaol, built into the base of the massive promontory on which Nottingham Castle perched, was fronted by a trio of barred cave openings, as if the massive rock was something alive and with mouths open and eager to devour any who approached below.

Isabella couldn't help thinking of the queer gills in the demon that the archer Robyn Hoode had beheaded. She shivered, recalling how it had come back to life, and quickly buried the memory.

Vertical bars lined the trio of cave mouths, but only the center one, the gate, could be opened. Isabella was a frequent visitor to Passelewe's gaol; as the leader of the foresters, she reported to both sheriffs any news on poaching or thieving or assaults in the king's preserve. She would have considered their working relationship close before today.

The first time she had come here Adam had been twelve and expressing a nascent interest in joining the Keepers of the Forest upon reaching maturity. After she'd introduced him to the sheriff, Passelewe had given them a tour up through the rock, showing them various cells that existed at different levels of dungeon within it, up the long winding stairwell that led from the gaol facing Broad Marsh all the way through the rock to the larger, southern keep on the plateau far above. As they climbed, he regaled them with stories— how it was believed by some that Lancelot had carved out many of the hidden chambers in the promontory to hide Guinevere from King Arthur once their adulterous affair had been found out. Surely, the man who told her that romantic story had not yet been turned by the demons. When had it happened, then? And how? She couldn't really comprehend what Orrels called *spinners*.

If Hoode's plan failed, how was she ever going to come calling upon the Norman sheriff again after this, knowing what lurked behind those eyes? How would she dare leave Adam alone in his company?

She *wished* she knew what lurked behind the eyes of that one who called himself Robyn Hoode. He had not joined them in this endeavor; he'd insisted that he would find another way in—that their contentious visit would misdirect the sheriff's guards (what did he call the demons? Yvags?) and afford him the opportunity to penetrate the promontory—yet she could not see how he might succeed at this. The Waits were known. She was known. But this outlier who'd suddenly appeared with answers and explanations, with direct knowledge of the demons in their midst, well . . . she didn't trust him. Then again, at this point, what could she trust?

Knights that weren't human and could suffer fatal blows and revive? Not just revive but resurrect as Jesus did. That she'd seen with her own eyes. It was unholy, and it should have sufficed as proof of what he told them. Nevertheless, his story felt . . . wrong. False somehow in a way she could not work out. Yet the quiet anguish when he'd mentioned his dead wife had been plain to see. His hunger for vengeance as he beheaded that creature.

No, it was more as if Hoode had left something out of his tale that she couldn't quite pinpoint. His facts failed to connect properly. For instance, he knew Little John by name, but didn't know that Little John wasn't Reynold Greenleaf? Absurd. Both could not be true. But as he had not accompanied them, she could not interrogate him further, and she very much wanted to do so. He was, well, intriguing.

At that point she set the matter aside, because they'd arrived at the barred caves of the Nottingham castle gaol. The guard on duty at the gate knew them all and she him. He was called Milo, and was surely not one of Passelewe's *Yvags*.

Elias asked that they be taken to the sheriff as if this were the most casual visit, perfectly ordinary. The Waits were always reporting to both sheriffs about things in the city, and she was always reporting about matters in the king's preserve. There might be two boroughs here but Nottingham remained essentially a Norman town. Passelewe received any news first.

The unlocked gate was thrown back and all of them entered the dark sandstone gaol. Somewhere deep in its recesses—if he was to be believed—Robyn Hoode would be making his way down from the keep to the cells that had no doors, the oubliettes, as well as those with more traditional entries. Little John and the Waits' own Benedict could be in either type of cell—she'd no idea how Passelewe decided on such things. The last she'd turned over a poacher to him was three months ago. She'd made no inquiry as to the disposition of the man, but also had neither seen nor heard anything further of him.

How would Hoode be managing? Mostly, how did he think he would actually make his way past the various guards and checkpoints in the first place when he sported no red mustache nor looked anything like that creature had done in its human guise? The Waits and she would provide a modest diversion at best. In fact, she expected the next time she saw Robyn Hoode, he would be occupying a prison cell of his own.

Or perhaps dead.

Escaping from the Waits proved to be the most difficult part of Thomas's plan. Geoffrey and Osbert both wanted to accompany him and had to be talked out of it—their presence would have kept him from penetrating the castle at all. They objected that he would not be known to any of the soldiers there. He countered that his unfamiliarity was the thing that would get him inside. There was no way to tell them how he would accomplish this without them all thinking he, too, was a demon. He argued that the more diversion they made, the easier his task. At last they conceded.

The body of the slain Yvag they put in an empty cell. Orrels oversaw this from his stool at the table. He had his leg elevated on the table. The ankle was bruised, but fortunately not broken. Still, it would be some days before he could walk on it without leaning on one of the pole arms for support.

In the cell, Thomas stripped the Yvag of its armor and surcoat. Most of the blood staining the fabric had been resorbed.

Orrels called out that he had multiple suits of mail for Thomas to choose from for his disguise. Of course, when he emerged from the cells in the Yvag's armor, he'd already glamoured it as mail. Orrels said, "Oh, I see you found one. Good."

He took the Yvag's magical sword, which was light as a cloud. The only thing he regretted leaving behind was his bow. But judging from the various descriptions of the tunnels beneath the castle, it would be useless anyway.

The rest of the glamouring was easy; the route up to the castle passed by any number of uninhabited caves. He simply ducked into one. He remembered the lantern-jawed and mustachioed face the Yvag had hidden beneath well enough. Besides, under mail and with the bright yellow and red cinquefoil surcoat on display, any minor discrepancies would likely go unnoticed. The surcoat was torn where his dagger had done its work, and, after rinsing most of the remaining blood out, he'd left it torn. It would give the enemy the impression that he'd not easily gotten his hands on the masonry bag, that he'd fought for it. He hoped that might work to his advantage, too, as he hoped the glamoured Yvags among Passelewe's guards would cluster close to the sheriff rather than mingling with the humans who might apprehend their oddness. The keep would be ill-lit inside, the steps down through the rock—which Isabella Birkin had described to him in detail—even darker. He was as prepared as he could be. The rest was in the hands of God.

As he entered a gate in the castle curtain wall, however, he was nodded to familiarly by a few of the guards. For a moment he worried that all of them might be Yvags, that Passelewe had been accruing a cohort here well before the prelate had been slain and the dights taken.

Now uncertain what to expect, he listened hard for the buzzing, the pressure, of conversing Yvags. But every soldier he encountered, every surcoated guard like himself, registered as human. So either they had seen his double in the sheriff's company or they simply recognized and acknowledged the coat of arms that he, like they, wore.

He crossed the courtyard straight for the donjon, walked in through the open portcullis door, and was immediately immersed in darkness and the smells of cooking, of fatty meat and onions, and a haze of smoke. It took a moment for his eyes to adjust to the dimness. Another guard stepped up, another mortal.

Thomas patted the mason's bag. "Sheriff Passelewe," he said.

Without so much as a word, the soldier ushered him across the wide stone floor. They passed two adjacent kitchens, and arrived finally at a large dark door in the rear wall. Small torches burned on both sides of it. Wide iron hinges and rows of studs decorated its face.

The guard dragged the door open and came smartly to attention. Stepping into the space, Thomas could just make out a flight of roughly carved steps disappearing in the blackness below. He reached for the torch beside him and held it over the steps. The flame guttered in a draft emerging out of the stairwell. Perhaps twenty feet below, the steps turned, leading out of sight. He glanced back at the guard and the banded backside of the door, then started down the steps.

Above him the door thundered shut.

The question now was how to find John. The bend in the descent led to another, and soon he didn't know which way he was facing as he walked down. Eventually, he came upon a horizontal tunnel that branched off from the stairwell. Everything below remained dark and no one was about, so he strayed into the tunnel and shortly encountered a locked grate set in the floor. The space below lay in utter darkness.

He knelt and held the torch close. It threw long strands of shadow into the chamber below, delineating a floor strewn with straw or perhaps dried reeds. There was an overturned bucket. Otherwise, the cell lay empty.

Thomas got up and continued until he came to a second grate. This one was unlocked. He opened it on loud hinges, and lay down to hold the torch deeper into the hole.

A figure lay in the straw far below. Short and thin, in ragged clothes suggesting that he'd been here for quite a while, the man was either dead or insensible. Beside the grate and tied to it was a coil of rope. Thomas supposed this was how the prisoner received water, or had his slops emptied if such a courtesy was even provided, which— from the stench—he doubted. But no exit for the prisoner, who could never hope to reach the opening. The cell reminded him of Taliesin and the inescapable Yvag prison, which he'd thought to be an oubliette, too. Was the old poet even there any longer?

Getting to his feet again, he idly kicked the rope into the open hole. If the man had any strength left, maybe he could climb out. Thomas stepped around the open grate, but the tunnel ended just ahead. There were no more oubliettes, at least not on this level. He returned to and continued on down the steps.

It surprised him how uninhabited the passages were. Then again, he was somewhere in the middle of a mammoth stone promontory with soldiers above and below him. It wasn't as if anybody this deep inside the castle rock was going to escape. Perhaps he shouldn't have bothered with that rope. It was offering false hope to a dead man.

The steps continued down in what felt like a random direction. Whoever had carved this path had not worried about straight lines. Other short tunnels branched off, but all appeared to be dead ends. No Yvag chittering reached him from any of them. He kept going. Here and there the torch guttered, and the steps echoed as with the sound of fluttering, causing him to look about himself.

Eventually, the way below glowed softly with its own flickering torchlight. Thomas followed another turn in the steps.

Before him was another tunnel offshoot, this one lined on each side with three solid doors set in the rock. Two guards sat on stools there. The nearest stood up at his approach. The one farther back was a bearded guard he'd already met, with the Yvag name of Simforax. His torturer in the caves of The Pilgrim had called him that. Simforax appeared to be sleeping, but the soft pressure and whisper of probing thoughts attempting to invade Thomas's mind suggested otherwise. He instinctively rebuffed them, and Simforax rose to his feet. No surprise how the nearer, human guard was maintaining as much distance as possible from the other. On some level, probably not even consciously, he would sense the odd stillness of the bearded soldier, poised like a mantis on a foxtail.

Out loud, Thomas said, "I seek Sheriff Passelewe." He closed a hand around the strap of the mason's bag and pushed the word *dights* to the forefront of his thoughts.

The Yvag soldier took an eager step forward.

Thomas gestured at the cell doors. "Are the prisoners here?" he asked.

The human guard answered, "You mean the outlaws?" The Yvag simply focused upon the nearest two doors as it buzzed something the equivalent of *outlaws*.

Thomas said, "I thought only one of them was considered an outlaw. The other man was simply found in his company. As it happens, he's an upstanding member of the Nottingham Waits."

The human guard nodded. "That were his defense, but the sheriff, 'e thought it wisest to hold them both for now while 'e draws up proper warrants." While he spoke, Thomas sent to Simforax the thought *We need to remove this one if we're to empty the outlaw for Passelewe.*

To the human guard he said, "What are you called, lad?"

"Er-Ernald," he replied as if no longer quite sure.

Thomas said, "Ah, well, worry not, Ernald, this should be sorted soon. Waits are even now down below with the sheriff."

The Yvag glided quietly forward. Ernald must have sensed the movement and glanced around. In that moment Thomas unsheathed the Yvag sword. He'd had no opportunity to test it, and could only hope it would activate for him as it had done for the creature in the Chandler's Lane gaol.

Trapped between them, Ernald looked at him, fearful now. "'Ere, what you about?"

"This," he replied, and thrust his arm out.

Without a sound the blade shot forward. It just missed Ernald but squarely impaled Simforax—so keen the leaping blade that the Yvag kept walking another step before it realized what had happened. By then the blade had retreated and black blood was spreading down the front panel of its surcoat. It shot him a look of outraged confusion.

"What have ye done?" shouted the guard. He drew his own short sword.

"Hush, Ernald," said Thomas. "See for yourself."

Warily, with his sword tip still angled defensively at Thomas, the guard dared a look behind him.

The Yvag's appearance melted away as it lost its glamour until, in surcoat over black armor, it swayed, its thorny face gray as death, fierce and inhuman, weirdly jointed. Not taking any chances this time, Thomas thrust the sword and ran the creature through a second time. The black-dripping blade snicked out and back to its normal state so fast that it sprayed Yvag blood after it across Ernald's own coat.

"If it puts your mind at ease, he was walking this way in order to kill you with that dagger." He gestured at it with the sword, which reacted by snapping forward and skewering the Yvag's hand. A barbed dagger fell from its grasp and clattered on the stone.

Thomas, deciding the sword was if anything a little *too* receptive to his gestures, sheathed it again as Simforax collapsed.

The guard waved his sword warily to keep Thomas back although Thomas was making no attempt to close the distance or attack him. "What . . . what was that?" he asked.

By now Thomas knew how to field such questions. "A demon, lad," he said, "in the employ of your sheriff. They've arrested these two men under false pretenses and we need to set them free before reinforcements are sent." He'd sensed the Yvag's dying squall. Even Ernald had winced—though the cause of that ringing pain would elude him. Whether or not the cry reached anyone, Thomas had to assume it had. Someone would be coming, probably from below. How many glamoured or reshaped Yvag knights would the sheriff have enlisted in the town? Before the theft of the *dights,* would their presence even have been necessary? The aldermen and magistrates he'd known in Melrose and Ercildoun had all acted solo. Unless Nicnevin had changed the rules, he assumed Passelewe would do likewise. Right now, however, he didn't know and didn't dare assume.

XXII. Passelewe

Little John came alert at the sound of the pull lock being disengaged. The door swung open, but he remained still in the putrid straw as if unconscious. His only concern was saving his strength for when the sheriff returned. He'd every intention of making one final effort to kill the man, if "man" even described Passelewe. This might be his chance: Minutes earlier he'd felt the queer ache in his head, same as he'd done with the prelate and soldiers on the King's Way, same as with the Queen of Faeries. Same as while he'd been tortured by that Norman bastard.

Instead he found himself squinting at two guards, one of them the bearded one who'd forced that horrible eel down his throat. He shuddered at the memory. His fists closed tighter. But then that guard turned to the other one and told him to "go let out the other Wait."

He knew that voice. The other withdrew, and the guard came and knelt beside him. The guard's form changed exactly the way those two soldiers on the King's Way had done—mail became shiny black skin like a sheath but hard like a shell. The wide toadish face became slim, dark-bearded and blue-eyed. A face he knew, too!

"Are you alive, John?" Thomas had a key and was unlocking each of the cuffs from neck to ankle.

Finally freed, Little John grabbed the clanking bar and used it to lean himself up and rest his back against the wall. "Woodwose," he said, "No denying this time. What *are* tha?"

"Someone who hates these villains at least as much as you do."

"I doubt right now tha can match me." As if to prove it, he flung the torturous bar across the cell and chipped a piece of stone from the wall where it hit.

The Woodwose grinned. "Let's plan to test each other on that point as soon as possible," he said, then clasped John by the hand and helped him to his feet. Glanced at the raw flesh on Little John's wrist and around his throat. "Fitted you up, did they?"

"And fed me something alive. Wet and awful it were. I think it maybe made me tell them things. Lots of things." He glanced down, ashamed. "Everything."

The Woodwose nodded as if that confirmed something for him. He gave the ceiling of the cell a once-over.

At that point Benedict of the Waits and one of the sheriff's guards emerged from the cell opposite. They had to step over a corpse lying in the middle of the tunnel. John smiled. Woodwose had been busy, same as he planned to be.

Looking up from the body, Benedict blinked at them both. "Robyn Hoode?" he said. "How are you here, and in Passelewe's colors?"

"John," said the Woodwose. "This is Ernald, a well-meaning member of Passelewe's retinue. So, don't kill him."

Ernald was gaping at him in disbelief. "How did you do that?"

Thomas answered Benedict. "Necessary to penetrate the castle's defenses. The sheriff will be on his way up. Your compeers have probably stalled him as long as they can down in the gaol."

"Passelewe a *lich*—like the bishop was?" asked John.

"Exactly like the bishop. He's expecting his man to deliver the things you stole." He patted the bag.

"The *dights*." Seeing the surprised look the Woodwose gave him at hearing the word, he added, "Was all the bastard could blather about while he tortured me. 'Where are me *dights*?' So what do we do then?"

"You won't enjoy it."

John guessed. "You want us locked up back in our cells."

"At least in *this* cell, along with him." Thomas nodded back at the body in the tunnel. "After all, there can't be two of me. Everything should look as normal as possible."

"Wait now," said Ernald. "What are you gettin' me into?"

John clapped him on the shoulder. "More like what we're getting thee out of. Or if tha prefer we could finish you." Ernald blanched, but John didn't mean it. He said, "Benedict, help me with this bastard," and stepped over to the dead Yvag.

Benedict stood over the gray-green body, looking disinclined to touch it. He met John's determined gaze, and finally, muttering, "Elves and fairies, just as I told 'em," he bent to the task.

They dragged the body by the ankles into Little John's cell and dumped it in a corner. John thought about it a moment, then leaned over for the creature's sword, saw that it had the same sheen as those that had guarded the prelate, and decided he would get along just fine without it. He took a few handfuls of rancid straw and threw them atop the corpse. Then he smiled at the Woodwose.

"I'm ready for him," he said.

The Woodwose nodded, then headed out of the cell. By the time he'd crossed the threshold, his armor had turned into mail again.

Sheriff Passelewe and his glamoured personal guard, Kunastur, climbed the steps to the cells with a kind of determined ferocity. The meddling Waits had continued to take up Passelewe's time after the call from the cells had reached him. It was troubling: Simforax had been placed here to ensure that nobody and nothing interfered with that outlaw from whom he intended to extract every scrap of information before executing him. There was much about the goings-on in Sherwood that Passelewe wanted to hear. It was as if someone with far too much knowledge of the Yvag agenda was at work.

On the way up the steps he awakened the hob that lived in the stairwell—the one he hadn't dropped down the throat of Little John—hanging like a sleeping bat, and sent it ahead. But by the time he reached the level of the cells it hadn't reported back yet.

He rounded the stairwell, anticipating trouble of some sort. And there stood Simforax in his bearded glamour, on duty as if nothing out of the ordinary were occurring. Then Passelewe realized Simforax was patting the bag containing the *dights*, slung over his shoulder. No wonder he had called out so urgently. This was a triumph. But where was Tozesđin, whom he'd sent to the Saxon gaol to retrieve the bag? Nowhere in sight. They hadn't passed him on the way up, so he must have returned to the castle. Why he'd left the bag with Simforax was something to hear about later. For now Passelewe wouldn't even reprimand him. This was all working out splendidly.

Simforax nodded at the rear cell door, then turned and strode into the cell. Perhaps they would use one of the *dights* on Little John instead of its attuned victim—such readjustments were easily made—and send the outlaw back into Sherwood Forest as a spy. Although the means of creating the devices was limited, dependent upon the efforts of the mercurial Þagalwood creatures, it would be worth sacrificing one to learn these mortals' plans while also embedding a spy in their midst. The remaining two would still be used to core out their original targets. He would need to confer with Zhanedd on this, get the changeling's approval, but the Queen had placed the two of them in charge of recovering the *dights* and now they had done it. It was up to them both to allocate those *dights*. At least one Yvagvoja was waiting impatiently and impotently in a Felley Priory crypt even now as a result of the theft on the road. The sooner that one was embedded in a human, the better.

From below came the sound of the Waits calling for him to, of all things, *wait*. They were coming up the steps after him! There was no time. Kunastur and Passelewe hurried past the nervous human guard, who started to say something even before the sheriff turned and clutched onto him. "Tell the Waits we went on up the steps, Ernald," he ordered. "Do not let them past you here, whatever you do." He started to leave, but turned back. "You'll find yourself well rewarded." The guard looked positively terrified, and glanced around at the cell doors. They would likely need to dispose of him once all plans were carried out. That would be his final reward. Ah, well.

XXIII. Everything You Know Is Wrong

Inside the small cell, both of the human prisoners now lay against a hump of putrid straw; both were unfettered. The bar constraint was on its side in the corner as if flung there. Thomas/Simforax had released the humans—but of course, if the Yvags were going to empty Little John, they would want him relaxed, receptive, and in a position for the *dight* to do its work.

Then Thomas turned and offered Passelewe the bag. The sheriff snatched it, and untied the flap. "All three?" he asked ardently, so excited that he spoke the words aloud.

Glamoured Thomas nodded and thought in the affirmative.

Shouting echoed up the stairwell, the Waits getting ever nearer. As if fearing their arrival, he circled behind the sheriff to close the door completely. Kunastur stepped aside to let him.

Passelewe felt about for the *dights*. He pulled one out, a look of ecstasy on his ruddy face.

Thomas projected the thought of using one of devices on Little John as though he were debating the matter with himself. He and Passelewe had forged some sort of link at the archery contest, and the sheriff had practically been bellowing his thoughts all the way up the steps. He'd also snidely uttered the name *Zhanedd*. Thomas got the impression that the doxy in The Pilgrim and the sheriff were in a competition of sorts. More than that, the sheriff's disparagement seemed to confirm that she was a changeling. Although he'd loaned her two of his guards, the Yvagvoja riding Passelewe considered itself vastly superior to those who merely glamoured, but especially superior to changelings.

"Here, watch them both," the sheriff called. Kunastur gave Thomas an odd look—had the knight heard his supercilious thoughts, too?—but walked up beside the sheriff, one hand on the pommeled hilt of its sword, which for once appeared to be a normal arming sword.

Passelewe rolled Benedict aside, then knelt down and pushed aside the straw in order to clear a spot on the floor where he could start the *dight* spinning beside the unconscious Little John. Thomas knew it wouldn't take long.

Almost immediately the sheriff encountered a large piece of cloth. It was the corner of one of his cinquefoil surcoats, a yellow flower on red. He tugged to free more of it, and a thin arm sheathed in black armor slid out of the straw. He sat up on his haunches, puzzlement on his face. He reached out, pushed away more straw, and shortly uncovered the true, unglamoured face of dead Simforax. Quickly, he glanced around. Thomas as bearded Simforax stood at the door, returning his stare darkly.

"What—" he started to ask.

Little John's eyes opened. He grabbed the sheriff's left wrist. Passelewe whipped about to face the outlaw, unconscious no longer. Exhausted brown eyes now stared daggers at him.

"Kunastur!" Passelewe shouted.

Kunastur drew its sword, but Thomas reached around its shoulder and pressed the point of his dagger to its throat. "No help from you," he said, relinquishing his glamour. When the Yvag stared back in shock, he said, "You should do the same. Conserve your energy. Nobody in this room believes you're human anyway." Kunastur glared at him, but the glamour evaporated.

John sat up while continuing to grip Passelewe's left wrist. The sheriff dropped the *dight* as he reached blindly with his right for his own dagger. Grasping it, he attempted to stab, but John caught that hand as well, twisting hard to make him drop the blade.

Passelewe tore his other hand free and struck John in the face twice. John took the blows and spat blood. Then he laughed and, letting go the sheriff's wrist, grabbed him around the neck with both hands while he climbed the rest of the way upright. He dragged his captive along with him. Passelewe was tall, but John lifted him off his feet. The Norman sheriff kicked desperately at the straw, and pummeled the torso before him.

Benedict meanwhile sat up and collected the fallen *dight*.

"Wait, John," called Thomas just as the Waits and Keepers threw open the door and charged in, Geoffrey in the lead and Elias dragging Ernald with him, all of them armed and ready to kill... something.

The Yvag Kunastur tried furiously to tear itself free of Thomas, preventing him from interceding further.

"Greenleaf, stop!" Will Scathelock shouted. But instead, with one quick gesture, John snapped the sheriff's neck.

Passelewe's final look of amazement moldered in an instant. A burst of fine red droplets sprayed John and the straw. Unlike the prelate on the King's Way, the sheriff withered as if all the water in him had evaporated at once. His eyes fell in, his mouth collapsed into a grim rictus. A dried crust crumbled off him. Horrified to be touching it, John hurled the corpse away, yelling, "Why's it me gets all the rotten ones?" He wiped his hands madly down his front. The dried-up body hit the wall and slid down, where it appeared to be sitting up and listening.

Isabella, Scathelock, and the Waits stared in horror but made no move to challenge John. The young guard, Ernald, fled.

Thomas slapped Kunastur's helm, which receded. He pressed his dagger deeper into the guard's neck. "You're next for the chopping block. Now where lies the Yvagvoja that rode him?" Gray-green and mottled, the Yvag attempted to sneer at him, but behind the contempt was outright fear—either at Thomas's use of that word, or because he, a human, had altered his form as easily as they did.

Little John drew Benedict to his feet. Both stared, repulsed, at the husk of Passelewe, but their looks became feral as they considered the revealed Kunastur. "You want us tae ask him for you?" John said. "Just for makin' us lie down in the smell of piss, I'd beat him into the stones." He bent down, collecting the bag and taking the *dight* from Benedict, who continued to stare owl-eyed at Passelewe's corpse.

"Perhaps after a moment." Thomas stuck the dagger into the

Yvag's flesh enough to make it jerk. "Where do I find Zhanedd, then?" The name clearly surprised the creature. Thomas leaned closer. The barbed blade pricked deeper, drawing a trickle of black blood from its throat. "You'd be amazed all I know of your kind, beginning with your Queen, Nicnevin."

The black rings of the Yvag's pupils expanded in distress as it tried, against the knifepoint, to get a better look at him.

Geoffrey bellowed, "Egads! Another demon!" He'd dragged a poleaxe up the stairs with him and despite the small space, managed to lower it. Thomas let go, and the Yvag scrambled back against the stone wall, Geoffrey striding right after it.

Isabella and Elias stared Thomas up and down. He could see that they were wondering how he came to be dressed in the same clothing as their demon. "My other way in," he said, acknowledging the black-and-silver armor.

"But how did you get down the steps? How...?" She stopped, shook her head.

Elias asked, "Is that truly Passelewe?"

Benedict said, "Aye."

Geoffrey looked back over his shoulder as he menaced Kunastur. "It is certainly his clothing," he said, then added, "And his red hair."

"He was a bit more lively earlier." Thomas held out his hand for the bag. John happily gave it away. Thomas held it up. "And if you're wondering at John's ire, Passelewe was just about to spin one of these to life—which would have been the end of John."

Isabella asked, "The one you killed in the gaol—why didn't it go the same way?" Even as she spoke, Benedict and Little John were dragging the twice-punctured corpse of Simforax out of the straw. She looked down with horror as it emerged.

Thomas replied, "I realize this is confusing, but Passelewe isn't like these two. He's what John would have become if he'd spun this little device—namely, an empty repository possessed by a demon, what they call Yvagvoja. These other demons are hidden in crypts and tombs—probably some in caves here in Nottingham. If you came across one, it would appear to be asleep. Think how many places there are to hide in hereabouts."

"I'm to believe you have lived with these...Yvagvoja?" she asked.

He replied, "We're acquainted." For an instant he stared again into the past: at Waldroup shoving one through a ring he'd sliced open; at Baldie resurrecting for one final moment before his body melted; at the little screaming hobs that guarded the creatures populating the crypts. But the Waits and Keepers were waiting, no doubt, for some elaboration. "The instant that John killed Passelewe, the demon controlling the sheriff, wherever it was, awoke. The umbilical between them was severed. It'll have fled by now, probably out of our world and back to its own."

"All right, but why did he rot thus?"

"Because—" He paused as the door opened and the young guard, Ernald, stuck his head into the room. He looked at all of them, at the corpse of the sheriff, and hesitantly came in.

Thomas gave him what he hoped was a reassuring smile. "Because," he said again, "in truth, like your bishop of Doncaster, Passelewe actually died some time ago, I would guess years from the look of him. Doncaster was much more recent. Someone used one of these to empty each of them for occupation, same as he was going to do to John."

Osbert said, "Well, what're we supposed ta do nar?" he asked. "Sheriff's dead, an' who'll believe it?"

Thomas answered, "I don't know. Ask Ernald here what he thinks. Probably best to tell anyone he fought off a demon at the price of his life. At least there's an element of truth in it." He gestured at Kunastur, that Geoffrey held at bay. "And you can show them this one as proof, same as the one in Chandler's Lane gaol."

"You mean, cut off its head?"

"I do. It's the only way."

"It's not," Elias argued. "We should ask it questions. Who has ever had a demon to interrogate?"

Thomas tried to explain that interrogation would be pointless.

Osbert interrupted him. "What—what do we do tae keep it if we're keepin' it?"

Scathelock said, "There's oubliettes on a level higher up where the Normans put people they want to forget about. Even this creature shouldn't be able to get out of that space unless it can levitate. Can it levitate?" Will asked him.

"No, I think it can't, but you see—"

"Ernald?" Scathelock asked.

The young guard nodded enthusiastically. "No one can get outta them. None e'er has."

"What about Passelewe, then?" Benedict asked. "There another like 'im comin'?"

"There won't be another like Passelewe. It takes one of these—"

"Spinners," Will interjected.

"Spinners, yes." *And they'll look for someone else influential; maybe it will be Orrels this time. Or Isabella. We need to get her away from here and warn the sheriff, too.*

Isabella said, "Like Passelewe or no, the town will need to elect someone new to oversee the Norman borough."

Thomas replied, "Yes, and we don't want to be around for that. Far too many questions. Why not make Ernald here your sheriff while that's decided? After all, you've captured a demon yourself."

"Me? But I'm no one."

"My reasoning exactly. You might stand a chance."

Ernald clearly didn't like the sound of that at all. "Well, why not you? You seem to know everything about this."

"I'm not even Norman. I wouldn't be considered."

"You speak it as well as anyone."

Thomas smiled wearily. "No one else in this group can. Every one of us needs to get away from Nottingham right now, today. We're every one of us lures. John alone has killed two of their prized possessed; they'll want his head on a spike. But you, all of you, were present for this death and that of the demon they sent to retrieve these." He shook his bag. "Which we still have. They want these more than anything, and they are now after us all, believe me."

Will Scathelock scratched his head. "Well, I have a suggestion," he started to say. Thomas raised a hand to silence him.

"Discuss nothing further in front of this one." He indicated the Yvag. "It's capable of telling its marrows everything we say. We need to kill it."

Ernald reached for the poleaxe Geoffrey held as if it had just occurred to him to use it.

They all fell to arguing again, talking over each other.

Frustrated, Thomas said, "All right, keep it alive. But nobody visits it by themselves. No one can be alone with it ever. And whoever watches over the oubliettes needs to understand that the demon can mimic anybody. It can change itself into you or me or even Passelewe—anyone it can remember. You could open the oubliette and find your mother in there."

"How can it remember me mother?" asked Geoffrey. He released the poleaxe to Ernald, who immediately balked, reluctant to go off with the Yvag.

Osbert patted him on the back and said, "I'll accompany tha, an' if it changes inta anybody at all, I'll be pleased to cut off its 'ead like Robyn says." He gave the Yvag a smile of invitation, then stepped aside to let the "demon" pass. He poked it with his arming sword. It gave Thomas a black look as it walked by him.

This is not over whispered in his mind. Beside him, Isabella and Elias both cringed a little. Thomas supposed they had all heard or felt the threat.

"Osbert," he called after. "Don't hesitate to run the bastard through if given the least provocation." He followed them out and watched as they walked to the steps. A part of him felt it was a terrible idea to let them out of his sight. Even with Osbert guarding the lad, he knew he should simply have slain it no matter how this group reacted. They did not understand the Yvags. What would Alpin have done? Killed the creature in all likelihood here and now. No quarter.

With the creature gone, Will Scathelock said, "The King's Houses?" He was addressing Isabella Birkin.

Skeptical, she replied, "What, now we welcome in outlaws we've hunted?"

Scathelock looked insulted but restrained himself from answering in anger.

Sensing the transparent tension, Thomas said, "I don't know these King's Houses, but if it's a question of our being outlaws, then arrest us first. Consider John and me prisoners if it gets us and the Waits out of Nottingham tomorrow."

"I was referring just to this one," she said, although her look said that could easily change. "And his partner, who has remained curiously absent this Fair day."

"Robert Hodde, you mean. He is absent because he is dead," Thomas told her to her surprise. "He fell to them early."

Little John nodded grimly. "I seen his body myself," he said to no one in particular.

Benedict clapped him on the shoulder. "I'm sorry to hear it. He was a right pain in our arses, collectively speakin'."

Little John barked a laugh. "'E were that. E'en ta me."

Thomas said, "If you need to see for yourself, I can take you to where he lies, a hut in Barnsdale. Though my inclination is to go this instant, I suppose we'll remain here long enough to bury Warin on the morrow. Our belongings are in Chandler's Lane anyway." As he spoke, he ducked out the cell doorway. The Waits and Keepers followed. They went down the steps, which led to the back of the ground-level Norman gaol.

XXIV. Yvag Reversals

As Thomas and the Waits marched out from the shadows in back of the ground-level cells, three guards came to attention. To the left stood a trestle table not unlike the one in the Chandler's Lane gaol, surrounded by five stools. Parchments lay upon it, warrants by the look of them.

Thomas scrutinized the guards, listening for their unspoken chatter. None that he could detect.

Elias noted, "There were two more here when we arrived."

"Aye, they just up and run out afore yas come down," explained one of the remaining trio. "Where be the sheriff?"

"Lost his humors," said Thomas, to which Benedict added, "'Twas terrible to behold." The guards traded a worried look.

Elias told the guards, "You've a comrade making his way to the oubliettes with the one who slew your sheriff. You might want to assist him. We can, ah, look after ourselves."

The three men sprang into action, running for the steps in the rear.

Behind the table, a row of pegs had been hammered into the sandstone wall. On one hung a fat leather purse. "Hey, that be mine from the contest wi' Benedict here," John said, and pushed the table aside to grab the purse. Beside it hung the sheriff's distinctive red-and-green *chapeau à bec*. "An' that's a lovely cap, don't ya think?" Smiling delightedly, he grabbed the hat and jammed it on his head, which was too large for it, but he didn't seem to mind.

Scathelock remarked, "I think you'll be very easy to find with that on. You should definitely wear it." They all chuckled, even John.

Thomas was looking at the table—specifically at the open warrants lying upon it. They included one for *Little John passing as Reynold Greenleaf,* another for *Benedict "of the Waits,"* and a third one for *Robert "Robyn" Hodde or Hoode or Robbehood.* Taking no chances, it seemed. The sheriff had been in the process of filling these out when Elias and the others arrived.

Thomas rolled the warrants up and dropped them in his mason's bag.

Isabella frowned at him. "Now I see the outlaw in you, I think."

"Lady Isabella, later I'll make you a present of these and you can arrest and hang me, if that's what you choose. But I'm tired of playing by the rules of the Yvag. It's time they have to play by ours."

"You must tell me what they are, our rules."

"I surely will, once I find out."

To his surprise and perhaps her own, she laughed, then looked him over as if studying a new form of life. For a second he worried that he had somehow glamoured himself in front of her. Uncomfortable under her intense scrutiny, he caught up with Elias. "How are we going to explain all this to Orrels?" he asked. He pushed aside the iron door.

Elias replied, "I will convince him. I won't be going with you to the King's Houses. As the leader of the Waits, it's my bound duty to remain, and there are too many of us have not witnessed these creatures and so must be persuaded. It will be up to each man to decide if he remains and guards the town from these demons or goes off to safety. Geoffrey and Benedict, and Osbert, when he returns, can decide for themselves. But we are charged with protecting the town, and *some* of us must remain, ever-vigilant. Who can we trust but those we know?"

Thomas refrained from pointing out that "those we know" would be the first ones imitated by the Yvags.

Osbert was annoyed. First off, they hadn't gone ten feet before Ernald insisted they swap weapons, leaving Osbert with the long-handled, unwieldy poleaxe.

Second, the steps up were uneven, some narrower than others and worn. Worse, they curved to the left or right such that Ernald's torchlight came and went; in some places, masked by the young guard's body, it failed to highlight the turn altogether, forcing Osbert to call out for them to slow up and wait for him. Who would have thought the steps could go on so long? It began to feel like the demonic Kunastur was playing with them, casting a spell to make them climb the same steps over and over. Of course it was just that nervous Ernald was in a hurry to drop the Yvag in a hole. Osbert could appreciate that, but for him this was a trudge on tired knees. He should have let Geoffrey go in his stead. Besides, he wanted to hear what Scathelock's plan was.

Then came a fluttering sound in the darkness behind and below him. The first time, he whipped about and cut a gouge in the wall to his left, the poleaxe being almost the full width of the stairwell.

He squinted into the darkness below. Nothing appeared. Osbert supposed there were bats or birds in the stairwells, nesting pigeons at the very least. He turned back. Ernald's torch had gotten ever farther away. He groaned and hurried to catch up.

The glow of the torch revealed the tunnel where they'd gone to his right. Huffing, Osbert pushed himself up the last few steps to it.

There were two grates in the tunnel floor and both lay open. The second one had a rope dangling into it, but Ernald stood peering into the nearest one. He turned at Osbert's arrival. "He jumped!" he exclaimed.

Osbert hurried over to look in, too. *Something* lay in the bottom of the oubliette. Since both guard and prisoner wore the same surcoat, it took him a few moments to identify the features of Ernald down in the straw, his head twisted at a terrible angle. "Headfirst, can you imagine?"

Osbert turned back. "Ernald" grinned at him, and a dark green, batwinged monstrosity came flying straight at him, screeching, with teeth like needles. Warin had been attacked by such a thing. Osbert swatted a hand to ward it off, didn't even realize he'd stepped back until he was slipping, falling straight into the hole. The poleaxe caught across the opening for a moment, but snapped in half from his weight.

He fell into darkness, desperate to brace for the impact but not sure when the floor would arrive. His left leg took the brunt, jamming up through his knee, which shattered. He landed on his hip so painfully he thought certain it was broken, too. Pain radiated up the leg and into him like a stream of fire.

The axehead missed him but stabbed into Ernald's body next to him. The shaft clattered across the stone floor.

Osbert stared up, in such agony that his consciousness seemed to disconnect from his body. Above, the glamoured Yvag stood on the now-closed grate and peered into the second hole. There had been a prisoner there—if Osbert recalled correctly, it was someone Passelewe had arrested for being a pickpurse. The open grate suggested that the man had escaped, though where in these tunnels could he hide? Osbert wished he was up there, hunting for the thief right now.

His head throbbed with a terrible pressure, with whispers of some sort of incomprehensible conversation, as if the oubliette was haunted by the ghosts of all those who had died there. He supposed he was about to join them. His lower body felt terribly cold....

Kunastur, still glamoured as Ernald, patted his shoulder and the little winged hob dropped from the ceiling to land there. *"Tell Zhanedd their plans,"* it said. *"Big reward for Fleega, yes?"*

"Very big reward," Kunastur promised, sheathing the arming sword taken from the real Ernald. The boy had been so skittish and nervous on the way up that he noticed nothing as the Yvag distorted his perceptions, finally telling him to jump into the hole. "And for me, as well, I imagine. Not from Zhanedd, though. We are going to find the *dights*, Fleega. With no assistance, no interference from Zhanedd or any of the Queen's handpicked knights. An even bigger reward when we triumph."

Kunastur turned and started up the stairs. "The other knights do not know what we do, in part thanks to you—that they're fighting a human that can change its shape as I do. We will show them all up by killing it."

By the time the Yvag was halfway up the steps, it had glamoured itself as Passelewe. That was who various soldiers in and around the Norman keep beheld selecting a horse and riding off past the town and to the north. The sheriff said not a word to anyone, but Passelewe was often brusque. The only odd thing, in fact, was the queer bird or bat that rode like a pet on his shoulder until he was mounted and then flapped along beside him.

XXV. Winding Sheets

Early the next morning in the Chandler's Lane gaol, Thomas sat glumly beside Little John, looking on while Geoffrey and Benedict washed the bodies of Warin and Osbert with wine and balsam. The two were laid out on two boards across Orrels's trestle table. All was conducted solemnly and in silence.

Poor Osbert had been found alive in one of the oubliettes by some of Passelewe's men, but was by then already in shock. He lasted only briefly as the barber attempted to sever his shattered leg. The added weight of his loss felt powerful enough to extinguish the candles and torches in the gaol.

Geoffrey wrapped the bodies in their winding sheets, and Benedict made sure Osbert's severed leg was properly bound where it should be, below his knee, so that he didn't have to go hobbling along without it in the next life. "Be just like 'im to forget it," he commented.

They were the first words spoken in over an hour and were followed by further amused jibes at their dead friend, culminating in Elias saying, "At least he has Warin with him, so he might not get lost." That led to more stories about them both, good stories of decent men, which warded off the strangeness they had experienced. For the Waits and the Keepers the world had now become unnatural.

Sheriff Orrels and Elias had already set out to inform their families: Warin had just a mother left alive, in Holme across the Trent River; Osbert had a wife and two children living on Wheelwright Lane.

Once the families had come and had time with their men, the Waits picked up the boards and carried the two down Stoney Street to St. Mary's burial ground where a section was maintained for them.

Orrels had already informed and paid two gravediggers to make the plot ready to receive the bodies.

Representing the Keepers, Will Scathelock joined up with the procession on Stoney Street. Thomas carried his mason's bag with him.

It all seemed surreal. People on the street stepped back and watched them pass by—people who only yesterday had cheered on Benedict in a contest or spoken with Osbert and Geoffrey as they tallied the contestants. The world of yesterday was like a dream. Nary a trace of it remained.

The Waits plot of burial ground had barely seen use before this. Arriving there, Elias muttered, "I can't recall the last of us who fell in anything like battle."

Gathered around the two boards, they listened while the priest said a mass over the bodies and mother and wife bid their respective men farewell. At the end they lowered their comrades into the ground, with the gravediggers waiting in the shadow of the church to finish up. Then they returned in silence to the gaol—all save Thomas and Little John.

Those two unobtrusively followed the priest into St. Mary's. They knelt and prayed until the priest left them to preside over another, unrelated burial. Once alone, they picked up their bows and descended into the crypt.

It was decidedly smaller than the crypt of Melrose Abbey, containing three covered tombs. Thomas led the way to the tomb farthest from the steps. He made to grab hold of the lid.

Little John asked, "You sure if we open these the ghosts of the dead won't follow us out?"

Thomas leaned on the lid. "We find sleepers in one or more of these, any ghosts about will thank us for ridding their tombs of the villains." John looked undecided. "Well, would you want someone making use of *your* tomb?"

After a moment John stepped up and grabbed the other side of the lid. Together, they lifted it half off, enough to see that no sleeping Yvag occupied the space below. The condition of the corpse suggested none ever had.

They closed the lid and repeated it on the other two. No Yvagvoja inhabited those either.

If the creature operating Sheriff Passelewe had hidden in Nottingham, it hadn't lain in the tombs of St. Mary's. There were two other churches to investigate, and Lenton Priory of course, and who knew how many hundreds of caves pockmarking the landscape from there to Mansfield, any one of which might disguise a sleeping place for an Yvagvoja, caves dug behind caves. They would have to keep looking. Little John glanced nervously around.

Thomas reached into the mason's bag. He contemplated dropping the *dights* into the tomb, but decided it was too risky. The Yvags might commandeer it at any point, and having loitered here it was possible he and John were already being scrutinized. He would just have to carry them a little longer.

"John," he said, and together they replaced the carved lid on it, then made sure everything was the way they'd found it.

Upon leaving the church, Thomas said to John, "After we get to the King's Houses, I would like for you to show me the spot where you beheld the Queen of the Fairies." John gave him a quizzical look. "They opened a gate in that spot from their world three nights ago by your reckoning. They might have done so more than once, and it might have thinned the barriers between our worlds. Such openings—it's useful to know where they are."

Little John sullenly agreed to show the way there. "I'm sorry I e'er set eyes on them spinners. Wish we could go back to the split oak tree and stop Much and Robbie from trying t' rob anybody. Broke the world, tha' did."

"I wish I had that power."

"Make tha God then, wouldn't it?" John weakly tried a smile.

At the gaol, a keg had been opened and ale poured, a wake of sorts begun for the two fallen heroes. With all of the Waits there along with Warin's mother and Osbert's family, it was a crowded space. Thomas and John cracked dour mugs with Geoffrey and Benedict, the latter of whom asked where they'd gone off to.

"Church," said Thomas. John nodded.

Orrels came up to him. "So now to our list of those who are neither alive nor human, namely the Bishop of Doncaster, we must add Sheriff Passelewe. If that long-deceased body in the castle cell belongs to the real Passelewe—"

"It was no one else," insisted Geoffrey. "We'll all swear to it."

Orrels frowned. "Then 'twas his doppelgänger rode north out of town, identified by our own Calum. And no mistaking him."

Thomas said, "The doppelgänger was called Kunastur. Not that it matters."

"Ah, well, it matters in that they are not selecting another to replace him just now, as they expect him to return to the castle."

"It will prove most interesting if . . ." The words he'd intended to speak evaporated. The seizure had snuck up on him. Thomas realized he was thinking there were fifteen people in the gaol, and seven columns supporting the ceiling, and eighty diamond-shaped quarrels in the mullioned front window through which the bright sunlight was pouring in—light both intense and shimmering colorfully. Cold filled his head and crackling electricity caught him off guard. He stumbled forward, tried to hand off his mug to Little John, then crashed into Will and fell.

When he woke, he was laid out on the floor of the gaol with Little John. Will and Orrels knelt with him. He could feel the tickle of foam on his cheek, where it had churned out of his mouth. He lowered his head, squeezed shut his eyes. Behind his eyelids the darkness still sparkled lightly. "I had a fit, yes?"

"Yes," said Orrels. "Do you have them frequently?"

"I have them . . . sometimes. I've no way to judge if that is frequent or not. Thought I was quit of them, fool that I am."

"You know that you speak while you're laid low," the sheriff said.

He opened his eyes again and looked at Will. "I said something?"

"Yes," Will told him. "A sort of riddle from the sound of it."

They helped Thomas to his unsteady feet. He leaned against one of those seven columns. "Sure," he said. "It's always a riddle, and half of them make no sense. What did I say this time?"

"I *believe* you said, 'Another Janet for your bed, short-lived the love, though steep the climb to voice it.'" Will asked what it meant.

"I have no idea," he said. "Most of what comes out are crazy things. Sometimes they only make sense much later, as though I've seen things that have yet to occur. But even I don't believe it." He pointed at the front window. "Eighty diamond quarrels," and laughing, added, "I sound like the idiot of the village." He let out a sigh. "Another mug of ale would wash away the taste. I'll try not to shatter this one."

Later that afternoon, the Waits were called by the priest of St. Mary's because someone had disturbed every tomb in the crypt.

PART THREE:
SHERWOOD

XXVI. The King's House

To Thomas's eye, the complex of the King's Houses looked like an elaborate manor with two halls, a tower, a chapel, multiple kitchens, terraced gardens, and assorted other small buildings, and all of it surrounded by a shallow defensive ditch. Where a tributary of the River Maun called the Vicar Water ran past along its eastern perimeter, the stream had been dammed up, creating an enormous pond. Thomas, accompanied by the Keepers and two of the Waits—Geoffrey and the boy, Calum—rode along it and up to the Clipstone village street. The scattering of town buildings, mostly houses, lined the opposite side of the street. He guessed that some of those who maintained the halls lived there. Sir Richard atte Lee had mentioned both Clipstone and a "royal hunting palace." This surely must be the same. He marveled that for all the time he'd dwelled in and around Sherwood he'd missed so large a site.

Off the Clipstone street, they rode through the archway of a two-story main gate and across a wide yard to a long set of stables that could have housed twenty times their horses. A fenced paddock branched off the stables to the west and already had a few horses in it. A skinny, bearded old fellow in a drab gray cotehardie and brown leggings came forward to take their horses. Isabella identified him as Edrick and he greeted her as "milady."

Everything was built around the two large stone halls. The largest, in the center of it all, was an immense structure that she named "the Great Hall." It overlooked sloping gardens, fruit trees, and the pond. It included covered passageways beneath pentice roofs and windows all around.

The second, smaller stone building fit the description of "hunting palace" given by Sir Richard, and stood to the southwest of it. This was two stories tall and displayed large windows sectioned by bar tracery and topped with quatrefoil circles in the arches. A tower abutted the left rear corner of it and poked up another story higher than the hall, affording a view over the small chapel off the rear corner. Isabella referred to the second, smaller building as "the Palace." Its narrow lancet windows looked out upon a broad section of demesne land, no doubt offering a view of the denizens of the king's deer park when they passed by. At one corner a buttressed wall projected out from it, perhaps a repaired and reinforced section, which reminded Thomas of the many abbeys and cloisters he'd worked on over the years.

While the paddock and ditch provided a modest defensive barrier, these houses would hardly have withstood any serious direct assault. The two-floor main gate itself even contained a glazed window—hardly a protective feature. Clearly, this complex existed for the leisure of a monarch.

Will explained that the King's Houses were kept in perpetual readiness for a king's visit, although the likelihood of such a visit was almost nil. King Henry II, who'd had the initial buildings erected, had only traveled here a few times. King John, who had added the chantry to the complex, had visited but five times during his reign. Henry III and his wife, Eleanor, had initially spent more time here, and Henry had added chambers for his queen that overlooked the terraced gardens sloping down to the Great Pond.

The last official keeper of the houses, Robert le Vavassur, had died in 1247, and since then, as no one had been named to replace him, the Keepers of Sherwood had added his duties to theirs and made the household retinue's chambers in the Great Hall their own when they stayed here. Eventually, Will supposed, King Henry III would name a new overseer, or order the sheriff of Nottingham to do it. Thomas hoped that meant Orrels.

He listened to Will's history lesson while marveling how much the main buildings reminded him of the Château of Chinon, and all the more queer: He'd been working stone in France for Henry II at the very same time the king was having his hunting complex erected.

History seemed to be nothing but a map of crisscrossing lines.

❈ ❈ ❈

In the Great Hall, Isabella assigned them individual chambers. They would all lodge in retainers' rooms on the second floor, placed around the great hall chamber.

Of the Waits, only two had traveled with them: Geoffrey, who felt that he was in the thick of whatever plot this was and wanted to punish someone for Osbert's death; and Calum, a slight and freckled youth of sixteen who'd witnessed the flight of the false Passelewe. For him this seemed like something of an adventure. Curious about the "demons," he'd asked a lot of questions of everyone on the ride here.

Isabella assigned the Keepers and Waits rooms side by side, Adam, Maurin, and Will together. Shown his room, Geoffrey recited from some memorized text as though he were a priest advising her: "A maiden should separate from all male guests remain."

Isabella laughed. "No one is concerned with impropriety where I am concerned, Master Geoffrey. Least of all my profligate husband."

The Waits all knew him and the many stories of his dissolute behavior.

"To place your minds at ease, Geoffrey, I shall occupy a chamber on the first floor. The king and queen's chambers, of course, are to remain inviolate."

Little John snorted. He'd no care as to where she slept. His concerns were personal. "I'll ne'er be able to close both eyes in 'ere. Too comfortable a bed for one used to brambles, reeds, an' straw. An' for you, Woodwose, not much like your hut, neither." Then he told Isabella, "Wager you'll find us both bedded on the floor come morning, mistress." At the threshold of his chamber, he removed the bycocket hat he'd purloined from Passelewe and offered it to Thomas. "Doesn't fit me head," he explained, then entered his chamber.

Thomas took the hat. He brushed his fingers over the feather. Looking up, he found Isabella studying him again, and quickly went into his own chamber beside John's and shut the door.

It rained through the afternoon. The servants built up a fire in the main hearth and laid out a small supper feast on the massive table in the hall itself of roach fish from the pond accompanied by a parsley sauce, a cabbage pottage, barley bread and mugs of ale. It was the best meal Thomas could remember having eaten in decades, marred only by the conversation.

Isabella, Will, her son Adam, and Maurin each expressed their sympathies to the two members of the Waits. Isabella seemed unprepared to include Thomas and John in that company. Little John at the very least was still an outlaw in her eyes.

It was a grim conversation overall, as it might have been any of them who'd followed callow Ernald up those steps. Probably Osbert hadn't even considered that the two of them were leading a demon to a dungeon. Certainly, Osbert didn't know what it could do. But Thomas had known. Even witnessing Passelewe's death, and seeing the creature called Kunastur, these good people simply lacked any experience with the diabolical made manifest.

Back at the gaol, Elias and Orrels had described how the Norman soldiers went up and down the stairs and into every one of the side tunnels to search for that demon. They found the mummified corpse of Passelewe in the cell, of course, but despite the Waits' assurances as to its identity, they refused to accept it was their sheriff. It was some trick, a body pulled from a crypt and dressed up.

Geoffrey added, "The only one they found among all the cul de sacs was some cutpurse escaped from the other oubliette. Likely saw his chance and took it. Or possibly your demon helped him escape." This last was addressed to Thomas.

My demon. Yes, that was right. Of them all, he alone had known what Kunastur was capable of, but he'd let them overwhelm his concern and foolishly let himself be convinced that with two men guarding the Yvag, everything would be all right. He should have taken that poleaxe away from Osbert and cut the damned creature's head off right then. But he nodded noncommittally, saying nothing.

Geoffrey said, "Might have persuaded the remaining guards to accept that Sheriff Passelewe was dead and his corpse the withered thing in that cell if he hadn't emerged from the keep above and strode the yard in full view of them all. Everyone recognized him. Only thing odd about it, other than *we* know he was dead, is Passelewe picked out a horse wasn't his own. And then Calum saw him." He nudged the young member of the Waits.

Almost owl-eyed at this point, Calum said, "Was stationed at Carter Gate, me, didn't know nothing of those goings-on in the castle. I saw the sheriff on that horse, no mistake. And there was a small bird, maybe a sparrow hawk, keeping pace with him."

Thomas and John exchanged a glance.

"We should ne'er have left Osbert alone with that devil," said Geoffrey. "Ernald . . . what did that boy know of such things?"

"As much as the rest of us," Isabella's son, Adam, remarked sourly.

After the meal, Thomas borrowed a hooded brown ganache, took up his bow, and went for a stroll by himself around the grounds. The rain had let up for a bit, becoming more of a mist, but no one else was about. Still, he kept the hood up to disguise his identity.

He circled the palace, then wandered between the tower and the chantry as if randomly roaming the grounds. The chapel entrance faced the tower. Nothing small was flitting through the air, and no one was watching as he pushed open the door and went in.

It was dim inside, made darker by the wood paneling that lined the lower half of the walls. Three rows of pews faced a small semi-enclosed space containing an altar covered in an elaborate embroidery and bearing two candlesticks and a small cross in the center between them. No doubt it had been erected by one or another of the Angevins for private masses in their honor—but no, Isabella had said something about Henry III having visited in December of the previous year and the chapel being prepared in advance for him, the oak wainscoting added, and a glazier hired to seal the windows, hermetic and silent because the King attended three masses a day. As it was neither lit nor currently in use, it suited his own needs perfectly.

He crouched down, and lifted the embroidered altar cloth. A dark empty space greeted him. From beneath the ganache he drew his hidden mason's bag and reached into its depths until his fingers closed on the point of a *dight*.

The rains returned in the early evening followed by a drifting fog. As darkness set in, the forest lit up with strange fires. Geoffrey remarked this was exactly like the night the Waits had spent on the road from York. None of it was near enough the King's Houses to be directly visible, but enough that weird colors lit trees and mist alike. Through the rectangular panes of the second-floor windows of the hunting palace, Thomas and the others watched distant flickerings of green fire appear and just as quickly vanish, to be replaced by others, sometimes nearer and sometimes farther away, igniting and winking out.

A herd of deer swept across the park like ghosts, fleeing the strange fires. Odd sounds—howls and distant shouts or cries—echoed through the landscape. It was as if Sherwood had become haunted. Young Calum gaped at it all.

No one of them was foolish enough to go out and investigate the noises and fires in the pitch black of night, and anyway the fires like an *ignis fatuus* came and went too quickly. Run at one, the glow would light up elsewhere. Will Scathelock commented, "Who knows what we would meet in haunted Sherwood tonight?"

Eventually the sounds and fires diminished. The Yvags were not focused upon them at all—from here the opening gates appeared entirely random. If anything, the brief fires were moving away, not coming closer.

While they all sat together in the Great Hall near the fire and discussed it, Thomas sat off to one side. Little John, beside him, whispered, "This all is like what I saw the night the Queen come out."

Was it all a coordinated effort by Nicnevin, this systematic terrorizing of denizens of the forest, gates opening in different places each night...? Or maybe not entirely different. He urged himself again to have John take him to the spot where he'd seen his Queen of Fairies. If it turned out that *she* came through that same gate each time, Thomas might end the assault on the people of Sherwood with one single well-directed arrow.

Then John said, "Robyn," which he'd never yet called him. "If tha wanted ta, you know, investigate those fires, I'd go with." He paused, then thought to add, "I wouldn't like it, mind, but I'm yer man if ye go."

One thing the random fires made clear to Thomas: The Yvags obviously still had no idea where their *dights* were. He took a little satisfaction in that, though not enough to absolve his guilt.

They all continued talking, covering details they already knew, but Thomas withdrew into his own thoughts. He already blamed himself for the deaths—blundering about, missing things that his former self would never have. There had been one or more of those little monsters lurking in the shadows of the stairs and tunnels, and he should have known. His descent into the mad Woodwose had allowed a lifetime of neglect to blunt honed instincts. He might not look a century old, but his readiness had lain dormant almost that long. True Thomas had indeed become the Woodwose. He had to clear his thoughts, become again the warrior that Alpin Waldroup had trained him to be. How he wished to hear his teacher's ghost at his side again, taunting and provoking him, pushing him to risk everything. So, what now? The little bastard hobs were everywhere, and he'd already been assaulted by one in John's company. Kunastur, of course, was the resurrected Passelewe. By now that Yvag and its hob might be anywhere.

But, having failed, would Kunastur have fled to Ailfion? It would have to admit to playing a part in the deaths of Passelewe and Simforax. Nicnevin would not look favorably upon the messenger bringing that news, much less on a knight who'd stood by while the deaths happened.

And if he were Kunastur? What he would do was capture the *dights* himself. Prove his worth.

"Calum," he said. "This horse that wasn't Passelewe's and rode past you—what did it look like?"

The lad described a piebald gelding. Geoffrey interjected that it belonged to one of the castle guards, who was quite upset about it.

Calum asked, "Is it important?"

He looked at the group around him. "Imagine for the moment the creature knows where we've come. Passelewe had a pet hobgoblin hidden in the tunnels. The flitting thing that bit Warin on the road the night before I met you, Geoffrey? The sparrow hawk Calum saw? I think they are one and the same. If so, then the whole time we were inside the castle rock, that fae hob was lurking in the shadows with us, and I imagine it heard everything we said. Even when we moved off to keep Kunastur from hearing us, the little monster was listening, probably on the ceiling. Our demon might ride away and never return, but I think he will try again for those *dights*. He'll come after us. They've only lost compeers in the fight thus far and not retrieved a single one. I know the queen who rules over them. She does not make allowances for failure."

"But both sides have lost," said the previously quiet Maurin.

"Was never a fight we wanted," Geoffrey added.

"That's true enough," Thomas replied, "but it's not how they'll see it. We are supposed to go about, bovinely ignorant of their machinations, their very existence, allowing them to swap changelings, place skinwalkers, and select sacrificial tithes as they've been doing for centuries."

Isabella remarked, "Once again, you display a knowledge of these creatures as if you'd lived amongst them. I should like to understand how that is."

Yes, how was he going to explain all he knew? It had been three days here since Little John had slain that bishop. In their world—he'd called it Ailfion to Janet for so long that he'd almost forgotten the name Yvagddu—that would be, what, a few hours? Kunastur might return there to gather reinforcements. But in Thomas's experience, which admittedly was limited to the Yvag knight Aðalbrandr, such a knight might consider that an admission of failure, whereas, armed with the knowledge of where they were, why not come at them alone? Great honor no doubt awaited whichever knight returned with the devices. The Yvag race were not used to failure, and from what Nicnevin had said to him, there had been none before he stood up.

He answered Isabella: "Yours is a fair request, milady, but there is no time for the full story just now. We are here, but I believe Kunastur has arrived here before us. Must have, in fact. He'll have traded Passelewe's form for a new shape that allows him to move about here freely and approach us closely. I will wager my purse that he's in our midst even now."

Little John scratched his head. "But then there'll be two'a the same man."

"Or woman."

They looked at one another, and then around the immense hall, suddenly suspicious and uncertain. The retainers who'd stoked the fire, the ones who'd brought their food . . .

"What should we do? How do we make certain . . . ?" asked Scathelock.

"To begin with, we go nowhere alone. We haven't been poisoned or we would know it by now. And anyway poisoning us doesn't get him the *dights*. If he's here, Kunastur will adopt the shape of someone who attends to the houses, or the man who fishes the pond or tends the horses—somebody whose voice we don't know well or at all, probably someone not expected to speak or remain in close quarters. Glamouring will change his appearance, but not the sound of his voice, nor will it teach him how to bake bannock."

Scathelock brightened, understanding. "The *horse*," he said.

Thomas stood. "Get some torches. Let us go see who's grazing in the paddock."

XXVII. Mary of Clipstone

The piebald horse wasn't in the paddock. They found it in the stable, securely put away in a stall where it might go unnoticed for a day—long enough for what Kunastur wanted. He might have been here since the day before, giving him plenty of time to select the most useful member of the household to impersonate.

It was no longer speculation. The Yvag walked among them.

Neither the Waits nor Thomas nor John knew the retinue of the King's Houses. That left it up to the four Keepers of Sherwood to identify the glamoured pretender.

They left torches in the outside brackets on the walls of the palace and Great Hall, lighting their way to the kitchens. Fog swirled around them.

Thomas nocked his bow and belted his quiver; Little John grabbed his quarterstaff. They and the two Waits followed Isabella and her group at a distance, lagging behind to watch for anyone who might try to flee.

Isabella had barely mentioned that there might be someone in disguise among them, when the head cook gestured for the Keepers to follow her outside.

"This is Sehild," Isabella said, introducing the auburn-haired woman.

Sehild said, "Don' know about disguise exactly, but I've one that's afflicted now two day on."

She directed them through the pantry and finally into the pitch-black buttery, where casks of ale and bottles of wine were stored. Sehild brought in a candle from the pantry.

In one corner, behind three kegs, a girl in a coarse woolen overdress crouched tightly as if she might squeeze through the joints of the wall. Before they even moved the top keg out of the way to see her better, she started to wail. She kicked at the floor with her wooden-soled shoes, which slipped and scraped, and slapped the wall as if it might open and let her pass through.

Will and Adam took her by the arms and lifted her onto one of the kegs. She squealed fiercely. Only when they backed away did she calm down. Her eyes flicked about as if she was seeing things in the air around her, and she tried to climb back behind the kegs. Adam and Maurin stopped her, though neither of them seemed to want to touch her for fear that whatever this was might be contagious, but she wriggled and tried desperately to tear free of their grasp. This time they held onto her.

The girl had a prominent overbite and receding chin. Thomas asked Sehild who she was.

"Mary, of Clipstone," came the answer. Of course everyone in the kitchen was "of Clipstone."

Adam told the youngest and least threatening, Calum, to hold onto her. Then he knelt in front of her and gently caught her eye. Softly, he asked, "Mary, why are you in the buttery?" He stroked her hands, which seemed to calm her—at least, she stared with fascination at his hands upon hers. Thomas watched Isabella watching her son, as if she'd never seen this side of him before.

Mary of Clipstone replied almost in a child's lilt that another voice had compelled her to hide here.

Someone among the kitchen staff? She couldn't say but didn't think so. She thought it was a presence that had entered the kitchen. "I thought maybe a *bodach* but no little man did I see about me."

The cook crossed herself. "It's the devil, isn't it, girl?" she said, her tone sharp and accusatory, all but blaming Mary for letting it in.

Scathelock told her to hush up. Adam asked Mary if she had been speaking to someone in the moments before the Keepers found her. She didn't know. Her memory of the time before they found her was confused. "It's all smeary, the time. What day is it now?" Then, weeping, she added, "How I walked from home this morning, I can't even say that it was today."

Thomas whispered to Adam, "Keep talking to her."

While he engaged her, Thomas directed Calum to slide in beside her and pull aside the collar of her mantle. He did so, carefully. She flinched at his touch, and stared over at him as if fearful of finding the devil next to her, but she didn't scream. He folded back the material. The bite mark was raw where Kunastur's needlelike teeth had sunk into her throat.

Thomas said, "She would have been out of her mind perhaps for hours from one bite."

"How do you know?" asked Scathelock.

He tugged at his own cotehardie, revealing the bruised bite he'd received from Zhanedd. "The Pilgrim," he said.

While they stared at him, Sehild added, "Mary does nae work in the kitchen, but in your lordships' chambers and the hall, collects the bedding, passes the warming pan on chill nights like this."

Isabella said, "She's one of our chambermaids. I saw her just this afternoon."

"I think not," said Thomas. "Though I expect her double has gone through most of our chambers and belongings by now." Then to John, "Quick, come with me."

Beyond the buttery lay a serving passage leading into the Great Hall. The two men slipped into the empty ground-floor chamber. Will Scathelock followed. He'd also grabbed his bow. Thomas gestured for him to stay by the main door. Thomas and Little John quietly ascended the two staircases to the second floor, John emerging on the left and Thomas on the right. He'd anticipated that the Yvag would be in his chamber. They all seemed to know he had possession of the *dights,* maybe of ördstones, too.

Once Kunastur had those *dights,* he could open a portal right there in the chamber. Return to Ailfion in triumph and leave behind a gate right into Thomas's room.

The only drawback to this plan was that the *dights* were no longer to be found in the patched and empty mason's bag. It still hung on a peg in the room, an inviting target. Or at least it had at the point of the afternoon meal.

As he crept toward his own room, he heard a soft rustling, but it didn't come from his chamber. It came from Will Scathelock's. The "maid," no doubt having exhausted the possible hiding places in Thomas's room—there were few indeed unless one started prying the panels off the walls—had concluded reasonably that he'd given the *dights* to someone else. He glanced over and saw that John had heard the same sound. John would reach the door first, so Thomas took up a position behind him and out of the way of the door. He nodded.

John flung open the door and stepped in.

"Oh!" cried the chambermaid in a voice sounding just like Mary's. "Beg pardon, sir, I was just passing the warming pan down Master Scathelock's bed."

Indeed nothing in the room appeared to be out of place. A jug stood on the small corner table. Beside the bed was a wood-and-leather chair with Scathelock's bag upon it, seemingly untouched. The girl's voice was, well, the girl's voice. Not glamouring, then. The Yvag had reshaped itself, becoming her twin right down to the marrow. No wonder it had bitten her, sharing her memories, collecting some of her . . . self. No wonder her recent memories were now vague. More intense and exhausting for the Yvag, but who knew when or if it had shifted away and back again. Without her voice it certainly didn't dare wander through the various buildings here, where too many knew Mary of Clipstone. She'd probably spoken to some of them earlier when no one was paying any mind, to Isabella for one.

Then again, that was its undoing here. Adam and Calum were even now with the real Mary of Clipstone, identical to this one, right down to the wooden soles on her shoes. The only remaining question, then— he heard the barest chirr—"Mary" was communicating with . . .

"John, get out of the doorway!"

Kunastur's hob swooped down upon Little John, screeching, "Yaaaaa!" John swung at it, missed. It dove into his hair, bit his ear, then reached around and tried to gouge his eyes. It sliced into one eyebrow and blood flowed down his face. He spun around, swinging his staff, striking himself in the head in an attempt to smash the creature.

Chambermaid Mary turned and sprang for the window. Thomas didn't dare fire for fear of hitting the whirling John.

The window frame cracked. The many rectangular panels shattered.

"Will!" Thomas yelled. "Outside!"

He charged at Little John, took the arrow he'd drawn and skewered straight through the hob, nailing it to the doorframe. John continued slapping, spinning, even after it was off him. Blood from his ear and the gashes above his eye covered half his face. He howled with rage.

Thomas dodged him and ran to the window. In the light from the various torches, the chambermaid was visible, running hell-bent through the mist for the paddock, transforming even as "she" fled. A difficult shot, but he nocked, drew, and fired anyway.

In the same moment something flashed from below him on the right—a crossbow bolt. Both arrow and bolt struck Kunastur at almost the same time, throwing the Yvag off its feet even as it reached the rear of the palace. It ran up against one of the stone buttresses and folded over it, twitching for a moment. Finally it lay still. Thomas's arrow had caught it in the side. The bolt had finished it, impaling it at the base of its neck.

In the yard below, Will Scathelock and Isabella Birkin appeared. She emerged from the right, holding a crossbow. Will hadn't fired his arrow at all. He called out, "The door—I never had a shot!"

They all nodded to each other.

The others emerged from the Great Hall now and with torches strode warily, weapons drawn, to the other, smaller palace. This Yvag would not be resurrecting. Thomas went to assist Little John. He could do nothing to bring back Ernald or Osbert, but at least their killer would walk no more.

"Will," he said, "is going to need a different room."

Those who'd been on hand at Sheriff Orrels's office watched Kunastur long enough to satisfy themselves that it would not resurrect and come at them again. Then they buried the corpse in the paddock's midden heap. Thomas nabbed its ördstone, which flickered and skritched ineffectively at his thoughts. He was beginning to feel like the keeper of ördstones.

Knowing that the Yvag's body still lay out there seemed to worm its way into everyone's thoughts and attention. Calum, who hadn't beheld the demise of any other Yvags, seemed particularly ill at ease.

In the Great Hall where they all sat together, one or the other nervously cast owlish glances over their shoulders, at shadows, at the fire. It was as if, having seen one Yvag knight resurrect, they could not help but assume all others would do the same. Thomas could almost hear them imagining the black alien blood slowly flowing across the yard and back into its body.

Finally, he excused himself, went outside and, using the magical Yvag sword, decapitated the corpse. He carried the head to the far side of the King's Houses and threw it into the fortification ditch. Then he walked over to the long pond and tossed the creature's ördstone in it. The blue gems flickered as they faded, sinking. He was tired of collecting the things, and still did not know with absolute certainty that creatures on the other side of Ailfion couldn't identify its location and come through in that exact spot. Just because he hadn't witnessed or tried such a thing didn't mean they couldn't do it. Let them cut a doorway in the pond.

The surface stilled. He turned back to the hall.

He'd killed enough of the Yvags in his time, more than he'd ever wanted to encounter in the first place. Most of them had been sicced on him by the Queen or her consort, the one called Aðalbrandr. He'd never had to rationalize his deeds; he was running for his life. If anything, the killing took place in a white-hot blur of rage—or at least so it seemed from this distance. Aðalbrandr he could have killed and resurrected a half dozen times just to kill him again, though at this remove even that passion felt like a tiny echo of the seething fury he'd felt so long ago. This all needed to end but it would not end. His intrusion the first time had been mischance, the first time anyone had actively opposed the Yvags, disrupting their routine of snatching a *teind* whenever they were so inclined, a human they could glamour and sacrifice in place of one of their own. From the Yvag perspective it was a small blot, hardly worth troubling over. There was an endless supply of humans . . . until he'd cost them a dozen of their kind. He understood how they reacted to that—like the one in Orrels's gaol, they were *immortals* whereas his kind lived forty, perhaps sixty years if lucky. Using humans, tossing them in that well like tossing logs on a fire, they saw as an act of no significance. Humans were disposable. What he did in opposing them was monstrous to them. He could appreciate their perspective: He was the villain in their tale. Immortal beings had died by his hand. They would have had to be foolish indeed to think he would ever capitulate. But they thought him long dead.

The first time was the aberration, the oddity. Nicnevin had brought it upon herself.

What was this time, then? Another odd mischance, performed by an outlaw this time, one who just wanted the sparkling jewels that bedecked an errant bishop? And his longstanding friendship with that outlaw and his mates had brought the fight to his door once again. Happenstance? Perhaps.

But it was beginning to feel like destiny.

XXVIII. Night & Isabella

Awhile, Thomas lay in bed and thought about the latest riddle.

Another Janet for your bed,
short-lived the love,
though steep the climb
to voice it.

He could only interpret that one way, but wrestled with the notion that if he said nothing, then none of it would happen. "Short-lived" did not sound encouraging. Just before he fell asleep, he realized that doing nothing about it would ensure the "steep climb," and so he drifted off on the horns of a dilemma.

He awoke fully sometime in the night, as he often did, and walked out into the Great Hall barefoot in his long shirt and braes. The retainers had kept the low fire burning, though the misty evening brought only a mild chill. He wandered out to the privies on the south corner to relieve himself. The moon played among the tree branches. The torches were all doused and the royal demesne beyond the court was pitch black. The fog created unnatural shapes between the buildings. If Yvag knights were still coming through various rings as John and the Waits maintained, then they had moved to the north end of Sherwood. He listened awhile to the normal though no less strange sounds of an English wood at night without mixing in the entry and departure of the Yvags.

Returning to the interior of the hall, he spied Lady Isabella sitting in one of the chairs near the high hearth. She wore a dark green gown, and her golden hair was no longer plaited, but bound up in a snood off the back of her head. Tempting as it was to pretend he hadn't seen her, he was sure she had seen him and would conclude that he'd actively avoided her. Instead, he came over, dragged another of the chairs around, and sat opposite her before the fire.

"Missing your home?" he asked.

She drilled him with a look as if he were insane. "On the contrary, I find excuses to stay away. I regret that my husband has knowledge of my need to appear in Retford. He's particularly good at interfering when he wants to. With any luck, however, he will be somewhere else, seeking his pleasure as usual."

He didn't know how to respond to that. Finally, he said, "Your son travels with you."

"Adam," she said. "He is a forester in his own right. You know that, surely. Planning to take my place one day, the foolish boy."

"You don't advise that he remain in service with the Keepers?"

"It's not that."

He nodded slowly. *Your husband,* he thought. For someone who was not present, his lordship seemed to wield much influence. He did say, "I notice you do not acknowledge your son in your retinue."

"Oh, that is by Adam's request. He wishes no favored treatment and I have obliged him, although he will inherit the position whether he receives such treatment or not."

"For him a conundrum. I see. He can't earn the position because it's already his."

She asked, "Why does he call you 'Woodwose'?"

"What?"

"Little John. At least a half dozen times in my hearing he's called you that."

"It's his little jest," he answered. He couldn't immediately come up with a reasonable explanation. There was no basis for thinking Isabella Birkin would not react tempestuously if he showed her what John's Woodwose looked like. She was too perceptive, too analytical, as her question itself proved. He looked nothing like anyone's notion of a woodwose, while John dispensed it like a name he'd used for years, which was in fact the case. Still, he tried to shape some kind of defense. "I lived alone in Barnsdale. A beehive hut in the woods. I'd withdrawn from, well, all of this, and I had no visitors save John and—"

"Still, it's an odd sobriquet for someone who isn't hoary and ancient with a beard to his knees. I grant you, somebody unskilled has hacked at your hair and beard recently. Even so, *woodwose* hardly describes someone as young and prepossessing as you." He blushed, speechless at her forwardness. She seemed not to expect a response. "There's so much about you that appears contradictory if not simply false. You look like no hermit I've ever encountered, and Sneinton has plenty of them to offer for comparison."

He struggled for a suitable reply. Again, she gave him no opportunity.

"You live in a hut in Barnsdale, a wood often rife with outlaws, yet you are not an outlaw. I know all the outlaws in Sherwood and Barnsdale and they know me. They know to fear me. So then how is it I've hunted any number of them through Barnsdale Wood, and never once encountered you or your beehive hut? A monk's hut, that would be? I should remember if I'd seen its like, and that, again, rings false to me."

He wondered what she would say if he told her that she had once met him in the woods there, hairy and grizzled and wearing only rags, the remains of his clothing from Fontevraud; nor could he tell her how he'd built his hut in three days with some of those same outlaws bringing him stones just so they could watch him do it. It was wedged deeply in the wood and off every path, glamoured to blend into the forest when he was present so that she'd have had to run right into it to find it. Of course right now it would be standing visible and obvious, a tight heap of stones, and if she saw it her response, as he imagined it, would be to insist that she'd passed that very spot a hundred times and there had been no hut there. His living a hermit's existence only truly worked if no one encountered him.

"All right, then," she said. "How is it both Hodde and John know you, who are not an outlaw?"

He tried to make it as simple as possible. "We crossed paths is all."

She waved his answer away. "Tell me then about Robert Hodde, whose name might be your very own patronymic. And who by happenstance came to you as he was dying and now lies dead in your secret hermitage." She leaned forward. "Was he your father?"

He laughed at that, which at least covered his inability to defend himself. Every point she made poked a hole in the desperate façade he would have erected. It was as if he were hiding behind a tapestry that she methodically set about unweaving. Soon enough there would be nothing remaining of his small lies and obfuscations. They only worked in limited circumstances that allowed him an exit. Isabella Birkin had been paying close attention to everything he said and everything everyone else had said, and having gathered all the bits of misdirection, she could see they made no sense; they hadn't been designed to, not on her larger tapestry. Too late he understood that she was interrogating him. Thus far she'd left him squirming, but he'd engaged her. *Steep the climb . . .*

"Hodde is no relative of mine, I assure you."

"And yet, upon arriving in Nottingham you first sought out a relative of his, a tanner. You also told members of the Waits that Hodde the Tanner was your uncle. Why?" she asked.

"It was expedient, far easier than explaining how I was carrying out a dead man's request to deliver his takings—"

"His *stolen* takings."

"—to his family. And I'd given my word before I knew what he would ask of me. I wasn't going to renege on that."

"So is 'Hodde' even your true name?"

"My true name." He made a pained smile at that wording. "Yes."

He almost said it then, opened his mouth with "Thomas" on his breath, but then stopped. What was it that kept him from uttering it? That Sir Richard had known the name "from the ballads," which suggested that it hadn't faded as it should have done. Also the power and control the elven invested in names; look how Nicnevin had taken him over through the use of his full name. Just then it seemed to him that the knowledge of his name could only prove treacherous for the one who knew it, as well as for him. John didn't know it. The only person she could learn it from was Sir Richard atte Lee, who seemed to be long gone or a victim of these nocturnal events. "Let us just agree to leave it at *Robyn.* You can add *Goodfellow* to that for all I care."

That provoked a rare smile from her.

"All right . . . Robyn. You exhibit so much knowledge of these creatures. Explain to me the difference between the demons slain here and in Chandler's Lane and what happened with Passelewe. Why were their deaths so different?"

"Passelewe was a skinwalker. A *lich*. It means—"

"His skin walking around but not Passelewe on the inside."

"It sounds as if you didn't need to ask."

She continued, "And you have made it difficult for these creatures to lay hands on these things they call *dights*, these spinners, which are how someone *becomes* a skinwalker."

"Yes. That's right." He did not add that he believed one of them was intended for her.

"How difficult?"

"They can search everywhere here and will find nothing." He explained, "Three such devices were being brought south for some purpose, carried by a prelate. I can't tell you why they simply didn't bring three more, unless there is something unique to these three, something I wouldn't know how to find out. Or perhaps they are difficult to make. But the elven demons aren't used to interference from us. They have acted on the belief that a simple accident has occurred, from which they can easily recover. And in truth it *began* as a simple accident."

"So then, how do we know who are the inhabited men and women? How do we know, for instance, that King Henry isn't one of them?"

Thomas glanced down at his bare feet. Reciting, he muttered: *"Never kings, but always kingdoms."*

"What is that?" she asked.

"It's from another riddle. Spoken a long time ago."

"And you were the speaker of this one, too?"

"It was one who was called Thomas the Rhymer."

"Oh, I've heard that name in songs."

And so, he thought, how right he'd been once more not to admit it as his own.

"If I read that bit of riddle right," said Isabella, "these creatures work in the shadows then, behind the throne, influencers and manipulators. Someone like Peter des Roches, for instance."

"Who is Peter des Roches?"

"The Bishop of Winchester?" Surprised that he didn't know the name.

"Yes," he replied, "exactly like him." *Exactly like you as well, unfortunately*, he thought.

His agreement seemed to trouble her. Carefully as though edging along the question, she asked, "How can you recognize when someone has been taken over in this way?"

"You can't, always. Sheriff Passelewe was passing undetected until he made the mistake of grabbing on to me. I can...hear them sometimes, hear the strangeness of their thoughts. But I've also seen an Yvag wake up inside its *lich*. Seen the sudden cruel intelligence behind its eyes, the way it...leered. Once in a human body, the creatures seem to brim with lust as if they've never known the physicality, the pleasures of the flesh, before."

He thought of his own father ogling every woman at Cardden's Christes Maesse, and Forbes the Miller investigating his new form after a *dight* had emptied and replaced him.

"'Pleasures of the flesh.' I think you describe my husband perfectly, Master Hoode," stated Isabella Birkin.

"But has he not always been thus?" he asked. "So was I told."

"Always flirtatious, interested and willing to say so? Oh, yes. However, less than a year ago the shape of his perfidy changed. *He* changed."

"How so?"

"I know the very moment. Robert back from visiting Doncaster and at least one courtesan I knew he kept in that town. He always evaded my questions—I long ago grew used to the betrayals—but that day he behaved like someone I'd never met. The look of such an unquenchable appetite. He made overtures about our coupling, absurd in their depravity. We two were years down the road of being well quit of each other physically. We occupied the manor and barely shared in the raising of our son. For all of that, he was absolutely astonished by my rejection. It was as if no one ever rejected such opportunities."

He nodded slowly, seeing it all.

"I couldn't understand it. So I spied on him when he thought he was alone. He was studying his own body, his hands in particular as if they'd only just grown there. As if he'd never beheld himself, when the truth is, there isn't a mirror anywhere that Robert doesn't love."

The *dights* and their effect explained everything she'd witnessed.

"In that moment, I thought the devil had purchased his soul and replaced him with a demon." She frowned. "The saddest part of it, altogether there was so little change. Mostly to do with his interest in governing, in the running of things. Before then, he would walk out of a room rather than endure such a discussion."

He guessed the next part. "And suddenly he invested himself in matters political."

"Yes," she said. "And began meeting with men I didn't know he knew, while still feeling up any chambermaid fool enough to be caught alone by him. If anything, his lust increased."

"But not for you."

"Oh, it would have included me had I acquiesced to his overtures. He has ridden too far down that road. He covets not me but my inherited position, which goes to Adam next, not him. And there is nothing he can do about it. He's not the first, mind you—there was even a Nottingham sheriff named Philip Mark who tried to steal the title once."

Thomas nodded, relieved for the moment. The Yvags had possession of her husband, so didn't need her. Then doubt crept in. Maybe they'd assumed her husband would have all the influence, only to learn otherwise once they'd taken him over. One of those *dights* still might have been meant for her, or even for her son.

Isabella seemed to cast the entire matter aside. "Are you familiar with the writings of Gervase of Tilbury?"

"I am not."

"A wise philosopher, I think. He refers to things that seem miraculous or marvelous. He calls them all *inaudita*, 'things unheard of.' Some of these, he tells us, are true miracles of God. The rest are natural phenomena. It's his view that we simply haven't encountered them before and so they *seem* unnatural to us."

"I'm sure there's a point here?"

"You've allowed us to refer to your Yvag as 'demons.' I say 'allow' because I can see at every instance how you bite back your objection to the word. Demons are too much in the realm of God and the Church for you, I think."

"The Yvag are certainly no miracles of God, nor are they simply natural and misunderstood."

"But they are *inaudita* to me, and to the Waits as well. Not to you, though."

"Think you I've all your answers?"

"I wish to know what they are to you. You've said things that tell me you have been their captive."

He considered. *Onchu. Innes. Janet.* He folded his hands calmly in his lap. "That whole story's not for telling. They are and will always be my enemy."

"Yes, of course. I perceive that. But what are they? Not demons."

"They are the *elven*. In some places, faeries, fae, gruagach. Plenty more names. 'Demons' was what everyone in the Waits took them for, so I simply agreed."

"I see," she said. "You do that rather a lot."

He lowered his head again to hide that he was laughing. Yes, he supposed he did do that a lot.

"It matters not what you call them," he said, "they will come at us again as they did today and tonight and every night. They will try to infiltrate the retinue, mostly by replacing people, I imagine. That is, unless we give them the *dights* or they steal them back. My intention is to keep them away from their intended victims." *Starting with you.*

"And you are the only one among us who knows where they are hidden."

"I find it's safer for us all if that's the situation."

She thought a moment. "You are their sworn enemy, yet they don't seem to know you exist," she said.

"They believe I'm dead. I let them be for a while. And I . . . retired."

"You protected your wife above all else."

He nodded. "Yes."

She replied, "Now perhaps I understand 'woodwose' a little bit, I think."

"If say you so."

"I do say so." She smiled. "Tomorrow, Will and I travel first to Rufford Abbey. Sehild informed me that a message was delivered some days ago. The abbot wishes to speak with me regarding the use of my foresters for some purpose. I imagine it will not take long, and the two of us will continue on from there to the forty-days court in Retford to give our testimony."

"Testimony in what?"

"It regards a case of illegal pannage. A trio of men we arrested some weeks ago, nothing to do with this. It happens every year when the acorns drop."

"Have to say I feel sorry for the poor fellows. They stand no chance against you."

She seemed to find that comment amusing, but continued, "You asked about home, if I'm missing it. Laxton Hall is positioned such that I must needs visit it at some point in that journey to appease D'Everingham. Only, now, thanks to you, I go forewarned."

"You must allow me to accompany you. You might be watchful, but I know the exact signs." The riddle ran through his head again. *Another Janet...*

If he had only a short time, he needed to apply himself, however bold, however decidedly foolish. "Also, I have a request of you, milady," he said.

"Yes?"

"I should like to spend every minute of the time until you depart tomorrow in your company."

She looked at him, astonished. For once he'd taken her completely by surprise. "Oh," she said. Then repeated it. "Oh," again. Finally, she cleared her throat and gathered herself up. "I believe I assigned you *that* room, Master Hoode," she said. He nodded to it. She took him by the hand, then walked barefoot across the wood planks without a look back. He followed her. They passed his chamber and all the others in which members of the Waits and Keepers slept, and descended silently to the chamber she'd given herself.

XXIX. Zhanedd in Ailfion

Sir Richard atte Lee lies at the feet of the Queen. He is naked save for a collar connected by a chain to Nicnevin's throne. His memory of how he arrived here is a chaos of impressions—of things done to him and with him, handed off to one creature after another like a jug of wine, and like a jug of wine there's a little less of him each time. Some of the creatures have assumed shapes not their own, even stolen them from his memories. Some have somehow changed him to match them before they make use of him. He no longer knows if it has been hours or months, but he is drained, feeble, certain that he is near death. They will never let him go. They will use him up. He knows this because, at some point in his various transformations, something happened and he began to understand their speech. He can now overhear their silent, humming conversations.

He raises his head as the one who captured him arrives.

Zhanedd in that strange shiny armor strides in like some military captain reporting to their commander, in this case the Queen. He looks back at her. She is seated on her dais under a richly textured baldachin, and dressed in a long red gown sewn with columns of pink pearls. The flush of rose at her throat all but glows, extending up into her cheeks, making her large golden eyes seem almost to ignite as they track the Yvag's arrival.

On the opposite side of the Queen stands the strange creature called Bragrender, its forever-transforming shape—warping from grotesque to exquisitely beautiful—hypnotic and stupefying to behold. The creature can pin you to the spot—at least, it did so to

191

Sir Richard when he looked directly at it. He had to be dragged away. The Queen and the other creatures do not react so strongly to it.

The Queen interrupts his drifting thoughts, scowling at approaching Zhanedd. "You have no *dights*. You were tasked with acquiring them."

"True, I have none." Zhanedd stops to strike a defiant pose. "And that is thanks to your various fledgling, meddling knights, who've repeatedly interfered in the belief that they will triumph easily over the humans."

The Queen stiffens. "Well?" she says. "And why wouldn't they?"

Zhanedd makes a dismissive gesture. "Surely you must know that Kunastur is dead. I passed through a gate in time to watch his head severed from his body by a human wielding one of our marvelous blades."

The information appears to surprise the Queen. She glares down at Sir Richard and for a moment he thinks she's about to kick him.

Zhanedd says, "So you did not know."

Lips unmoving, she speaks to Zhanedd. "The humans are dolts. They do occasionally intrude; once in a great while they manage to overwhelm one of us or stumble into our way."

"Are you presenting an excuse for the loss of our precious *dights*?"

The Queen seems to grow taller on her throne. Sir Richard flinches.

"The loss of the *dights* is a perfect example," she says. "They know not what or where we are, nor have enough sense to organize any resistance. Using them as an excuse for failing to acquire our property is beneath you, Zhanedd. You come to us empty-handed and seek to be rewarded for it."

Sir Richard can hear the resentment boiling up inside the Yvag knight. Apparently, so can the one called Bragrender, which stares fixedly upon Zhanedd. He wishes he knew what these *dights* were, other than something precious that's been taken from them. And there is some manner of bond or relationship between Zhanedd and Nicnevin that he cannot quite distinguish, something akin to a master and apprentice or parent and child different from the Queen's relationship to the Yvags who've passed him among them. If he knew more about Yvag relationships, he might understand, but he's too exhausted to pry, his mind too tired to do more than passively listen.

If they come to blows over this, he will lie here helplessly in the middle of their battle.

"Empty-handed," Zhanedd repeats, "against *doltish* mortals like him." She points at Sir Richard, and he clenches, anticipating that this will be his end. Instead, Zhanedd says, "Let me begin with your soldier Tozesđin, who decided he alone would recover the *dights* rather than informing me of their whereabouts as he should have done. He, like so many others, knows I am a changeling, but one singled out by you for special treatment. He refused to obey me, and warned me off instead, telling me to 'stay away and let the genius that is Tozesđin triumph.'"

"..." The Queen emits a sound like a slapped hornet's nest.

"The genius that is Tozesđin now has no head."

The Queen waves the news away dismissively.

"But not of the consequences of his meddling. *I* had captured and interrogated one of the involved humans. I followed him across Nottingham to where he was keeping the *dights*, in one of their gaols, which is also where Tozesđin was claiming his victory right up until the moment they cut off his head. I might have pulled victory out of this defeat, but your superior Yvagvoja running Passelewe determined that he would take the *dights* instead. I am sure that voja has returned by now to explain how he failed, given that Passelewe is dead as well, along with Simforax. But you know that."

The Queen sits absolutely still. Sir Richard would be anywhere but caught between these two.

"My point is not merely to criticize, my Queen, or complain about how unfairly you've treated me in this after having assigned to me the task of recovering your *dights*. Nor is it the almost constant prejudice I deal with among your various soldiers. I know, because you have told me, that few changeling-bred Yvags even recollect their transformation. Thus many of those who affect a superior attitude are themselves changelings and unaware. You might consider making them aware to teach them some humility."

Instead of the Queen, Bragrender speaks. Even its unvoiced words sound inhuman. "Enough. What *is* your point, Zhanedd? Time is passing."

"It is this: We are making a mistake in treating the humans as hapless, bumbling creatures that occasionally wrest a victory from us. My opinions of your knights aside, this one small band of mortals has slain all four of these as well as the *lich* of our Yvagvoja of Doncaster. And they seem now aware of our regenerative abilities. There is nothing accidental in this. We have an enemy."

"Who?" asks the Queen.

"I cannot be sure. It might be more than one. However, one of them when interrogated gave up your image."

"Mine? How is that possible?"

"You told me once of changelings who did not transform right, who went insane after immersion."

The Queen looks at Bragrender, who answers for her: "Especially during the time the pool became corrupted. Yes, what of them? They were all put down."

"Are you certain?"

No one says anything for so long that Sir Richard glances up at Nicnevin.

Finally, through Bragrender she replies, "A few in Þagalwood were lost. But we know what happens to the unprotected in Þagalwood. The situation resolved itself."

"Of course. Nevertheless, I want to speak with Passelewe's voja about the sheriff's encounter with this same human as well as the others. He might be some manner of changeling, too. Possibly one who eluded you."

"And now sides against us with humans?" she asks, her tone suggesting how absurd the idea is.

"It's a theory. Passelewe established rapport with him, which is why I must speak with his voja."

"What is the name of this supposed changeling?"

"He goes by Robyn Hoode, but I believe this to be a false identity."

Sir Richard mishears the name at first. But it's not Robert Hodde they're speaking of. A false identity, though. He can't help thinking of his brief acquaintance, Sir Thomas, hopes that he has escaped the campaign the Queen is waging, fled to another country.

"In any case, the *dights* are still kept from us, and all of the gates you've opened throughout the forest have turned up nothing, because none of those outlaws had anything to do with the theft."

"My gates yield a trove of *teinds* at the very least and terrorize the gowks. They're all as weak as this." The Queen places a foot against

Sir Richard and idly pushes him onto his back. Unprepared, he blinks in confusion. "This one is almost used up."

"I don't suppose the Þagalwood assemblers have produced any other *dights* yet?"

"I am told, one has been completed."

Zhanedd's eyes glisten. The knight says flatly, "Then I want it."

"You? Why should I give it to you, Zhanedd?"

"You assigned me this task. Had your knights not interfered, I would have the missing ones by now and we would not even be at the mercy of the strange assemblers. Besides, from our experience so far, if you give it to anyone else, you will lose it as well. Whereas I have a plan of attack and a target."

Through Bragrender, the Queen derides Zhanedd: "One target is the same as any other." But she sits tapping her fingers against the arm of the throne. At last she says, "Very well. I will entrust the new *dight* to you. See that your plan is successful."

Zhanedd bows and withdraws from the throne room.

Sir Richard finds the Queen's golden eyes contemplating him as if he was her next meal. She looks to the other creature in the room, the one Sir Richard dares not look at.

"Of course, we won't do as she suggests, either, will we, Bragrender?"

The terrifying, constantly shifting creature faces her and then glances down at him. Once converged, he cannot look away from this horrifying thing, and almost immediately he finds his mind emptying, like sand through a net.

"Now, now, don't devour him, my pet." The Queen cups his jagged, ever-changing cheek. "Our toy may yet prove useful before we bid him farewell."

XXX. Rufford Abbey

The band set off early the next morning. The two Waits remained behind in the King's Houses. They must shortly return to Nottingham, but until then would ensure no further visitors intruded to hunt for the *dights*. To add to that confusion, Thomas carried the empty tool bag with him, fully on display across his horse's rump. Lady Isabella and her son rode up front. Thomas and Little John rode behind them, followed by Will and Maurin.

The River Maun road to the King's Great Way was strange in the morning fog, but not so strange as the Way itself. Seemingly overnight, breaking wheels had been erected on poles along the wider road. These emerged like giants out of the fog. Most displayed the broken bodies of outlaws fitted to the wheels. Between them, the Keepers and Little John were able to identify some of the dead.

"Being very methodical about depopulating the forest," Thomas said after they'd encountered their fourth breaking wheel. "Do they truly believe all of the outlaws in Sherwood know who is in possession of their devices? Or do they just enjoy torture? This will only ensure that everyone flees."

"But this suggests," said Will from behind, "the one we killed last night shared none of his information with any others of his kind. I mean, if 'Mary of Clipstone' knew you have those spinners, why attack these innocents instead of the King's Houses?"

Over his shoulder Adam called back, "To scare them?"

"They're doing what they're told to by their murderous queen," Thomas said darkly.

John pointed out words cut in one of the poles. "What's it say, then?"

Isabella read off, "It's in Latin. 'Return what you stole.' You're right, Will."

Thomas said, "John being an excellent example, that will only threaten people who know how to read. I do not imagine there are many outlaws with that skill."

"Those killing them make no such distinctions," she replied. "Yvag?"

"Murderers and torturers who take reading for granted? Undoubtedly. Even Sheriff Passelewe would have known better."

"Educated walkers, then," said Will.

Maurin added, "Monks, priests, poets, and councilmen."

Thomas laughed. "I've never trusted any of those."

"You don't feel terror in the face of these wheels?"

"Terror? No. Regret, certainly. Regret that these innocent people have been harmed because of"—he glanced at them all—"what some or all of us have done. That is what they want us to feel, what these wheels are for. Enough regret that we willingly give back—"

"Why *don't* we give them back, then?" asked Adam. "These . . . these *things*."

"The answer of the moment is, we do not have them to return."

Silence followed, until Little John suddenly clapped his hands and laughed. "You hid them!"

"I did, yes, and the less specific your knowledge is, the better. Broken on one of these Catherine wheels, there is not one of us wouldn't tell them all they want to know and then make up more answers."

"You're all *horrid*," Adam proclaimed, "and your keeping them hidden is the cause of this. People dying needlessly."

Thomas replied, "Not so, and I wish I could make it easy for you to understand, Adam. It's been us dying needlessly at least since Warin's death. If he died for nothing, if Osbert died for nothing, then we should by all means return to the elven their devices, and let them get on with coring out more Passelewes. Which is what they intend. But what does it matter, so long as we don't have to witness it nor learn of the victims, hmm?" He rode up beside the young man, but spoke gently. "And what if your mother is an intended target? Or both of you for that matter. That might easily be the case. You are exactly the sort of well-placed influential patricians the Yvags prefer to occupy. And if not you, it's sure you know one who would be. Will you trade their lives?"

With no counterargument, Adam muttered under his breath, kicked his horse, and galloped on ahead. Isabella did not look at Thomas, but rode after her son.

Thomas let his horse drop back. He kept his own counsel on the matter; he agreed with Adam it was unfair for innocents to die over this. That was how it had all begun for him—with innocent Onchu as their sacrifice, with drowned Baldie hollowed out and possessed, with Innes tricked and obscenely used. That wasn't his, that was the Yvags' cruelty, random and uncaring. And no matter his or the others' submission on any front, the elves would go right on killing as suited them.

Rufford Abbey was less than a century old. It had displaced an entire town in order to be erected. A few thatchless stone houses remained as testament to the church's dominance, ghost dwellings in the fog. Most of the village stones had been repurposed as part of the abbey itself.

White-robed monks met them near the north transept and took their horses away. Another one led them inside, and across the nave to the central cloister, where more Cistercians scurried about. The monks seemed, one and all, to be attending to injured local persons who were either sitting or lying upon cloister benches. Thomas counted eight of them, and all appeared to have been assaulted. Most were bloody in some part; one had a severely broken limb as if he'd almost been attached to one of those wheels before escaping or being let go. The cruelty of the Yvags was playing out again, and he hoped the example wasn't lost on Adam. The campaign of terror deserved a response.

The abbot came up and greeted Isabella. His name was Godwin. He was a squat and barrel-chested man, and jovial. He recommended they go to the lay brothers' frater for a meal while he and Isabella spoke in private. The two of them strode off before anyone could even think of something to say. Another monk offered to lead the way to the frater.

Meanwhile, Maurin had walked over to the people being treated. Thomas patted John on the shoulder to go on without him—"I'll catch you up"—then turned and followed Maurin to the nearest wounded townsman, who looked as though he'd been bashed in the forehead.

"Who attacked you?" Maurin asked.

The man, in shock, only then fastened upon him, and then upon Thomas behind the lad. It was as if the man sought the familiar in their different faces.

"Them knights. Come outta the dark, the swamp where there ain't no place, come outten it like off a battlefield."

Thomas thought, *You've been a knight yourself.* He did not interrupt.

"All dressed for like the last crusade, like the Templars had sailed up our river. An' all they wanted to know was who stole the dice? Not one us knew what they spoke of, didn't while they cracked and hoisted 'em, still don't now."

"We do," said Maurin.

"Well, then they shoulda talked ta you all and not ta us."

"They want to," Thomas said, but the man wasn't listening, lost in reliving the event.

"They cracked Ealar's knees, elbows, bent 'em all wrong ta fit 'im to the wheel." The man's eyes suddenly found his. "Their arms was bent wrong already, them knights. Them terrible, terrible knights." The townsman lowered his head, shaking it.

Leaving Maurin and Will to continue speaking to the wounded, Thomas walked off. He could hardly remain unmoved by the poor man's plight and that of others. He determined that before leaving here, he was going to pay a visit to the abbey's crypt. Maybe he would get lucky.

The monks looked on while the visitors indulged in bread, eggs, and ale. By the end almost all of the locals had been sent home to recover. Only one was going to lose a limb. There were far worse situations every day, provided you didn't count the dead men hung from wheels.

Isabella's business with the abbot concluded, and she joined the rest of the Keepers in the frater. Thomas asked what the abbot had wanted.

The abbey, she said, had requested and received approval for its own private forester to tend to its holdings. As Warden she was to select one of her Keepers to take on that role. Thus she had to choose someone who would no longer dwell among the Keepers but live instead in the abbey surrounded by monks. She suspected her husband's hand in this—stripping away a confrère reduced the number of Keepers she could rely upon. Sherwood Forest might be the King's preserve, but she admitted to a very personal relationship with the land and a cold determination regarding poachers. She was more suspicious than ever that her husband was "like Passelewe."

From her abrupt silence then, Thomas could tell that wasn't all.

"Also, my husband requests that I return to Laxton Castle immediately rather than delaying until we've resolved our business in Retford." The reason for this change of plans had not been provided to Abbot Godwin although it seemed clear he thought no woman should be entrusted with leading a group of foresters in the first place. She asked that Thomas say nothing to the others for the moment.

"Of course," he promised. Instead he asked one of the serving monks where the entrance to the abbey's crypt might lie.

"Dorter Undercroft, you mean?" the monk replied.

"I—I suppose I do. 'Undercroft,' most definitely."

The monk led the way. Thomas caught John's eye, gestured with his head for him to follow.

From the frater behind him, Isabella called out.

Thomas turned back.

"Don't stray far, you two. We leave shortly for Retford," she told him.

Emerging from his chambers, the abbot said, "Don't you mean—"

Isabella cut him off. "No, I do not. My appointment is at the Moot Hall of Retford while the forty-day court is in session. We'll go to Laxton when our business there is concluded, and not before."

The abbot glared at her. "'Wives should submit in everything to their husbands,'" he quoted.

"What a meaningless string of words coming from one who's known only celibacy," she told him. She matched his glower until he finally marched back into his chamber and slammed the door.

"In the end, not the friendliest sort," Thomas observed.

Isabella said coldly, "We're leaving for Retford."

"Of course. And unfortunately that exchange poisons the request I was going to make that you take an extra day and join John and me. There's someplace I need for him to show me, and we have Robert Hodde's body to bury, which, whatever you thought of him, is overdue. As the Warden of the Keepers, it does concern you."

"In your hut?"

"Presumably he's still there. It will be brief. We would be in Retford tomorrow, but it concerns me to leave you alone here, when—"

"I think you forget who fired a crossbow last night that brought down the demon at King's Houses," she told him angrily. "I am more than capable of rescuing myself, Master Hoode. If you need to make this side trip, then do so and join us in Retford when you can. But I won't wait for you. As I told the damned abbot, I will not be delayed."

Again he said, "Of course."

She turned to leave, but hesitated, and faced him again. "However, when I face D'Everingham," she said, "I should very much like your company. He is pulling the threads of this, I'm certain, and you know more than the rest of us about these matters."

He thought of their time together last night and this morning in the darkness of her chamber, her fierce passion and joy, matched now by her fierce anger. "We'll be there," he said.

He watched until she was lost from sight in the cloister.

Thomas and Little John followed the Cistercian, who showed them the steps down into the crypt. Thomas asked if the monk would by chance have a winding sheet they could have—he'd noticed some in the cloisters, and there was someone, he explained, who hadn't survived the attacks in the forest. The monk nodded and hurried off.

Thomas drew his dagger and Little John gripped his staff as they started down the steps.

Was there a spell, a repulsion at the top of the steps? Thomas thought he sensed it even as Little John walked a complete circle down two steps and back up without seeming to be aware and then said, "I don't know, Woodwose, should we e'en go down there?"

That answered the question. Thomas pushed through the spell, and suddenly it vanished. Would that alert the monk who had cast it?

That might be the abbot. He had sensed nothing odd or otherworldly about the man. But then they had spent two minutes in each other's company. No doubt any Yvag could maintain a silence longer than that.

Little John charged right past him, went straight down the steps, came to the first tomb and without hesitating lifted the lid with its effigy of a knight. Hurrying after, Thomas hissed, "No, we start at the far end! Oh . . . Never mind." Because the nearest tomb was empty, containing no remains at all. But the space looked as if it was prepared to accommodate someone or had done until recently.

Thomas said, "I think someone has been installed here."

"Passelewe?"

"Him, or possibly the one in your prelate. Would the bishop have stopped here if he'd come this far? It's not out of his way, and you confronted him well north of here."

Little John shrugged. "How's it matter?"

"Someone among the monks here is not what he seems. Someone put that dissuasion spell in place."

"What dissuasion spell?" asked John.

"You didn't sense it, but it was there at the top of the steps, running you in circles."

"Nah, I never. But here, would take two men ta carry body outta this hole."

"True, but if it's the bishop or the sheriff, then whoever it was awoke on their own and probably jumped straight back to Ailfion. Didn't even disrupt the spell."

"I say there were no spell."

"I understand that. For right now, since we're already here . . ." Thomas said, and circled the second tomb. He pushed at the lid. John caught a corner and lifted it. The moldering corpse within remained undisturbed, exactly what a normal death should look like. He thought of the tombs in Melrose. "They were only using the one, then, for someone special." It was possible they'd taken to keeping all of their voja separate. He would be the cause of that. "They'll be keen to replace both losses. With Passelewe's death, they may be reconsidering just where to apply the *dights*, and if anything more urgently." The bishop of Leicester and Simon de Montfort might have gained a reprieve. He still didn't know who the third device was for.

"We shouldn't give them demons the chance then, hey?"

He nodded. "We'll do well to revisit this undercroft at some unannounced point." They reset the tombs and quickly left. If any monk was watching them emerge, he hid himself well. The young monk who'd led them there reappeared with a bundle of plain linen for them. Thomas thanked him for his hospitality, and he and John walked through the cloisters, across the nave and out. They had a long ride ahead of them. He only wished that Isabella Birkin was riding with them.

XXXI. Burying Hodde

From the abbey Thomas and Little John headed west. They'd ridden for an hour or so in their individual silences when John abruptly spoke up. "Tha know spot where I seen the Queen is near thi hut, Woodwose. Certain ya are you wanta go back there? I mean, Robbie ain't exactly waitin' on us."

Thomas had been thinking of how to frame this discussion. He had to get Little John to the gate at night, and knew that wasn't likely to be easy. "I want to learn," he said, "if you discovered a gateway favored by the Queen of Faery."

"Oh." Another silence, then, "Why's 'at important?"

Thomas answered, "The first place I encountered her was called Old Melrose, a place where an abbey once stood. Nicnevin, the Queen, came through that single green ring many times. Don't ask me why—she just seemed to favor it. So I thought, if the place you saw her is another favored gate, I want to see it. But more important, we might get the chance to kill her there and put an end to this invasion, stop the Yvags from torturing whomever they catch, get them to leave, for a year, a decade, forever."

"An' take that target off Lady Isabella."

The statement so startled him that he just stared open-mouthed until John started laughing.

"Ah know tha fancy her, an' I know what bed tha didn't sleep in last night."

"How?"

"Oh, I'd somethin' ah wanted t' tell tha, middle of night."

Thomas couldn't help but smile. "You're a sly one, Little John."

John shrugged. "Ah just see what I see. Tha hope to kill their queen an' they'll all pack it in and go home, leavin' Lady Isabella safe."

"I do."

They rode a little farther. "Think tha he's still there? Robbie, I mean."

"Still there, and probably the worse for it. I doubt anyone would have moved him."

"Like, the wolves will'a been at him."

They rode on across Sherwood, past the great split oak where John's troubles had begun. The bones of the prelate were gone from the King's Way. It could have been the Yvag knights had collected him, or someone who imagined they were in the presence of some holy relics.

As they neared his hut, Thomas put aside his mulling over of matters concerning the Queen and Isabella Birkin. He said, "You mentioned you had something you wanted to tell me in the middle of the night last night."

"Oh, ah did, yeah." Then he continued without saying more.

Thomas asked, "Well, what was it?"

"Oh, it were just that—I mean, I wanted t' say that, well, whatever we're undertaking here and what comes next, I want tha to know that I'm yer man."

He almost refused, but had the presence of mind to stop himself. It would have been like rejecting Alpin Waldroup's offer to teach him the bow. And John had now stated this twice.

They rode a little farther then before he said quietly, "Thank you, John. I wouldn't want anyone else."

He smiled, John nodded, and that was that. Some bridge had been built in their relationship. He was becoming Robert Hodde's replacement, from the Lincoln green cotehardie to his knowledge of Sherwood and his bond now with the last member of Hodde's band. Everything that needed to be said had been.

They rode on.

Robert Hodde's body had somehow escaped the various predators roaming the forest. The glamouring spell he'd placed upon the hut might have played a part even though the hut stood in full view. The stink of it did spill out past the stone walls now.

However, someone—he guessed the same two Yvag knights—had

tortured the corpse, running it through with blades and feathering it with crossbow bolts. It must have made for rousing target practice among the frustrated knights. They couldn't torture anything out of him. Other than that, Hodde's body had ripened, swollen, and gone pale and blue, against which his auburn hair seemed artificial.

Thomas found a surviving clay jug and carried it to the same stream where he'd washed the blood out of Hodde's clothes, then returned, tore a section of the winding cloth, and used it and the water to clean the body.

"Robbie didn't much care for bathing," Little John observed.

"I'm sure those nearest him noticed."

"We knew better'n ta stand downwind."

Thomas laughed.

"Last time 'e had one I think was when I knocked him into River Went."

"Still inadvisable to swim there, is it?"

"Well, the fish all died." Little John was grinning as he said it.

Then they were grim and silent, paying attention to their friend's body as they wrapped him completely. After, Thomas went in search of discarded stones. He knew there were a few in the rejected pile of hut stones that were vaguely shell-shaped, suitable as digging blades.

The body didn't weigh all that much. They carried it some distance into the depths of the forest, to a place between oaks where acorns covered the ground but it was otherwise level.

"'Ere's good," said John. They set the body down and, from their opposite ends, dug out a hole deep enough to bury him. It took the rest of the afternoon to fill it back in. Then they covered the signs of digging with leaves. Satisfied with their work, they stood one stone at each end of the grave as markers. It seemed most appropriate that Robert Hodde enjoy his final rest hidden deep within his forest.

It was growing dark as John directed the way along a narrow footpath by which he'd fled only a few nights before. They'd left their horses back a fair distance just to be safe.

The trees thinned, oaks giving way to a field of birch and alders, which grew in tall grasses surrounding a depression of standing water. Past the grasses, the ground rose into a wide hillside splashed in purple heather and growths of fern.

Little John pointed but even in the settling dusk it was easy to identify where the ring had been. Everything in one spot on the heath was trampled as if by a dozen horses just riding about in small circles as they might have in taking positions flanking their queen.

Thomas walked to the spot. In one place the plants were scorched, as though a torch had been dropped there, more or less the very center of activity according to John. Hoofprints gouged the dirt and grasses here and there, but the prints that could be seen had been left by no horse. Thomas could almost recreate in his mind's eye what John had described.

Carefully, he drew his ördstone and held it out on his palm. It flickered, the tiny blue gems lighting as if the stone contained agitated fireflies. It had been a long time since he could recall seeing it so active. Holding it out, however, he watched amazed as a tiny blue line no wider than a hair stretched from the stone to that center of activity. The air seemed to pucker, something like a bubble, and the view of the heath through it distorted. He half expected to see Þagalwood or Yvagddu through it, but that vision didn't manifest—just a circular area of distortion, the otherwise hidden ring itself. The world had been thinned by the presence of the Queen's gate.

Little John had been leading the way. He backed up from the distortion, turned and followed the blue thread of color to Thomas's hand. He appeared ready to bolt should Thomas produce anything else, but approached the stone out of obvious curiosity. Thomas was tempted to slice the air, but was sure a terrified Little John would flee, no matter his allegiance. More than that, this might open onto the middle of one of their plazas, a staging area. The lensing effect revealed nothing on the other side of the gate.

"What is that blinking thing, Woodwose?"

He walked over and showed it to John. The blue "thread" maintained its line to the gate. He held out his hand, but Little John refused to touch the ördstone. "It's a key that opens doors we can't see," he explained, closed his fingers over it and dropped the ördstone back into the quiver at his belt. "Doors between our world and others."

"You took that off the demon in Chandler's Lane gaol."

"Actually, that was another one."

John glanced back, but the circle of distortion had vanished. "You open this one, we going t'be fighting off a horde a black knights?"

"That's the problem with a door you can't see past. You've no idea what's behind it."

"Tha know I'm with tha, but if thi intent is ta open that one, I would be elsewhere."

"You're a wise man. And, no, I won't open it. But we need to take up positions for when *they* open it. If Nicnevin comes through, I might only get one shot."

The sun had almost set—just stripes of pink and yellow clouds remained—and already odd sounds, howls, and cries echoed across the forest.

With his bow, Thomas climbed higher in the upland heath to look over the woods. He glimpsed a distant spark of color—presumably another gate opening. By now surely this was a simple tactic to frighten. Anyone who'd traveled a pathway or road in Sherwood now had seen some of the wheels and the mangled dead, and would have had the good sense to flee. All for show, this nocturnal haunting. But it meant the gate below would probably open soon. He hoped so.

As he climbed back down the hillside, he thought again of Isabella Birkin. He assured himself she would be busy anyway with the trial in Retford; besides, she was safely surrounded by the Keepers. Tomorrow he would catch up to her in time to ride to Laxton Castle and confront D'Everingham.

His contemplation of her was interrupted by a line of sizzling green fire that appeared in the air. It seemed to reach for the ground. The line flexed and split into an oblong, widened finally into a perfect circle. By then, he had taken up his position behind a tree, in sight of Little John.

Behind the circle the darkness of night no longer showed. A shimmering silvery surface filled the ring, and it took him a moment to recognize one of Ailfion's many plazas—a staging area, exactly as he'd feared. The shining backdrop was one of the city's towers, close enough that it filled the view. No doubt its needlelike tip would stretch into the red-black sky that couldn't be seen. The pavement of the plaza was not visible, and the first of the Yvags to cross over stepped up to pass through the ring. It might have been the very spot where, in his escape, he had cut open the way to Þagalwood.

Both John and he held their bows at the ready, waiting for the Queen.

The knight that had cut the ring stood and stepped up and through, followed close-on by another. They took up positions at the sides. Once again they had bothered to glamour as crusaders. There must have been a reason. Maybe they assumed any outlaws would be less frightened of human knights. The number of bodies hanging on wheels suggested it had worked to some degree. He doubted it did any longer. Nobody was foolishly going to approach a gate at this point.

Two more knights emerged, these on horseback though he knew the black steeds to be no horses. The two rode about in sweeping circles that kept the gateway in the middle.

The hoofprints he'd already looked at told him this was a repeat of previous appearances. Were they just showing themselves to be formidable? To throw a scare into . . . someone? Who, in the middle of the forest? What would be the point?

Then, as he speculated about the knights and the gate, two more knights came riding slowly along the same path John had followed earlier. One held a torch. The hairs on the back of Thomas's neck stood up. Between the two knights walked a naked man, slow, keeping pace with them or them with him. From his face, it was apparent he was in a trance. There could be no doubt: This was the escorting of a *teind* to Hel. The knights guarding the ring stood still and watched. Maybe Nicnevin would arrive for this, but any further waiting and their captive would be walked right out of the world. However much he wanted Nicnevin dead, he could not let this poor hapless soul be taken. He would force them to sacrifice one of their own.

John was watching him. Thomas lifted his chin. Then he stood up, one arrow nocked and two more between his fingers. He took careful aim, then fired at the nearest escort, following with a second shot at the one with the torch. The first arrow plucked the Yvag knight right out of its saddle. The second knocked the other knight askew, causing the torch to sail to the ground. The Yvag desperately righted itself just as Thomas's third arrow, as if anticipating this, punctured its armored breastbone. The stallion bounded forward. It knocked down the naked man and galloped straight through the opening. "A real horse," he muttered. Where had they stolen that?

Little John meanwhile had shot two of the other four knights guarding the ring, one on foot and one mounted. The remaining two had drawn their swords. He and John both knew what that meant.

Thomas ran for the nearest mount. Little John ran erratically back and forth from tree to tree to avoid the deadly sword blade, but continued firing all the while at the two remaining knights.

Thomas swung up into the saddle as one sword blade cut the air close enough beside him that it nicked his forearm. Turning the beast, he grabbed the stumbling naked man by the hair. Instinctively, the man reached both hands up. Thomas caught one of those and hauled the man like a sack over the horse's rump, kicked his heels, and the beast shot off into the darkness away from the guttering torch.

With their *teind* gone, the knights quickly retreated back through the portal and sealed it up. The tip of the stone glowed bright blue until, with one last spit of green fire, everything vanished as if it had never been. With the ring gone, Thomas drew up and waited for John.

Back there four Yvag knights lay dead or regenerating. He would have to make sure the latter didn't succeed while Little John roused their rescued *teind* from the spell cast over him. The poor man could count himself lucky. Not Thomas. He'd missed a chance to eliminate his nemesis. This would do nothing to protect Isabella, but instead likely sealed up this gate and told Nicnevin that her soldiers were being hunted again for the first time since Ercildoun.

XXXII. Retford to Laxton

The Moot Hall of Retford had begun life as a motte and bailey fortification. The ditch around the steep scarp remained. What might once have been a drawbridge was now just a walkway. The hall looked to be a modified wooden keep sitting atop the mound, thatched roof visible behind the crenellations at the top. The castle was now given over to meetings of such entities as the forty-days court and other legal proceedings. That nothing in particular appeared to be going on did not strike Thomas as odd. He didn't know what to expect, but assumed a Woodmote court would have a backlog of matters to hear.

Little John said he preferred to stay with the horses. His name might be all too familiar to members of such a court. There were owed fees at the very least.

It wasn't until Thomas had climbed the steps and entered, to find no sign of a court in attendance at all, that he became concerned. The table where the judges would sit was obvious across the room, but unoccupied. Isabella ought to be here right now, weighing in sharply against the three men accused of illegal pannage, her arguments irrefutable, damning.

Instead, he found one young man with bowl-cut hair at work at a small table outfitted with an inkpot and dozens of papers, copying a document and acting as if he hadn't come in. He asked where Lady Isabella Birkin might be found.

The young clerk paused, looked up at him with some annoyance, and replied, "Gone home," then went back to his transcription.

"What do you mean, 'gone home'? Where?"

The clerk held his stylus up, pausing between words. "That would be Laxton Castle, yes?" he said. "Left for it this morning after the fiasco." He returned to his copying.

Increasingly irritated by the uninformative answers, Thomas snatched the stylus out of the scrivener's hand. Ink spattered on the document. "What fiasco? What happened to the case of pannage?"

"Thrown out. The accused trio produced a document"—he pushed through those he had and dangled one in the air—"granting them permission to herd their pigs onto the King's land. Thereby maintained their innocence, they did."

"And Lady Isabella accepted that evidence?"

"Well, she had to, didn't she?" he said. "The document was written and signed by her husband."

"What?"

"See for yourself. His signature and seal."

Thomas slid the page over. As the scrivener claimed, it read like a legal document granting the parties full rights to graze their pigs, signed with a flourish and below that wax imprinted with a signet. If he'd known nothing of the matter, he would have believed it, too. He said, "But Robert D'Everingham has no legal standing to grant such permission."

The clerk grinned. "And that's what propelled her home, good sir. The accused insisted they'd no way of knowing that. Her 'usband, he misrepresented himself as a Keeper of Sherwood. So it become a matter of a dispute between Warden and him. The court, it suspended, and she departed with such speed, all her companions were caught off guard. I can tell you, her ire all but set the room ablaze. I wouldn't want to be her 'usband for nothing."

A pall of foreboding wrung the irritation out of Thomas. "Believe me," he said, handing back the stylus, "you wouldn't want to be him anytime at all. The other foresters—did they ride out with her?"

"After her, more like."

"And how long ago was this?"

"Oh, hours nah. It were the first business took up by court this morning."

Little John was surprised at how huge an estate Laxton proved to be, the entire settlement bordered by both an outer ditch and a low curtain wall, which in turn framed a second smaller curtain wall containing what were likely the original settlement houses. At the far end, its gatehouse opened to the motte on which Laxton castle itself perched—a round shell keep enclosing a two-story hall and other smaller stone buildings within. Their thatch roofs peeked over the keep wall. Defensively, it was the very opposite of the King's Houses.

The road led straight through the larger main gate to the second enclosure. On either side stood smaller houses, most with attached crofts, reminding him both of Clipstone and of the small vill in Barnsdale where his own brother and family dwelled. The people toiling in the crofts paused to watch as the two of them rode by. They looked like people everywhere.

John and Thomas rode on into the smaller enclosure where they dismounted. Stable and paddock were part of that smaller yard. In the stable, John identified horses belonging to the Keepers, horses that had pursued him on more than one occasion. So, they'd arrived in timely fashion. All the way from Retford, Robyn had spoken of his worries regarding Lady Isabella, how her husband was surely another of those walkers like the prelate had been, and more treacherous than she appreciated for that, and how he hoped the others had caught up with her before she reached Laxton. Now he was saying nothing at all, but at least it appeared they had accompanied her.

One of the villeins in the yard scurried off through the gate and up the slope to announce their arrival. Robyn, unable to stand still, paced the yard.

Instead of D'Everingham it was Lady Isabella herself who descended from the motte to greet them, although John did not recognize her until she was crossing the yard. He'd never seen her in such finery before. She wore a blue surcoat, white gown, and a pale yellow mantle trimmed in fur. On her head a crespine of gold wire held her hair, a narrow fillet and barbette securing the wire frame. She walked boldly up to Robyn, took him by the face, and kissed him deeply. A little embarrassed and surprised, John looked around, and noticed how the other villeins were gawking. It seemed they'd never seen such behavior in their mistress before, either. The unnaturalness of it shook even Robyn. He stepped back from her, though he must have been pleased to find her safe.

"I feared," he said, "you had either killed your husband or he you."

She laughed. "As you can see, neither," she replied. She could not keep from touching him, and ran her hands over his shoulders, then down his arms as though one touch invited another and another. "We have resolved our disagreement—that is, he apologized for his part and I for mine."

"Yours? What part of your outrage owes him an apology? He usurped your authority as if it was his own." Even John could see how this made no sense. The lady seemed herself somewhat ill at ease, and he wondered if she had struck a bargain of some sort with her husband to protect her lover. Her unease caused John to look up at the walls around them; he half expected to see armed bowmen taking aim, but there were none. Still, nothing about this was quite right.

"The others, then, caught you up before you rode this far?"

"Oh, they've come and gone." Robyn didn't react, but John couldn't help glancing again at the stabled horses, a look she must have identified, because she added, "We gave them fresh horses back to Clipstone."

"The Keepers without you?" Disbelief dripped from the question. "That's positively *inaudita*, wouldn't you agree?"

"Yes. Certainly." John wondered what that exchange meant. It seemed to mean something to Robyn, though not to her. She continued, "Once they understood that Robert posed no threat to me and that I would remain to await you, my dear, they rode off. I told them to go. They should not be on the road at night. And it allows Adam an opportunity to lead." She lifted her arms. "You see? Robert has his pursuits, and I have mine." This last was barely shy of an invitation. Even he heard that, and found it odd, given how angry she had been with Robyn at the abbey. "But come, both of you, it's well past midday. You'll be hungry if you rode as hard from Retford as your horses indicate. Come meet the capricious Robert, fill your bellies, and spend the *night*. We'll return to Clipstone in the morning." She gestured for two of the serfs to come take the horses.

They handed off their horses to a bent-backed old man. Robyn lingered a moment. He insisted they collect their bows and other possessions.

"Oh, you've no need of all that," Isabella insisted.

Robyn replied that it was better to know they were at hand than not. "No telling who besides three pig farmers would like to skin your husband alive," he said. He belted his quiver and shouldered the empty mason's tool pouch. John grabbed his staff.

She laughed, but it was an uneven sound.

With everything to hand, they followed her through the gatehouse and up the steps to the keep.

Robert D'Everingham had a pitcher of wine brought into the hall. He was already drinking from a full goblet. He watched intently as they each accepted theirs and a servant poured for them. Isabella passed him to sit, and he reached out with one hand to grope her. She twisted away from his grasp and slapped his hand away. In that moment, Robyn looked to Little John and gave his head a small shake. John wasn't sure if it was a sign not to drink the wine or disgust with their host's rude behavior. D'Everingham laughed, while Isabella gave John and Robyn a look that seemed to say "What can I do? This is who he is."

They sat at a table that could have served ten. D'Everingham preferred to stand. He was slightly taller than Robyn and soft, a man who had never toiled in fields or fought in battles—not fat but someone who'd known much comfort. His curling hair was a blond so pale that it looked almost white, his beard a darker, straw color.

He walked around as he spoke, as if making a great speech. "My wife claims you're an astonishing bowman. Says you split another's arrow straight down the middle."

"Then she exaggerates my talents." Robyn set down his wine as if he'd just drunk from the goblet.

D'Everingham scrutinized Isabella. "Does she? Well, I'm not at all surprised. She exaggerates all sorts of things about me, as well. And you"—he turned to point at Little John—"I hear that you shot and killed some sort of creature—a *demon*, was it?" He swiveled for confirmation from his wife. "Yes, my old friend sheriff Passelewe of Nottingham claimed it was on the King's Great Way. Demon disguised as a bishop no less." This seemed to amuse him. "Hardly much difference there, really." He took a large drink of his wine. "Tell me, how did you recognize the . . . irregularity?" He bared his teeth in a grin.

It was evident that Robyn wanted to retrieve his bow from the chamber where they'd laid their things and murder the man. John paid that more heed as he answered. "I recognized nowt of the man, who were no man at all as it ended."

D'Everingham stared at him for a moment, then slapped his thigh, laughing harder. "So, for all you knew right then, you shot an actual bishop! Why, any other outcome, they'd have you drawn and quartered in Nottingham."

"Was jammy, aye."

"I'm sorry. Jammy?"

"He means he was lucky," Robyn explained.

To Little John it looked as if Lady Isabella also wanted her husband to vanish, no doubt so she could spend time with Robyn. He couldn't make out if she was playing some part to keep her husband at bay. She was definitely not acting like the Lady Isabella of yesterday.

Then two maidens arrived from the kitchen next door, carrying a board of sliced venison and large boule of bread, and bandy-legged D'Everingham wove his way back to the table. He set down his goblet, but then approached the nearest maid from behind. He took her by the hips and ground himself against her. As he turned the girl around to slobber a kiss in the vicinity of her mouth, Isabella made straight for him, passing by Robyn who, in that moment, leaned over and switched his goblet with D'Everingham's.

Even as Isabella reached her husband, he was clutching for the edge of the table. The girl had kneed him in the bollocks. John couldn't help guffawing. The girl ran from the room while D'Everingham, half doubled over, muttered painfully, "Feisty." No doubt there would be trouble for the girl, unless his lordship was so in his cups he wouldn't remember the specifics of this later. But the man righted himself and insisted, "Come on, come on. Food's near chilled being carried here from the kitchen." He swiped up Robyn's traded goblet and drank deeply. "Sit," he said, "and where's the sauce for the meat, Edme?" The remaining serving girl raced off to retrieve it.

Robyn pretended nothing out of the ordinary had happened, picking up the conversation as if they'd only paused momentarily. "So, Adam led the return to the King's Houses? I'm a little surprised."

"Why so?" Isabella answered. "He has witnessed enough of his father's *exemplary* behavior already." She cut D'Everingham a sharp look, but he was paying no attention. "There was nothing for him to learn here. He wants more authority. So I gave him some." She watched her husband shakily take another deep draught of wine as the girl Edme returned with whatever sauce had been prepared. She set it down on the corner of the long table and fled before D'Everingham even noticed.

Robyn said, "'Tis a wonder you have any servants at all."

"They are well compensated for his excesses."

"They must be quite wealthy."

Lady Isabella laughed.

Thirst got the better of John then. Robyn was drinking now, and he decided he would trust the wine, too. His host had drunk now from two different goblets and was still upright. He enjoyed a deep drink from his goblet, stopping only when the sediment rose to the top. Even so, it tasted sweet.

D'Everingham, overcoming his discomfort, stabbed at a slice of meat, and gnawed on it. He stared wickedly at John. "Jammy," he said, and shook his head, chuckling.

It was half an hour before he fell out of his chair. John thought his host had simply drunk too much wine until he stood to help Robyn lift the man back up, and the room began to echo strangely, the crackling of the small fire became very loud, and suddenly it was Robyn bracing him and saying, "Come on, John." They abandoned D'Everingham and Isabella to their servants. Robyn muttered some apology, and then they wobbled together from the great hall to the chamber Lady Isabella had shown them upon arrival. It seemed suddenly that he was lying down, no memory of passing through the doorway, and Robyn was saying, "It won't kill you, I think."

Then, oddest of all, Robyn fell down next to him, sound asleep.

"Sleep, sleep, sleep," said someone from the doorway who sounded a great deal like the lady herself. Obeying her command was the easiest thing in the world. The last sound he heard was the door closing.

XXXIII. In My Lady's Chamber

✠

"Sleep."

Thomas listened to Isabella Birkin's soothing voice. Not that it emanated from Isabella Birkin at all. If he'd had to guess, he would have submitted that it was the same Yvag who had befuddled him and tried to hand him over to Passelewe's guards in The Pilgrim, the one called Zhanedd. She had been attempting to gauge the real Isabella's relationship to him—probably had plucked images, memories from Isabella directly, the way she'd pulled them out of him in the cave—but in a hurry: She didn't know how angry Isabella was with him at the moment, and so had gotten much wrong. Her not knowing the reference to the word *inaudita* confirmed his doubts. Had Isabella become a skinwalker, she would not have gotten it all so wrong. But, then, he had all three *dights* at the moment and thus the upper hand. They weren't turning anybody just now. He wondered if the others had caught up with Isabella before she reached Laxton, or whether they, too, had endured a performance by D'Everingham and been made to down drugged wine. Either way, not that much time had passed, so presumably they were somewhere nearby. He hoped they were all still breathing. They couldn't have been interrogated yet.

Having cast her spell over him and put John to sleep, "Isabella" crept into the room. With one eye, he narrowly peered at her going through their belongings. She was quiet but methodical. She reached deep into his mason's bag, feeling all around inside it before returning it to its peg. Finally, she held his quiver, drew the arrows out, placed them on the low chair. Not letting himself smile, he watched her feel about in the quiver. Unsatisfied—as he'd known she would be—she replaced the arrows and hung the quiver off the chair arm again. If she wanted to search his clothing, to seek the pouch that hung from his neck, she was going to have to roll him over. He had a dagger at the ready if she did.

For a moment she stood still and stared at him and he kept his eyes shut, listening for the sound of cloth in motion. Pressure swept his way, within it the strong impression of the *dights*. Did his mind answer the call?

Finally, with a sigh of frustration, she closed the door and walked away. He let out a long, held breath and opened both eyes.

Soon enough she would discover that her husband was not simply drunk, but had swallowed whatever potion they had prepared for him and Little John. When she did, she would return, no doubt armed and ready to kill him.

It was time to hunt for the Keepers and Isabella. Other than as a gauge for how long D'Everingham himself might remain unconscious, snoring John was going to be useless. There was no time to waste. He rolled John on the bed, then pushed up the linen-wrapped straw and dug his arm deep beneath it until he touched the Yvag knight's armor. As no one had found it, he supposed he could assume that all the servants were human, no one glamoured, else they'd have gone pawing through everything in here while the lord and lady distracted them.

Out in the great hall, Isabella was directing four servants to carry D'Everingham to his chamber. Her voice fairly dripped with disgust.

Thomas peered around the doorway. Lifted up, D'Everingham tried unsuccessfully in passing to grab onto Isabella with his one free arm. She turned and slapped him. "Idiot!" she said. "And your like are supposed to be *so* superior. Get him out of my sight." He tried to latch onto one of the female servants tasked with dragging him off, but tawny-haired Edme took her cue from her mistress and swatted his hand away. Thomas hid behind the large open door and let them pass by. Small bursts of pressure in his head suggested that the Yvagvoja was attempting to complain to Isabella, perhaps to say that it had been poisoned. She ignored the communication, turned, and followed the servants out the far door.

As carefully as possible, Thomas searched through the main hall. He avoided the few servants who came and went, carrying off the food and drink that had been laid out for him and John.

With each turn of a handle he expected to find bodies, poisoned, drugged, or spelled into a trance. But there were none. The bed chambers all lay empty, unused, save for D'Everingham's room. His lecherous host lay alone and snoring within the draperies of his bed, and still fully dressed. No doubt nobody wanted to be near him.

The next chamber along he assumed would be Lady Isabella's. He had a dagger out as he cautiously opened the door, but that room, too, was empty, as if nobody used it.

There were no cells, and no cellar lay beneath the stones of Laxton Castle's ground floor. He wondered if there was some other hidden room, but then why would it have been built and where? The exterior shape of the hall conformed with the chambers he had already investigated.

He exited the main hall, and stood awhile at the top of the motte, from where he studied the various inhabitants below where most of the houses, buildings, and a small church stood, inside the second curtain wall along with the stable and paddock.

Nothing about the scene suggested anything odd, and he very much doubted D'Everingham shared any of his dealings with the villeins who farmed and worked Laxton.

However, the main hall itself was flanked by two smaller sets of buildings. Thomas glamoured himself as one of the men he saw below and walked around to the buildings on his right. He knew from the smell before he reached them that these were the kitchen and pantry houses, and behind them the adjacent buttery. Peering into each, he got some odd looks from the staff, including two of the women who had served in the great hall, but no one interfered with his search and he found no one. Nor in the well, where the elves seemed to like to dump their enemies.

He walked around the back of the hall to the single smaller version of it on the opposite side. Two stories like the main hall, and with two smaller mullioned windows in the front, echoing the larger ones in the hall.

He lifted the latch and pushed open the door.

The ground floor comprised just a single chamber, with a low ceiling of thick beams, and a stone floor again; there was an empty hearth, old tapestries and a few X-framed seats, a row of benches, and a small table. Lady Isabella's blue sleeveless surcoat and gown lay across the table. To his left, a stairway hugged the outer wall. Thomas crossed to it and followed the stairs up. As carefully as he tread, he didn't know these steps, so it was impossible to keep the stairs from creaking in places. At the top, the bare stone wall became paneling. Directly ahead stood a closed door. He paused to listen and caught the faintest hint of Yvag thrumming.

Delicately, he opened the door. It gave a loud creak.

In the center of the room, Isabella turned with a gasp and in the same moment dropped the large curtain around her bed that she'd been holding up. He glimpsed a limp hand before she stepped forward, capturing his attention. She was dressed in only her undertunic.

Her probing stabbed at him. Thomas could see that she wasn't pretending to be surprised. She'd really thought him laid out by the potion in the goblets. He closed the door behind him. The bed stood on a riser. Three sides of it were hidden by an elaborately carved set of screens. The posts almost reached the ceiling. There was a padded stool near its foot. A small writing table across the room, and a hearth with protruding and carved stone hood. In the hearth stood an incongruous well bucket with a ladle handle protruding from it. On the far side of the room, he thought something shifted in the shadows near the darkly beamed ceiling.

He smiled to Isabella. "Do you know, I've tried and tried, but I simply cannot find your foresters anywhere."

"Robyn, my heart. Whatever do you mean? I'm . . . I'm surprised—and delighted—that you found my own apartments. Why ever would you want the Keepers with us?" Even as she spoke she was trying to enchant him with a hummed note or two. It was hardly enough, no competition at all with Alderman Stroud's wordless tune long ago. She strolled away from the bed to her table.

"Tell me, did they catch up with Isabella before she arrived at Laxton, or were you forced to improvise when they interrupted your capturing her? And then we showed up. You didn't have time for a proper interrogation, not like Passelewe gave Little John."

"I told you," she replied, "they all rode off together."

"'Together' is a certainty. You haven't had time to deal with them one by one. But none of them 'rode off,' now, did they?" He gestured at the curtained bed. "Must have been difficult carting them all up here. So, tell me, was it the same elixir you used at The Pilgrim, or something different?"

Isabella's expression hardened. Her probing changed to images flung at him—of the weird ley where he'd seen Nicnevin's changeling babies before they were transmuted; the Queen carrying one into the pond for the ritual. He could not help recalling how he'd nearly drowned in that glowing pond before learning to breathe the lucent fluid. From fragments of her thought storm, he understood that she believed as Passelewe had that he must be one of them. He did not disabuse her of the idea. Better that than she learn who he truly was.

Instead he reacted to the images she invoked: "Why show me the Pool? Nicnevin isn't transmuting Keepers this week, is she?" He walked closer.

This close, she exuded lust like a perfume. Unlike her skinwalker husband, she controlled and directed that lust. She was very much like the Queen herself. But she was also frightened.

"Or was that your memory of when *you* were made? Yes, it's always there, isn't it? But I thought changelings forgot they'd ever been anything but Yvag. I met one who derided them all as inferiors, never for a moment considering he might be one himself."

She faltered then. She knew herself to be a changeling and under all of her cold and efficient achievement, she doubted herself. She fought for recognition. He read it as if it were written on her skin.

She redoubled her effort to wrap him in her desire. She shrugged and the undertunic fell around her feet. Naked, she faced him.

The lure of her compelled him, but he denied it. "You are not Isabella," he said.

She tilted her head, looking at him. "And you are not human. So." She shifted. Her body rippled and knotted, twisted and flexed. It lasted only a few moments but must have been painful to endure. He remembered reshaping all too vividly.

The form of Isabella Birkin was absorbed into the true insectoid form of the Yvag from The Pilgrim, her belly ribbed with yellowish muscle, rose sprinkled at her throat, arms ending in taloned fingertips. But above it all was the face of Innes; it was impossible not to see his sister in those greenish-gray features despite the spicules, the metallic hair, the hungry, golden eyes.

I am Zhanedd. Embrace me. Her desire was a rope around him. He must obey. Everyone obeyed. She smiled, baring her needle teeth.

He knew what she was expecting: another changeling like herself. He could only conclude that she believed him to be one of the rogue Yvags driven insane by the transmutation, that Taliesin had spoken of forever ago as his "mad companions." Her lust rolled over him, but he had been here before, with Nicnevin. He would not give in, but he let himself stumble closer as if she had him. She backed up to the bed.

Tell me now where you've hidden the dights. As she asked it, she turned away. Reached under the bed curtain.

She swung back quickly. He'd already closed the distance. Now he charged, rammed her with one shoulder, threw her against the curtained frame of her bed. The Yvag sword she'd just drawn leapt and stabbed into the wall across the room and back again. Splinters of paneling flew. Zhanedd struck her head on the thick bedpost and dropped to the floor. The sword fell beside her. Had he succumbed to her overtures, it would have plunged right through him. So much for giving in to any Yvag.

He knelt beside her. He ought to kill her with her own sword… Only, unconscious, she bore an even more uncanny resemblance to his sister. Finally what had been obvious even at The Pilgrim smothered his long-held desire for revenge.

This *was* Innes's child, the one the elves had snatched and replaced. There was no cause for her to maintain that face now: It was her own. Alderman Stroud had lied and claimed Innes had borne a son, but Innes had given birth to a daughter. He was certain of it, just as he was certain that he ought to kill her with that sword, but he could not make himself do it. At war with himself, a voice that once would have belonged to Alpin Waldroup, his mentor, warned him that no good came of showing mercy to an Yvag, while his own argued that there must be some part of his gentle sister in this changeling, and he might yet find it. Right now, however, he had no time.

He picked up the elves' elongating sword, stood up, and drew back the curtain. Four bodies lay across the bed. From behind it came an unholy shriek.

XXXIV. Zhanedd's Gambit

Three-quarters of the way to Laxton Castle and just as she was about to leave the King's Way, Will Scathelock, Adam, and Maurin Payne caught up with Isabella Birkin. Adam pulled up alongside her while there was still room, but she barely acknowledged him. She was pushing her horse, focusing on or lost in her fury with his father. Adam had no doubt that this time, when she confronted him, she would kill him. He thought he would not stand in her way if she did.

Then they were on the path home, and he had to drop back. They rode the remaining distance single file. The forest oaks gave way to a rolling landscape and the view of the low curtain-walled estate through the trees. Then they broke through the trees onto the grassy slopes, and the full view of the three different enclosing walls, with the bailey perched on top of the motte at the far end. Beholding it should have brought some sort of joy of homecoming, but Adam felt nothing but darkness and unease. At the same time, he caught sight, above the main gate, of a bird or maybe a bat. But bats didn't come out in daylight, did they? No, but they carried messages to the devil, and that made him think that his father must be home.

They rode through the first gate. The people working the land there paused to watch. A few removed their woven hats and waved them to Lady Isabella, but she acknowledged none of them. Adam did, in her place.

Through the second gate, and his mother barely slowed down until the last moment, then reined in suddenly and swung off her saddle, dropping to the ground. She must have been stiff after that hard ride, but she showed no sign of it.

Their old equerry came shuffling up to take the lathered horses, saying, "M'lady," and handing each horse in turn off to the stableboy.

At the same time one of the serving girls came down through the motte gate. She carried a bucket and ladle. It was the tawny-haired one, Edme, who had recently turned fourteen and who Adam knew had been hand-fast betrothed to the smith's son, who was a year younger than she.

She made a leg before Isabella and gave her the ladle, the first drink. Isabella paused to drink deeply of the well water. It must have calmed her a little. She turned to Adam and said, "Do not try to stop me."

He, accepting the refreshed ladle, said, "Would you like my assistance?" He drank his fill. The water was cold and wonderful.

"What? Invite my son to commit patricide?" She took off her riding glove and touched his cheek. "It's enough that you might have to watch me face execution later." Then she turned and marched off.

Edme carried the water to Will and Maurin in turn while Adam waited. Then, refreshed, they all followed after her. Maurin asked, "Would she really kill him?"

"I believe this time she might," he answered. "He's intruded into the unspoiled part of mother's life this time where he had no business."

Adam thanked Edme, and the girl followed them up the motte steps to the tight inner courtyard with its main hall and adjoining buildings. Isabella had no doubt entered the hall—at least Adam thought so until Edme, coming up behind, said, "Lady Isabella went into her house. I'm sure I saw."

"Thank you," he said. No doubt his mother was selecting a weapon of choice, maybe loading a crossbow. "We'll wait for her below, then," he said, or tried to. His mouth was suddenly inflexible. His fingers did not want to unlatch the door. They slid off it, and he found he couldn't raise them again. When he tried to turn around to view Will and Maurin, his legs gave out and he corkscrewed to the ground from where he watched the two Keepers topple after him.

Young Edme with her ladle was providing each of them another drink whether they wanted one or not. "Mustn't have you waking up on your journey," she said. And then it was his turn. He stared into her eyes and saw something there, an expression, a knowledge, that didn't belong to the girl at all.

His head lolled back, and he thought, *We're all poisoned.* He remembered nothing after that.

Thomas dodged back as a dragonfly-winged little fae hob came shooting around the bed curtains in Lady Isabella's chamber. It grabbed at his face and he ducked. It swung in a wide circle, screeched, and dove straight for him again. Already gripping the Yvag sword, he hardly gestured his hand before the blade sprang out and bisected the creature. It stabbed a ceiling beam, too, and came snapping back in an instant. The halves of the creature plopped onto the carpet. It oozed and melted into a puddle of goop. The jellylike viscera of the little monster were absorbed into the nacreous blade.

He turned back to the bed and drew the curtain all the way open. Lady Isabella, Adam, Maurin, and Will Scathelock lay there side by side. He thought they were dead, but when he tugged on Will's boot, the archer mumbled incoherently. They were alive.

He needed to get them away, but must first deal with Zhanedd.

Thomas grabbed hold of the bed curtain and tore it from its rings. After setting the sword aside, he took a dagger and ripped through the cloth, cutting three strips. He tied one around Zhanedd's ankles, with a second bound her hands behind her. The third he tied around her throat and then to a bedpost. It was as close as he could come to the way they'd hobbled Little John.

Satisfied with his handiwork, he stood, then pulled Isabella across the bed to himself. He drew her up, folded her over his shoulder, picked up the sword, and carried her from the room. Down the stairs and then out of the building. No one was nearby. He entered the main hall, and hurried over to the nearest bench, laying Isabella down upon it. He set the Yvag sword on the floor beside her. Then he turned and ran.

Back in her chamber, he grabbed Adam and carried him across to a different bench. A third trip delivered Will Scathelock into one of the leather chairs. It was at that point he worried that he needed to check on Little John and D'Everingham. He ran up the steps to the upper floor and down the hall to his chamber. There Little John slept on unharmed.

Thomas drew a dagger and ran back along the hall. Even as he caught sight of D'Everingham's door, a green light flickered beneath it.

Thomas charged, and flung the door open, ready to defend himself against Yvag knights. What he saw instead stunned him. The face of Zhanedd peered out from the remaining opening of an Yvag gate. Behind her was a wattle and daub wall—it might have been any house here or in a nearby settlement. She leered and said, "Thank you for our *teind*!" Then she sealed it the rest of the way up and was gone.

In terror, he ran back out and down the stairs.

Isabella, Adam, and Will all lay as he had left them on the benches there. What then...? "Oh, Christ," he said, "Maurin." He snatched up the sword and ran back to Isabella's house, taking the stairs two at a time. Her chamber door stood open. Inside was no one at all. The curtain that he'd torn up had been cut again, the pieces lying or dangling empty. He drew his ördstone and laid it on his palm, then slowly turned.

A blue line stretched out, and a ghostly circle formed in front of the large hearth. A ring had been opened in this chamber scant moments after he'd rescued the three Keepers.

He should have rejoiced that he'd rescued them, because there was no question but that the Yvags had entered the chamber for everyone. Zhanedd had gone to too much trouble for anything less. But he'd failed to get Maurin out, worried as he was about Little John. He couldn't be everywhere at once, no matter how hard he tried.

XXXV: Return to King's Houses

Within the hour, the three Keepers came around. Little John remained unconscious, but Thomas wouldn't leave him alone, else lose him, too. Carrying him was much more difficult than the other three. He dragged him down the stairs and propped him up at the bottom.

Once they were all situated, he hurried to the kitchen and requested the servants bring them some water.

When he returned, the first thing Isabella wanted to know was why Maurin wasn't with them. Thomas explained to them that the Yvag called Zhanedd had taken Maurin as a tithe to Hel.

Adam glared at him. "How do you know that?" he asked weakly.

Before he answered, the serving girl, Edme, arrived with a pitcher and cups. She went first to Adam and offered him a cup. He knocked it aside, which soaked Will, who fell out of his seat trying to get away from it.

Thomas took the water pitcher from the girl and set it down on an empty bench.

"Don't let her go," Adam said. "She's not what she seems. One of those *things*."

Thomas looked her over. Then he reached for her hand and held it. There was not the least hint that she was Yvag. "She's not," he said, and gestured for her to go. He picked up the pitcher again, sniffed the contents, swirled it around, then drank a cup. "Water's cold. Fresh." He offered the cup to Isabella. She looked darkly into his eyes as she accepted it. He asked, "What happened? Tell me everything."

She described their arrival, a false Edme who'd met them and how she'd given them a potion in the water she brought. Having climbed the steps up the motte, Isabella had suddenly felt dizzy and tried to reach her private chambers. The others had been tricked the same way.

"John and I were greeted by a false Isabella."

"False Isabella?" Isabella repeated, then said, "Oh."

"She and your husband put on quite the performance for us. They tried to dose us with the same potion, I think. In our wine. John's thirst got the better of him, which is why he's still asleep, but I switched mine with D'Everingham's drink."

"If he's asleep upstairs, I want to kill him before he wakes."

"He is a skinwalker, for certain. I think this was all about capturing you," he told her. "But he's gone, hauled through an Yvag gate by the one that impersonated you."

For a moment she remained silent. Then she said, "You promised to catch us up at Retford." Her tone accused him.

"And lucky for us all that I didn't, or arriving together, we would surely have succumbed to the same treachery. I wouldn't have known the serving girl at all, but I recognized that you weren't you. The Yvag was the same one as at The Pilgrim, that wanted to hand me over to Passelewe. She's the one who named you as a target of one of the spinners. Also, she knew nothing of the word *inaudita*."

The word drew her glance. He smiled, but it was not returned.

Across the room, Little John yawned, which sounded more like a bear than anything human. Thomas walked over and offered him a hand to pull him up. "How did you sleep?"

"Woodwose! Was it you set me here or did I walk?"

"I put you here."

"Good job, then. For how long have I slept?"

"Hours. It was intended to be your final sleep, too."

John, spying Isabella watching him, said, "Your 'usband imports a mingin' wine. Speakin' of, where would our host be lurking? I have an urge t' thank him proper for 'is hospitality."

"Gone, I'm afraid," said Thomas.

"So what's our plan now, then? Back to King's Houses?"

Across the room, Lady Isabella said, "We who were almost taken by demons would like a meal first."

John leaned around him and waggled his fingers in greeting.

Thomas concentrated on his boot. "All right. A meal and then we go. We'll be riding at night, though."

"Don' get dark nar till compline."

Isabella went to the kitchen with instructions. The others climbed the stairs up to the dining hall, at which point Thomas excused himself and returned to the dark room where he and Little John had collapsed. His empty toolbag still hung on a peg there, and he grabbed it in passing.

Then, standing in the center of the room, he pulled up the pouch around his neck and drew the ördstone it contained. He closed his eyes to picture the interior of the King's Houses chantry, the pews, the ornate arch fronting the altar, the candlesticks and cross. Eyes closed, he cut the air.

When he looked again, there was the chantry before him, the shadowy chapel space empty.

He stepped through the ring, crossed past the pews, and knelt before the altar. Lifting the cloth, he felt for and removed all three dights. He dropped them into the bag, smoothed the cloth back into place, and stepped back through the ring. He sealed up the gate and returned the stone to its pouch. Hung the mason's bag on its peg again. The room had been searched, the bag found to be empty. It seemed the safest place for them. At that moment John entered.

"I wondered where ye'd gone," he said.

For an instant Thomas scrutinized and listened to him. Zhanedd might impersonate someone other than Isabella, and it would be foolish to think the creature would only don the guise of women. Kunastur had portrayed both Passelewe and Mary of Clipstone. It was Thomas who thought of Zhanedd as "she" because of the striking resemblance to Innes. Who knew how many others she'd been and of what sex? In any case, there was no hint of oddness to John's manner. He was the very essence of John. Doubtful anybody could mimic that. Still, the first rule now in every encounter must be to trust no one to be as they appeared.

He said, "I just recovered the—what does Will call them? The *spinners*. A good name for them."

Little John, with a worried look, said, "Tha had 'em here all this time?"

"No, hidden elsewhere. I worried the false Isabella or her husband would find them if I brought them in that old bag with us. She would have, as it happens."

"Too much blood's shed over them things already. I wish we could smash 'em."

"That is the truth." Isabella and Sheriff Orrels, too, had called them *spinners*. It felt right. What was *"dight"* to anyone but an Yvag, after all. "And so you and I will know they're back in our possession, but let's not mention it to the Keepers. Adam would certainly do something foolish if he knew."

"Oh, aye. He's a narky one, all right."

Thomas tied up the mason's bag again. Slung over his shoulder, it looked as empty as before. "Now I'm ready to tackle that meal."

"That's good, for I came to tell they've got venison pie and rabbit in gravy for tha."

Just hearing the words caused his stomach to rumble. "Lead the way," he said and followed John out.

It was twilight when they arrived at the King's Houses again. The two Waits they'd left there had returned to Nottingham. The houses were empty.

Isabella hadn't spoken to him for most of the ride, furious over the loss of Maurin. He couldn't disagree with her—in thinking they were coming for Little John, he'd all but given Maurin to Zhanedd. More than that, in Barnsdale he and John had disrupted the Yvags' capture of a *teind*, so it was doubly on his head that the boy had been sacrificed.

Isabella wanted to go after D'Everingham. Upon departing, they'd found his horse gone from the stable. Thomas concluded that Zhanedd had simply opened a gate down to one of the eighteen houses inside the largest curtain wall of Laxton. That was in keeping with his as-yet-unproven notion that skinwalkers could not be hauled off to Ailfion when their host was here, not without perishing. A local gate, though, appeared to be a different matter.

Isabella said, "I have a fair notion of where he would run, and other men who would side with him. But what do I do when I catch up to him? It would be my word against his. Even if I could get him arrested—"

Thomas replied, "You'd have to kill him. There's no way to separate him and the Yvag that's taken up residence in him, no unbinding I know of that doesn't destroy the host. And he will come back after you until he has you."

Her mouth compressed into a thin line. "I suspected as much."

"The situation will never return to how it was before the Yvag invaded your life."

"It's *you* invaded our lives," Adam snarled.

"Adam!" Isabella snapped.

"No, he's right," he said. "Under any other circumstances, we would have said a few words at The Pilgrim and gone our separate ways. Might have met in Barnsdale, but we will never know. And if I could point the elven, the demons, in some direction other than yours, I would do so gladly. But too well do I know them and they will not let you be until they have what it is they want of you."

She said, "And that's me."

"One of the dights, the spinners as you call them, was designed with you as the target. One for the bishop of Leicester. One for Simon de Montfort. I've no idea what schemes they have for the other two, but you're the Warden of the Keepers of Sherwood. It's a position of influence. I think they turned your husband in the mistaken notion that your title would go to him. They misjudged the line of succession, and now they need to correct that error."

"So they're coming after us again."

"You today, and tomorrow assuredly Adam. Of that much I'm sure."

"And what of you? What do *you* want out of this? I know you want something," she insisted.

Thomas looked to John, who shrugged. This wasn't his argument. Thomas said, "When this all began—when Robert Hodde died in my hut—I would have told you that all I wanted was to continue to be left alone in Barnsdale."

"But no longer?" asked Isabella.

"Now I see that, like it or not, I'm a cumber to their schemes. If I go back to living in the forest again, a hermit, they will roll right over everyone and everything else hereabout like some sort of fearsome siege engine. They become *inaudita* again, something unheard of, with no one paying any attention, no one recognizing the pattern of their cruelties and manipulations. They've only come out because of the spinners, which must be terribly precious. My time for withdrawal from the world because of what was done to me is over. You're both welcome to be furious with me—you'll be no more angry than I am with myself. Blame me for everything you care to, but don't allow that fury to blind you to what the elven are doing and who it is they're replacing."

Will Scathelock had sat silently through the arguing. He suddenly piped up. "Fine. What do we do about that?"

"We need to recruit the outlaws of Sherwood Forest and beyond to our cause."

Isabella spluttered, "You what? You want me to pardon the very people I'm obliged to arrest and punish under forest law? Criminals? They will get their way, your demons, if I do that."

"Listen to me. You and they disagree on how the resources of Sherwood and Nottinghamshire should be used. Some of them are merciless bastards, no question. But many are just hungry and providing as they can."

She started to respond hotly. He held up one hand to stop her.

"I'm not trying to undermine you. I'm saying just that this is their land as it is yours. You're willing to protect it, to fight for it. I'd argue they'll do the same. They're the ones under direct assault by these creatures, after all. Their bodies adorn the wheels along the King's Way. That's another burden on me. They're dying because I choose to protect you in thwarting the plans of the Yvag. So, we have a common enemy. And not just the outlaws. The Waits, even Orrels and any other local sheriffs if they aren't skinwalkers already. Especially those with martial training." He wondered again if Sir Richard was still about somewhere and if they could locate him.

"You make it sound like a war," she said.

"Not like a war. It *is* a war." Before mother or son could respond, he said, "And as part of that war, tonight Will and I will be in the woods north of Clipstone."

"We will?" replied Scathelock.

"These rings, these gates, seem to open near habitation, including the outlaw camps in and around Sherwood. There happens to be such a camp above Clipstone that outlaw bands sometimes use—"

"Aw, Robyn, she don't need to know that," Little John complained.

Thomas smiled impishly. "She already knows it, John."

John looked at Isabella in some surprise. She nodded to him, and he frowned.

"One thing I observed that night before we traveled to Rufford Abbey, was that numerous of the rings we saw seemed to be lighting up in the vicinity of that camp. I want to go there. And I don't want to waste another night."

"But me and not Little John?" Scathelock said.

"You, my friend, are likely the best bowman amongst us. If the situation required close combat with a quarterstaff, I would pick John for this. He shoots well, too, but you and I are going to kick a hornet's nest, and while we're kicking I want him here with Lady Isabella and Adam in case some of the hornets get in here. That's more likely to require his staff."

"So, we're to do what, guard an outlaw encampment?"

Thomas replied, "No, Will. Tonight you and I are going to show the Yvags how costly it is to open these gates any longer. But because you'll be recognized as a member of the Keepers, I need to have John accompany me to the camp first."

In darkness, Thomas and Little John arrived outside the outlaw camp north of Clipstone. They had come to it alone, in case the encampment was currently occupied. John was the perfect envoy for encountering other outlaws here.

For years an impenetrable wall of brambles had been encouraged to grow around it through which nothing could be seen. But the smell of meat cooking on a spit rode on the air, and that told them the camp was inhabited.

They came to the entrance, marked by three stones. John did the honors, carefully reaching into a section of the berry-dotted leaves and pulling it out to reveal a low tunnel through the briary growth. They ducked into it, and John drew the clump back into place behind them. As the two of them stood upright again, they found themselves facing three drawn bows. These lowered almost immediately at the sight of Little John. Thomas in Hodde's Lincoln green and the bycocket hat was still a stranger to them.

"Fouke!" cried Little John, and he embraced the elder of the two men and one woman. He made introductions between "Robyn" and

Fouke III, Fouke's son, and Sybil, Fouke's wife. Thomas knew of Fouke by name but not of his family.

Their bedrolls were laid out beneath the broad canopy of a wych elm and away from the small fire where a shoulder of meat rode suspended upon a trio of skewers, its fat hissing into the flames below. The family invited the two of them to share the meal. The meat was from a hog they'd found killed beside its herder, who'd been left dangling from a breaking wheel. "Pig was going t' go to waste otherwise," Fouke explained. While they politely refused the food, it seemed like a perfect introduction to the subject at hand.

"We've been traveling with some foresters," Thomas said.

Fouke and his son looked about themselves nervously.

"Don't worry, we're not inviting them in. We've all bigger game to hunt—namely, the creatures who hung that poor herder up like so many others on wheels all over Sherwood."

"We've seen 'em. Been careful, have we, settling in each night to one of the camps before dark when them green circles appear. Lots'a others hereabouts all scared out of their wits. Some vills attacked, and camps like this one tore up. We heard de Cuckney's abbey were molested, too."

Thomas agreed. "They do seem to be everywhere. It's my hope to put an end to these night terrors by facing them down."

"Knight terrors is right. Knights come out of 'em, only to my thinking not knights at all."

"It's elves," Little John said matter-of-factly.

Sybil Fouke looked between them. "I thought elves were little stubby folk," she said.

"They'll be delighted to hear that," said Thomas. "Believe me, they're as tall as you or I."

"Elves." Fouke scratched at his beard. "Always been dark and mysterious, ain't they? So why are they comin' out in the open here all of a sudden?"

Before Thomas could answer, John said, "Robbie and me held one of them up on the King's Way. They killed young Much."

"Aw, that simple lad," said Mrs. Fouke, and she hugged her son to her. He looked appropriately embarrassed.

Fouke clicked his tongue. "It's what comes to us all finally, I suppose."

Thomas paused to let that sentiment fade away. "If you're traveling anywhere tomorrow, spread the word, too, invite others to join us at King's Houses or even to take heed of where these green fires appear and stop the elves on their own. We run and hide, they'll keep coming until they've emptied the forest."

"Halfway to doing that already, they are."

"Which is why we need to stop them now."

"Well, count on us to spread the word," Fouke assured them. "Though to take on your elves, I would like the company of a small army."

"So would we," Thomas agreed. "Hence, the invitation." He clasped their hands, while John hugged both of the Foukes and shook hands with the son. Then the two of them left the family to their meal. They replaced the brambles behind them.

On the way back to the Keepers, John asked, "If we're not askin' them to fight alongside you tonight, why'd we visit them?"

"Mainly to make sure they don't respond to whatever is about to happen by coming out in the dark and shooting me and Will."

John considered that for a moment, then said, "Good idea."

XXXVI: Closing a Gate

"I still don't understand," said Will Scathelock. "How do we know where this ring will appear?" In the dark, the outlaw camp of the Foukes lay a short distance behind them. The cooked pork scent still lingered.

Thomas paused to draw the pouch from around his neck. He took out the ördstone. "This will tell us." Its blue gems glittered, their light edging Will, glistening in his wide eyes. "At least, I hope so. In Barnsdale Wood it led us straight to a spot John had seen. Let's see how it works here. If they haven't given up their terrorizing, it shouldn't be long now."

Will still stared, goggle-eyed. "What is that?"

"It's called an ördstone. It's how the Yvag slice open our world and step through from theirs." He laid the stone on his palm, then slowly swept his arm across his body. At three different points in the arc, the stone emitted a whisper of a filament. The first and the third were insubstantial as smoke and extended farther than they could see among the trees. The middle line of gossamer ran straight to a point not far from them. The blue line there appeared to spread out like a spiderweb or a ball of mist, its surface rippling, pulsing.

"That is where the nearest gate will open. I suspect, should we follow the other two lines, they'd lead us to two others more distant. Let's hope this one opens first."

"You know, when you speak of their world, these elves, you're like someone sharing stories of the Sidhe or the Fomóire."

Thomas closed his hand over the stone and dropped it back into the pouch. "I imagine those stories are all about these same creatures. The stone can cut an opening in the side of a hill or in the air—anywhere you like really—but it seems that spots where their gates open repeatedly become weaker, like a door whose hinges are wearing out."

As he spoke he took his bow in hand and drew three arrows. Will grabbed his bow and laid an arrow across it.

"There's a tree just there you can stand behind." He took a few steps away until he was standing behind a bush that came up above his waist. "Two things to remember. First, their armor can be almost impervious to our arrows. It offers small targets so try to aim for points where they aren't covered."

"And the other?"

"When they step across, some of them will likely have those clever swords of theirs, so be prepared to dive aside if they point anything at you. For all we know, those blades can pass right through trees."

"You might have told me all that earlier so I could say no!"

Even as he objected, a spot in the darkness flared bright green, so bright it was painful to look at. The spot sank toward the ground on a diagonal, leaving behind it a duller green line that unfolded into two, curving, as the spot reached the ground, into a large circle that simply hovered in the air.

Thomas drew his bow. "Let them come all the way out," he whispered.

Two foot soldiers emerged, their black articulated armor reflecting the green fire and the reddish darkness at their backs. Behind them, another two knights on black steeds were visible.

The first rider came out of the ring.

"Now," Thomas said, and let fly with his first arrow. He struck the knight in the helm. The arrow stuck partway. The material flexed and withdrew, but with the arrow attached, its point cutting a line straight back over the creature's skull. Black blood flowed in a sheet down its face. It wiped fiercely at the blood and grabbed for its sword.

Will's arrow had hit its mark, puncturing a foot soldier's throat. That knight stumbled back into the ring, hung for a moment upon the threshold, and then fell backward into the red-eyed black beast behind it, which stopped to let the body fall before proceeding around it. Thomas shot a second arrow at the remaining foot soldier.

It went straight through its silvery white hair, penetrating from side to side. The Yvag dropped. Will fired at the second mounted knight, flummoxed when his arrow hit the threshold and seemed to hover in the air a moment before flying on. The knight caught it in one gloved hand, and kicked its mount into a gallop, charging. It flung the arrow away and reached for a sword at its hip. It did not seem to recognize that there were two enemies aimed at it.

Thomas tracked it carefully, and as the knight aimed the sword and Will dove behind the tree, Thomas shot the knight through the skull. The punch of the arrow knocked the creature sideways out of its saddle. The sword blade jumped, striking nothing before it returned, by which time it was falling from the knight's grasp. The charging beast slammed its rider against the tree behind which Will crouched. The knight landed so hard that the ground seemed to shiver.

There was movement inside the gate. Another figure in black ran forward, knelt, and hastily sealed up the ring. Thomas watched in silence. The Yvag's abandoned black mount stood as still as a statue, its form skeletal and only suggestive of a horse. The red eyes focused on Thomas. He drew his ördstone again to let the blue jewels guide him in the darkness. The gossamer line shot out into the depths of the woods again, but he wasn't interested now in chasing the openings. He knelt beside the slain knight, and dug around in its flexible armor until he found its ördstone. As Will walked over, he held it out. "Here," he said. "With this you can control that beast as well as cut open the world."

Scathelock eyed the monster askance. "Why would I ever want to do either?"

"Point taken," he answered, and withdrew the offered stone.

"I wouldn't mind a suit of that armor, though."

Without a word, Thomas rolled the body over and began stripping the flexible material off the Yvag. Will knelt to assist, but then sat back on his haunches as more and more of the creature's physiognomy was exposed.

"Gills like some giant fish? Talons. And those legs—it looks as if it could spring into a treetop. The armor makes them all seem—what should I say?—normal."

"They are anything but normal." Thomas handed the armor to Will, who expressed amazement at its lightness.

They could climb up on the beast and pursue the other openings hinted at by the ördstone, or just take the mount back to the paddock. Thomas recalled the one he'd ridden out of Ailfion upon his first escape. It had proved to be surprisingly tractable. In the end he'd sent it through the Old Melrose gate to the elves before departing Ercildoun. Perhaps he should do the same with this one. An abandoned riderless steed certainly sent a message. For now, he concentrated, and the beast became a white stallion. Will Scathelock gasped.

By the lights of the ördstone, Thomas walked around, collecting his arrows that had remained on this side of the gate. He would need to acquire more of them soon. He wondered if there might be a fletcher in Clipstone or Edwinstowe. Otherwise, he must pay a visit to Mansfield. The need for arrows was about to become pressing.

With the Yvag sword, he decapitated each gray body. None of these were coming back to life to torture and kill someone else. He collected the ördstones of each as well, intending to sink them all in the pond.

From the armor of another corpse, he removed a sheathed dagger and gave that to Will Scathelock, laid the armor across the beast's saddle. "For that you might find a use," he said. "Especially as it clips into the armor."

Will accepted it without comment.

They walked the riderless beast back through the woods. He thought he glimpsed Fouke III standing very still against the brambles and watching as they passed by. He suspected the lad had witnessed a good part of the fight. Whether or not the Foukes would join their cause, he would have to wait and see.

XXXVII: A Threat
to Little John

Thomas and Will returned to the King's Houses to find that Sehild had brought them all a late meal of fried pork pies and bean tarts. The two of them sat at table and greedily consumed the small pies and tarts, and drank good ale. The other three had already indulged. Little John was enjoying his ale while watching Isabella Birkin and her son. No one showed any inclination to leave the Great Hall, even after hearing of Thomas and Will's rout of the demon knights. Will showed off the pooled material of the Yvag suit of armor. When Adam looked up, envious, Thomas handed him the second suit he'd collected.

Thomas suggested they would want to repeat their ambush at the other two identified gates and send out more archers to confront others, creating (he hoped) a fear of opening the way from Yvagddu to Sherwood at all. "With luck, we'll soon attract more bowmen and be able to compel them not even to try and come through. And this will all stop."

"Yes, but by suspending forest law," replied Isabella.

Thomas picked up his ale and walked to where she sat nearer the fire. "Forest law is objectionable," he said as he sat down. "Preserves of deer and fowl for royalty only, who only come here when they remember to make use of any of it. You said yourself that no one has used this estate or the deer preserve in so long that the caretaker's died and not been replaced. All while people go hungry."

"It is the rule of law."

"Then the law is inadequate."

Adam, perhaps fed up with the conversation but more likely eager to try on the elven armor, got up and left. John followed him, leaving Thomas to look after Isabella. Will Scathelock arose then before he could be drawn into the debate. He bid them a good night and departed.

Isabella sat and studied him again, a disposition she seemed to be perfecting. He sat uncomfortably under the scrutiny but made no further argument regarding forest law. Finally, she asked, "What is the truth of you, Robyn?"

Caught off guard, he didn't know what to say in reply.

She continued, ticking off each point as she made it. "You know who the spinners have been made for. You know the workings of them as well as the elves do, and you say you saw your wife cored out by one. You descended through Nottingham castle rock with the ease of someone who can shift their shape at will—and I suspect that's true, isn't it? You know things about these demons—these elves—that no one else knows. In fact, you know too much about too much. So, I ask again, what is the truth of Robyn Hoode?"

He had to smile—she'd been carefully observing and assessing everything that had happened. "The truth is," he said carefully, "there is no truth to Robyn Hoode. As I said before, you'd be as accurate calling me Robyn Goodfellow."

"You're a *puca*, then." She stared. "Battling elves?"

"That's as near accurate as any other story you might concoct."

She shook her head, dismissing all nonsense. "All right, *puca*. Where do you come from? When were you born?"

He ignored the first question. "I was born in the Year of Our Lord 1121."

She laughed. "That's impossible."

"Everything about my life is impossible. You want the truth of Robyn Hoode, you'll first have to embrace that." And then he told her a version of his story just to show her how impossible. He left out where it took place, left out Janet and Morven, said only that the elves had tormented his whole family while he served as a soldier and he had decided to put an end to them. He told her what the gleaming city of Ailfion was like, how time was somehow unhinged there and that twenty years could pass in a matter of weeks or months, he couldn't be sure.

When he was done, they sat without saying anything for some time. Then as a coda to his story, he added, "That's how I know the Yvags won't stop coming after you so long as they can find you. You and Adam both, I fear. They want someone to rewrite some part of forest law for them, perhaps to give them control of Lincolnshire and Derbyshire. Somewhere lies a plot involving de Montfort and the bishop."

She said, "So in the end this all boils down to a grab for power."

"The core of everything they do, yes." He anticipated more questions from her.

Instead, abruptly, she stood up. "Upon that, let us retire. You've given me much to think about, not to mention impossible visions of spires that stretch to the stars." He got up with her. Stern in demeanor, she said, "I want to believe you, and to embrace your tale, I do. But there is much in it that remains *inaudita*. Perhaps once all of these threads are knit into a whole, I will see the picture and understand. Perhaps then we will know each other again."

She turned and walked away.

Left to interpret that, Thomas retired to his own chamber, pulled off his clothing down to his braes, and collapsed on the bed. He couldn't very well blame Isabella for keeping him at a distance now. At least, he thought, she wasn't furious with him.

Pounding at the door awoke him, and a voice calling out, "Robyn, it is Isabella!"

Thomas rolled off the bed and answered the door.

It was indeed Isabella. The nearby chamber doors opened. Will and Adam peered out. She said, "Little John has ridden off. One of the serving staff came and woke me just now." The woman in fact stood in the shadows behind her looking distraught. He thought it was the woman in charge of the kitchen, Sehild.

"What's caused this?"

"A body has appeared. At the gatehouse."

Thomas turned to grab his clothes, and that was when he saw that the flap of the mason's bag had been untied. He reached in but knew already the *dights* were gone, stolen while he slept. Hastily he pulled on the Lincoln green surcoat and leggings, and bolted from the room.

Across the hall, down the steps and outside, he ran, all the while thinking how John must have taken off in pursuit of whoever stole them. *Fool*, he called himself, to think that just because Zhanedd had searched and found nothing, they wouldn't look there again. The Yvags desperately wanted those spinners.

Beyond the paddock, the gatehouse stood like the remains of a fortress wall built above the outer ditch. Running for it, he took in everything: the black Yvag beast in the stable still, motionless but tracking him, or more likely his ördstone; in the archway of the gatehouse, the King's Houses equerry, Edrick, standing over a body; no one else in sight. Even at a distance, he could see that it wasn't Little John's body. Closer, it became a young man, no more than fifteen at a guess. From the look of it he'd been run through with one of those terrible swords.

Edrick began explaining as Thomas drew near. "Don't know when nor how this one showed up, good sir, but wasn't here before this dawn."

These details only reinforced the idea that John was in pursuit of the thief. Maybe there had been more than one—but John wouldn't have wielded one of those swords, wouldn't have touched it. Who—

"Beggin' yer pardon, good sir, whoever left him left this with him." Edrick drew from his tunic a crumpled piece of parchment and gave it to Thomas. It read:

> To Little John,
>   Your brother from Palavia Parva sends this greeting to you via his eldest.
>   Return us the dights or we shall take another of his family— one for each day until you do.

"But the writing would have meant nothing to John," he said, and held the parchment up. "Did you read it to him?"

Edrick shrank a little bit. "I confess, good sir, that I did. I did not understand all of the words, but enough of them. The mistress of the kitchen has long been trying to teach me how to read, mostly Latin. This man, John, could not but squint at it. I'd no presentiment what I was about to say, how terrible the news."

By then Will and Adam had arrived. Both stared at the dead boy. Isabella, roused last of all, was just coming along the path.

Thomas handed the scrap of parchment to Will. He turned for the stable. As he crossed the paddock, he saw that John's piebald mare was absent. He saddled the Yvag beast and led it out of the paddock.

"Will," he told Scathelock, "I don't want to do this but no one else here has a chance of stopping Little John. If he gives up the *dights*, the Yvags will surely destroy Lady Isabella. You and Adam must keep to her side at all times, let no one near her, not even those you think you know."

"I swear it, Robyn," Will answered.

"I as well!" added Adam.

"You'll swear what?" asked Isabella. Then she saw the body and gasped.

Thomas didn't stay to hear them answer. He kicked the beast into a gallop, and in moments was beyond Clipstone and on his way to Barnsdale.

The vill of Palavia Parva was on the far side of that wood, not far from The Saylis. John had spoken of both places. If only Thomas had visited it, he could conjure its location.... Abruptly, he tugged on the reins.

Maybe he didn't have to. He didn't need to arrive at the destination; he needed only to get ahead of Little John.

He climbed down from the Yvag beast.

XXXVIII. Spinners

The question was where exactly Little John would pass by. Sherwood and Barnsdale were full of footpaths and trails, many known exclusively to outlaws. John would know more of them than he did. Robert Hodde was buried, and it seemed unlikely he would ride near his hermit's hut and the grave, and even less so that he would go near Nicnevin's gate. But there was a reasonable destination on his route.

Thomas closed his eyes. He imagined he stood in the shadow of the immense limewood tree he'd climbed only days ago though it felt like an ancient memory now, and as he did, he recalled the riddle he'd babbled long ago in the presence of Robert Hodde:

A parting of ways,
The band dissolves.
Before is met a new friend,
The survivor to the Great Limewood will be summoned.

Well, he'd thought he understood it, but what if he'd got it all wrong the first time? Or what if the riddle could mean two things? Who said the nonsensical byproducts of these fits only applied to a single situation? The citizens of Ercildoun certainly thought they could recast his riddles to align with any event they imagined. Why couldn't he?

This was a parting of ways; John had grabbed the spinners and ridden off on his own. The dissolved band could be the Waits—they had returned to Nottingham—or the Keepers or even Hodde's original band of outlaws. He'd thought Sir Richard to be the new friend, but what if that referred to Lady Isabella herself? Then Little John would be the survivor—certainly he was the last remaining member of Robert Hodde's little band. That left the question of how to summon him to the Great Limewood tree. But even as he climbed up on the beast, he knew the answer to that, too. That left only the question of how to stop him from giving up the *dights* and endangering Isabella and Adam. He must capture John's attention before he could capture John.

He withdrew his ördstone from its pouch, and focused again on Hodde's old camp.

Everyone else seemed to have some critical task to perform. With Robyn and John gone for an indefinite period, Isabella Birkin's tasks included overseeing whatever needed doing in the King's Houses, riding the adjoining park to tally the number of deer in it, and looking for any signs of poaching or illegal clearing of timber in the park. She had plenty to do. She did not like being someone else's task.

All morning Will and Adam followed her everywhere as if she cast two shadows. She couldn't so much as walk to the stable without the both of them jumping up and joining her, silent and ever-vigilant. They would not let her be, and she cut short her circuit of the deer park and returned to the houses early.

When Sehild came up the stairs with a supper for her, Will met her at the ready, his bow drawn, which caused her nearly to drop the wicker tray she carried. Even after Isabella said, "It's only Sehild," Will kept her in his sights. Not until she withdrew did he put away the arrow. Meanwhile, Adam was sampling the food and drink to make certain it wasn't poisoned. And if it was? What then? Her son would die protecting her? She didn't want that.

Finally, she put down her spoon and said, "Enough. Robyn's gone to retrieve the spinners. The demons don't have them, so they aren't going to harm me. Honestly, you two, how many outlaws have we chased down and arrested together? You never worried about me then or if you did, you had the good manners to keep it from me. I am quite capable of looking after myself. Which of us brought down a demon right out there with a crossbow?"

Will folded his arms in silence.

Adam said, "Robyn told us to stay by your side and to trust no one."

Isabella frowned. "'Robyn told us.' You sound like a child, my son. Before this turn of events I know you were both planning to ride to Nottingham and get as many of the Waits as possible to join us here so we can close all of these gates the demons open, and put an end to their incursion once and for all. The sooner that's done, the better. Why don't you go off and do that?"

"But we'd be leaving you alone," said her son.

"You would also be leading the devils a chase through the forest. They might actually pursue you and let me be. Besides, Nottingham is so much closer than Barnsdale, you could ride there and back before Robyn returns."

"You could ride with us," suggested Will.

"I could not."

It was clear they wouldn't leave her unattended no matter what she said, and finally in frustration, she got up and told them, "Figure out what you're going to do. I'm going to walk the perimeter as I've done a hundred times or more." They both made to accompany her. "No," she said. She drew her long dagger. "I'm armed and perfectly safe until Robyn comes back with the spinners. No one is rewriting forest law today. I'll only be out of your sight a half hour."

She left them in the Great Hall and exited beside the recently rebuilt king and queen's chambers, past the currently idle "king's kitchen" with its clay and straw daub walls, and walked toward the main gate. From there she followed the palisade and ditch around to the Great Pond. It gave her time to think.

What was she going to do about Adam? How could she propose to kill D'Everingham and explain it to him? "You watch, he's going to melt like Passelewe"? That should be the case, knowing what she did of him. But it was still his father, whether demon, monster, or awful man. She could easily go to the gallows for her actions no matter what he was. In Adam's position, she would probably step in, or try to, just as she was proposing to interfere with her husband's plot to murder her and her son, none of which she could prove at the moment but all of which she believed. The body of that boy in the gatehouse, now laid out in one of the stable stalls, only reinforced her notion of the cold-bloodedness of these creatures and, by extension, her husband.

And then there was Robyn. What was she to make of him? A *puca* who'd lived a hundred years? It was ridiculous and she knew he wasn't telling the truth about himself. So many questions that he simply flowed around, giving answers that answered for nothing. Yet, he was loyal to his friends—to the outlaw Little John as much as anyone. He didn't seem to care whether any of these outlaws had broken the law—she supposed because many of those who made or upheld the laws seemed to be themselves possessed—Passelewe, her husband, the bishop of Doncaster. She could not deny the unnaturalness of them. This loyal Robyn seemed alternately merciless and gentle, forward and shy, forgiving of almost anyone, but also naive. Didn't he understand that without forest law, the people in the towns and vills and manors would strip the forests of every tree, every deer and boar? People were not thoughtful, and some form of order must be maintained. *Inaudita*, indeed. What would Gervase of Tilbury have made of him?

Along the length of the Great Pond, with the terraced garden and fruit trees on her left, she strolled as she watched the fisher wading in with his net. No doubt he was catching tonight's dinner. He saw her and gave a cursory wave, then went back to seeing what he'd caught.

Coming full circle, she returned to the paddock, passing the smaller Queen's Hall and kitchen, and beyond it the tiny, single-story apartment known as Rosamund's Chamber, built apparently for King Henry's mistress, Rosamund Clifford. Odd, however—the door to Rosamund's Chamber stood open. She approached it cautiously. She'd stayed in there a few times, back when Adam was a baby, so that he would not keep other foresters awake if he wailed at night. It was a dark, warm house in the winter, but rarely put to use.

Isabella drew her dagger and stepped across the threshold.

The bed, the bench and table stood empty and unused, the room deserted, musty. Then why?

There came a sting on the back of her neck. Isabella slapped at it and swung about, ready to thrust with her dagger at some invisible source, but already the venom in that sting was locking her muscles. Her thrust died, the tip of the dagger barely poking something solid but unseen. A hand gently removed the dagger from her grasp. The figure seemed to step out of nowhere, out of the room itself. Glamoured to the shadows of the room. She understood now.

Isabella stared into a perfect copy of her own face.

"Zhanedd," she guessed. The word sounded garbled in her mouth. The venom made it difficult to speak.

The Yvag bowed theatrically, smiled as if to reassure her. "This will all be over before your protectors even notice you are missing."

It was strange hearing such an inhuman voice emerge from her mouth, more strange oddly than the double itself.

"You mean to kill me."

"Yes, and no." Zhanedd raised into view one of the spinners.

A cold horror of anticipation and helplessness closed over Isabella. "I thought you had none—your knights . . ."

"It's true," Zhanedd said, while carrying the *dight* to the small table. "We have failed to recover those, and they are most difficult to come by. But not impossible."

So the demons still didn't have the remaining three. She hoped that meant Robyn had been successful.

Zhanedd returned and gripped her by the shoulders to guide her to the bench.

"You've been told how these work, yes? So I won't bother to lie and say you'll feel nothing," said Zhanedd. "I will say, you won't feel it very long. Consider that a blessing."

Isabella had placed herself in this position. She should have listened to the wisdom of Adam and Will instead of taking umbrage at being ordered about, followed around. She'd let her rage at how Robert D'Everingham treated her provoke her into this fatal mistake.

Zhanedd pulled her down to sit on the bench. One slender gray-green hand reached around her and turned the spinner over, stood it somehow on its point. Then the hand hovered above it. The device began to spin.

At least they'd come for her and not Adam; at least she'd protected him from this. Green light flashed out from the spinner, which whirled and whirled, rising aloft, the green line rising with it. God protect her son from both his parents now.

The green line climbed, and Isabella Birkin was scoured out of existence. It hurt beyond all imaginable pain.

✣ ✣ ✣

Thomas could only guess when Little John would be within range of the ram's horn. He knew it could be heard far from the tree because he'd heard it any number of times while in his hut or wandering the woods, most of the time blown by Much, if Hodde had been telling the truth.

The call might draw more than John alone—the horn served as an alarm, after all, whenever their woods were threatened or invaded; it was how they had so often eluded the Keepers—assuming there were any others left in this wood.

Sitting high up in the limewood tree, he leaned back, gathered his breath, and blew long and hard into the ram's horn. The note echoed through the woods. How far, he could not be certain, but it had been loud the times he'd heard it in his hut, times it had given him enough warning to glamour the hut from sight. So at least an impressive distance. If John passed anywhere near the old camp on his way through Barnsdale, he would have to hear it.

In the first hour, perhaps three times he blew the horn. Understandable that no one arrived after the first call. Even if Yvag gates hadn't opened to slaughter night after night, no one would likely be sure they'd heard this horn. He tried to recall when last it had been sounded. A year or more, perhaps. Also, anyone who did hear it would almost certainly know by now that Robert Hodde was dead; they would have to wonder who would be sounding the call, if not his ghost.

Four times he blew the horn before Little John appeared. As he rode up to the limewood tree, Thomas put away the horn and dropped down out of the low branches to meet him.

Little John stared at him in wonder. "Woodwose, what are tha doing here and how did tha ever get ahead of me?" Off to one side of the small clearing, the glamoured black beast stood still, and John cast it a wary glance.

Thomas pointed at the worn leather satchel hanging off John's right hip. "The spinners," he said.

John closed his hand around the strap. "I can't give 'em up. You know that. Young Wilkin they killed. 'E was apprenticed ta my brother, Drustan, learning a craft, an' they think that was 'is son. They'll kill one'a his family for certain next if I haven't delivered these soon as I can. Three girls my brother has. I can't let them come to harm."

Thomas came forward. "John, listen to me. You take those to the vill and they'll kill you *and* those girls. Your brother's whole family. You've had enough experience with them to know I'm not lying— probably you've seen more than anyone else I know." He nodded at the quarterstaff tied up under John's leg. "They'll pull those damned swords of theirs and cut you to ribbons. Your staff won't save you. Your bow would have been of more use."

"Nah, I got to get close enough t'hand these things over."

"Says the man who saw them up close on the road and in the gaol, saw them skewer his best friend and innocent Much."

John sighed, head lowered. Finally, he climbed down. He drew the staff before turning back to Thomas. "I have t'go. Have ta try." It was obvious John would knock him down if he came any closer. He had an idea why.

"How did they find out about your brother and his family, John? I've been by your side for most of a week and I knew nothing of them."

Little John's expression tightened, darkened. He looked furious but unable to direct that fury anywhere. His hands turned and turned the quarterstaff that seemed to have nowhere to strike. He said finally, softly, "I told 'em, I think. When Passelewe had me under castle, he and t'other demon asked me things, all about Robbie's crew and my own. Who was I and where'd I come from—like that."

Odd, Thomas thought, how much this was about brothers—Onchu so long ago, the Lusks, Hodde's brother the tanner, presumably harmless and useless to the Yvags, and now John's, who was proving of far more use to them. He said, "It's not your fault, my friend. You were ill—" He tried to say "ill-used" but his mouth suddenly didn't work. A fit had snuck up on him. His head throbbed with cold, and lightning jolted through his skull. He reached out a hand. "John," he managed to get out before he dropped to his knees. It was like the time with Hodde. Did this limewood tree trigger seizures? Its scent? He suddenly smelled a burning, heard his trembling, jagged voice choke out the riddle:

> "*Palavia Parva another millstone*
> *'Round your neck it weighs your fate.*
> *A prick of poison to end you,*
> *To welcome death's embrace.*"

He came to his senses with John kneeling beside him. A look of relief crossed Little John's face. "Robbie told me this of you."

"What did I say?" He'd heard himself this time, but wanted to confirm that his mad riddle had named Palavia Parva. John repeated it. Yes, it was as he'd heard, pulling John into it.

Thomas got up, wiping spittle from his chin. "A millstone 'round *my* neck, not yours? That makes no sense." And yet ... A "millstone"? What was his dark self trying to tell him?

John got wearily to his feet. "Robyn, I have t'go, else they slay another before the night. Surely you see that."

Now, Thomas had spent his hour in the limewood tree thinking about their situation. Like John, fearful for his family, the longer Thomas left Isabella Birkin unattended the more certain he became this was all a devious arrangement. At the same time, he couldn't let John ride to his death, either. The plan he'd conceived was mad to be sure, but it did hang the millstone around his neck. With false confidence, he said, "There's another way, John, a way where maybe nobody dies and you get all of your family out safely."

John stared at him as if he were insane. "What about the rest of those living in Parva?" he asked.

"They aren't leverage. If the elven have no other plan, they *might* leave the vill altogether."

"But they might not."

"No, and to that end we must do more." Thomas steepled his fingers, bowed his head. Without seeming to realize it, he walked away, around the enormous tree bole, ducking under one after another massive branch.

The remaining population of Palavia Parva weren't leverage, more like expendable to their captors. What if he leveraged them first?

He returned to John, grinning, and reached out his hand. "Let me see the satchel, John."

Very reluctantly, Little John lifted the strap over his head and handed it over.

Thomas untied the cover and flipped it aside. He took out the spinners before handing the satchel back. "Now," he said, and all but danced back under the tree. He swung up into the branches, vanishing in the greenery. He found the tree hollow where the ram's horn was kept, and carefully removed the horn and set the *dights* inside the hole. Then he climbed back down. "There. As before, we both know where they are." He tied the ram's horn to his belt.

"What good does it do for tha t'give me this?"

"That will come into play later. In fact, for this part don't bring the satchel at all. We'll put a spinner in it later."

John looked around himself. "For this part?"

Thomas drew his ördstone from the pouch around his neck.

"Ah, not that thing."

"It's not for me, it's for you," he said. "*You* are going to wield it."

John stared at the black, glittering stone in horror. "I would nah touch it."

"You'll have to," said Thomas. "Because between us you're the only one who's been inside your brother's house."

XXXIX. Split Decisions

Drustan Liddel, baker for the vill of Palavia Parva, sat dejectedly in the dirt, his back against the clay daub wall, while his wife and three daughters mixed and kneaded dough that was to rise overnight for tomorrow's baking. Two loaves, the last of the day, browned in the oven. Drustan was supposed to be slicing some stale bread into tranchers for the others in the vill, but his heart wasn't even in that. The cruel knights that were keeping the entire vill prisoners had taken Wilkin, son of his brother Odel, and not returned him.

It had almost been his youngest daughter, Annora, but Wilkin had interfered, shoving the lead knight back out the door and daring the two of them to take him instead. They'd obliged the lad without hesitation. It seemed it didn't matter to them who they took. In fact, when Drustan worked up the nerve to ask why they were doing any of this, the knights said it was to punish his other brother, John, which made no kind of sense. John was an outlaw who had not spoken to Odel since the day he'd gone off with Robert Hodde, that terrible little man, an awful influence who'd convinced John to choose the rough life in the forest over anything remotely civilized. The wonder was John hadn't yet been arrested and hanged, drawn and quartered. Drustan wasn't much closer to him, either.

They'd killed Wilkin; he knew it, although none of them would say. But with the loss of Wilkin, Drustan's resolve had deserted him. He just couldn't keep baking as if nothing had happened.

Five knights had taken over Palavia Parva. Where they came from was a mystery, but there was something unnatural about all of them.

For one thing, they were dressed in suits and hoods of mail as if for a crusade, with surcoats displaying a yellow cinquefoil, which he recognized as the badge of Nottingham's Sheriff Passelewe. Very odd that Passelewe would be engaged in something so far from his town. Even the Keepers of Sherwood didn't visit here.

Drustan wasn't certain he believed they were men. They seemed more like creatures carved out of wood, often standing motionless, sometimes for hours. Other times their actions seemed identical, like it was one man instead of five.

After two had taken Wilkin that morning and despite their warning to stay inside, Drustan had sneaked from the bakery to his house behind it and, once they'd passed the mill, followed them a ways. As the sun balanced on the horizon, they marched Wilkin straight toward it through the orchard. Oddly, the lad, who'd just defied them, went along willingly, clearly under a spell.

On the far side of the orchard, they'd created some sort of green fire—at which point Drustan thought he'd been seen, and fled back to the bakery. Whatever he'd seen, his nephew had not returned, nor been anywhere about since this morning. He feared they had burned Wilkin alive.

Recalling the strange business in the orchard, he was utterly astonished when a spot of that very same fire appeared in the middle of the air. He blinked, then became fearful that the knights or the queer fire itself had overheard his thoughts and now came for him.

The spot sizzled and began to grow.

Young Annora gasped. Peripherally, he saw his wife react, putting a hand to her breast before gathering all three girls to her.

The green spot became a line and then expanded into a circle. Inside the circle was some other place, woods as far as he could see. In the center of the space stood two men. The first was down on one knee, having made the circle with whatever he was holding. His brown hair was perhaps longer, his beard scruffier, but there was no mistaking it was Drustan's brother John. Behind him, with a drawn bow as if about to kill Drustan, stood a black-haired and bearded man with wintry blue eyes and a determined expression that only relaxed as he took in the scene in the bakery. He lowered his bow. "You did it, John."

John stood up. "Was the smell of it did the trick. Can't forget smell of 'is bakery." He grinned and, as if it were nothing, stepped into the bakery from the forest. Seeing his brother, he opened his arms wide. "Drustan," he said. The girls waddled their mother closer without letting go. "Girls," said John brightly, and he let go Drustan to bend and hug his nieces.

"An' who's this, then?" Drustan asked of the stern man who stepped through after.

"He's Robyn Hoode, come to take tha from here." Over his shoulder he said, "This be all of them."

With the bow strung across his back, Robyn Hoode crossed to the ovens and used two long-handled paddles to slide out two brown bread loaves. "No point in letting these burn," he said. "Don't want the bakery harmed when you know you'll be returning, once we're rid of your knights." Then he finally smiled a little. "Besides, these loaves might be all we have to eat today." He handed one of the paddles to Drustan. "Come on, John. We need to vanish before those elves come calling."

"Elves," repeated Drustan. It made weird if perfect sense. He was right about the knights.

John propelled the women to the circle, at which point they balked. He picked them all up and carried them into Barnsdale Wood. Annora shrieked.

"Oh, that's not good. Drustan, you have to go now." He pushed the paddle to herd the dazed baker over to and through the opening, then stepped through himself. "Now, John, finish it," he said, and Drustan watched his brother kneel and begin erasing the opening with a slow diagonal wave of the sparkling black stone as he rose to his feet. One final green spurt and Palavia Parva was gone.

Robyn Hoode patted Drustan's back. "Bring it with you," he said of the bread. Then he took the stone from John, who looked desperately happy to give it away. "We'll need to use this one more time."

Around midday, Little John rode undisguised into Palavia Parva. The vill appeared uninhabited, and he decided the elven knights had discovered his brother's absence and slaughtered everyone else in retribution. He rode slowly up the main road, fearful that he'd entered a trap or was about to encounter a pile of corpses.

By now Drustan and his family should be at King's Houses and all well. They were far away and safe with Robyn, which was what mattered. He was going to have to stop calling him the Woodwose after this adventure.

They'd used that magic stone of Robyn's to travel. He had not. He never wanted to touch one of those stones again, and anyway from the limewood camp it was only a couple hours' ride to the vill. Those stones were the devil's handiwork, or elves' according to Robyn; also according to Robyn, no danger awaited John in Parva. The Yvags had invested in him specifically. If this ploy worked, they would redouble that investment. "The important thing," Robyn had reminded him, "is that, no matter how angry they might make you, do not kill any of them. Not yet."

He rode past the mill, across the river bridge and on to the well. His brother's bakehouse, in which he'd stood only hours ago, lay dark and quiet. A dissipating ribbon of smoke rose up from the oven as if everything inside was normal. At least it hadn't all burned down. John drew up and dismounted. He dragged out a bucket of water from the well for his horse.

In the central hall the door opened and an old man shuffled out. Robyn had warned that anyone he didn't know might likely be a glamoured Yvag, but short of killing the old man, John doubted he could tell.

He carried his satchel. Despite what Robyn promised, he knew full well there was a slim chance the greedy elves would kill him before he showed them what he had, so he called out, "I'm here t'bargain wi' those killed my nephew. I got some'a what they want but not the lot. We're gunna have t'strike new arrangement, you an' me."

The old man paused, glanced around himself as if expecting a trap, then shimmered into the shape of one of Passelewe's soldiers. "We do not bargain," he said. Except for the different design to his surcoat, he might have been one of those John had met on the King's Way. His smugness annoyed John.

"That so? Then what d'you call killing my nephew and more t'get the spinners?"

"Spinners? Oh, I see. The *dights*, you mean."

John reached into the satchel and flung the single spinner into the dirt at the knight's feet. The Yvag almost went to his knees to keep it from hitting the ground. The creature seemed to revere the device. The knight glanced up, golden eyes glowing in the shadows of his helm. "The other two?"

John grinned. "Well, that's where tha *learn* to bargain. I ain't yet got 'em. Have to ride back to King's Houses to find where they be hidden."

Getting to his feet, the knight shook his head. He wouldn't allow it.

Reading the gesture, John said, "All right, then, and best of luck to ya." He turned toward his horse.

The Yvag called out, "Wait."

John fancied he could feel them talking to one another, probably forging a list of conditions. He didn't give them the opportunity. He turned back and promoted his own. "I'll bring other two if I can find 'em, but you kill no more people here."

"What do you mean?"

"I mean, tha ain't got my brother and his family no more." He gestured at the bakery, and from the knight's look read that they had been unaware of their absence. "Ya want your *spinners*, ya leave off threatening the others hereabout. I know 'em, every one," he lied. "I'll know an' tha harm any."

A pause then, the knight as still as a statue. From the odd pressure that made him want to clear his ears, they must have been buzzing like a hive of bees. He admitted to enjoying this a little bit.

Finally, the Yvag reacted. "Three days we'll give you. No more. After that all of these people are ours to dispense with."

Not quite the bargain he had hoped for. Robyn would have to make it work. That little black stone was going to be very busy. "Three days, then," he agreed, and climbed back upon his horse. It would be a long ride back to the King's Houses.

When Drustan Liddel's family arrived, Isabella Birkin busied herself immediately; first she assigned them chambers in the smaller palace, then took their partially baked loaves of bread to the kitchens.

In her absence, Thomas went looking for Edrick, only to find that the old equerry had disappeared entirely, as had the body of Wilkin, Little John's nephew. The stall where the corpse had been laid out previously proved to be empty, nor was the body laid out in the chapel. Neither Will nor Adam had noticed anything strange. Isabella had been her usual headstrong self for the better part of his absence, but much calmer since his return, so much so that they set off for Nottingham to gather as many of the Waits as they could, and anyone else who wanted to join up, leaving her in his care.

By now, Thomas supposed, Little John had delivered the one *dight* to the Yvags occupying Palavia Parva. From here on he must be doubly vigilant. If they came for Isabella, there wouldn't be long to wait.

The King's Houses still seemed safe: Kunastur had acted alone and no one else had yet been replaced by a glamoured Yvag. He hadn't known he was going to ride after Little John, so how could they have done? Yet the dispatching of Wilkin seemed designed to force that exact situation. Wilkin was bait and John had taken it. He had reacted predictably to the obvious threat. Second-guessing himself, Thomas worried that the obvious threat had hidden a far darker one. And why was Isabella taking so long in the kitchens over two loaves of bread?

He was about to go see, when she returned. She immediately busied herself with Drustan Liddel's three girls and their mother. Their conversation must have encompassed the events occurring in Palavia Parva, because the girls' and their mother's expressions turned fearful as they spoke. All the while Isabella did not look his way. He supposed she was shunning him, still angry.

This saddened him more than he could say. She'd shown him how to feel again. It wasn't love by any means, but a deep tenderness, and he regretted its loss. Still, whether or not she was disgruntled, with Will and Adam gone, he needed to speak with her directly. She alone had been here while he was absent.

Thomas interrupted her interaction with the Liddels and took Isabella aside. He said, "Will mentioned that you went for a walk, circling the palisade and pond. I wondered if you encountered Edrick or know what became of Wilkin's body. I can't locate either."

"I've no idea," she replied curtly. "I saw no body—that is, of course I saw it just after you did. But after that, I've no idea. You left here in such a hurry." She reached out as if to squeeze his hand, but hesitated and drew her arm back without touching him. "Have you looked in the stables? Or the chapel?"

"Yes, both." The only thing he could think was that the Yvags had come back while he was gone. Unable to get to the others, they had grabbed Edrick and the body. But, why? That they'd dumped Wilkin here to get John's attention meant they knew where the *dights* were, at least approximately. But having left the body . . . They *should* have left it. The Yvags were being too tidy for their own good—which was not his experience of them. *Calculating*, he would have said. Look how long the prelate's body lay ignored on the King's Way.

He excused himself and left Isabella to the Liddel family.

Late in the cloudy evening, with a steady rain now drenching everything, Little John rode through the main gate, his horse lathered after the long, hard ride. Thomas poured him a cup of ale.

John smiled wearily at his brother's family, rescued and safe, went over and hugged them all. Returning, he asked if Wilkin had been buried yet. Thomas answered him, "Wilkin's body has disappeared."

John took him aside and asked what was going on.

"Edrick and Wilkin *both* are missing."

"How's that possible?" John asked.

"Indeed. I've a couple of notions, but nothing yet proven. I've searched the obvious places and found no trace of either of them so far; it's time I think to look in the less populated parts of the estate. Of course, they could have been dragged into Ailfion, too, so I need to seek for gateways."

"Wi' one a them stones?" he said. It was obvious from his tone that he had no desire to participate.

Thomas nodded.

John sighed while giving his brother a concerned look. "They got inside King's Houses, then."

"For all we can tell, they've been inside it all along. The one we slew knew we were coming here. Who knows how many he told. And because of how they used Wilkin, we know they know we have their spinners."

"But they think they're here still."

Thomas nodded. He glanced surreptitiously at Isabella, who was sitting again with Drustan's wife and daughters. He leaned close as John slurped his ale. "I wish I didn't have to say this, but keep a close eye on Isabella, John. I can't be absolutely certain yet, but I fear the worst. Just pay attention to everything she does."

✠ ✠ ✠

An hour later a party of seven came riding in. Everyone was hooded or keeping their heads down. Thomas went out with a bow at the ready and John with his, but the group proved to consist of Elias, Will Scathelock, Adam D'Everingham, Benedict, Calum, and two others who Elias touted as having participated in the Nottingham archery contest and who happened to have been at the gaol looking for work.

Isabella welcomed them into the hall, then led them all to the main hearth to dry out by the fire. It was the most inhabited the King's Houses had been in quite some time.

Once they were all settled, she came up to Thomas of her own accord, this time with a creased brow, to ask if he'd learned anything further regarding Edrick's unexplained absence. Her response, so delayed, struck him as odd, as if she had studied on the concept of being worried, concluding it would seem peculiar if she failed to express some disquiet. Instead, her sudden concern raised his hackles. "He has been gone much too long now," she said. "He would never desert his post." Then, eyes wide with worry, she asked, "Do you think these demons have found him?" In that moment, he recognized her expression—he had beheld it only a short time earlier on the faces of the Liddel girls. She matched them perfectly.

"I do," he replied, and then, just to see how she reacted, he added, "They made a grave error if so."

"Grave?"

He paused, as if thinking over how to express it, but he was provoking her eagerness, watching it take hold. "They should have left Wilkin in place."

"Should they," she said thoughtfully, then dismissed it and smiled, all of that concern erased in an instant. This time she laid her hand upon his arm with rekindled tenderness. He met her gaze, which seemed to be watching his expression to see how he reacted. She said, "Well, it's no matter. Our food is here."

The Liddels' fully baked loaves of bread were brought to the table by Sehild and two other cooks, along with more of the bean tarts, a wedge of cheese, and pitchers of beer. Nothing in the staff's demeanor suggested they'd noticed anything out of the ordinary about Isabella, but for dour Thomas all doubt had been erased.

While they ate, Elias sat down beside Thomas and asked what

their plan was. But he in turn insisted, loudly, that Little John tell his story of Palavia Parva beginning with the delivery of Wilkin's body at the gatehouse here.

Once that tale was engaged, he quietly retreated as if to his room, but instead descended to the first floor. He followed the covered passage to the kitchen and pantry in order to cross the yard at the closest point to the stables and mostly out of anyone's sight.

He stood in the dark awhile, watching to see if anyone followed him in the rain.

Upon their arrival Isabella had given him the grand tour. He knew that many of the smaller buildings across the estate remained empty and unused, just as the king and queen's chambers remained unused. There was a separate Queen's Hall—a miniature version of the hunting palace, with its separate kitchen—and another, smaller building the name of which escaped him now. He would need to look inside both. But first . . .

Entering the stables, he drew out his ördstone and floated it on his palm as he turned in a slow circle. The glamoured white stallion watched him, or more likely the stone, carefully.

He turned. Turned again.

A blue gossamer strand shot from the stone to a spot in the middle of the empty stable. The air there warped slightly—a gate recently sealed.

Thomas made a complete circle but from there no other threads extended. He had a grim notion now where both Edrick and Wilkin might have gone, or at least where the King's Houses had been breached. There was, however, no point in cutting into the sealed gate, no point in pursuing when anything might be waiting on the other side. No, better to investigate the other buildings first.

He turned to leave only to find himself facing Adam D'Everingham. Lit blue by the stone's glow, Adam, one hand gripping his dagger, stood glaring at him as if barely able to contain his rage.

XL. Adam's Dilemma

Thomas half expected Adam to draw the dagger and attack. Instead, Adam's anger seemed to collapse upon itself. He lowered his hand against his thigh. He said, "She's not right, is she?"

Thomas knew exactly what the question meant. Head slightly bowed, he answered, "I didn't want to think it was so—that there might have been a fourth *dight* we knew nothing of. The Yvags seemed so intent on recovering the three . . . What I don't understand is when it might have happened. You and Will were with her until I got back. When—"

"We weren't. Don't you see?" His trembling scowl was self-directed, his eyes full of pain. "She tired of us watching her every move, and went off for a walk across the entire grounds." A tear slid from the corner of his eye. "She *insisted*. You know how she can be."

"I do, yes. Stubborn."

The word almost made Adam grin in his misery. "We shouldn't have listened, but we did. *I* did. I obeyed her like always."

Thomas nodded in sympathy. "It won't be much consolation, but I think if you'd followed her, either you'd have taken her place or they'd have slain you and Will both. This was too carefully executed."

Adam sniffled and wiped at his face. "What do we do? How do we undo—?" He finally shook his head.

"You know already we can't." *Can't bring her back*, an admission to himself finally that the worst had come to pass. If Adam sensed it, too, there could be no doubt. Isabella had been cored out and replaced. He wanted to grieve, but neither the situation nor Adam would allow it.

"Where are they, then?" Adam demanded. "Where lies the sleeping thing that's inside her?"

"I'm not certain. Not hereabouts. Too obvious, too easily found, impossible to defend. Perhaps at Laxton, where your father can guard the site, but then where does his own possessor lie?" It was a question he had turned over repeatedly without a resolution. "At one point I did think I knew. John and I found an empty crypt at Rufford Abbey, but whether it had been vacated because of our visit or just awaited habitation, I can't say. It had been made ready for someone."

"The abbey?" Adam said. Then he seemed to understand. "Where you went while we waited. You were looking for these sleepers even then?"

"I've found others in sepulchers before. I couldn't determine that Abbot Godwin was involved, but someone there surely is. Someone cast a spell upon the entrance that kept Little John from descending, and I've seen that magic before. He didn't even recognize that he'd been turned aside, it's that sly."

"Then how did you get past?"

"A curious trick, usually taking more than one run at it. You have to acknowledge that you don't wish to fight it at the same time as you plunge through. You . . . muddle things a bit. I'm not sure that's helpful."

Yet Adam nodded, as if grasping the idea. He seemed about to walk off, but then hesitated and turned back. "She was fond of you. It surprised her. And me. I was . . . I was angry because it wasn't my father. But he hasn't been my father for years, has he?" Another pause and then he remarked, "I'm the only one left." Then he marched out of the stables and cut away from the Great Hall as well, no doubt, thought Thomas, to wallow alone in his misery.

There were still outbuildings to investigate. He headed as he'd intended for the nearby Queen's Hall, a miniature version of the so-called palace with a separate and unused kitchen attached to it. The hall was kept in good order; the kitchen not so, dusty and strung with cobwebs. Nobody had visited either of them recently. The even smaller building beside the hall was a one-story apartment. Inside was a single room with a bench, small table, and a large bed. He found himself staring at it. Despite the uninhabited appearance of the chamber, the bed curtain was drawn. Zhanedd had tried to hide the Keepers at Laxton by drawing the curtain.

He pulled a dagger before crossing the room and sweeping back the curtain. He should have been prepared for the two dead bodies, but took a step back in shock. Wilkin was facedown in the bedding. Edrick lay on his back, his head tilted at an impossible angle. "Zhanedd," Thomas muttered. This was surely that Yvag's handiwork, instinctively hiding the bodies to protect their newest asset. A mistake, as he'd told Isabella.

Thomas drew the curtain again and left everything as it was for now. Went out and softly closed the door. He would have to tell Little John and his brother, but not right away.

Isabella had been put in play to betray them all. He was sure of that. The only unanswered question now was how she would do it.

Overnight, the woods continued to flare with green fires, but fewer than before, as if it was now all for show, a reminder that the Yvags could do as they liked. Late that night another man arrived through the main gate—a tall and gaunt figure with long graying hair and a dark beard. Elias, guarding the King's Houses, brought him inside.

Thomas could not help but grin, even at the sight of him so worn down and thin. "Sir Richard!" he called.

"Sir Thomas!" answered the knight, no doubt to the confusion of Elias and the others.

Thomas said, "So I *will* have opportunity to repay your hospitality. I'd hoped as much, but with these nightly invasions I feared you might have been scooped up." They embraced.

Stepping back, Sir Richard said, "Oh, but I was scooped up, as you say."

Everything fell silent. "What happened?" Thomas asked.

"The—what did you call them?—the Yvags, yes, they killed all five of my friends, the green-fire brigands, before dragging me off to . . . I really don't know where."

Thomas thought he'd called them nothing at all, recalling no conversation with Sir Richard where they discussed the Yvags. Then again, he and the knight had consumed a fair quantity of ale.

"Torture tha?" asked John.

"Oh, yes. They forced me to swallow a—a creature, I don't know what to call it." He shivered at the memory, and John nodded. "Asked me over and over about some missing objects. 'Course, I knew nothing of them." He looked at Thomas. "So then they asked about you—if I knew where you were. Of course I didn't since we had parted ways, but then I didn't know you were going by Robyn Hoode, either. I thought I met him a few times—a much smaller man, and older."

"That was Hodde, who I'm afraid is dead at the hands of those green-fire brigands."

Sir Richard scratched at his beard. "So you're as practiced at the bow as at the staff."

"More so, I would hope. I've thus far avoided a good drubbing when applying arrows." Thomas introduced him to all those gathered. He said, "You were tortured and had no answers for them. How did you escape?"

Sir Richard accepted a cup of ale. "I didn't. Don't believe I could have found my way, either. No, they opened one of those rings of theirs and threw me back out."

"Tha were lucky."

Lady Isabella asked to be introduced to him. Thomas could feel the pressure of her probing. Sir Richard exclaimed, "This is the personage who has chased me across all of Sherwood? My lady." He bowed.

She canted her head. "I've pursued you? I don't believe I've had the pleasure."

"That's because we know how and where to hide," replied the knight. If he also felt the intrusion of her thoughts, he didn't show it.

"Well, no more hiding now," Thomas said. "We are all on the same side for once."

Sir Richard glanced at Thomas. "And how was that accomplished exactly?"

"Come eat, at the very least some bread and more ale, and we will discuss it all." Sir Richard followed Isabella to the table.

Little John came up to Thomas to ask how this strange outlaw knew him. Thomas explained, filling John in about poor Sir Richard's situation at the hands of some mercenary turned abbot who was known by the name of "Red Roger."

"Oh, I know of 'im. Roger'a Doncaster. Bad as they come." Behind him, Elias was nodding in agreement.

"When this business is over, perhaps we should pay him a call."

Little John laughed.

Elias came up and said pointedly, "Sir Thomas?"

It was some time before the company discovered the absence of Adam D'Everingham. While it occurred to Thomas that this Isabella Birkin might have dispatched her own son after their previous conversation, he first checked the stables and paddock, discovering that Adam's horse was missing, his livery as well. He was sure now that Isabella's son had not returned to the Great Hall after their encounter. It might be that Adam was riding through the wet night to exorcise his own demons, but it seemed far more likely he'd set forth to hunt for the Yvagvoja of Rufford Abbey exactly as they had discussed.

However, upon returning to the company, he explained that Adam did not like Thomas's evolving relationship with Isabella, and had earlier confronted him about it—which was certainly true if not exactly accurately portrayed—and proposed that, furious and sulking, Adam had gone off on his own to work through these feelings. Everyone, especially Isabella, seemed to accept that. Her Yvagvoja would know of their difficult history.

One significant limitation of skinwalkers was their inability to share information freely the way Yvag knights did all the time. If Adam's absence became a cause for concern, Isabella would need to make a report of all she'd learned, either to a flitting little hob or to another Yvag in their midst, if there was one. Thomas was listening now and would sense any such communication. Even then, she would know nothing of his destination. Adam was as headstrong and rebellious as his mother had been. Whatever happened now, Thomas's own sharp-edged guilt was one more stone around his neck, one more sorrow to carry afterward. If he was right about Adam, it was a pain that would soon be shared. In the meantime, he would have to watch Isabella as much as possible to interrupt any attempt to alert a third party, added to which there was now Sir Richard atte Lee, whose story, while convincing enough, raised questions about the remarkable benevolence of Nicnevin.

It was surely well past midnight by now. Adam D'Everingham had ridden a perilous path; although the storm had passed and the moon was out now, the trail had been soaked, making it difficult to distinguish the burrows and other treacheries that could easily trip a horse. But he knew the way, and was careful. That he reached Rufford Abbey without incident would have made his mother proud.

Against the moonlit darkness of the woods, the abbey glowed with the smallest of light—a large, sharp-edged structure with one or two candles burning behind the windows of the nave. He walked around the presbytery and slipped silently into the south transept, careful not to be obvious. If what Robyn Hoode had told him was true, then someone in the abbey must be involved in what went on in the undercroft.

He'd been here as a boy on at least two occasions, left on his own to wander about while his mother and the abbot hashed out the details of various agreements: how many deer the abbey was allowed, how much they could interfere with travelers on the King's Way—things of that sort, which had meant nothing to him at the time. Compared to racing around the cloister or playing hide-and-seek with Brother Piers, it was all tedious and ignorable, but it meant he'd had experience of the undercroft on occasion, too busy with his game to be afraid of who or what was buried there.

From the nave he entered the cloister, where he borrowed a thin candle to light his way across the covered walkway and to the steps into the undercroft.

He reached the entrance down into the crypt...and found himself walking away, hand out to push open the door to the outside. He slowed.

What had just happened?

He turned around and went back.

Almost immediately he felt the urge to turn away creeping upon him. He started to follow that urge. His thoughts collected around the unnecessariness of visiting the crypt.

Stopped again.

What was happening here? The opening to the crypt insisted he was de trop. Whatever approach he took, the spell—for it was surely a spell as Robyn had said—would send him elsewhere, out into the night.

Adam paused to reconsider Robyn's suggestion, the way to deny the spell's manipulation. Something pushed at his head, invading his mind.

That was when he spied the grinning monk watching him from the covered walkway to the monks' frater. No one would be eating this late. Somehow, the monk had been alerted to his arrival. The spell itself? Perhaps proud of his handiwork, he'd had to come and witness its efficacy. Or else he was on guard.

The quiet laugh emerged as a wheeze. "You'll never get in," said the monk.

No doubt that was true. The spell would continue to redirect him. The monk stepped nearer, pushed back his pale cuculla. It was Brother Piers! But that was impossible. Piers had died four years ago from a fever.

"Adam," he said, still grinning, but now tenderly. He held out one hand. "Come away now, come along."

Adam turned and retraced his steps back through the cloister and presbytery, out to where his horse stood tied. He stood the candle in the dirt. It was not Piers, could not be. The voice was wrong, that wheezing. He squeezed shut his eyes. What he had seen was a lie.

Now he reached into the bag he'd carried and brought out what appeared to be a congealed mass of night itself: the Yvag armor, borrowed from Will Scathelock. Having not tried it out, he didn't know if it fit over clothing, so he quickly stripped down to his braes before stepping into and tugging the armor on. Even as he pushed his hands into the sleeves, the armor came to life and flowed up his body, over his shoulders, around his neck. It continued up and over the top of his head like a hood of mail, leaving his face bare. The dagger Will had shown him hung attached above his hip. And though Will was considerably taller than he was, the armor fit him as if it knew his body.

This time he walked the dark path around the outside, guided by the candlelight, back to the undercroft door. He opened the door and went in.

The monk still stood in the shadows. His grin faded at the sight of Adam in the shining black-and-silver armor.

"'Never,' you said," Adam told him. "Let us find out if that's so."

"No, withdraw!" the monk snarled and launched himself at

Adam, slammed against him, arms thrown over his shoulders to wrestle him to the ground. Almost instantly, "Brother Piers" sagged in his arms. Adam pushed him away, but held onto the Yvag dagger he'd stuck into him.

The monk collapsed at his feet, a look of surprised horror on his face, continued limply to reach up, fingers sliding down the slick armor, finally slipping to the floor. The monk gurgled one final breath, and the glamour faded. There in the candlelight lay an Yvag in armor much like Adam's, its sharp face gray, though it continued to look something like Brother Piers as if caught in the middle of transition. Had that monk always been one of these demons? Recollecting Maurin's story about the one that had come back to life in Nottingham, he dropped to his knees and made himself stick the barbed dagger into its throat. Perhaps it was that which made him acknowledge the quest he was on, what he proposed to do. Then he noticed that the Yvag also had a sheathed dagger. Why hadn't it tried to kill him, unless it and its kind wanted him alive?

Climbing to his feet again, Adam sheathed his dagger, picked up a candle, and walked to the steps. The pressure of the repelling spell poked at him, pushing him away as before; now, somehow, he was outside it, like someone looking through an odd doorway before entering a room. As Robyn had advised, he projected thoughts that he was no enemy of what it protected as he pushed hard through its resistance, found himself on the far side of it, and, undeterred, descended the steps into the crypt.

The lid of the first tomb was sculpted, a gisant of a recumbent knight with mail-gloved hands pressed together in prayer. Adam wondered who that was supposed to represent—a king, a knight, some benefactor? Surely not his father. It set him to wondering whose body would lie beneath it. There were two other tombs, as well, but Robyn had described this one.

With great effort he pushed against the lid. At first it wouldn't budge, and he speculated that he would need a mallet instead to smash the cover to pieces. And then, as if another spell had broken, the lid moved—a grinding slide away from him.

Something small as a trapped bat flitted out of the opening and right past his face. "Raaaah!" it screamed. Its claws tore at his cheek, and he fell back.

The creature came about and dove at him. Adam swiped at it with the dagger.

"You not us!" it yelled as though he'd claimed otherwise. "You pretend!" It dove again. Below it, in the shadows of the tomb, something moved. Adam ducked the darting hob, bent over the edge of the tomb, and stabbed hard into the darkness there again and again. The interred creature kicked and flailed. Seeing his target more clearly, he thrust again. The hob landed on the back of his neck now and tore gouges across his cheeks. He slapped at it as the demon in the tomb fell still.

The screeching hob suddenly sprang away and flew up and out of the undercroft, and Adam at last tucked away the dagger. Blood ran to his chin from the many inflicted cuts.

Unsteadily, he slid down with the tomb against his back and tried to feel nothing, no anguish, no loss. But it was there, up the steps and out of the crypt, awaiting him: Whoever this Yvag had been inhabiting, they were no more.

Now that it was done, Adam dreaded that he had either just murdered his father or his mother.

XLI. Seeking Balance

Knowing what Adam intended and what the outcome might be, Thomas accepted Isabella Birkin's invitation. He drew a chair up to her bedside.

In front of him she undressed and, then naked, invited him into her bed, expressing a hunger discrepant with the reserved Isabella he knew, whose lust had only emerged at moments in private. It was pure Yvagvoja hunger on display, as urgent as Zhanedd's venom or Queen Nicnevin's, the difference being that she had nothing to infect him with. This was someone he didn't know. He nevertheless caressed her, stroked her, and did all he could to satisfy her without ever undressing and coupling with her. And it seemed to work. His touch was enough to send the Yvagvoja into a delirium of desire. Her eyes rolled back and she lost herself in pleasure that aroused him as well. He wished he could forget that this was not Isabella but Isabella displaced.

Eventually, she rolled away, naked, bawdily displaying herself, relaxed and teasing him with soft calls of "Robyn, oh Robyn," until, finally, she lay back and drifted to sleep. By candlelight, Thomas watched her. He was not sure if he knew whether the creatures slept. He'd never before had occasion to watch one do so beyond their dormancy in crypts.

He fully intended to remain awake beside her, but he also finally dozed off. No doubt he put himself at some risk in doing so; had she been pretending, he would have been powerless to stop any attack.

He awoke to the sound of Isabella gasping. She sat straight up and almost blindly, she reached for him. "Robyn!" she cried, "Oh, my lovely *puca*," and in that wording and the longing of it he knew it was she, and what had come to pass: Adam had reached Rufford Abbey and they knew now whose voja lay in that crypt.

He lunged for her even as a red mist like some scarlet ghost burst out of her and evaporated. Red glistened on her pale skin and on the coverlet beneath her. He caught her as she fell forward, her body already waxy and cold, bluish, lifeless, a *lich* but only recently dead and so not showing anything like the decay of others he'd beheld.

He hugged her tightly to him, and shed his tears before finally laying her back on the bed, whispering, "I'm sorry, so very sorry. I failed you." He covered her nakedness, left her looking peaceful, and wearily rose to shuffle off to his own room, the room she had chosen for him.

One or more of the elven might have been lying in wait to kill him then and there—he had little resistance to offer—but none did. If there were any, they no doubt thought Isabella had him well in hand. Or maybe there were none in the mix at all, and all of the archers and outlaws were as they appeared. Tonight he was not going to sort that out.

On the bed he collapsed, exhausted and sick of the forever game being played. Here, at Melrose, at Wariville in France . . . Everywhere, no doubt. Now the game had pressed a young man to kill his mother, whom he loved, a woman who—

He made himself stop. *Who loves her, Tom—her son or you? Or is it both?* He knew exactly what Alpin Waldroup's ghost would have asked.

Today . . . Today would he try to find some balance in the universe and save the lives of twenty or so people who were otherwise going to be executed by the Yvag to prove a point that did not need proving. Isabella Birkin, he tried to tell himself, had perished that those people and John's family might live. She would have agreed to such an exchange if told of it. He imagined she'd gone to her death at Zhanedd's hands hoping to have saved her son by doing so.

It was Sehild who screamed and brought everyone running to Lady Isabella's door. Isabella was dead, evidently had died in her sleep. Will Scathelock and Little John both eyed Thomas askance.

Both knew of his relationship with her; both half expected him to be
in bed with her, although John at least had an inkling of his
suspicions about her transformation. Sir Richard and the other
archers joined the Waits and Keepers crowding the door to her
chamber. Still missing from the scene was Adam D'Everingham.
Elias asked what it meant that Adam hadn't returned. Should they
look for him? Thomas recommended they search the whole complex.
They would no doubt find Wilkin and Edrick and so resolve that
mystery. They all started to leave, but he held up Will and John. "I
need to talk to you both."

Sir Richard edged over to join them, but Thomas told him, "Go
on, Sir Richard. We have duties to the late Lady Isabella to discuss."
He waited until the reluctant knight accepted this and left with the
others. Then he led Will and John to his chamber. Thomas closed
the door after them and said quietly, "Adam returned to Rufford
Abbey and found a skinwalker in the crypt—at least, I'm assuming
that's what's happened. Neither he nor I knew for certain what
awaited him there."

"What, like Passelewe?" Scathelock asked.

"Yes. He left last night and must have arrived before morning."

Scathelock blanched. "They turned her. We let her go off alone
and they turned her."

John, distressed, said, "No, it's I killed her," he said. "My rash act
on account of Wilkin—"

"No, John. Will." Thomas cut them off; he'd now had hours to
come to terms with how the Yvags had manipulated them all. "Do
not start blaming yourselves when we were dealt choices
irreconcilable. Had you and I remained here to guard her, your
brother's family would be dead right now. So, probably, would Adam
and you, Will. It's going to be terrible for Adam when he learns the
news. He was hoping it was his father's parasite asleep in that tomb."

"These monsters," Scathelock said sadly. "With him absent, it falls
to me to accompany her body home to Laxton. Even if D'Everingham
knows already, he won't be bothered with recovering her. I doubt he'll
be on hand for the interment. It's my duty."

Thomas nodded, and went to where his quiver hung. "Whatever
you do, don't tell him Adam's part in any of this. She died in her sleep
is all we poor mortals know."

Will nodded. "Adam's life still won't be worth a bent penny. His father wants her position—*his* position now."

"That's a problem for another day, though if you find him, bring him back with you. But you take her home, Will. And here." He handed him an ördstone. "Take the white stallion. John and I and the rest of these men cannot tarry. She died because of this plan of the Yvags, and on foot it's a full day's journey to Palavia Parva. We only have two days now."

Little John said, "Why don't ya use magic stone, cut us a way there?"

"I can't. We are certainly being scrutinized. The demons have opened a gateway into the stables and probably elsewhere in the complex as well. Last thing I want them knowing is that we have an ördstone or two. It might prove to be our only way out of the trap they've set in the vill."

"Tha think it's a trap."

"I *know* it's a trap, John. We hand over those remaining spinners, they'll no longer have a reason to spare any of us or their hostages. I'm guessing we'll encounter new outlaws joining us on our march. Sooner or later if not already, we'll have elves in our midst."

"All right. I'll come back from Laxton soon as I'm able," Scathelock promised. He hurried out but was gone barely five minutes before he returned in the company of a balding man in a sepia-colored tunic. "Says he's the fletcher of Clipstone and that you ordered two dozen arrows."

"I did," said Thomas, and greeted the man.

The fletcher swung the long narrow leather satchel off his shoulder, and carefully removed the arrows in two small bundles. Thomas paid him. He bowed and departed. Will followed him out, saying, "This time I mean it."

"'E didn't say one word," John observed, "that fletcher."

"True." Thomas drew one of the arrows. "But his craftsmanship speaks for him." He handed the arrow to Little John.

While admiring it, John said, "You're leading us, hey, Robyn?"

"*We're* leading us, my friend. The location and details of Palavia Parva are known to you, not me. You tell me what you think."

"What I think." John pursed his lips, his brows knitting as if thought was painful. "I think," he said, "we'd be wise to dispatch someone ahead of us to The Saylis to watch road." The Saylis was well known to Sherwood and Barnsdale outlaws. It offered a perfect, secluded height for concealed observation of all activity upon the King's Great Way as it ran below Pontefract in the north. The vill lay a short distance from it. "If there be troops amassed against us, would be best to know of it."

He expected no amassed troops but agreed to it rather than dispute John after requesting his opinion. "Ask Elias to choose one of the Waits. We'll pretend he has to return to Nottingham."

"Aye, that'll work. And we'll say 'e's guidin' my brother and 'is family. Him wants to come wi' us back to Parva, but I'm havin' none of it."

"Good," Thomas agreed. "I'd hate to have rescued them only to hand them back to the fiends."

John left to speak with Elias.

Alone, Thomas thought back to the campaigns in which he'd fought, remembered the time when their captain had fallen and Alpin Waldroup had taken charge, though leadership was not what he wanted, either; he remembered Alpin calling out, "They pay us to go and be killed where we're told, so let's go and die as ordered!" It was an odd thing to proclaim, he'd thought at the time, but the men rallied to that honest assessment by one of their own and followed him back into the battle. He could use Alpin's common sense about now.

Adam, he hoped, would return to them, although it might be days. After Rufford, he no doubt had ridden to Laxton Castle to learn if his father still lived. He would be devastated when Will arrived with Isabella's body if not before, and because of the position she'd occupied, there would be an Inquisition Post Mortem before her title among the Keepers was awarded to him. If Robert D'Everingham was on hand, would he try to muddy the waters, claim that Isabella's "death by natural causes" was in fact witchcraft and blame Adam? He did eagerly want her title, and probably enough to murder his son. The creature wouldn't shed a tear. On the other hand, if the voja occupying Robert knew that Adam had discovered its secret, D'Everingham might make himself scarce.

A perilous situation—it was a shame they didn't know where that voja slept. But as he had told Will and John, that was for another day.

This morning they marched for Palavia Parva.

✠ ✠ ✠

The group of ten—archers, outlaws and Waits—headed north past Worksop to join the King's Great Way again. Along the way, Thomas thrice paused to blow into the ram's horn.

Elias asked him what he was doing.

"It's an idea Will Scathelock gave me—to invite all of Sherwood's outlaws together under one banner."

His call went out through valleys of woods and across hillsides of heather. They went on across the Ryton and past Blyth, where he blew the horn again.

Outlaws did trickle in, one here, one there, sometimes two. They included Fouke, his wife, and son, all armed with bows. The trio looked tired, harried, ill used by the "green-fire brigands," as Sir Richard had named them. None of them knew of the situation in Palavia Parva, but news, which had traveled freely through the forest in the past, had all but stopped, so many had fled or died at the hands of these creatures. Two women were among those joining, whose partners or husbands had fallen afoul of the "demon inquisition." That this Robyn Hoode was taking the fight to the enemy was all the motivation they needed to join up.

At one point Thomas fell in beside tall and gaunt Sir Richard. He asked, "Does this feel like another crusade to you?"

As if it was difficult to assess, the knight considered the question awhile before answering. "What we're collecting is as diverse a band as the Children's Crusade was. Might even be someone else here who endured that. Still, we have no more sense of our enemy than they did. If anything, less. So I answer, yes and no."

"At least there's no siege machine here to drop a stone on either of us." They both reflected upon that.

The knight glanced around at their group, now sixteen strong. "The forest is far less inhabited than when you and I met. Once, that horn would've brought fifty." He walked on, silent again, awhile, then said, "Know you, it was Lady Isabella I suspected of executing my band. Instead, these . . . these demons as you say . . . well, they're quite outside my experience. How do we approach them?"

Thomas found that an odd sentiment from one who'd been tortured by the "demons." He answered, "I have something they want, while they hold the population of a vill to ransom. We are exchanging property."

"Sounds more like battle lines, soldiers, than unholy creatures."

"They are perhaps both, though their army is of another world and so has ambitions we can only guess at." Sir Richard cut him a sidelong glance, as if shocked by the idea. Thomas added, "I would prefer not to give them what they seek, but right now I see no way to avoid it."

"But where are you keeping this property? You've brought no satchel, no bag," asked Sir Richard.

"Where it's safest," he replied.

It was obvious that Sir Richard wanted to ask more, but he said only, "Another riddle." After that they walked on in silence. Eventually, the knight wandered off into the woods to relieve himself, and Thomas fell back to speak with the new arrivals. He was also listening for the buzzing of any Yvag communication, but hearing none. If Yvag had taken up with them, they were being cautious. The group were anywhere from wary to downright fearful of the inhuman enemy. One of the two women had, by green firelight, watched horrors unfold, barely escaping with her own life. Why hell was releasing its fiends into Sherwood Forest, no one could comprehend, though there were suppositions ranging from Divine punishment to hell itself overflowing to witches (known to couple with demons) having birthed such monstrosities in the wood.

That night they camped in Barnsdale. They could have pressed on, but Thomas wanted to meet the enemy after a night's rest rather than after a long, exhausting hike. He ended the day with another blast on the horn.

The next morning, they numbered twenty-two.

PART FOUR:
THE DEATH OF ROBYN HOODE

XLII. The Limewood Monster

Calum came down from The Saylis without calling attention to himself, and fell in with Elias and Benedict as if he'd walked beside them from the start. His horse he said he'd left with someone in Wentbridge.

Thomas was walking alongside Little John. Benedict came up to speak with John. "Calum says nothin's happened along the road. If anything, it's been unnatural quiet hereabouts. Not anything like knights gathering."

"That's good, innit?" John asked.

Thomas replied, "I hope so, but we can't let ourselves think they haven't cut portals into every house in the vill to call up who knows how many more if needed. Still, if the road remains clear, it leaves us to focus upon the vill itself. How soon, John?"

"River's just over that rise ahead. Vill's on t'other side and up a ways."

Even as he said that, Elias called out and pointed. A rider on a blazing-fast white stallion was riding the thin road through the heather toward them. Thomas recognized the disguised beast well before he identified blond Will Scathelock on its back.

Will dismounted the beast and went straight to Thomas. He was dressed in black, articulated armor. Behind him, some of the outlaws were staring at his odd apparel. Others looked over the strangely still horse. "Am I too late?" he asked. He craned his neck, looking at all the outlaws standing or sitting among the gorse.

"Now, why would you think you were?"

"Green halos like to the other night. Two or three, back there just off the road. Could easily be more of them deeper in. The fire doesn't show so much in the daylight. Anyway, I thought sure they must be engaging you already."

"No," Thomas said, understanding at once why the road here had been devoid of activity. "I think they're waiting for a signal from the vill. They mean to trap us between the vill and them."

He gathered everyone together, and studied the faces: the Fouke family, Elias and the Waits, the archers who'd competed against him and Will, Sir Richard, and the various outlaws he didn't know but all of them vouched for by Little John, who seemed to know everyone.

He climbed up on a fallen tree, overlooking them all, and for a moment he was cast back in time to a sloping, grassy plain that was about to become a battlefield in France, and where a short soldier stepped up onto a tree stump to direct the infantry, the mounted knights, and the archers. He'd become that soldier.

"The . . . demons are coming up behind us," he announced, and many looked back to where the edge of the woods began with a scattering of birch trees. "Will says they're in the woods near the road, maybe deeper. Now, clearly, they are in league with the five who've invaded Palavia Parva, and my guess is, their intent is to squeeze us between the two forces, but they're waiting for a signal. Archers, I want at least four of you to engage them on your own. Their armor is like this that Will is wearing, regardless of how it appears. It is difficult to penetrate. You can waste countless arrows firing at it. If you do, try for these openings along the sides, assuming you can see them. They breathe through those. Personally, I recommend you marksmen aim instead for their throats, mouths, eyes. And get out of the way if they draw their swords. Those have special properties that Little John can tell you all about. Also, some are like to be riding creatures such as this one. Don't waste your shots trying to bring these mounts down, either. They can't be killed. Ultimately, you want to drive them back through those blazing green rings. Every ring that closes up is one less way in for them.

"Elias, will you take the other archers back into The Saylis? If any of those demons get through, you rain arrows down on them." And there was Waldroup again in his thoughts, in his words: *"Once you know the other side's plans, change the rules to bring them down."*

"The vill," said Little John, "it's on t'other side of river, too. Only one bridge across to it. We'll be ducks in a pond."

"Can we wade across elsewhere, upstream perhaps?"

"Aye."

"All right, then, Will, you take five and ford farther up. Come around from there."

"That'll put ya comin' in behind church," said John. "Fields up that way, too. And orchard trees."

Scathelock nodded. Young Fouke III walked over to John, parents in tow, to volunteer.

"All right. John, you're leading the way over that bridge. You're the face of us, giving up the spinners. They'll be expecting you to come bargaining. See how long you can keep them engaged, how many of the villeins you can get released before those coming to get us strike. Sir Richard, the Foukes, and these others are yours to position as you see fit. Sir Richard is near as good as you with a quarterstaff if there's to be close combat. If there is, it means some of the elven got past Will's bowmen."

"I know. What about tha, Robyn?"

"I'll have go to collect our ransom now that we need it."

"I could accompany you," offered Sir Richard.

That boldness erased any remaining doubts Thomas had about Sir Richard. He replied, "Let us see the situation first, before we do anything."

They came up a hillside that proved to be a field lying fallow for the season, the first indication that the vill was near. Thomas had the remaining force hold up. He went to Will. "I hope you didn't use that stone to cut a gateway to here."

Will glanced back at the white stallion. "Didn't need to. That creature all but flies on wings. Without it I would still be on my way here and likely riding a dead horse. Here." He tried to hand the stone back to Thomas, who insisted he keep it for now. "By the way, D'Everingham was nowhere to be seen, nor was Adam, though he'd left my armor at the castle as if he'd known it would fall to me to return his mother's body. The whole household wailed over her. They were still grieving when I left."

"I'm sure they were. My heart is with them." He let out a deep sigh. "Let's avenge her here."

"My thoughts exactly."

"Oh, once you're in position," Thomas said, "you might let them catch a glimpse of you in that armor. It might unsettle them a bit."

Will embraced Thomas, then led his five off below and along the ridge. The archers ran off into the woods, and Elias's band headed down the road and climbed up into The Saylis to watch for more trouble.

Thomas dropped the stone into his quiver, then alongside John crawled atop the ridge. From there they beheld their destination.

Palavia Parva comprised fourteen thatched houses, spread over the lowland around and along the river. A wheat field lay below, half harvested, dotted with "angels"—sheaves of wheat bound together near the top and stood up in neat rows to await threshing. From here they did indeed look like golden-brown long-skirted maidens. More fields lay on the opposite hillsides beyond the town.

As John had described, the church, ringed by a low wall, stood slightly apart to the northeast of the rest of the vill, separated in part by an orchard. Will would be coming from there. Smoke wafted out of the holes in most of the fourteen roofs. A few figures strode about, some feeding the animals penned up in the yards beside their houses, some walking the dirt lanes as if taking a morning stroll, but accompanied by at least one knightly figure that hung back as if watchful of the group. No one, despite the bound sheaves, was wielding a flail over any laid-out stalks of wheat—they must have known that the baker was gone.

In fact, John pointed out that his brother's bakehouse was dark and smokeless. It stood nearest the mill. No one was attending to the animals in its yard, either. Starting from the bakehouse, John identified a cooper's, a blacksmith, a tannery, and, farther back, a main hall, which was a larger version of the thatch-roofed houses, with four windows along its sides. Almost all the houses had smaller outbuildings on their properties. Had it not been for the knights and the lack of threshing, the scene would have been deceptively idyllic. Smoke floated out of the main hall chimney.

"John, if you had but five men to hold a population of, what, twenty-five perhaps? What would you do with them?"

Little John pondered a moment. Then he replied, "I'd be keepin' them in one place, all together."

"Agreed."

Thomas studied the bakehouse and mill. If John could hold the Yvags' attention on the bridge long enough for him and Will to get in place, this might yet work.

"All right, then," he said quietly, "it's over to you, John. I won't be long, and next time you see me, I'll be in your brother's house."

"You'll what?"

"Or maybe the mill. Once I'm back, though, you stay low—just for safety's sake." Then Thomas patted him on the shoulder, rolled aside, and took off running down the hill and below the others watching the vill from the ridge.

Back along the road and away from the vill, he drew up beside the white stallion. "Well," he told it, "at least I know you won't talk." He stepped close to the beast. Someone in The Saylis might see everything, but that couldn't be helped. He took out his ördstone and concentrated on his destination. Eyes closed, he focused upon the chantry in the King's Houses once again, then sliced the air and quickly stepped through the portal, turned and sealed it up.

He stood a moment in the empty chamber, then crossed to the altar and uncovered the hidden space where he'd stuffed his masonry tool bag. The bag only had one ördstone in it now. He took the one Will had given him and dropped it in. The two stones skritched and burbled, a sensation like insect legs trying to communicate, to twist his mind as they'd once done to Alpin. He closed up the bag and drew his own ördstone again.

Thomas stared up at the massive limewood tree. He removed his bow and leaned it against the corrugated trunk, then hauled himself up and out of sight. The spatulate leaves shivered as he made his way around to the hole where he'd left the remaining two *dights*. Those he quickly dropped into the masonry bag along with the ördstones. These fluttered and flickered as if agitated in the presence of the little pyramids. The skritching grew louder; the pressure in his head became a dull headache.

He grabbed onto a lower branch and swung down to the ground again. Facing him as if he'd grown there stood Sir Richard atte Lee.

"Sir Richard," Thomas said, not terribly surprised. "Aren't you supposed to be observing the vill?"

"So," replied the knight, making no pretense of innocence, "this is where the *dights* are safest, is it?"

Thomas could not help smiling at that. "Seemed so to me and they're still here. You and your kind were so busy turning over the King's Houses, I couldn't very well hide them there any longer."

"Kunastur found them, then?"

"He did not, though he tried. And you—is this the weary *flesh* of Sir Richard or have you reshaped yourself into him? I know it's not mere glamour. You have his voice."

"His *fetch*, am I? Which do you think?" Sir Richard closed a hand around the hilt of his sword.

Thomas guessed its blade would throw off a multicolored sheen. He estimated the distance to where his bow leaned against the side of the limewood tree. "I think you reshaped. I noticed on our way here you've periodically gone off on your own—once even as we spoke—no doubt to unspell yourself and regather your strength."

"You suspected all this time? How could you?"

"Where Nicnevin's concerned, I've a suspicious mind."

Sir Richard's brow furrowed. "How come you to know the Queen's name?"

"You asked me that before. Does everyone on your side insist on learning that?"

"Before?" The knight gestured dismissively, then extended the arm. "Hand to me the *dights* now."

"Tell me first—how did you arrive here of all places?"

Sir Richard showed his annoyance at this delay but reached into his kirtle, then held up between thumb and middle finger an ördstone larger than Thomas's own, more like the ones Waldroup had once collected. "You thieved our hostages in Palavia Parva. A simple matter it was to track you here from there."

"Ah, the portal." They were like apparitional doors along a hallway, each opening to a specific destination.

"I should care to know how it is *you* come to have and use such a stone."

"That's a tiresomely old story, *Zhanedd*. Do you have that much time, or would you prefer to discard this shape first? We both know you aren't Sir Richard atte Lee. I assume he's past suffering?" The knight said nothing. "If you care to conserve your energy, I won't prevent you."

Sir Richard bowed slightly as if in thanks. His body began to ripple and contort. It broadened into something more powerful, even taller. The voice, becoming a croak, replied, "He might be dead by now, your Sir Richard; he is certainly otherwise vacant."

As the transforming Yvag knight spoke, Thomas dove over the nearest roots of the tree. The nacreous blade of the sword bit into the trunk where he'd stood. He rolled, snatched the bow as he passed it, and sprang up behind the limewood's massive bole. If that damnable snaking blade could bend around the tree, he was doomed.

"There is no escaping," said a voice no longer belonging to Sir Richard, but deeper, a growl like a rusted hinge. The sword did not shoot around the tree.

"I was going to say the same," Thomas replied. He stepped out, bow drawn to kill the Yvag that had tortured and dogged him.

And did not fire.

He had never beheld anything like the creature that confronted him. Tall and muscular in the Yvag armor of black and silver, it stood its ground. Its face portrayed the very essence of beauty, an allure that compelled him, tugged at him. He stumbled a step toward it before that visage and the entire creature changed to something jagged and skeletal at once, propelling him back but without releasing its hold over him; then again it warped into a hideous, distorted form bent on devouring him if he remained, and then again into achingly enticing beauty . . . It flickered, shifted, transformed while he stood his ground but barely. Its bewitchment teased and tangled in his mind no matter how the shape of it focused upon him and fluttered through glimpses of things, moments, people he'd known. Onchu swirled past Alpin swallowed Innes melted into Baldie becoming Aðalbrandr, and so on too fast to name, a ceaseless coruscation into new forms stolen from his memory. Whether he stared at it straight on or turned to view it sidelong, the creature flickered hypnotically, its identity always becoming something or someone else—Yvag, human, animal, frond, stone, lightning, darkness, death, and through all of these it grinned maniacally, basked in its effect, which it must have known, a living cockatrice.

Five minutes staring upon it and almost anyone would be driven insane, robbed of their memories. As it slid through new forms, Thomas hurled himself back behind the limewood tree before he became rooted to the spot.

The thing asked again, "How know you the name of the Queen?"

"What is your name? You're not Zhanedd."

The creature made an eerie creaking sound. Thomas realized it was laughing. "Zhanedd," it said, "that weak changeling. I am the only one the Queen trusts."

He replied with mock disdain. "Oh, the Queen again. She trusts you?"

"I am her wean."

"*You?*"

"I am Bragrender mac Nicnevin."

"Nicnevin?"

"Jumalatar Nicnevin Ní Morrigu. My mother, Queen of Ailfion, for whom I will kill you and collect the *dights* you stole. Now, come out and face me!"

They would be dying in Palavia Parva, a battle surely engaged in the Barnsdale Wood without him by now. This monstrous spawn of Nicnevin would hold him here forever if he didn't act. However fast he was, he knew it would be faster. No help for that. He drew two arrows, stepped quickly out, fired the first knowing the creature would block it, shot the second at the ördstone it still held. The arrow pierced its hand and drove the stone away, into the brush. But the sword in its other hand had already jumped, and though he dodged, it cut through his thigh so swiftly and sharply that he didn't quite realize until it snapped back. Then the cut burned.

Lurching away, Thomas collapsed. Bragrender could have killed him then but went racing to retrieve its escaped stone. He hastily drew his, focused on the bakehouse of Parva, and sliced his way back there again. His vision blurred though, the cold creeping agony of his wound skewing his arrival. The gate opened not in the bakehouse but beside the mill—not where he'd intended to arrive. He threw himself through the ring, then turned and sealed it up. The creature was bellowing his name—"Robyn"—which rippled and warped away as the gate vanished, becoming a loud bleat above him. He looked up to find a goat staring him in the face. He was in the bakehouse yard.

Not far away, Little John stood staring down an occupying knight.

Thomas lay there, arrow drawn and pointed at where the gate had been. If Bragrender even started to open it now, he would eat an arrow. But the air did not spark. Bragrender would know Thomas was expecting him this time, and not yet how severely he'd been wounded.

When, after a minute, nothing appeared in the air, Thomas gathered his strength and rolled over. The goat bumbled out of his way. He was seeing spots in a collapsing swirl of darkness. There was no time to prepare or protect himself further.

He stumbled up and lunged into the empty mill, managing not to pass out before he'd shut the door after him.

XLIII. Another Millstone

Leggings soaked from fording the Went, Will Scathelock sent three of his group into the orchard near the small church. Once they were situated behind three trees, he led his remaining two bowmen around the priest's house and the church and took up positions behind the low front wall surrounding the burial ground.

From there, he watched Little John stand upon the bridge awaiting some sign that the demonic elves had seen him. Perhaps, thought Will, he should shoot one of those guarding the humans who were outside and feeding their animals. At any moment he expected to hear a clash of archers, swords, Yvags, *something* from back down the road. And where had Robyn gone? He was nowhere to be seen. Was he in the thick of that fray Will couldn't hear? More likely he'd gone to fetch the spinners (although Will had thought they were in the tattered old bag he carried). He had probably cut open one of those circles in the air for himself. Will shuddered at the thought. It had been strange enough riding that beast while holding one of those stones. He hadn't mentioned to Robyn the one time he'd dropped it and the beast had come to a dead stop until he got down and found it again.

From here he couldn't see the other members of their band, either, including that tall skinny outlaw whom Robyn addressed deferentially as "Sir Richard." He was almost certain the Keepers had come across that one before with three or four others. How did Robyn know him?

Or maybe Robyn was leading a group around the vill right now to come at the demons from the half-harvested fields on the slopes above it? There was a lot Will wished he'd been privy to, but returning Isabella's body to her castle had been a task he could not shirk.

Just then a knight in a surcoat of alternating red and black panels abruptly came out of the cooper's house close by and took up a position facing the bridge. The knight did nothing further, just stood and waited. Little John started down the slope from the bridge.

For what? wondered Will. And odd, his surcoat. Drustan Liddel had said the knights were dressed in Passelewe's colors. Not this one. He didn't look demonic, either—just choleric, as if occupying this hamlet was a waste of his precious time. But upon his appearance, the other knights ushered the villeins away from the animals and herded them into the larger central hall. Will got the impression the whole vill was being kept in there.

After a minute, the same four knights emerged from the hall. Two of them carried crossbows. Like the first, they took up positions just outside it and then stood, still as statues. Unlike him, they tilted their heads back as though they could see all the way to The Saylis from here. None of them seemed aware of the presence of Will and his men.

To the two beside him, he said, "Take aim, good yeo—" when, on the far side of Little John in the narrow space between the mill and the bakehouse, the air suddenly lit up bright green. Will nearly shouted to John, sure that the demons were invading the vill from without. Instead, who should bound out of the fiery ring but Robyn Hoode. He seemed dazed for an instant, but then lay there aiming his bow at nothing. A small goat gamboled up to him before he finally lowered the bow, turned, stumbling awkwardly, and scrambled for the mill. He was wounded, that was clear—one entire leg was slick with blood. But when had he changed into that same black armor Will had put on? Little John, having walked down from the bridge, didn't even see him. Neither did the first knight outside the cooper's. The bakehouse itself must have blocked his view.

What madness had overtaken Robyn that he'd openly revealed his ability to work the demons' magic? Did he possess the spinners in his bag after all? He still carried it with him. But who had wounded him so grievously?

Even as he wondered all of this, from the direction of The Saylis came the blast of the ram's horn: Presumably, the archers had engaged the demonic knights in a skirmish. From behind Will came an odd pressure, as if someone's fingers were pushing up through his hair. He could not help glancing back. The door of the church had opened. A white-robed priest stood there. The priest might have *appeared* human, but there was no mistaking the nature of that pressure: He was communicating with the knights. Without a single word he was telling them of the bowmen in the graveyard.

Will found the four knights staring his way.

"Well, that's just enough of that." He pivoted about and raised his bow to aim at the priest.

Thomas opened his eyes to find Isabella Birkin kneeling beside him. She was pale and bloodless in death as he'd seen her last. She had torn a cotton flour sack apart and ripped a long strip of the cloth to tie around his thigh. Having ministered to his wound, she looked upon him with seraphic joy; yet the first words out of her mouth were, "You'll lose that leg."

"I won't," he replied. "I heal quickly."

"So you do." Astonishment filled her voice. He followed her gaze to his own leg, which was indeed whole once more, the blood gone, even Robert Hodde's legging knitted whole once more. "I do not," she told him sadly, "I'm dead." Then she confessed, "I never expected to know love again."

"Nor I." But vaguely he was aware that he wasn't conscious, and had passed out propped against the wooden bin where the flour poured out of the chute below the millstones. His head swung side to side and his eyes fluttered open. He raised his head up. No Isabella greeted him. No, of course not. The realization stabbed at him. His leg was indeed tied off with a strip from a flour sack, but he had done this himself in his last lucid moments. Blood had darkened the floorboards beneath him, but at least it had stopped flowing. His leg was wetly carved and raw but the wound didn't look quite as bad as before. No doubt the glamoured Yvag armor had minimized the damage that Sir Richard, whatever he was, had inflicted. "Bragrender." Another elven name.

Thomas looked around. Unlike Oakmill, there was no table or stools, no Forbes or Janet, no Aðalbrandr seeking revenge. No Sir

Richard in any form, only two short, thick planks leaning against the walls, one by each of the two doors. The miller could bar his doors, probably so that no one could inadvertently open them in the midst of a grinding and set the wind to whirling through. Those would prove useful.

He must not have been unconscious for more than a few minutes. No one was shouting or fighting outside. It sounded like John was talking, and having to bellow his words at that, so at some distance from whoever he addressed.

With some difficulty, Thomas got to his feet and hobbled to a shuttered window. He pushed against the shutter, opened it only enough to see out. Something pressed against his good leg and he looked down: An orange-and-white cat twined itself around his legs. "You the local rat catcher, are you?" he asked it. "Shame on you for letting the vermin invade." The cat looked up at him, seemed to determine that he was not about to supply it with a snack, and wandered off across the floor. "Best you not remain here long, puss. Go hunt mice elsewhere."

Outside, John was explaining that the "spinners are gunna take a little longer to lay 'ands upon," and glancing worriedly back at the bakehouse.

The listening knight appeared impatient enough to run John through where he stood below the bridge. There was no time to waste.

Thomas grabbed his toolbag and carried it up the steps to the grinding stones. Partially ground grain lay around and in the center hole as if the work had been interrupted. He untied the bag and reached in. The ördstones buzzed in his head like angry bees, as if they knew his intent. He winced but carried on, dropping the two ördstones into the hole. He was about to add both the spinners, but hesitated. If this worked as he hoped, Nicnevin and the Yvag would assume that all the spinners had been destroyed. He could not say why just then, but he felt that a time would come when he would be glad of holding onto one of these. He returned it to his tool bag, then leaned over and covered the three pieces with the grain while muttering, "Millstone around *my* neck, Alpin. So obvious, hey?"

He limped to the rear door of the mill, nearest the large vertical wheel. Just outside, beside a narrow stone walkway, a lever protruded that released the exterior wheel. The walkway or jetty continued along, paralleling the mill, to the end of the channel, where a sluice gate attached to a rope and pulley controlled the water's flow past the wheel.

Back inside, Thomas gathered his bow, belt quiver, and toolbag and carried them out beside the lever. He glamoured his Yvag armor, turning himself into the incarnation of Robyn Hoode once more—Lincoln green cotehardie with red trim. His whole thigh throbbed, though the wound looked better.

Grabbing a broom on which to lean, he hobbled through the mill to the door on the opposite side, through which he'd crashed. He opened the door and limped outside, this time toward the base of the bridge.

John turned just then, and a look of great relief came over him. The knight he'd been speaking with had already spotted Thomas and headed straight for him, hand on the hilt of his sword.

"No closer," Thomas shouted. "If you want your *dights*, you release all your prisoners first from the hall."

The knight drew up, sourly replied, "Then we'll have none to bargain with."

Thomas laughed. "With another force coming up the road at our backs to trap us even now, you feel you need hostages? We know what you have planned." He gave the knight a moment to consider that. "You want the *dights*, send the people over the bridge with my friend now. Once they're safe, you are welcome to repossess the two you don't have. I am leaving them in the mill for you."

John looked as if he wanted to object but Thomas shook his head. He must get the inhabitants of the vill to safety, which was to say, over the bridge.

The knight was communicating with more of the Yvags scattered about. The humming pressure of it pushed into Thomas's head.

He marked Will Scathelock in the kirkyard, aiming an arrow at the doorway of the church, as if he expected someone to come out. Or maybe he'd already sent them fleeing back inside. That led him to wonder if other Yvag knights might be glamoured to blend in with the inhabitants. He knew they'd never intended to deal fairly with John, but they also probably thought five of them could easily finish him off. No wonder the knight looked so dyspeptic.

"Very well," the knight agreed finally. "We will release them all but you remain in the mill, your friend upon the bridge. And those behind the kirkyard wall must withdraw."

Thomas gave Will a nod to retreat, then limped on the broomstick over to John.

Will and his two companions climbed over the low graveyard wall and made for the bridge. Passing Thomas, he whispered, "Three still in the orchard if you need reinforcements."

"Good," Thomas replied. Turning to John, he said, "You heard?" John nodded. "Among us you're the only one knows the inhabitants here. Watch them carefully as they cross over the bridge. I fear there might be a substitution or addition. Will was aiming at something beside the church. So watch there." John nodded again. "And remember what I said about staying low."

The four knights, meanwhile, had gone into the central hall. Almost at once, people emerged, clearly more than happy to escape their captivity. As he headed back to the mill, Thomas wondered if they knew that their captors weren't even human.

The citizens of Palavia Parva walked up the bridge around John. One, a barrel-chested man with a red apple of a nose, tugged on his sleeve and said, "'Ere, whatcher doin' to me mill?"

"Using it t'save your life today," he replied, watching Robyn go in. The miller looked forlornly from John to the mill and back again; shaking his head, he continued up over the bridge, muttering, "Outlaws an' knaves."

The knights came last of all. John watched them suspiciously: two with crossbows, and two sporting those lethal swords. In the air around them circled little flitting creatures. One darted ahead and dove at John. He smacked it with his quarterstaff so hard that it flew against the bakehouse and fell to the ground. It did not get up. The other flitting hobs circled back and kept their distance.

Despite the threatening presence of the knights, Little John was glad to see all of the vill set free and not so much as an arrow fired or a sword drawn, but he didn't trust the luck. Did the knights know that their forces in the woods had met with resistance? The sounding of the ram's horn had told him that much. Maybe those coming out of the rings were too far away to communicate with these five. Maybe the archers had sent them all packing before they got through. He recalled Robyn explaining how the elves were so long-lived beneath their resistant armor that they hardly believed death could touch them any longer. He wondered if that might make them terrified of the fight: Geoffrey had described the one in Chandler's Lane gaol, petrified with fear at the prospect of death. If you lived forever, what did death even mean to you? He scratched his head, thinking about terrified demons while the citizens of the vill passed him and went up and over the bridge, until only Little John and the five knights remained.

The knights looked him over, menacing, cold. To each he returned the look twice as darkly. They still didn't have their spinners. They didn't dare harm him, not yet. He stood his ground and they all turned away and headed across the croft to the mill.

They're all yours now, Woodwose, an' God help tha. He started up the bridge. Will Scathelock awaited him at the top.

XLIV. The Death of Robyn Hoode

With the knights heading for him, Thomas ducked inside the mill and immediately barred the door. He hobbled across the room, gave the grinding wheels a last look. He'd done this before; he knew how it ended.

The knights began battering the door as he opened and retreated out the back. The bar wasn't thick. It wouldn't hold for long.

Thomas gathered his bow, quiver and bag. At the lever, he pushed to release it. The wheel rocked free on its spindle. He charged clumsily along the walkway. The leg was improving with each passing moment.

Reaching the end of the walkway, he drew up the sluice gate and the water poured through. The main millwheel began to turn.

Inside, the five Yvag knights broke through the door. The split wooden bar clattered to the floor. Two hobs zoomed in and whirled about the space. Robyn Hoode had gone. Then the vertical interior wheel began to rotate on its axis, driving the mechanism that turned the millstones. They bombinated fiercely in increasing panic. Where were the *dights*?

The millstones gave out a terrible crack. One knight bounded up the steps to the wheels and glanced down into the hole in their center. The tip of a single *dight* pointed out of the heaped half-ground grain. The soldier dove for it, reaching frantically into the hole. Got its fingers on it just as the stone caught a different corner and snapped the pyramid between the wheels. Fingers became caught between it and something else hidden in the grain. The Yvag screeched. The hand was pulled in and relentlessly crushed. A second knight tried to assist. Another crack, and a streak of blue lightning shot out of the hole and right through that knight. Its glamour vanished in an instant. Smoke curled out of its chest, and it toppled from the platform into the flour bin below. More lightning, green and yellow this time, stabbed the air, and crackled up the second knight, whose trapped arm pulled it relentlessly down.

A keening rose out of the hole, mechanical and yet the wail of something in agony, of a soul released from captivity.

The one who'd led them in buzzed: "Ördstones in the bottom, too late now, get out get out!" That knight charged for the rear door and out onto the walkway, to be met with an arrow in the chest and another in the neck. The two following backpedaled and turned to retreat out the smashed door, led by their flying, terrified hobs.

More green flashes erupted as the twisted *dight* ruptured. As if doused in flammable oil like a torch, the trapped Yvag knight burst into green flame and a moment later was yanked over the turning stone and straight into the center hole. The last two made it out as green and blue streaks connected and spread, sheathing the whole mill in an aquamarine glow. Luminescent, the mill burst like a bubble in a flash as bright as a miniature sun. In its wake it left nothing.

The structure was gone. The remaining stone floor smoldered like the floor of an oven.

Little John was standing on the ridge on the far side of the river when the mill exploded. The force knocked him down the embankment. He got to his feet and ran back up the slope, calling out "Woodwose!" and "Robyn!" again and again. The last John had seen, Robyn had been standing right beside the main wheel when he shot that demon knight—far too close when all the colored lightning struck. The millwheel had been sheared straight across with the top half gone. The squat miller was screaming at him in outrage.

There was no trace of Robyn Hoode on the narrow walkway, now cracked and strewn with rubble. Little John sat down on the ridge and put his head in his hands.

✠ ✠ ✠

Downriver, Thomas crawled up onto the opposite bank with his bow and quiver, the latter full now of both arrows and river water. Dazed, he sat in the mud and poured the water out of the leather quiver and out of his mason's bag, and stared back the way he'd come.

The river had carried him farther than he'd intended, but he could still make out what had happened after he'd jumped. The mill simply wasn't there any longer—not surprising, given he'd used two ördstones and a *dight*. He was somewhat amazed that the rest of Parva was still standing.

It looked like two of the elven knights had survived. One fired his crossbow at someone across the bridge that Thomas couldn't see from there, one of their archers no doubt. Beside the bridge, Will Scathelock and two companions jumped up and fired back. As arrows fell, the knight who'd led them ran back the way it had come, in the direction of the hall. Thomas expected, by the time someone pursued the knight, they would find the hall empty. The knights had lost and they knew it.

Unsteadily, Thomas stood, and winced. The leap from the walkway had done his wound no favors.

He sloshed on up to the road. He was back among the birch trees, back the way they had come, halfway to The Saylis. The archers would be in the woods somewhere, and he began looking for them, heard shouting from deeper in and followed it. He soon came upon two archers, one dead and the other alive but just barely. It looked like those impossible swords had done their work, straight through one and into the side of the other. He took a legging from the dead man and gave it to the other to press against his wound. It did not look lethal and he told the archer as much.

As he went on, he encountered more bodies—mostly fallen Yvags—one here, one there, and he suspected these represented places where gates had opened and the archers had been ready and waiting. Ahead, someone yelled, and he limped along as fast as he could, nocking an arrow, which proved fortuitous as he came up a draw to find two remaining archers rushing to aid a wounded third and fourth against yet another glamoured knight. They didn't need his help; nevertheless, as the Yvag knight directed its blade, he fired. His arrow impaled its arm and the magic sword spun out of the

Yvag's grasp before it could span the distance to another archer. The Yvag fell back through the open portal and, on the other side, a figure hurried forward and sealed the gate. A second arrow struck the closing circle and fell as if it had hit a wall.

The archers cheered. From behind him a familiar voice said, "Well done, Robyn," and something stung his right shoulder through the glamoured Yvag armor. He twisted about. Sir Richard was backing away from him, smiling.

"Bragrender," Thomas said, and reached out to grab the false knight, but his legs gave way and he fell face-first into the leaves.

The first of the archers reached him. "What happened?"

Thomas stared and tried to answer. Nothing came out. The potion, whatever it was, had paralyzed him.

Sir Richard said, "I know not. I came forward to congratulate him on his shot and he collapsed. Here, see, he is wounded."

"His leg, oh—"

"He must have been in another skirmish. Can there be more of these treacherous demons in the woods?" Sir Richard asked and glanced about.

"Someone go tell the others!"

"I'll stay with him," Sir Richard promised.

"We will also," one of the archers replied, indicating he and his friend would remain there with their wounded company as well. Another bowman ran off toward the road. One of the remaining bowmen said, "He came to our aid despite his wound."

Sir Richard shrugged. "As you like."

Thomas, helpless, tried desperately to move, but could not even shift his gaze to focus.

Shortly, Little John and Will arrived, followed by Elias and Calum down from The Saylis. "His eyes are open," said Elias. "We have to seek aid for him and the other wounded here and at the vill. What do we do?"

Keeping his distance from the body, Sir Richard suggested, "I know the prioress at Kirklees, Sister Amille. A hospice there she runs, with nuns quite sanative. Had we a cart or wagon, we could bring him and the others there. It's not terribly far."

"What do you think?" Elias asked of John.

"There are wagons in the vill," John said, but his final, suspicious glance was at Sir Richard, who strode farther off away from Thomas. John remained at his side.

Will and Elias returned with a wagon drawn by two horses. They already had the miller, shot through the shoulder with a crossbow, lying in it. They added Thomas, the two wounded archers, and two other outlaws who'd defended the vill in the wicker-sided wagon bed, one of whom had a broken leg. Sir Richard offered to ride along to show them the way. Little John replied, "Oh, ah know way to Kirklees well enough. You can walk along wi' the others."

Smiling, Sir Richard said, "Of course," and joined those on foot, including Geoffrey and Will. The family Fouke and two of Will's men opted to remain behind and help in the vill. But most accompanied the wagon on the off chance that more circles would blossom along the way.

Beyond a gatehouse, the Priory of Kirklees was three sides of a square, with a wide, open courtyard in the center surrounding a garden where various medicinal plants were growing. As the wagon passed the gatehouse, the prioress came out from the center of the larger structure and stood watching their arrival. Sister Amille was a small, compact woman with dark hair. To Little John as they neared, she seemed self-possessed and still, not in the least shaken by the arrival of so many. She seemed to count the outlaws accompanying the wagon as they passed by. Following after her was a monk in a brown frock, the hood up. His shadowed face was pale, and mostly what could be seen was his red beard. He was perhaps the local prelate here to interfere in matters at the priory.

John jumped down and led the sister to the back of the wagon, telling her, "We 'ave wounded from battle this day who need your ministrations." He wanted her to know that no one here intended her any harm.

She walked after, giving each of the wounded a cursory examination until the wagon drew up. "Bring them in to the south wing of the priory," she told him. "That's our infirmary. We have pallets enough in there to accommodate all of these. Come." Those who'd followed along on foot helped the wounded down, save for the Woodwose himself, who didn't move. At some point along the way his eyes had closed. John directed her attention to him. The rest had superficial wounds. There was something truly wrong with him. "Bring him inside," she said. John obediently dragged the Woodwose out of the wagon and picked him up.

Sister Amille darted a glance at the quiet monk, who remained on the opposite side of the wagon, provoking Will Scathelock, beside John, to ask her who he was.

"Why, he's the abbot of St. Mary's," she said. "Sir Roger Doncaster."

"That's 'Red Roger'?" Will said to John, but too softly for the abbot's ears. They both kept an eye on him.

The abbot continued to watch the men helped past him but did not make a move to assist with them. He seemed more interested in observing Sister Amille than in attending to the wounded. Everyone had been helped past him before he turned and followed after them all.

At the door Sir Richard disentangled from a slightly wounded archer and let the man hobble inside alone. The tall knight remained by the entrance. John stared daggers at him while carrying Robyn in last of all, but Sir Richard appeared to take no notice.

The infirmary space was long and narrow, like a converted cloister. They had left a pallet in the front for Robyn.

John placed him on it alongside the others. Robyn's head lolled. He didn't even seem to be breathing. "Oh, Woodwose, don't tha die on me now, and leave me ta face that angry miller alone."

Sister Amille entered last and closed the door after her, but not before John glimpsed the abbot and Sir Richard chatting outside. That made no sense at all. Robyn had told him the story of Sir Richard and how he'd been done out of his lands by that very abbot. So why wasn't he drawing his blade and stabbing the bastard eighteen times? It's what *he* would have done. Instead, they behaved like old chums.

Sister Amille knelt beside the body of Robyn Hoode.

Little John asked, "Where are the rest'a your nuns?"

"They were . . . all afraid of your small army." She smiled. "You're all quite terrifying, you know. Like men who've just barely survived a battle. We don't see much of that here."

"Us? We're no threat to no one." He exchanged a doubtful look with Scathelock. "No other sisters?"

Will stood a moment longer, then began working his way to the back of the cloister while pretending to look closely at the other wounded men on their pallets. He came to where Elias, Geoffrey, and Calum stood chatting. He leaned close and said something to the three Waits. Then he walked on, continuing to observe the wounded.

The Waits turned and ambled toward the main door, raising their voices as they went. Calum said, "I'll bet my mother's salve would fix old Robyn's wound!"

Geoffrey all but leapt backward. "Your mother? She's a notorious witch!"

"What's that?" asked Elias. "You'd have us dabble in witchcraft? They'll burn us at the stake for your mother's concoction."

Geoffrey addressed Sister Amille. "What say you, Sister? Is such a liniment nought but witchery?"

"What's she put in it?" Elias asked.

"I—" said the sister.

"Aconite and belladonna," Calum replied.

"*Monkshood*, the very devil's helmet, and you dare suggest it's not a witch's brew?" Geoffrey rose to his full and incensed height.

Calum insisted, "It ain't witchcraft. I'll show it you. In the wagon. You come and see. That's where I keep it." He jabbed Geoffrey. "I'll rub some on *you* and maybe cure your *temper.*" The three continued their loud squabbling as they threw open the door and went past Sir Richard and the abbot as if oblivious of them. The abbot and the knight watched them for a moment, then came inside. No one other than Little John noticed that Will Scathelock had absented himself from the infirmary altogether.

With things calmed down, Sister Amille told John, "I've little hope for your friend. My recommendation is that we bleed him awhile, hope to balance his humors."

John scratched his head. "Been wounded in leg, 'e has. Surely he's already lost all the blood he can afford."

The prioress glanced past John. He knew the chummy Red Roger and Sir Richard stood where she looked. He felt more than heard an odd susurrus in his head. To John, Sister Amille made a perturbed face. "I'm sorry," she said, "I feel you should go with your friends outside and let me work with these poor men. The abbot can assist me, and that is enough."

"I don't mean to leave his side," insisted John.

Sir Richard called, "Now, now, we must let the sister do her work. She knows more of healing than any of us could."

Under his breath, John muttered, "Then, when's she gunna start using it?"

The prioress didn't hear—she had walked to the back of the infirmary, to return with a dull metal bowl and two sharpened blood irons. She shooed Little John. "Go on," she said, "it will all be better after this."

Sir Richard opened the double doors. The few other archers and outlaws filed out until only John remained. Robyn seemed as still as death.

The prioress was humming something quietly under her breath. Little John barely noticed before his thoughts became confused, and she whispered to him, "Go outside, and all will be well." Sir Richard followed all the others, stepping outside as well, and making of himself an example. He gestured to John to follow.

John found himself on his feet and plodding up the aisle. The red-haired abbot stood at the door. John knew he should not go outside, but seemed to have no control over his actions. Sister Amille's humming led him along as if she walked before him. He stared at Red Roger, thinking, if Doncaster was like the prelate on the road, then what was the prioress? What was Sir Richard? Then he was out the doors and shuffling toward the wagon, where everyone else was gathered in the dull late-afternoon light.

Halfway there, he was met by Will Scathelock, who emerged from the north wing of the priory. "John," he said, and his name seemed to draw Little John out of his spell. They reached the wagon together.

Geoffrey said, "Well?"

Will asked, "John, are you all right?"

"I . . . No, she spelled me."

"Who?" asked Calum.

"Sister Amille."

Will declared, "She isn't Sister Amille."

They all stared at him.

Elias said, "What?"

"Sister Amille is dead, along with all the nuns of the priory, stripped of her tunic and veil." He gestured back the way he'd come.

"Then who is she? What is she?"

Little John said, "She's one'a them things like we met in Orrels's gaol." He picked up his bow. "Likewise Sir Richard and the abbot."

Elias replied, "Is every prelate in the land turned into one of these creatures?"

"Would not surprise me," said Geoffrey.

"But Robyn, he vouched for Sir Richard, right?"

"Vouched for who he used to be. Not who he is." He turned to face the doors. Sir Richard had quietly gone back inside. "Come on!" he yelled.

Will drew and nocked his bow. The others drew theirs.

They marched for the infirmary door and were almost upon it when Calum cried, "Look!" and pointed to one of the quarrel-paned windows. A reflection of green fire flickered in the panes. John broke into a run.

XLV. The Little Stone of Robyn Hoode

The prioress slid one of Thomas's arms off the side of the stuffed palliasse and over the bowl, took up a leaf-shaped blade by its thin metal handle, and cut along his forearm. The thick red blood began to flow.

Sister Amille continued to emit an odd tuneless humming, and the other wounded men on their straw pallets lay in a daze of the same spell she'd cast over Little John. Doncaster leaned over and studied the cut. "A good job of it," he said. "But you drain him dry and he'll be of no use as a *teind*."

Sister Amille broke off her humming. "Oh, I won't let him perish. There is something I would know of him."

"How he is still alive?" Sir Richard asked the question as he closed the priory doors behind him. "I should like to hear that, as would Mother. That is, the Queen."

The sister briefly smiled. "So it's official. We all want to know the answer. He is too good at what he does, the way he interferes. The Queen does not seem to appreciate this. But she will. Tonight I put an end to all his obtrusion."

"*We* put an end to it, you mean," corrected Sir Richard. The doors had no lock, no bar. He tugged on one instead, as if it were no great effort. The top hinge creaked and twisted, the wood deformed, and the two doors stood jammed together tightly in the middle. "I do hate to bring this up, but that John is soon going to realize he was spelled. This appraisal of yours is best finished on the other side."

"Where it was always going to finish," agreed Doncaster, "and him tossed into Hel."

"Fine, go about it," she answered in a tone that said she would not participate. She was hovering over her victim, watching. What she saw seemed at first an optical illusion—that the thin stream of blood had reversed direction. But it was no illusion. Blood was flowing up out of the pewter bowl and back into the incision she'd made. "Yes!" she hissed triumphantly. "Look! He is *Yvag*."

"What?" Doncaster hurried over to her while Sir Richard, armed with an ördstone, began to cut an opening in the middle of the aisle directly in front of the palliasse on which Thomas lay.

The spitting ring of green fire opened onto one of Ailfion's plazas, surrounded by glass and silver spires and needles pointing into the nocturnal blood-dark sky.

Something hard struck the heavy doors and then struck them again. There was yelling. Recognizable voices.

Doncaster tucked away his stone to draw his blade. Sister Amille unglamoured in an instant into Zhanedd, her gray-green face and golden eyes all that showed of the Yvag beneath the tunic and veil she wore. Zhanedd grabbed onto Thomas to pull him upright.

Sir Richard turned from the gate he'd opened. "But if he's Yvag—"

Thomas came up easily and swiftly, eyes open, and he buried a black dagger in Zhanedd's throat, then wrenched it down.

Wide-eyed and burbling up black blood, Zhanedd stumbled back out of reach and fell across the next patient who, spelled, flopped off the straw-filled bedding. Thomas hung onto his barbed dagger.

In that moment the broken door cracked further and was dragged partway open. Outlaws ducked in one at a time. Little John came first, his bow brandished as if to ward off a blow, followed by Will Scathelock, who fired even as he stood up. John's shot followed close on. Arrows flew like winged vipers, and Calum charged in after them with a quarterstaff and a dagger. He went for Sir Richard, but halfway there, Sir Richard reshaped into Bragrender, who rose up to its full height as it flickered angrily through multiple forms snatched from those all around it.

"Stop!" cried Elias. "Calum, come back!"

But Calum did not hear. Basilisklike, Bragrender's irresistible transformations stole Calum's will. Even at the distance of the doorway the bowmen could all feel the creature's bewitching effects and knew to stay back.

Will and another archer managed to fire off two arrows. Little John cried, "I don't dare for fear of killing Calum!" Will's arrow struck Bragrender, penetrating the armor, but just barely. The other arrow hit the opened gate and slowly passed through it.

Doncaster tackled Thomas and both tumbled off the pallet. He tried to stab Thomas with a thin quillon dagger. Thomas grabbed the abbot's wrist with one hand and punched him in the face with the other, once, twice, the second time slashing across his face with the slick dagger. It hardly seemed to faze Red Roger.

Bragrender clutched Calum as a shield and sidestepped to where Zhanedd lay, black blood still bubbling from her long wound. Bragrender lifted her as if she weighed nothing, then hurtled across the aisle and through the open gate. An instant later, it tossed Calum back out, then sealed up the gateway. Seeing the gate close, Doncaster tried to get up and away.

As the last of the portal sparked and was gone, the outlaws and Waits raced to Calum and Thomas's aid.

Will fired into Doncaster's back, the arrow coming out the front. Doncaster folded forward, nearly impaling Thomas on the protruding head of the arrow.

Little John reached down and grabbed Red Roger by his hair. Thomas raised his dagger and stabbed the abbot through his heart. Knowing what was coming then, he pushed the body off him and onto the nearest palliasse, where the miller of Palavia Parva lay. Doncaster erupted in a mist of red.

John found himself holding up an already rotting corpse, which he flung away. It sagged across the miller, who was just beginning to stir and who shrieked in coming face-to-face with the moldering Red Roger.

"Woodwose!" bellowed Little John. He pulled Thomas up. "Ye yet live."

"Thanks to you and Will, I—" He stopped. Behind Little John, Elias and Geoffrey were kneeling with Calum, whose lifeless body they held between them.

Elias's head swung like a bell. "Such a good lad," he said. "He was the best of us."

"He was. So, too, Sir Richard," said Thomas, "whose likeness they stripped from him to deceive us. Their idea of a jest."

"We should kill them all."

"I wouldn't disagree with you."

Elias continued to embrace Calum, his head bowed.

Will said, "But you were *dead* in the wagon—we couldn't so much as rouse you."

Thomas answered, "I was poisoned. A dagger, a ring perhaps, wielded by Sir Richard who was not Sir Richard any more than that rotten thing was Red Roger of Doncaster."

"Skinwalker." Will all but spat the word. He told Thomas, "They slew Sister Amille and the others."

Thomas considered that. "This was a coordinated plan."

"But how could they know we would triumph in the vill?"

"They didn't have to. If we had lost there they would simply have abandoned the priory. It's possible the Yvag—the demon—Zhanedd, didn't kill the sisters until she knew we were on our way. Sir Richard sent word ahead. I could only listen, since they had me paralyzed in the wagon. I knew before we arrived that the prioress was false, but at that point I could say nothing."

Geoffrey asked, "But why then did they bleed you? It's as if they were trying to heal rather than kill you." He grabbed Thomas's wrist and inspected his forearm. "Why, that's near healed," he said in wonder.

Thomas drew his arm away and replied, "Their plan seemed to be to keep me alive but weak so they could take me through that ring they opened."

"So, the sister was nah part'a this," John said. "Another innocent sacrificed."

"All of them innocent," said Elias. "Calum. Warin." He met Thomas's gaze.

"Isabella," Thomas added. "The creatures are pitiless. Which is why we have to remain vigilant and drive them out wherever we find them. For those they've killed already and those they'd kill down the road."

Elias pointed to the spot where the gate had been. "What about that?" he asked.

"I don't expect they'll come through here again. What can it gain them? The spinners are no more, destroyed in the mill, and John's sure to be more cautious now about who he robs on the King's Way." That caused some laughter. "But we still need to take care of these men's wounds."

"Aye," they all agreed, save for the miller of Palavia Parva. He'd gotten free of Doncaster's corpse and was sitting up. The wound in his shoulder had stopped bleeding. "What about my mill?" he wailed.

Thomas said, "I think most of us here will pitch in to rebuild it for you, good sir. I've some skill myself as a stonemason. We'll make it for you better than before. Your sacrifice, after all, was critical to our carrying the day."

"And we *have* carried the day, haven't we, Robyn?" Will Scathelock declared.

Wounds were dressed, a bone or two was set. Elias and Geoffrey started a fire in the hearth.

Thomas and Will left the bowmen and outlaws to tend to each other, while the two of them, now with lit candles, walked around the priory cloister to the dorter where Will had found the nuns. They lay still as death. Yet, upon closer inspection Thomas didn't believe they were dead. He believed he was looking at the same situation as with the Yvagvoja he'd encountered. They could lie in a suspended state for months, years, decades. Seeing the sisters tore open his memory of Isabella that final night, though no one was inhabiting these women, no cruel monsters wearing them like clothing. "There must be a simple way to wake them," he told Will. Even while riding their conveyances, Yvagvoja could awaken when one of their little hobs screamed out an alarm. This magic must be similarly and simply broken. He only had to identify the means.

Zhanedd and others hummed a kind of music that invaded the mind, sapped the will. Alderman Stroud had done that to him long ago in an attempt to get him to kill Alpin Waldroup. Zhanedd had sent Little John out into the night with a few simple commands, once he was under her spell. So these nuns could have been sung to sleep. But Zhanedd was gone and they remained as lifeless as ever.

Looking closely at them, Will remarked, "They are dead. Look at them. As still as that beast you had me ride." He reached into his purse and took out the ördstone Thomas had given him.

As he held it, the blue jewels of the stone twinkled in a sequence. Then a gossamer strand extended from the stone to the nearest woman. She seemed to tremble and then drew a deep breath. Astonished, Will backed away.

As if it was tracing the way to another portal, the stone emitted a second strand of light, and then another to the sleeping girl nearest him. She also began to stir as a spiderweb of thin lines connected to all of the sleeping nuns.

The first turned over as if to go back to sleep. Others stretched or yawned. One raised her head and looked right at them. She gasped.

Will stood, dumbfounded. Thomas took him by the arm and whispered, "I think it best we not remain in the good sisters' dorter, brother Will. Come on." They picked up the candles and hurried out into the night through the doors where Will had exited before.

Once outside, Thomas began to laugh. Will eyed him as if he was mad. "It was right in front of me all this time." He held up his own ördstone. "All the tombs I opened with Alpin and on my own, the sleepers had two items on them, three if you count their armor: these barbed black daggers and an ördstone. The daggers are protective, of course. The stones open the way between here and Ailfion. 'Twas all I thought they did."

"Yes. Who's Alpin?"

Thomas waved the question away. "Then I discovered they can take you to anyplace from anyplace, provided you focus on your destination. And they point the way to previously opened gates." He held up the stone. "Now, what if they also signaled the sleeper to wake in the first place? What if this one stone does *everything*?"

Will asked, "What mean you by *everything*, Robyn?" He held his own stone away, observed it askance.

Thomas could barely see his, save for the sparkling jewels that twinkled in some sort of sequence. He lifted the candle closer. Seven blue jewels scattered randomly across the surface of the near-circular black stone—but not random, because tiny etched lines connected them, fifteen if you viewed them one way, nineteen if you considered each tiny segment its own separate line. The jewels weren't all the same size, either. The one set against the top scalloped depression—there were four—was tinier than the rest. The candles made the stones glitter as if grains of something sparkly were worked into the black stone.

He knew how to hold it to slice open and seal the world. He'd learned of necessity that he had only to recall a location for the stone to take him there. This one Alpin had lost in þagalwood, where Thomas had recovered it. It had saved his life then, and was attuned to him now. And yet it had taken Little John straight to his brother in Palavia Parva—perhaps because Thomas had remained close by? Because it *knew* he wanted it to assist John? That made it, what, aware, alive?

Inside his head, Thomas could sense the stone, a tightness as if his hair was standing on end. The jewels brightened and flickered in a new pattern. He held the candle away to find the stones bathing him and Will in their blue glow. He said, "I don't understand. I knew them to be dead. They didn't breathe."

"Yes, and you returned them to life—with that."

Will stared at him, horrified.

Thomas realized that could not be the story that got around. He slapped Will Scathelock on the shoulder and said, "They were under a spell, Will. That's all it was. Created, I imagine, by another of these. Shatter the spell was all you did. No one's been brought back to life."

Will gave an unhinged laugh. "No, 'course not. Just spells and demons ever since the Nottingham fair." He handed his own ördstone to Thomas. "Here, you keep it. I—I need some communion wine. A hogshead should do." He was backing away as he spoke, then turned and walked quickly toward the wagon they'd arrived in, saw the unearthly white stallion nearby and immediately changed direction, heading for the broken doors.

Thomas could only grin after him.

With the two ördstones in one hand and a candle in the other, he wandered around the priory and through a garden wall. There was a stone bench among the shrubbery, and he sat, putting the candle down beside him. He held up the two stones. "You aren't made by God, now, are you?" he said to them. He turned his over, laying the jewels against his palm. The fluttering candle flame revealed the intricate array of etched lines on the back. "But surely you are another of Isabella's *inaudita*."

The words were hardly out of his mouth and then she was there. In front of him, exactly as she had been on that night in the King's Houses when they had finally talked: her dark green gown, and on the back of her head the netted snood into which she'd drawn her hair. She was sitting with her bare feet up on the edge of the leather chair, her expression teasing. She said, "Are you familiar with the writings of Gervase of Tilbury?" Then it had been a question out of the blue. Now it was asked in response to his saying *inaudita* aloud. This was more than mere memory of an event. The interchange itself had transformed.

He tried to recall the conversation. One thing he remembered: "I have a request of you, m'lady."

She focused upon him on the stone bench. "Yes?" she said, as clearly as if she were right there.

He was about to repeat what he'd said to her then, but he hesitated, recalling the riddle that had joined them: *Another Janet for your bed, short-lived the love . . .*

Was it possible there was some memory of his wife he might ignite? He tried recalling her the night he'd first caught her bathing in the river. Isabella vanished, but nothing replaced her. Janet's face was vague to him, the memory too far away to reach. Nothing appeared.

But he hadn't possessed this ördstone then. It had come to be his only later, after Ailfion.

He thought about that. What did he remember of that jump from Italia to Melrose? Lying beside her after his escape, he'd asked if she remembered the first night when she'd snuck into his bed. He'd been out that first night, watching the Yvags take their new *teind*, and didn't come home till morning. And Janet—

Janet was lying naked beside him. He was *right there*. He felt the linen cloth beneath him, watched the firelight at his back throw its flowing shadows over her and against the wall. "I did not *sneak*," she said. "You weren't home, so you've no right to characterize it as such!" He laughed, and then laughed again. He couldn't stop, couldn't believe it. He could see her, smell her, wrap her up in his arms and hold onto her. She wasn't gone. She was warm and alive, and her face was crystal clear. He pulled her tight and clung to her. "Oh, my God, my God," he whispered and closed his eyes in bliss.

Elias and Geoffrey and Little John found him in the morning, stretched out on the bench in the priory garden. The candle had melted away. To them he seemed overcome with joy at seeing them. Tears ran from his eyes. He behaved as if he'd shared substantially in the wine they'd drunk during the night, after the nuns and the prioress had awakened.

"We gave her a fright, whereas she *terrified* us," said Geoffrey. "Thought it to be the creatures come back again. But Will set us right. Proclaimed they'd all been under a spell and you and he discovered how to lift it. Miraculous."

As Geoffrey was speaking, Thomas tucked the stones into the pouch hung from his neck and silently vowed never to lose them. Janet, Isabella—they lived still, whether in his mind alone or in the world when he called them up, what mattered was that he could find each of them by recalling the exchange of a word or two. By some means the ördstone contained his life from the moment he'd recovered it.

Little John said, "Adam D'Everingham's turned up last night, but we couldn't find tha nowhere. 'E wants us both to join 'is Keepers of Sherwood."

"So now we're to be Keepers *and* Waits?" Thomas laughed. "That can't last. Orrels will never allow it."

"Oh, he might," said Elias. "If persuaded. We shall tell him all about it before we bury poor Calum in St. Mary's with his comrades."

True, there was Nottingham and Sherwood to protect from another Yvag incursion, and more sleepers to hunt down. For as long as it lasted, he supposed he would live the part. The Woodwose was dead for all save Little John and Thomas resurrected as Robyn thanks to Isabella Birkin. "And how is the prioress of Kirklees this morning?" he asked.

"Come see for yourself," said John. "She says she would like ta meet the fella who brought 'er back ta life."

"That was Will."

"Not according to 'im."

"Is there any wine left at all?"

They strolled back to the broken doors, while, following behind in theatrical fashion, Geoffrey proclaimed, "Thus ends our performance here, and with our good lady waiting perfervid to thank her savior, the infamous Robyn Hoode!"